AWOKEN

BRIDGET E. BAKER

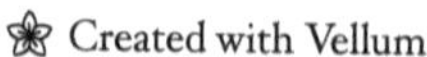 Created with Vellum

For my children

You will always have each other.
You may not yet understand the value of that gift.
One day you will.

Cherish one another.

PROLOGUE

One of my favorite games to play as a child was space captain and alien invader. Jesse and I would throw down a rock-paper-scissors match to determine who was stuck as the alien, and the other person would make something into a laser blaster. A wad of paper. A nicely-shaped stick. Legos formed into an 'L,' if we had any handy. We'd play for hours on end, rolling in elements from other games to keep it relevant.

Sometimes one of us would hide.

Sometimes we'd run races.

One thing never varied: the alien was bad. The space captain was good. Our make-believe world was drawn in stark, bold lines of black and white.

No one told me at school, at home, or in the system that the world is painted almost entirely in shades of grey. I had to figure that fact out for myself, and here's my dirty little secret: I stink at parsing out the heroes from the villains.

It's a little like picking a watermelon at the store. You can analyze the sound of the thump, the color of the sunspot, the gradation of pollen marks, or the presence of bee stings . . . but at the end of the day, you won't know whether it's delicious or mealy until you cut that sucker open.

The thing is, cutting *people* open is frowned upon.

And I've reached the point that my judgment matters. In fact, the fate of nearly eight billion people sort of hinges upon it. I can see people's souls, and I'm still shocked sometimes. People can want to do the right thing, and still make the wrong decision. They can desire to do what's right and still burn down a house, for instance. Inadvertent errors can occasionally be as bad as intentional harm. Entire shows are predicated on that, like *Tom and Jerry* or *The Minion Movie*.

The great literary minds of our times have repeated this adage enough that everyone knows it: the road to hell is paved with good intentions.

They had no idea how right they were.

And when you're on that path, often, you don't even realize it.

ANCIENT EGYPT

When she has time to rock me to sleep, Mother always sings the same song. It's not very long, and she always says her voice isn't very good, but it sounds perfect to me.

I've grown so large that my feet dangle off her lap. I worry that she might stop singing to me any time, so I sit very still and I am very quiet when she does it.

Her breath blows against my ear as the familiar words wrap me up and keep me safe.

My heart is happy.

Just as she finishes, Shu's head pokes around the corner of the doorway. "She's still awake?"

If I wasn't, his whisper would have woken me, but I'm guessing he knows I'm not sleeping because he heard Mother singing. I beam at him.

No one in the world is as fun as Shu. My feet hit the ground and I'm running across the floor before Mother can stop me. He swings me up in the air and around and around.

Our laughter bounces off the walls of my spacious bedchamber. When he finally puts me down, Mother's mouth is compressed into a flat line. She's standing up, with her head cocked sideways. "She was calm and ready to go to bed." If I hadn't already known she was mad, her tone would have conveyed her irritation perfectly.

Shu isn't worried. He knows his grin is contagious. He tosses me up in the air again as if to tell her he doesn't care, and I squeal.

"You'll have to read her another story or she'll never go to sleep," Mother says.

"It's fine, Mother. I'll go right to bed, I promise."

She rolls her eyes, but the sides of her lips curl upward. We're both glad Shu is back. I wish he never had to leave. "Did the meeting go super great?"

He chuckles. "It wasn't so much a meeting as a—"

Mother cuts him off. "It went well, or he'd be talking to your father right now instead of in here, trying to make you puke up your dinner by tossing you around like a sack of dates."

Shu finally sets me on the floor and bows his head. "Duly chastened," he says. "I promise I won't rile her up any more until tomorrow morning."

Mother arches one eyebrow. "See that you keep that promise."

He's finally off the hook, and he knows it. He crouches down so that we're at eye level. "Why don't you pick out another scroll?" He taps the end of my nose. "I'd be happy to read you one."

I walk toward the chair, not toward my shelves. "I'd rather you tell me a story. Something new and exciting. Like what happened at your meeting."

"When you're done, put her on her mat," Mother says, "and let Bastet know she's down. I'm going to get dressed and ready, and then I'll be with Imentet. We may be out late."

"She hates when you call her Bastet," I say.

"Excuse me?" Mother asks.

"Aha. She doesn't like the name Bastet."

Shu sits in the chair Mother just vacated, and I climb into his lap.

"Bastet is her name," Mother says, "her family name."

I shrug. "She doesn't like it. She wants me to call her Aha."

"That name reminds her of a time she'd like to forget," Shu says. "I'm sure Mother can relate to that and remember to call her Aha from here on out."

Mother's shaking her head as she walks out the door.

Shu doesn't rock me, but that's alright. I like to sit on one knee so I can see his face. He doesn't tell me a new story, but he tells my favorite one, which makes up for it.

"Many, many years ago, before you or I were born, and before Father met Mother, he had another child. Her name was Hatshepsut."

"And way back then, Dad would always ask the child he trusted the most to manage everything for him," I say. "That's how he could get a break sometimes. He called them Pharaohs."

Shu smiles. "Are you telling this? Or am I?"

I press my lips tightly together and shake my head.

"Alright, then. So, Hatshepsut was bold. She was fierce. And like her mother, she was a powerful telekinetic."

I love the next part.

"But when she asked to be made Pharaoh, Ra turned her down. Although he made sure that women had the same legal rights as men, he had never selected a daughter to rule in his stead because he knew the people would make jokes and disrespect the ruler when things were bad. He had too much love and adoration for his daughters to allow this to happen, and he didn't want his soldiers to have to kill people for something as commonplace as joking and horsing around. He felt it best that his daughters not take up the title of Pharaoh."

"Dad was wrong," I say.

Shu shrugs. "I'd be angry if someone said something rude about you."

I swat him as hard as I can. "I can defend myself." My words come out in a partial growl.

He laughs. "I know you can, little cub. I know."

I sniff. "Don't forget it."

"But Hatshepsut knew she was a better choice than Father's other child, Thutmose. She couldn't stand the thought of him muffing things up."

I beam.

"She put on a beard and used makeup to convince him that she was a male, and she presented herself as his long-lost son."

"And she challenged Thutmose to a fight to pick the winner!" I bounce on Shu's knee.

"Why do I even tell these stories?" he asks.

"Because you love me," I say.

"I absolutely do," he says, "and I would never fight you, whether you were dressed as a man or not. I would recognize you right away."

"Well, it's too bad Thutmose wasn't smart enough to recognize her. Because she beat him, and then she whipped the beard off and showed Dad that she was the better Pharaoh."

Shu laughs. "She surely did, but Father got her back, too, in his own way."

I cross my arms. "I'd have been so *angry*."

He chuckles, his whole body shaking slightly. "You sure would have. Father granted her wish—she was named the next Pharaoh—but he made her pretend to be a male at all public functions, using the same makeup and beard with which she tricked him and Thutmose so that people didn't realize until later, after she'd grown tired of managing things, that she had been a woman all along."

I shake my head. "So stupid."

"We don't use that word," Shu says, "little cub, as you know."

I huff. "Well, if Dad were here, I'd use it anyway, and I'd tell him what I think of him making my much, much older sister dress up and pretend just so he would let her do a job. And I'd—"

Shu stands up, his hands under my armpits, lifting me into the air. "And on that note of treasonous rebellion, I think it's time for bed."

"It's not treason to tell Dad what I think, even if I use words he doesn't like."

Shu sets me on my mat. "Well, whether it is or not, he'd never do a thing to harm you. Ever."

I can't help my smile. "I am his favorite."

He presses a kiss against my forehead and drags a blanket up to my chest. "You sure are, and I'll try and pretend I don't mind."

"I'm your favorite too," I say. "That's why you don't mind. And that's why you'll stay with me until I go to sleep. Right?" I whine, just a little bit, because he almost never says no when I do. A breeze blows through my room, and I shiver. I think it makes me seem just a little more pitiful.

"You don't need me to stay, cub."

I nod my head vigorously. "I do."

"Why?"

I don't want to tell him about my nightmares—of armies with shields and spears. I shiver again.

"It's chilly outside tonight," Shu says. "Why didn't Mother order a fire?" He glances over his shoulder at the fireplace. There are logs handy, but they're not lit. "I'll run grab—"

"Don't go," I say.

"I will stay," Shu says. "I promise. Just let me run—"

"You don't have to go. I can light it."

Shu frowns. "You don't even have a striking kit."

"I don't need one." I point at the fire, palm out, and *push*, and the flames lick at the dry logs.

My big brother's eyes widen and he straightens. "Oh, Sekhmet. What did you just do?"

I swallow. "Is it bad? I didn't know. I won't do it again, I promise. Please don't be mad."

"I have to tell Mother and Father. They'll want to know right away."

My mat tangles in my legs as I scramble toward him. "Please don't."

He lets me climb back into his lap, even though it means he's holding me while sitting cross-legged on the stone floor. "You don't need to be afraid." He brushes the hair out of my eyes. "It's just strange for someone to have not one talent, but two."

"Mother has four," I say. "She's Fire Called and Earth Called and Wind Called and Ice Called."

He nods. "Technically they're all in the same category, though. She's an Elemental."

I swallow.

"But Lifting and Shifting and Calling Fire as well . . . " His forehead crinkles up.

"It's really bad?"

"Well, not bad," he says. "But . . . strange."

"Strange is another way to say bad." I lean against his chest. "Do you love me less now?"

His arms tighten around me. "Father will be pleased."

"Not Mother?"

He shrugs. "I don't always know how she'll respond."

"What about you?" My voice is small, even for a little person like me.

He shifts me until he can see my face. "If you could Call

Wind, and Earth, and Ice, and if you could shift into a lion and an eagle and an ant, I would feel exactly the same about you as I do now."

I swallow.

"No matter what, Sekhmet, I will love you forever."

"Promise," I say. "No matter what."

"No matter what, cub. No matter what."

And I believe him.

❧ 2 ☙

ANCIENT EGYPT

M y stomach growls—I'm unaccustomed to missing meals, and Dad hasn't let me eat since last night. It wouldn't be so bad, except that we've been hiking all morning. Not exactly how I expected to spend my sixteenth birthday.

"Are you ever going to tell me why we're out here?" The sun rays manage to cook me, even though it's not yet midday. Sweat rolls down my cheek and streaks down my neck. Ugh.

"I'm not a huge fan of traipsing around in nature either." His words are belied by his appearance—Dad doesn't wipe his face with his sleeve. He isn't even sweating. He looks completely at ease, as though the angry sun isn't even touching him. No wonder people joke that he's a Sun God.

I stop walking, wondering whether I could simply refuse to take another step. "I look like a wilted lotus blossom. Why are you so fresh?"

Dad's eyes crinkle when he smiles at me over his shoulder, finally stopping. "If you applied yourself a little harder in basic shaping and forms, you'd be as cool as I am."

He's using magic. Of course he is. Anat did mention something about heating and cooling when we went over the simpler forms, but with my ability to Call Fire and a cadre of Wind Called servants to keep Dad's palaces cool, I've never bothered paying much attention to that type of thing. It's not like I anticipated Dad dragging me out on a forced nature walk.

"So that's a no? You won't tell me why we've been walking for miles?"

"Bastet will meet us soon," Dad says.

Why can't anyone else remember to call her Aha? I grit my teeth.

"I'm sorry. I know it's Aha. It's just that she was Bastet to me for quite a long time. It's harder for me to change gears than it used to be."

"How old are you?" I ask.

Dad laughs. "You're full of questions today."

And he's evading all of them.

"Ah, we're here." Dad sits on a rock at the top of the rise, surrounded by trees, including a few sycamore trees. They're my favorite, with their expansive canopy and brilliantly green leaves. I sit next to him and look around. The air is clear here, and the view of the pyramids in the distance is beautiful, even knowing they house dead people.

But I don't see Aha anywhere.

I'm not sure why we'd need her. She's transitioned from a nanny to more of an unofficial guard. They don't think I've noticed, but I'm sixteen, not blind. With the way she paces, growls, and bristles at anyone and everyone new, you'd think I was a basket full of gold debens, enticing the interest of every person who entered the palace instead of just another young person in a world full of young people.

Dad inhales and exhales slowly, practically daring me to ask more questions. I snap my mouth shut to keep from being predictable—he says I broadcast my feelings like a male cuckoo. Loud and unsubtle.

Well, not today.

I can wait as long as he can.

After quite a few long minutes of silence, he exhales. "You've exercised restraint. I'm impressed."

"I'm sixteen, Dad, not two."

His mouth twitches in obvious bemusement. "In this case, it's not your impatience that has caused me to hold my tongue."

This is the opposite of anything we've ever done to celebrate my birth prior to this year. Typically Dad throws parties with feasts or we take extravagant trips to other palaces, or he brings exotic animals or impressive dignitaries. I feign indifference by shrugging nonchalantly. It feels like I've pulled it off admirably . . .

Until he rolls his eyes. "For several years now, I've told myself that on your next birthday, we would have this talk."

I scrunch my nose. "Eww, Dad, don't. Anat has already answered any questions I've had, I swear."

A look of terror crosses his face, his pupils dilating to the size of large olives. "By Nut and Geb and all that's holy and right, *that* is not why I brought you here."

Awkward. "Okaaaay."

"Maybe I've made this into a bigger deal than it should be, but in all the time I've been alive, I've never had a child who could shift into an animal form." He stares at his sandals.

Dad always meets my eyes. He's never uncomfortable. What's going on? Is he embarrassed that I can shift? Why? "You don't like Renders?" He's certainly surrounded by plenty of them at the palace—Ammit and Pakhet are almost never more than a room away.

"It's not that I don't like them." He runs his hands

down his legs, his fingers splayed, and he inhales deeply, his nostrils flaring.

"You can tell me, Dad. Whatever it is."

"There's no one else I would tell all of this to," he says softly.

Something in his tone convinces me not to say another word. This seems hard enough for him without my intervention.

"You've been adored since the moment you were born," he whispers. "I hope you've felt that. There hasn't been a single part of your life or existence that has brought me anything but pure joy."

I meet his eyes then, so big and open, and I smile.

"I've messed up plenty of things in my long life—"

"How old are you?" I'd never thought to ask him before.

"I'm not quite sure," he says.

"You're so old, you've lost count?" I arch one eyebrow. I don't believe that for a second.

"My childhood wasn't like yours," he says. "No one celebrated my birth. No one delighted in my existence."

How depressing. "But you must have some idea," I press.

"What's your best guess?"

If I aim really high, maybe he'll think I'm joking. "Five hundred?"

He chuckles. "Not quite, cub."

"Two hundred?"

He shakes his head. "Wrong direction."

"You're *older* than five hundred?" I can't help it. My eyes widen.

"To the best of my knowledge, I was born close to twenty-four hundred and twelve years ago."

I suppress a cough. I must have misheard him. I know he's old, but that's . . .

"My father had several wives, and most of them struggled constantly to maintain his favor. My mother was different. She refused to try to curry favor, and she was too valuable to toss into the pit of vipers that was Dad's court."

I don't understand.

"Mother was quiet, and she wasn't particularly powerful, for all that she was an Assimilator. She was clumsy with shaping the power she siphoned, and her capacity to siphon wasn't great. But there weren't many Assimilators alive at that time, and my father quickly learned that it was precisely her lack of prowess that made her so valuable."

I'm so confused right now.

Dad drops his face into his hands, and I give him a moment to regroup. "The world was very different then. It was savage, and there were very few rules. Your great-grandfather unified Egypt. He was the first man to call himself the leader of this region. King Menes." Dad's voice is so bitter. "My father, Amun, ripped his own father's throat out to take that crown. From what I hear, Grandpa had no one to blame but himself. He always said he'd be succeeded by the child who could defeat him."

I blink.

"That's not even the surprising part," Dad says. "If I had to guess, I'd say that Menes was proud in the split second before he died that his son was strong enough to wrest control from him. It's how Renders worked at the time, and even now, to a certain extent."

He was proud of his son for murdering him with his teeth? I can't help it. My lip curls.

"I've neglected your shifter education badly, because of my own . . . history." He shudders.

My dad *shudders* at the thought of whatever he's going to tell me—the unconquerable, unflappable, omnipotent ruler of half the world, practically.

I put my hand on his. "What's the surprising part?"

He flinches, so I pull back, but he catches my fingers.

"Never ignore a kind impulse, cub. Thank you." He squeezes my hand. "Thank you for bringing me back to myself."

I wait.

He continues, finally. "My earliest memories are of life in a very, very small room that I shared with my mother. She was trotted out occasionally when my father felt he was aging so that she could siphon the life force of whatever individuals he instructed and renew his own life. Otherwise, he didn't bother us. We had enough food to survive, and if we were lonely, at least I felt my mother cared for me somewhat."

Somewhat? I have to try not to clench my hand for fear it would agitate Dad further. I'd slap my grandmother right this moment for the hurt she caused him—except it makes me wonder what she must have endured herself. Being held captive in a tiny room?

"But those were the only fond memories I have."

Fond? Memories of the time he spent in a tiny room, waiting for his dad to force his mother to kill people to keep him young . . . were fond?

"I was not quite nine years old when my mother was killed by an assassin sent by an enemy of my father. They realized she was the source of his immortality, and she was much easier to reach. Eliminating his font of youth seemed simpler than trying to kill him. That was the first time I ever siphoned anything at all—I withered the man who stabbed my mother."

"That's terrible. I'm so sorry." I scoot closer to him on the rock. "I can't even imagine having no family or friends or stimulation of any kind. You didn't even have books?"

"My mother taught me to speak. She taught me the basics of reading and writing as well, using rocks on the floor to carve letters into the wall."

I can't even imagine the great Ra, scratching letters into

a wall with a rock. I can't imagine him stuck in a room either—the dad I know would have destroyed everyone who tried to restrain him. The thought of him as a helpless child, desperate for love, then dealing with the death of his mother and the guilt of killing someone at the same time, is heartbreaking. "I'm sorry." Sometimes no words are the right words, but an expression of sympathy is the paltry best I can summon.

"I should explain something else to you first, or the rest of this won't make sense."

I almost dread learning any more.

"You know that alpha shifters are rare, but they serve an important purpose."

I nod. "They lead."

"In order to help other Renders control their aggression, or for Reapers, to help control their fear, the alphas have telepathic abilities, and they can control the emotions and desires of those around them."

"Like forcing a shift." Aha forced me out of my lion form and into my human one often enough—usually when I needed to be disciplined for something.

"But most of the Renders and Reapers can't shift into an animal form at all. They can only force it on the Renders or Reapers who are physically capable of shifting forms."

I think about the kitchen staff—when I startled them the other night in lion form, one of the girls washing dishes squeaked and rabbit ears popped out of her head. "It's odd that many of them can only shift a tail or ears."

"It's not odd—it's the way of the world." Dad sighs. "The strong must guide and protect the weaker among us. But sometimes instead of doing their duty, they pervert ma'at."

"It's not like people are weaker for being unable to turn into a rabbit," I say pragmatically. "Right?"

"Shifting provides many benefits," Dad says. "They can

hide, for one, or move more quickly. But beyond that, when you shift, your cellular structure reorders itself. Terrible wounds can be entirely healed in a powerful enough shifter. Being unable to take an animal form means that you may have an affinity to a certain type of animal, but no real strength. If you're something weak like a rabbit or a sparrow, you'll have stronger impulses to flee instead of fight."

"Which an alpha can control, if you're lucky enough to have one close."

"The reason Bastet left my service as a warrior—she was one of the best—was because you were born. She hates being called Bastet, not for whatever reason she told you, but because of the criticism from the general public when I appointed her as your caretaker. No one could believe I'd ask a destroyer of thousands, perhaps hundreds of thousands, to watch over my infant daughter."

A destroyer of hundreds of thousands? "Was she really that terrible?"

"She was my most impressive Render general."

"Why did you pick her? To make sure I was safe?" Has she always been a bodyguard?

"Alphas can always shift into an animal form, and they're almost always more physically powerful than your average shifter. They occur about one per one hundred individuals capable of shifting and there's a reason for that. A strong alpha can prevent about a hundred individuals from shifting in times of crisis, or force the same number to take their animal forms."

"If two or three out of one hundred shifters can actually take an animal form, that means it's about one in five thousand Reapers or Renders who are alphas?"

"Something like that."

"Why would alphas need to prevent their community from shifting?"

"The power of shifting to an animal form is primal.

It's said to be a gift from Geb himself, to help protect us from the animals that would otherwise have eaten us. A few shifters, stronger than their animal counterparts, stronger than the other humans, could protect an entire town. But the cost of such power is also great. It ebbs and flows as the earth and nature ebb and flow, specifically with the changing of the seasons. And it's tied to the moon."

"I've never noticed anything odd about my shifting when the moon—"

"Because of Bastet." Dad's lips are set in a hard line.

"What?"

"I hated doing it, Sekhmet, please believe me, but it was absolutely for your own good."

"*Doing what?*"

"An alpha can prevent the pull of the moon from forcing you into a shift. A forced shift will cause you to behave erratically—in ways you never would if your human side was in control."

It takes me a moment to process what he's saying, but little things fall into place. How clingy Aha becomes sometimes—how she won't leave my side. I'd never thought about the timing, but it makes sense. "She keeps me . . . safe . . . from the pull of the changing moons."

"She does it on my command," Dad says. "But that's not even everything." He sighs. "In order to do this, alphas must be able to control their packs. That's one of the reasons they can communicate telepathically. I've forbidden them from doing it in the palace until now, because I knew it would lead to other questions."

What questions?

"Alphas' ability to compel others to do their bidding varies, but according to Bastet, your ability there is quite strong. She said she's never been able to compel you to do anything, even when you were quite small."

And Dad's father . . . "Wait, did your dad make you and your mom do things? Is that why you stayed in that room?"

Dad gulps. "The last thing I haven't mentioned is that there's something called a supra alpha. That's an alpha who can compel other alphas." He pauses to let that sink in.

"Is Bastet . . . ?"

He nods. "Not exceptionally strong, but yes. That's the precise reason I chose her instead of, say, Pakhet. She's a strong alpha, and possibly better suited to caring for a child, but she's not a supra."

"Okay."

"I have lived for a long time, but my father was the most powerful supra that has lived during my lifetime. Most alphas can manage a pack of up to one hundred, but how many they can handle varies widely."

An alpha who compelled others is a concerning thought.

"My father assembled a pack that was thousands of alphas strong."

Thousands of alphas. With packs of a hundred or so each. The thought of that many shifters gathered. . .

"My father used my mother to rejuvenate himself, and he forced her to provide the same service to any alphas he deemed worthy of a prize. He didn't love her. He didn't respect her. He didn't even like her. And he certainly didn't care for me at all."

"Then why did he . . . " I trail off, unsure how to ask.

"Why did he make a child with my mother?" Dad's voice is flat.

I nod.

"I was his fallback plan. In case something ever happened to her."

"And when she died . . . " I can't quite bring myself to ask.

"I was forced to take over for her, yes," he says. "Only, I

wasn't like my mother. He figured that out pretty quickly. He'd ask me to siphon, and once I figured out how to both control the assimilation of energy and use it to make him younger, which took a lot of . . . *encouragement* . . . I realized that the person didn't have to be within my reach. Had I known how that would impact my life, I'd never have shown him that I possessed that talent."

"Why not? Surely he was pleased you had more power than your mother."

Dad shakes his head. "It made me a threat, you see. He could compel me to do most anything—and I always followed. I had no idea how to resist, nor did he ever soften his compulsion enough that I might learn it was even possible, but when he realized what I was capable of . . . " He pauses. "He was unwilling to risk his font of youth. He hadn't met another Assimilator. They were surely keeping well away from him, having heard of his eternal youth and my mother's capture."

"No one came to help you?"

"Not for a very long time," Dad says.

"I can't even imagine being stuck in one room—"

Dad tuts. "Not a room. Amun realized that might give me ideas. I needed less space or I might get creative. He locked me in a box, compelling me not to fight the confinement. He had me removed once a day to trot a few circles around the courtyard, eat a meal, and evacuate my bowels, and then I would go back in the box, assuming no one needed to be rejuvenated."

That's horrible. Ghastly. Inhumane.

"I didn't know any better," Dad says. "But with very little else to do, I became hyperaware of the presence of all the energy sources around me. They pulsed and practically burst with life. I had been compelled not to touch them, and I had no choice to obey, but I began to notice a difference between the varying sources of power. Some of the individuals Dad ordered me to siphon were bright and light. Some were dark and twisted."

Their souls. Dad began to see the light of their souls.

"I had to follow his instructions, but I found a loophole. He'd pull me out of the box, and he'd order me to siphon the enemies he brought. But he didn't order me to siphon them all fully—I think he assumed that was a given."

My eyes widen.

"If I'd left the light and bright ones all healthy and strong, he'd surely notice. If I only took a bit from each, he'd see that I hadn't executed them and he'd order that I drain them fully. I had to be quite careful in my small rebellion, but I was. I siphoned almost all of the life force from the light souls, but not all of it. I knew that if my father dumped them somewhere, they would eventually regain consciousness. I'm not sure how many survived, but some did, for sure."

I want to ask how he knows, but I'm worried interrupting him will be disruptive.

"I know you, cub. When you're curious, you twitch—wanting to open your mouth, but stopping yourself just in time. Ask your question."

"How do you know you saved any of them? How do you know they recovered?"

"It would be child's play now," he says. "But at the time I was untutored. I'd been in that box for a very, very long time before the idea occurred to me to spare some of them. I'm ashamed to admit that, but in my defense, not even my mother had taught me anything. I was acting entirely on my gut feelings, guessing everything."

"Okay."

"But after a very long time, in spite of my father's massive and terrifying power—the people already worshipped him as a god, of course—a few of the people I'd spared banded together. Word had gotten out that the child of the monster might be *good.* Might be *compassionate.* And they were stalwart enough people, bright enough souls, that the thought of my father keeping a good person in a box horrified them."

"Who?"

"You know some of them." Dad smiles. "Mehen organized it."

My heart expands. I already loved him, but now . . . to think of how he saved my dad.

"His attempt to save me failed utterly and completely. He was set to be executed, of course," Dad says. "My father was far, far too powerful, even for a gifted Lifter."

His words are like a rock to the head. "They failed? But Mehen's alive."

"They were set to be executed, I said. But in that moment, when my father was subduing the band of fifty of the people I'd saved who came back for me, his compulsion on me lifted. Even supras can only do so much, you know. That was always my father's weakness. He didn't have any loyal subjects. He employed brute force to control them at all times, and being that tapped, relying entirely on your own power, however great, is a terrible liability. The power needed to compel his men and the energy it took for him to deflect the unexpected attack pushed him too far and for one glorious moment, I was free, for the first time in almost two hundred years."

Two hundred years in a box?

"Of all fifty of the people who came to save me, only Am-Heh, Ammit, and Mehen survived. If I had attacked sooner . . . but it was what it was. The past is done. I killed my father in that moment, as surely and savagely as if I'd ripped out his heart. I imagine it hurt, too. I didn't simply siphon him, no. I sucked him dry." His smile is terrifying. "If I had it to do over again, I would be much, much slower."

Most people on Earth would probably be terrified by my dad in this moment, but not me. I think he was justified in what he did—and understandable in wishing to have inflicted more pain on the man who ruined his life for so very, very long. "I understand why you didn't want to tell me about supras."

"It's not that I didn't want to talk about my past, although I did need to wait until you were old enough to understand everything."

"Then what—"

"Bastet can't compel you, Sekhmet. That means you're not only an alpha. You're a supra—you must have inherited that from my father, which is not even unusual or rare. It's . . ." He sighs. "It's unheard of, really, for an ability to pass down from a grandfather. But it happened, no matter how unlikely, and if you have a fraction of your grandfather's ability, no one on Earth could stand against you."

Aha lopes up the hill behind Dad, her fur shining in the sun, her mouth open a bit, her sides heaving from her run.

"I brought you here today so that you can hunt for the first time—a rite of passage for any Render—and so that you can learn what it means to be a supra."

I really, really wish he was kidding.

❦ 3 ❦

EARTH

I shouldn't have woken up at all.

My brother Jesse's dying—when I ripped him out of Terra and slammed him onto Earth, I thought I'd saved him, but actually I left him with a hole in his soul or something like that. I've been funneling energy into him as a stop-gap measure, but if I don't find Ra's reservoir stones full of power, the next time he fades may be his last.

There's so much fighting and arguing amongst my supposed supporters that it feels like an afternoon talk show. Kahn and John have been going at it for a long time.

I certainly didn't expect to wake up in a Louisiana National Guard building in Bunkie, Louisiana, also known as the middle-of-bumpkis-nowhere. Apparently my dad left while I was unconscious, dismantling Erra. It's not like that surprises me, really—it's the most consistent thing about him, the abandonment. I'm more surprised at how much his absence disappoints me. At least it's one less person working an angle.

Devlin stepped away as well, for the same reason as Duncan, but before he left, he found us a safe place to hide. The Followers of Isis snatched up control of the US government and now control most of the military bases as well. Amun gave up once they'd lost the upper hand to avoid massive human casualties and focused instead on securing supply chains or something like that. I'm not saying that was a stupid decision, but he who controls the tanks kind of controls everything else.

I mean, if Amun was in a position to dominate Isis, would Devlin have sent me to huddle in a National Guard building that looks like a daycare and a barn had a baby? It has a metal roof with small, sliced windows surrounding it on all sides. I'm pretty sure the interior was decorated with whatever was available at the closest Goodwill storefront, mostly a combination of saggy, outdated seating, and scuffed, worn laminate tables. The floor tiles are a depressing checkerboard of black and white tile. It's not very secure, but no one would ever, not in a gazillion years, think to look for me here.

When I started dismantling Erra, almost seven million people who had never had powers before (women, yes, but also a lot of men who weren't Awake) suddenly started setting people they didn't like on fire (inadvertently, probably), or freezing their enemies into icicles (like, literally). It's made for a bumpy couple of days for the Followers of Amun and the Followers of Isis, and well, most of the people on Earth.

The news anchor on the television playing in the background is still bleating about it. So a few people have barricaded their homes inside a bubble made of ice. So what? And if the fire department can't keep up with calls right now, well, that'll be resolved soon enough. Once the Fire Called who know how to douse fire are able to round up the newbies and teach them basics, and ditto for Ice, things will mostly go back to normal.

Or maybe not normal, really, but they'll be less turbulent.

I do care about the world. It's just that every single one of the new elementals wreaking havoc right now are better off enduring the mania here on Earth than they would have been if I had allowed Erra to collapse on top of them. Alive is almost always better than dead, which is why I'm not bowing under the pressure that Kahn and John keep applying to pick a side and step into my role as supreme ruler of all the things. Using the behavior in this room as a microcosm by which to measure, I would not lead very well anyway. No one here can even look at me without scowling, or entreating, or chivying me.

The Healers are huddled in the corner, trying to avoid annoying anyone.

Henry's sitting by Jesse, and neither of them are commenting. They both look a little bit lost—like two kids watching their parents argue.

Mehen can't understand anyone but me.

John hates his dad, allegedly, but he's zealous in his support of the Followers of Amun.

And Kahn—to whom I'm still irritatingly drawn—is the most obnoxious of all. He's clinging to whatever Isis has told him like a small child enforcing his parents' safety rules.

"None of the small details matter. She needs to focus on reinforcing the structure that supports Rra, and making sure she doesn't have to dismantle it, like the others," he says.

For the nine hundred and fiftieth time.

And they're arguing with each other as though I'm not even here.

"Alora won't be able to avoid that, just as she couldn't miraculously stop Erra from unraveling," John says. "When those prison walls start coming down, she has no choice. She either allows those people to die, or she saves them." He grunts. "For a smart guy, you're remarkably dense."

"I understand that she did the best she could with the limited information she had, but the future is a chance for us to improve. Always," Kahn says.

"But is rebuilding it an improvement?" John asks. "I mean, she may have created it in the first place—we don't know for sure—but you can't live your life in a prison. I think when it was created, it was meant to be a reset button. Her rebirth was the sign that the time for humans' abilities to be suppressed is past."

"You have no way of knowing that," Kahn says. "But most importantly, Rra must be shored up so that it never gets close to Ā. Ra cannot be released. You've seen the histories about him—he's the whole reason Terra was built in the first place."

"I'm not at all sure that's true," John says. "I haven't seen any evidence of his evil. I've heard people among Isis' followers tell me how terrible he is, but just as many people with the Followers of Amun think he poops rainbows."

Mehen's following their conversation like a spectator at a tennis match, his head turning back and forth between the speakers, in spite of the fact that he can't understand a word.

"Do you have anything to add?" I ask in ancient Egyptian.

He shrugs. "You won't let me behead the evil one, so, not really."

Mehen has been frozen in some kind of bizarre stasis for more than two thousand years, awaiting the deterioration of Terra so that he could be revived. He's convinced that Kahn's the rebirth of Ra's mortal enemy, Apophis, in the same way that I'm apparently the rebirth of Sekhmet, Ra's daughter. I'd argue with him, or ignore the claim as complete delusion . . . except that I keep having dreams— vivid, specific dreams—of my childhood where Ra is my dad. It's a little hard to refute his nonsense when I appear to be sharing aspects of this specific delusion.

"The evil one?" I roll my eyes. "I swear, it's a good thing you can't speak English. You'd embarrass me. He's my friend, Mehen, I promise he is."

"If you insist." His nostrils flare, but he doesn't argue. "I would never bring dishonor on you. Never."

Because he loves Ra with every fiber of his being. "Ra mentioned that you saved him from the tiny room his insane father was locking him into," I say. "I'm not sure whether I ever thanked you for that a few thousand years ago. In case I didn't, I wanted to let you know that I appreciate it."

Mehen's smile is broad, his white teeth shocking against the deep brown of his skin. "You did thank me on your sixteenth birthday. It was quite touching." He tilts his head. "Did your dad mention it when you visited him on Ā recently? Or are you now remembering the first time he told you?"

I cough. "The remembering thing."

His smile broadens. "Excellent. That's the best news I've heard."

I'm not nearly as convinced as he is that it's good news, but at least someone's happy. And he's not trying to force me to join team Amun or team Isis. That's something. Meanwhile, Kahn and John are still arguing.

"I'm sick of listening to you guys." Jesse plops into the chair in the corner and tosses another handful of M&Ms in his mouth.

The Piggly Wiggly had a moderate amount of supplies —or at least, enough M&Ms to keep Jesse happy for a few days. The one nice thing about Bunkie, Louisiana is that the people don't stress or worry about 'national issues' overmuch.

"They're not helping me make up my mind," I say, "and

last I checked, I'm the only one who can dismantle or rebuild Rra, so . . . "

John and Kahn don't even glance in my direction—too locked into an epic argument about the merits or evils of Ra. Since neither of them have met him, that annoys me.

"Other than deciding the fate of, oh, seven billion plus people," Jesse says, "what are your plans for the day?"

That finally shuts them up. John beelines to my side and sits down on the sofa next to me, slinging an arm around my shoulders. His proprietary behavior kind of irritates me.

"I'm sure this has already occurred to you," Jesse says, "but I think you're pretty likely to pop up in Rra when you go to sleep."

"You really think so?" Kahn asks.

I grimace. "For my entire life, when I went to sleep, I was trapped in Terra because I could Lift. After I dismantled Terra, I went to sleep and wound up in Erra because I can also Call Fire. That's why I was caught there—and Kahn too."

Kahn shrugs. "But you've dismantled Terra *and* Erra now."

"Whoa—you can Call Fire here now? Finally?" John asks.

I shake off his arm and extend my hand, palm up. A tiny flame dances over my fingers. "I *can* Call Fire, but I think I always could have. It was my own lack of faith in my ability that kept me from doing it. Don't you think?"

John scratches his head. "Uh."

Jesse and Kahn exchange a glance I don't quite get.

"If I'm the warden of a prison, I can walk around in it freely, right?"

All three of them frown.

"This isn't actually a prison," John says.

"You're saying that you can move between Rra and Ā right now?" Kahn asks.

"It's like I have a key that will let me into any cell and any floor. Or, at least, it'll let me stumble around, take the elevator, whatever."

"I have no idea what you're saying." Jesse scratches his head.

"It's maybe not a perfect parallel, but everyone on Earth has some kind of powers, which is why everyone also exists on at least one prison world. In order to use our powers on Earth, we must be Woken—but I was also the only one with a key to navigate the structure itself. It's why I could see Terra as it truly was once I realized it wasn't real. That's why I saw those bundles of intricately woven ropes of energy. I saw that *before* it began to unravel. Now I think there are two ways that I can get into Rra and eventually, Ā. I can use my key and *slide* over, or I can get there in the way that all humans who can see it do, by going to sleep."

Kahn blinks. "But you'd have to be a shifter to fall asleep and wind up on Rra, so that won't work this time."

I haven't really been sharing my dreams of my past life as Sekhmet. Talking about old memories I'm not entirely certain are real feels . . . strange. And yet, these people have thrown their lot in with mine, so it feels like they ought to know. "I am a shifter," I say.

John scoots away, possibly to allow him to focus on my face a little better. Or maybe he's uncomfortable around my ability. "Say what?"

I grit my teeth.

"I never got to Terra by going to sleep," Jesse says.

Bless him for refocusing us. "You're a guy, but all women who could dream of Terra reached it the same way I did, through their dreams," I say. "All this to say, I do think I'll wind up in Rra as soon as I drift off. And like the last two times, I won't know who I am or remember anything about my life."

"What can you turn into?" Jesse doesn't look disgusted at all, or even afraid, only fascinated.

"Someone must have looked up Sekhmet, daughter of Ra, after Mehen said that's who I was. Anyone know her symbol?"

"Um, I do," John says. "We had to learn all about her in my Egyptian Studies class. She's a lion goddess."

"Are you saying you can turn into a lion?" Kahn asks.

I shrug. "I haven't done it on Earth, but I think maybe I could."

"Whoa," John says. "That's amazing. You should try." So maybe he wasn't uncomfortable, maybe he was impressed.

"Before we gloss over this part, can you move from here to Rra right now?" Jesse asks. "Like, without sleeping first?"

"I'm not sure. I've tried a few times, and nothing has happened." I sigh. "Which means if I have the figurative key I was talking about before, I don't know how to use it."

Which is only one of way too many things I don't know. The world around me is a strange mix of familiar things and the completely insane. I lean back against the sofa to try and think. It's old, and it's squishy, and I've tried not to examine it too closely.

"But you went there before, right?" John asks.

"On accident, when I was already in Erra—and I'd become aware of who I was while inside the prison itself."

"So somehow piercing the veil of ignorance that's in place when you reach the prison naturally—while sleeping—that's your limitation? Is that what you're saying?" Kahn asks.

"Yeah, I think so," I say. "I'm like a kid who *can* ride a bike, if I can find it. And if I can figure out where to sit, and how to balance on it while also moving forward. Otherwise, I'll just fall on my face."

"How are you planning to wake yourself up to the truth there this time?" Jesse asks.

"It requires strong emotion," I say. "Something has to be important enough to remind me of who I am and what I want, or perhaps *need* is a better word."

"What did it before?" Kahn asks.

"Needing to save Jesse, both times," I say. "And I got the message to myself by carving something into my arm. I have a few ideas for what my message tonight should contain."

Kahn frowns. "I don't like that idea."

"Oh, please," I say. "Even if I can't heal the injury on Rra, the next room over is chock full of Healers, sleeping off their night guard duty. One of them will patch me right up."

"And once you're aware of the stakes there? What will you do then?" Kahn's like a dog with a freaking bone.

"The next person to ask me whether I'm going to shore up the prison or free all the inmates loses," I say. "How's that?"

"Are you ten years old?" Kahn asks. "Because if so, that's a great plan."

"If she's ten, you'd go to jail for the way you've been leering at her," John says.

"I'm not the one kissing her," Kahn says.

"Don't I know it?" John smiles.

"These men are both jesters," Mehen says.

For once, I actually agree with him. I stand up. "I need access to the Internet." Now that I'm caught up on my options—which haven't really changed much in the last few weeks—I've got an artifact to locate. Jesse looks just fine now, but if I've learned anything over the past few weeks, it's that he can deteriorate at any time without much warning.

I need that reservoir Ra said I could borrow. With me, it's less 'in case of emergency' and more 'when the emergency happens.'

"It should be working again," John says. "As far as I can tell, the network was set up by Fred Flintstone's tech-confused grandfather, but I think I optimized it as well as anyone could."

"Perfect," I say. "I'll take Mehen to help me."

Kahn's eyebrows shoot up. "I'm sorry, did you say you need *Mehen*, the ancient Egyptian, to help you navigate your super secret Internet search?"

"I did."

A girl needs a bit of mystery now and then to keep the guys on their toes. Jesse catches my eye and lifts his chin infinitesimally, asking whether I'll explain to him later. I close my eyes with a half-smile, acknowledging that I will. Eventually. If I can find anything that makes my success even somewhat likely. No reason to distress him before it's necessary.

Kahn and John and Jesse all insist I eat another sandwich before they leave me in a small side office with a desktop that Mehen probably used before he woke up in modern times. At least the keyboard has the letters in the right places.

And at least we're alone. Even though no one else understands me when I talk to him, I worry about what they may infer from context clues.

"How can I help, Your Majesty?"

I groan. "Please don't call me that."

He takes my reproach in stride. "You didn't like it as a child, either."

"Listen, what I really need to do is place the timeframe when Terra was created, so that I can identify what era artifacts—"

"You want to research your powers and past history before picking a side." Mehen smiles approvingly.

That's an excellent idea, actually. For an ancient guy, he's still pretty sharp. "Yes, that's what I need to do." I can always explain about the reservoirs later. "But to do that, I need to know when exactly I was alive the first time, as Sekhmet—and when things became . . odd."

"In your memories, you still love Ra?"

"Do I not always love him?" I should probably have thought that through. Ra mentioned he didn't think I betrayed him, but that sort of implies that there's evidence I did. Or that the world believes I did.

"As far as I know, you always cared for your father, but I don't know everything. I have no memory of how I wound up in stasis for so long, for instance." He shrugs, not pointing out the obvious. I'm the Warden, and Ra's locked up.

"Can you tell me about any notable events, or maybe famous people, from just before Terra was formed?"

Mehen blinks. "Notable events, other than the creation of Terra, you mean?"

"Since no one on Earth remembers that Terra exists, I don't think there will be much record of that. So, yeah."

"Well, just before everything went upside down, your father's empire was conquered—taken from him by force." Mehen's lip curls. "You knew about a lot of that, of course, but you can likely find records on the conqueror, Aleksandar Ar-Rumi."

I type it into the computer, wishing I'd spent a bit more time on learning to type efficiently, and then I spin around like a turbo-charged top. "Wait. Is that the same person we call Alexander the Great?"

Mehen's voice is flat. "You've heard of him."

"He's probably the single most famous person who lived before Christ was born."

"I've never heard of this Christ, but Aleksandar was certainly not more famous than Ra. And there were a good number of people much more impressive, much smarter, and far more influential than him." Mehen scowls. "All he did was ruin things."

Call it a hunch, but based on his reaction, I'm guessing he disliked the man who conquered Egypt quite a bit. "Who exactly was Alexander? In relation to my dad, I mean."

He's smiling when I look at him over my shoulder.

"He wasn't actually my father, was he? Was it some kind of ruse?"

His smile evaporates. "Alexander is most certainly not your father."

"Then what's with the goofy grin?"

"You called him 'Dad,' which is a term of affection, is it not?"

Shoot. He's right. I decide to ignore it. Stupid memories as Sekhmet are really messing with my head. "Who was Alexander the Great to us? And how did he defeat Ra?"

Mehen's lips flatten. "If I tell you, you must promise not to tell the others."

"Why?"

"He has a high enough opinion of himself as it is."

"Who?" What's he talking about? "Are you saying that I *know* Alexander? That he's *here right now,* reborn on Earth like me and Jesse? Or are you thinking I'll tell him back in 350 BC? Because although the memories feel utterly real, I don't think I can change what happened in the past. I'm just regaining my old memories, not reliving the events of the time period."

Mehen stares at me, like he's willing me to connect pretty obvious dots.

I only know of one other person alive today whom Mehen . . . "Wait. Is it Kahn?" I leap to my feet. "You're saying that *Kahn is Alexander the Great?*"

"Stop saying *great,* like he's wonderful. He's Ra's archenemy." He spits. Like, honest to goodness, the old man hocks up a loogie and hurls it onto the mostly clean tile floor.

Which is totally gross.

And I don't even care. My brain is still reeling from this new piece of information. For the first time in a long time, I'm not the most bizarre person in the building. Because Kahn is the rebirth of a freaking legend.

Oh. And he conquered my father. That's sure a wrinkle. No wonder Mehen hates him.

❊ 4 ❊

EARTH

I don't understand how Kahn could possibly be Alexander the Great. "I thought you said he's Apophis." Although Mehen disliked Kahn at least as much when he was saying he was the serpent god who was allegedly Ra's mortal enemy.

"Apophis is the name he was born with, but to the rest of the world, the lying spider pretended to be the son of Philip, the King of Macedonia."

I'm so lost. "He *lied* about who he was?"

"Of course he did," Mehen says. "It's what he does. That's what I've been trying to tell you."

"I don't understand why he'd change his name."

"He had no choice. His mother had made an enemy of Ra, and they had to hide somewhere to hatch the plot for their revenge."

"Who's his mother?" If he says it's Rosalinde or . . . I don't know . . . anyone else that I know, my head might explode.

Mehen tilts his head like I'm crazy. "Terra was created shortly after Alexander finished conquering your father's empire . . . at his mother's command."

"The queen of Macedonia? Why was she Ra's enemy?"

"Olympias was his enemy long before she married King Philip and set her brother on a neighboring throne," Mehen says. "The other name she went by, the name you'll recognize, is Isis."

He says it so nonchalantly, like he didn't even need to mention until now that the woman credited with creating the whole prison to which I hold the key was Kahn's *mother* back in ancient Egypt. He seems to think that I should have known that all along. "None of the records say—"

"Apophis was trained by his mother to hate your father from his infancy, and as soon as he was strong enough, he attacked Ra's empire with all the forces his mother had gathered."

"You're saying that in a past life, Kahn probably wanted me dead?" Actually, he probably wanted to kill me on Earth not that long ago. Maybe this isn't such an insane concept.

There is no world in which we are enemies.

I shake my head to dislodge the memory of Kahn embracing our bizarre connection on Erra. We felt the same thing on Terra, and even now, when I turn and glance his direction, or even when I think of his perfectly chiseled jaw, something inside me shivers with longing. With heat. With the weight of fate.

But I really can't afford to get caught up in emotion right now. I need to have a clear mind to work out what's real and what isn't. If people can be bad on Terra and good on Earth, or good on Earth and bad on Erra . . . how much more different could someone be in a second lifetime? Could he have been a villain back then, but be the hero now? Or could Ra have been terrible once, but be reformed? He has spent millennia locked up, pondering his past mistakes.

All this crap is giving me a raging headache.

Luckily, a tap at the door gives me the distraction I need. "Yeah?"

John looks nervous when he steps into the room. Why would he be nervous? "Everything okay in here?"

Right. I was shouting just moments ago. "Of course, yeah, we're fine."

"You weren't speaking English, so we weren't sure what happened."

Thank goodness for that. I'm not sure it's a fabulous idea to tell anyone else that Mehen thinks Kahn was Alexander the Great. "I got the information I needed from Mehen, so that's good." I need to figure out what museum or collection has the most relics from around the time of Alexander the Great's rule. Or even better, perhaps they'll have a list of what relics they've got.

Mehen's frowning at me.

"What?"

"Your father would take care of this if he was here, but he's not." He crosses his arms. "I feel obligated to act in his place."

I sigh. "What exactly would the great Ra do if he were here?"

"Aleksandar could chew this one up and spit him out," Mehen says. "But neither of these men are worthy of you. They should both be eliminated immediately so that more worthy mates can more easily approach."

I'm definitely more than okay with no one else knowing what he's saying. "Are you actually suggesting that I kill both of my friends? My most trusted allies?" He has got to be kidding.

"You could simply send them away, but I'd strongly encourage death for the one you call Kahn." His lip curls. "I'm happy to take care of it. These men of your modern times know *nothing* of their powers. It would be a snap. Barely an inconvenience."

"They haven't had the benefit of thousands of years to refine their abilities," I say. "Neither have I."

"You're unparalleled," he says. "That is as true now as it ever was. And those boys are entirely unworthy."

"Perhaps instead of being so condescending, you could teach them some things."

He glances back at John and shakes his head. "I can't teach this one anything. He's not a Lifter." Before I can even ask, he scowls. "And I won't teach Apophis a single thing. Ever."

Of course he won't. "What about me?"

He bows his head. "I would be honored to train you."

Well, that's something.

"You have much to learn, and the more you can do, the safer you'll be until your father returns to guide your education."

"I have to do a little bit of poking around on this machine." I point at the computer. "But after that, I would like to see what you can teach me."

Mehen smiles. "Excellent. I'll wait outside." He sniffs when he reaches the doorway, as if John *smells bad,* which I know full well that he doesn't.

"Mehen's going to wait outside," I say.

John shifts to let him pass. "So you're done?"

"I have a few things to search on the computer, and then I'm meeting him outside so he can train me a bit."

"Can that wait for just a moment?" John clears his throat. "There's something I wanted to talk to you about."

Ah, crap. He's been awfully clingy since I woke up. Part of me is very okay with it—the part of me that connected with him even more strongly on Erra—but part of me feels like the world has been in free fall for weeks and I can't deal with anyone else asking anything of me. "I mean . . ." I turn toward the computer. "I actually do need to find some answers here. I know you guys want me to pick a side, or whatever, but I don't have enough information yet." Maybe if I make him think that talking with me will make it more likely I'll side with Isis, he'll drop it.

At the end of the day, I care a lot more about figuring out a solution to Jesse's flagging energy levels than I do about picking Team Isis or Team Amun. Though, I really do need to come up with a plan for when I'm thrust into Rra tonight. I'm pretty sure I'll be stuck there without a clue again, just as I was the last two times.

"This will only take a moment, I promise. More than anyone else, I know how stressed you are, and how little time we have."

The plaintive tone in his voice gets me. "Alright." I swivel back around.

John grabs a metal chair out of the corner and drags it across the room until it's right in front of me. He sits down and folds his hands in his lap. "I wanted to apologize."

That I did not expect. "For what?"

He swallows. "A few minutes ago, in the main conference room back there, I put my arm around you—"

I shake my head. "Look, it's fine. I wasn't—"

"Let me finish? Please?" He looks practically ill.

I nod.

"I like you, Alora, a lot. I've liked you for a long time, since the first day we met. There are a million little reasons why I can't stop thinking about you. You're hilarious. You're smart. You're resilient. The more I learn about you, the higher my opinion of you rises . . . And now I have memories of you on Erra." He runs his hands through his perfectly shiny black hair. It looks far better than it should, given that we're camping in a bizarre National Guard office building and taking showers in the bathroom sink. He looks upward slowly, his eyes tracking from my knees all the way up to my eyes and then freezing. They spark golden, and a tiny thrill runs up my spine. "Erra was even better than Earth in some ways. It was simpler. There was less riding on our actions, and fewer people *watching* us."

"It does feel like the whole world is weighing me down sometimes," I say.

"That's why I wanted to apologize." He closes his eyes. "I felt so close to you after our experience there. You and I bonded, and what we shared was electric and—" He clenches his fist and opens his eyes. "At least for me, it felt almost primal. I would have burned the world to ash to save you, if that's what it took. But instead, I *failed* you. Completely."

I shake my head. "It wasn't like that."

"It felt like that to me," he says, "but I'm not apologizing for that. Nothing I say could really atone for the way I failed you—but even that didn't destroy what we shared. You blaze too brightly for something like that to end us. No, you saved me instead. You forced the Earth Called to heal me, and then you brought me back to Earth." He swallows slowly. "And I repaid you by trying to . . . I don't know how to describe it. It's like I was trying to claim you, or something, draping my arm over your shoulder and glaring at Kahn for looking your way." He stands up. "I said I wouldn't take much of your time, and I swear I won't. What I wanted to say was that I'm aware there's something weird between you and Kahn. Anyone with eyeballs and probably some without can see it, plain as day. Every time he looks at you and the air in the room heats up ten degrees, I want to destroy something, and that's not fair to you. So I'm walking out of the room right now, and I won't act like I'm your boyfriend anymore. Because I'm not. You only said I was to keep him away—I don't know why, but I don't think it worked like you wanted it to. I saw you flinch earlier when I touched you. I'd never, ever force myself on you, and I don't want to complicate things for you, either. I can't think of a way to ruin things between us, whatever they are, faster than trying to force something that you don't feel as strongly as I do."

My hands tremble slightly. He's not wrong—I'm both insanely attracted to him and terrified of what that means. I was using him as a shield from Kahn, because I'm far more scared of whatever I feel for him. "I'm all sorts of confused right now."

"What you need is friends," John says. "Allies. People who aren't trying to force you into anything, and I vow that I will be that. I may not be your fated soulmate or whatever —I may just be an average Joe . . . or John." He chuckles. "But I'll do *anything* you need, and I'm on your side, first and foremost. I said it before, and I want to reiterate it. I got caught up arguing with Kahn before, but that had more to do with being a stupid, territorial, possessive male, and less to do with what you need. So I'm fixing that. You won't deal with it again." John pivots on his heel and strides toward the door.

"Wait," I say.

He freezes, his broad shoulders motionless.

"Can you help me with something? As a friend?"

He's back at my side a moment later. "Anything."

I point at the screen. "It's a computery thing."

He shifts the chair so he can see the computer. "What do you need?"

I sense that he was being utterly truthful, and for once, I feel like I can trust someone. I tell him about the reservoir Ra offered me on Ā, if only I can find its mirror on Earth. And I tell him about what Mehen said about Kahn when I asked what time period I should search for artifacts.

John groans. "That guy's bad enough already—when he hears that he's some kind of epic, empire-conquering icon, he'll be impossible to live with."

I can't help laughing. "I'm honestly worried about his ego if we tell him."

"Then let's not share." John's smiling. "But it's good to know what era to search." He points at the computer. "Can I?"

I shrug and slide over. "Please do. I have no idea where to start, and I'd normally ask Jesse to do it, but . . . "

"You don't want to tell him about the reservoir in case he objects, and he doesn't remember enough about computers to be helpful."

"Bingo," I say. "Is that wrong?" I bite my lip. "I've never kept anything from him, but I'm not sure how he'll react."

John sighs. "I've been meaning to talk to you about the whole Jesse thing, but I didn't want to upset you. You're stressed enough as it is."

"The ethical part feels like, I don't know, like an assisted suicide issue," I say. "Like, if a patient wants to die, and a doctor knows they will anyway, some people think they should allow the doc to help, and some don't. But in this case, I know we can save Jesse from the *murder*—"

"That my dad inflicted wrongly," John says, his eyes somber.

I nod.

"But you're not sure Jesse will agree, since we're not sure where the power in that reservoir originated." John crosses his arms.

"But it's not like we can give the power back, no matter where it was first obtained." I drop my voice, just in case someone is listening or about to enter. "But John, I've had a lot of memories popping up, and I'm pretty sure I know where it came from. Ra and his magistrates in Egypt judged people for what they did. Whenever possible, they retrained and educated, but when someone was truly evil . . . he . . . " My foot begins to tap. The way it felt in my dreams wasn't the same way it sounds. I can't help cringing as I say the words. "Well, he kind of harvested them for the magic in their life-force, or whatever, instead of just executing bad people."

John frowns. "Is that worse somehow? Turning them into something good instead of just chopping off their head?"

"It *feels* kind of worse to me," I say. "Maybe because I could benefit from their deaths. I think, if I had to guess, that's what landed him in the Terran jail, turning people into battery power for spells."

"What do the other Assimilators do?" he asks. "Have you seen that?"

Now that he asks, I realize I haven't. "I mean, in my memories, I can harvest the life-force from beings in the same way that my dad can, by simply siphoning it from a distance. I know other Assimilators have to physically touch the person or creature or whatever to take their energy, but I'm not sure whether there's some kind of code or something that they follow."

"It's possible some of the answers to those questions could be found in the records that would accompany Ra's relic you're looking for, right?"

I hadn't considered that.

"Mehen might know some things that could help."

Maybe.

"You should let him train you, too," John says. "So far you've been remarkably lucky in that you've been able to stay sheltered." He grimaces. "I think that may be changing, and soon."

My heartbeat accelerates. "Has anything happened?"

"Dad says Isis has seized the US military from the top and they're shutting things down."

"What does that mean, shutting things down?"

John slides to the computer and starts tapping, pulling up headline after headline. INTERNATIONAL

AIRPORTS CLOSE. And MARTIAL LAW IN EFFECT. Also, RATIONING MEASURES INITIATED.

"Ohmygosh." My words come out all run together, in an alarming whoosh.

"The citizens in small-town locations, such as where we are, aren't too keen on any of the new orders, even though they're being spun as government action 'for their protection.'"

"What's your dad doing about it?"

"Amun has focused its efforts on the energy and resource chains in the United States," John says, "including food supply and whatnot."

"Which the military can take by force at this point," I say.

"Can they?" John shrugs. "Maybe. I mean, Isis and Amun have roughly equivalent numbers of supporters, and I think our abilities here will render a lot of the traditional firepower obsolete. If I had any suggestions to make for Mehen and your training, it would be learning to counter modern technology in particular."

"Which he'll have no idea how to do," I say.

"I imagine he could learn if we show him the basics of how those work, but first and foremost, if you want to locate the reservoir, then all our arguing about you picking a side may be premature. Perhaps you have more information to gain before you can do that—namely, what can you *do* exactly and what you're *willing* to do. I guess that means I owe you another apology, for getting so caught up in what I wanted that I failed to ask what you needed."

He's right, and it's nice to have someone else thinking outside of himself for once. "We need to figure out where the collar might be and how to get to it."

John said he was good on the computer. He even mentioned he was a hacker in the past.

He dramatically downplayed his abilities.

Over the next forty-eight minutes, he hacks three museum networks and filters through their confidential catalogs of artifacts, narrowing down with wicked precision the exact items in their collection that might be of use to us. "That," I say at last, leaping from my chair when I see Ra's collar on the screen—exactly as I saw it in Ā not too long ago. "That's it."

"It's located at the British museum, in London, in the Bloomsbury area." He clicks a button and prints the page. "If things hadn't been so chaotic worldwide, I'm not sure I'd have been able to hack their system with this decrepit machine and sluggish connection, but thankfully, I don't think their security chief was bringing his A game." He stands up. "Now we just need to figure out how to get to London."

"Thank you, John."

Only a few inches separate us, and in spite of the things he said and the space he's giving me, I'm not sure I want it. He's the one person I can tell *everything* to without worrying he'll judge me. I inhale his scent—a tangy sweet sort of green tea—and memorize it in this moment. A veritable obstacle course of choices yawns in front of me, and it feels like the least important is the guy I want to kiss.

But John gets me. He supports me no matter what. And that's an undervalued trait. Mehen may not be impressed, but I am. I sway a little closer, and his arms circle my waist.

"Alora."

My name is a warning in his mouth. He's telling me that he offered me space—he stepped back of his own free will, and maybe that's what makes him so irresistible. The fact that he's not asking for anything.

And that's why I kiss him.

Because he's demanding nothing and offering everything and that's what I need right now. Someone who comprehends that my life is balanced on the edge of a blade and doesn't want to tip me over or force my hand.

His lips are firm, his hands are strong, and the chemistry I feel when I'm with him is very compelling. It's stronger, even, than it was on Erra, or on Earth before we went through what we did on Erra together. "This is real," I whisper, pulling back just enough to whisper. "And I care about you a great deal."

"But you're drawn to Kahn in some bizarre way you don't really understand." His smile is wry, and he releases me.

I can't argue with him. "Thank you for your help. Today. Always."

"I'm not going anywhere," he says. "Now let's figure out how to fly you to London before your dad starts shooting down planes."

EARTH

There's actually a breeze outside—it's nice, for the South in the early fall, anyway.

"Before you can travel anywhere, before you leave this miserable little dwelling," Mehen says, "I insist that you select your Court. It's a fluid group. You can appoint members and remove them the same day, but you need people sworn to protect you before we come out of hiding and begin traipsing around the world. Especially since, based on the magical box's moving images, the world isn't stable right now."

The magical box? He must mean the television. I suppose with his experience around magic, that makes more sense. I don't bother to explain. But that wasn't the only odd thing he said. My *Court*? "I'm not a princess," I say. "And I don't need a crown or a court or a team. I have friends, and they're already invested in protecting me without swearing to do it."

"Tell them what I request." He gestures pointedly at Kahn, John, Jesse, and Martin, who are all watching us argue with rapt attention.

Our training was an abject failure, which is probably the

source of his anxiety. Mehen knew nothing of guns, but he managed to crumple every single firearm we possessed inside of five seconds, before I could explain that we wanted to work on methods of disabling modern day weaponry. Then he irritatingly told us that our modern day weapons wouldn't be a problem, as he had already proven. He has such unfathomable control in his Lifting that I couldn't even begin to compare at that level. He realized the gunpowder in the bullets was a problem after the first shot was fired and instead collapsed the gun chambers, but he can't possibly predict the variety of weapons man has developed in the absence of much magic. Which means his refusal to learn is going to be his undoing. And probably mine as well.

"You may be able to Lift this entire structure." Mehen gestures at the building we've been hiding inside. "But that won't save you from a dagger, or even a carefully placed needle to the heart. You need people you're positive will protect you. And you need individuals who will repair the gaps in your education."

"And you'd be perfect to lead this Court, I presume?" I arch one eyebrow.

He blushes—like actually turns pink. "Only until someone more qualified is a viable option." He bows.

"Why's he bowing?" Jesse asks. "What's he jabbering about now?"

I'm pretty sure, based on the heat in my cheeks, that I blush as much as Mehen when I explain what he's requesting. "He thinks I need to create some sort of formal *court* of people." I cringe. "So that there's a pecking order and protocols in place to keep me safe. I told him that you guys will already work together, and that no one needs an official position or to swear oaths—"

"I'll do it," Jesse says. "I think as your brother I should

get a pretty cool title. Like, Chief Loyalty Expert. Or maybe First Lieutenant."

He's kidding. Thank goodness he's cracking jokes. It's not like I *wanted* anyone to join my *court*.

"I'll swear whatever oaths you want from me, obviously," John says. "And until someone better with fire comes along, I am happy to keep training you. Even if Mehen thinks my skills are subpar."

"He thinks we're all subpar," Jesse says, still grinning.

"We're also all she has, and I want a neat title too." John shrugs. "Maybe Fire Chief." Unlike Jesse, John doesn't appear to be kidding. He looks a little embarrassed about his title suggestion, but he seems legitimately interested in swearing an oath.

"Of course someone who has Lifted for hundreds of years while Ra prolonged his life would have more refined control," Kahn says. "That speaks much more to the kind of leader Ra was than to the skill we have, but if my Lifting isn't so rudimentary as to render my participation useless, I'd be happy to swear an oath. Certainly, I think keeping you safe and healthy is my top priority, and it's a good idea to make sure we're all on the same page."

Kahn seems serious, too. What is happening?

"I'll probably be more helpful than anyone else in keeping you healthy," Martin says.

"And me," Thomas says the same time that Rosalinde says, "And me too, of course."

Martin frowns. "We really only need two Healers, and I'd prefer if Rosalinde and Thomas stay here, safe and out of harm's way."

"And let you and Roland have all the fun?" Thomas clenches his fists.

"I'm not sure whether you'd trust me again," Oliver says, "but I'd be happy to swear any oath you prepare. And since you're an Assimilator, perhaps you can tell whether we're sincere."

Mehen's smile is irritatingly smug as he leans against a lamp post. "They're all offering to join your court, are they not?"

I scowl. "I already trust them," I say. "This isn't necessary."

"Soon thousands upon thousands will flock to you," Mehen says. "They are the first, and they deserve some kind of acknowledgement of that, even if they will soon be replaced by more competent supporters."

I nearly choke.

"You should give them that—they'll love you more for it, and they'll continue to support you in their limited roles for as long as they live."

Is he for real? Their limited roles? People flocking to me? But when I look around at my friends, I see something I didn't notice before. Vulnerability. They've expressed a desire to be given an official position—and I'd be rejecting them in a bizarre way if I turned them down now. This is idiotic, but they don't see it that way. If they follow me on this trip, this international flight, and my subsequent attempt to locate all of Ra's old belongings and writings, it won't be safe, not for me or them.

Also, I trust each of them, but they don't trust one another. Mehen may be eccentric and out of touch, but he might also be right about this. Having them all promise a few little things that they're already willing to do might help unite us as a group. It might make them more likely to listen to me and work together when I need help.

"Alright," I say in English. "But I'm not making up different titles for everyone."

"So that's a no to Chief Loyalty Officer?" Jesse half-smiles, his eyes squinting up, and I'm relieved that at least one other person sees the ridiculous nature of all this.

"Oh, I'm calling you that now," I say. "No way around it."

In the end, every single one of my friends insists on swearing to protect and serve, which is insane. The birds chirp like nothing bizarre is happening. The sun shines down on us like the world hasn't turned on its head. And all my friends get down on one knee and pledge to protect me.

Except for one.

"Can I talk to you alone for a minute?" Kahn's voice is low and urgent.

"You don't have to do it, and you don't need to explain anything, either," I say. "I'm the first one to admit this all seems bonkers."

He shakes his head. "It's not about that."

Uh. What else can it be about? He's the only one who hasn't sworn to protect me. "Sure."

"Good news." John slides his cell phone into his pocket. "Dad located a jet big enough for all of us and as many of his people as you'd like to take with you not far from here at a private airfield. We need to leave ASAP, since Isis is tightening airways—they're saying they'll be patrolling them with Air Force and Navy personnel soon."

"Sounds like the United States is turning into quite a fun place to be," I say.

"You're sure you want to leave?" Jesse asks. "It might be hard to get back home."

"Home for me is wherever you are," I say. "It's never been about a particular place." And my best bet at keeping Jesse safe is getting my hands on that battery power Ra offered. Once I have that, ready to use as soon as Jesse begins to fade, I'll feel a lot better.

"It won't take long." Kahn's voice is low, reminding me that he asked for a minute of my time.

"Sure," I say. "Yeah, that's fine." I pretend that my heart doesn't race and my pulse doesn't beat loudly in my ears at the thought of being alone with him. Even pretending that I'm fine, I can't quite bring myself to look directly at him.

He heads for the all-glass front door of the Louisiana National Guard building and I follow, my eyes tracing the shape of his broad shoulders and muscular back before I force myself to behave and focus on the back of his head. Which still gives me glimpses of the strong cut of his jaw when he shifts and yanks the door open. It's hard not to get distracted when I'm around him, but I'm going to figure it out. Even if he doesn't want to serve or protect me.

The second we walk into the small foyer—alone—a thrill races up my spine and my muscles clench with excitement. Which is stupid. Nothing's going to happen—not right now, probably not ever. He walks to the reception desk and leans on the table, several feet away from where I've stopped in the open foyer, as if he, like me, needs space between us to think clearly.

"What do you want?" I wish I didn't sound so abrupt, but it's the best I can do. I glance behind him at the doorway into the room where I awoke. "I probably ought to gather whatever belongings someone thought to bring for me." Clothing and possessions have never been high on my list, but right now I care even less how I look and what I'm wearing. The only reason I want to grab them is to keep from having to stop somewhere and find more clothing. All delays are bad delays until I've found Ra's reservoir and Jesse's not at risk.

The past few weeks have thrown what really matters into sharp relief.

"I wanted to explain, but I couldn't do it with everyone standing around staring at me." The muscles in Kahn's jaw twitch and he looks at me intently.

"I wasn't kidding. I don't actually think everyone needs to swear to protect me." I don't admit that it hurt a bit when he wouldn't. Especially after his certainty back on Erra that we'd never be enemies.

"You have a lot of decisions to make, Alora, and I'm behind you, entirely. I want you to know that first. But I can't be here as some kind of subservient follower." He shakes his head. "That's not what you really need, anyway. You clearly have enough of those, with more sure to follow."

I open my mouth to correct him.

"Just let me finish?" He looks almost apologetic.

I shrug.

"I may disagree with you often," he says. "In fact, I expect that I will. We seem to disagree fundamentally about what to do with Ra. I know it's probably confusing for you."

"I don't disagree or agree with keeping him on Ā—I don't know enough about what happened or who he is to make any decisions right now."

"You did lock him up to begin with, if, as we suspect, you created Terra," Kahn says, "but that's not even what I came to discuss." He moves toward me rapidly, closing the gap between us in three steps. "Do you remember the moment on Erra, right before it all unraveled?" He shifts closer still, and the heat from his body warms me.

I sway toward him. I can't help noticing that he smells like woodsmoke and pine.

"You said something then, something I haven't been able to stop thinking about."

"All your memories of Erra and Terra . . . you have them all?" I risk a quick glance at his face.

His eyes are full of heat. His cheekbones are sharp, his lips slightly parted. He exhales, and his breath fanning over my face makes my own catch. "You said we were in love once, but maybe not in this time." His eyes sweep over me. "I thought I had gone insane, you know." His teeth grit and that muscle in his jaw tenses again. "When I met you on Earth the first time. I was supposed to be working for Isis' interests. They sent me because I had some connection to you on Terra and they hoped you'd trust me. But when I met you, all my duties and tasks flew out of my brain. All I cared about was keeping you safe. All I wanted was to take you in my arms and hold you forever." He draws a ragged breath, but doesn't move a single inch closer. "You thought it was the exordium, but I knew it couldn't be a connection we'd forged on Earth, leaking through to Terra. After all, we'd only just met on Earth."

I lick my lips and his eyes focus on my mouth. I want him to kiss me. Badly. I want his hands to circle my waist and pull me closer. I want him to pick me up and keep me safe, like he said he longed to do.

"But on Erra, it seemed like you had thought it through. And that made me think. What if Mehen's right? What if you're Sekhmet, and I'm Ra's enemy . . . and we did fall in love on Earth? Thousands of years ago."

The whole idea is insane. I'm regaining my memories slowly, so slowly. I clearly loved Shu then as I love Jesse now. But the thought that I might have met Kahn, that our connection from thousands of years ago might have been so strong that later, many, many years later, when we were both reborn . . . I shake my head. "It was a silly idea."

His hand lifts up slowly, so slowly that I can practically hear my heart beating a hole in my body as his fingers rise past my waist, past my chest, above my shoulder and toward my face, finally coming to hover in front of my mouth.

"Silly," he whispers, just as his index finger brushes against my bottom lip.

A shiver races downward, exploding through my body. My fingers and toes tingle. My core heats up, and I *yearn* to be closer. I *long* for him to touch me again. "Silly."

When his head dips toward mine, I practically leap into his arms, my right hand curling around the back of his neck, and my left hand grabbing his shoulder and yanking him downward. Our mouths collide softly, effortlessly, like we've kissed a thousand times. A million.

Like it's never been enough, never will be enough, even in another two thousand years.

Longing, like honey, trails down my throat, into my belly, and heats, curling through me like golden light. I can't quite stop shivering, but I'm not cold. I'm filled to the brim with delight, with energy and hope and unfettered glee. I want to laugh and to cry out in such exquisite pain that it's almost pleasure.

His mouth shifts, pressing hard against mine, like he's worried I'll pull away at any moment. Like he doesn't quite believe that everything inside of me is melting and reforming around the one thing I know is true: I love Kahn. And yet, it's happening anyway. All that I was and all that I will be have met in this moment and are crashing into one another.

I will never be as strong, as beautiful, as brilliant, or as powerful alone as I can be with Kahn at my side. I will never be this joyful, this confident, or this complete if I stand without him. And that thought scares me more than anything in the world, other than the thought of losing my beloved brother.

The horror of my deep-seated desire to be with him, to stand beside him forever gives me the strength to wrench away and stumble back a few steps, moving and moving until my backside bumps into the glass of the front door. I cough into my hand to buy enough time to recover.

Who am I kidding? Days wouldn't be enough.

"I don't know what that is," Kahn says, "but it's *something*. Something I never imagined I'd feel. Something I never want to walk away from."

"It's not something I've chosen," I say. "It's not something we've earned."

"You chose to create Terra," he whispers. "You chose to lock Ra in prison. You chose to cut people off from their powers."

"Or maybe it was someone else. Maybe this was all a mistake. Or maybe I did it, but only as a time out. Perhaps it was always set to expire," I say. "We've been through this."

"The only way you'll know," Kahn says, "is to regain more memories. Until you do, I swear absolutely that I will remain by your side. I'll offer my life for yours. I'll do anything and everything required to keep you safe until you know what you need to know to make the right choice. And once you have done what's right, corrected the wrongs that have been laced into our world, then I'll support you in accomplishing whatever you deem right, whether it's tearing Rra and Ā down, or rebuilding Erra and Terra."

My hands tremble at my sides. "You are swearing after all." I can't help a tiny smile.

"I won't lie about this, Alora. You chose Jesse before—his continued existence mattered more to you than restoring Erra." He sighs. "Someone has already died to save him, inadvertent or not, it wasn't a clean or easy thing. I don't think we know whether bringing him to Earth from Terra was right or wrong, not for sure. I still feel in my bones that Terra existed for good reason and was created at great cost, and that we should be restoring it, but we don't know enough yet. For that reason, I'm supporting you until we know more. I care about your brother deeply. We were close friends on Terra, and I know he's a good person. But if you pick to save Jesse instead of saving the world, even given the way I feel about you . . . it won't be enough. I won't support you in that."

"There is no world in which we are enemies," I whisper.

He freezes. "That's still true, you know. If you start to lose yourself . . . I'll always be here to remind you who you really are. I won't let you forget whom Jesse loves, and what matters the most."

I really hope it doesn't come to that. Because I'm not sure I care who I am without my brother. And I doubt Kahn can stop me from doing anything.

I'm not sure anyone can.

John taps on the glass with ridiculously eager eyes. I nearly jump out of my skin. It felt as though the whole world had dropped away, but of course, we've been standing in the foyer of a boring National Guard building this whole time.

He pushes the door open. "Dad says that there's another one of Ra's Lieutenants waiting for you in London who *just* woke up. Once they managed to explain to him that Mehen and Sekhmet were headed his way, he practically leapt for joy. Or at least, he started babbling so fast they couldn't make sense of what he was saying."

"I'm not sure it's a great idea for us to meet up with anyone," I say. "Especially another one of Ra's people." He's got to be an elemental, if he just woke up.

John frowns. "Dad wasn't too keen on this whole plan at first. He tried to forbid us from going, honestly, but I told him he doesn't have a right to dictate to you. The only reason he was willing to get us transportation over there was because I swore we'd immediately meet up with the Amun soldiers in London."

"I'm so glad you were willing to help her choose a side," Kahn says, "even though she made it clear that she's not sure what she wants to do."

"It's bad there," John says. "There's been a struggle here, but it's mostly been civil and the violence has been contained to people who understand what's going on— that's not true in Europe. Dad says it's an all-out war."

"Here's a thought," I say. "We tell your dad whatever we want, and then when we get there, we can choose whether to meet up with his men."

"To do that, we'd need to land somewhere other than where's he's directing us," Kahn says.

"Exactly," I say. "I think we should be able to manage finding a small airport that could accommodate us." I look from one man to the other. "Don't you think?"

"I have one friend I could call," Kahn says. "He has some British contacts."

"We can ask the others as well," John says.

Nothing has been easy since I woke up. "Let me grab my stuff and we can figure this out."

I push past Kahn, ignoring the unwelcome jolt of delight at being so near him, and stalk into the room I was sleeping in for the last few days. I look around, dismayed, because there's not a bag, or a box, or any kind of container at all.

There is a bright pink lotus blossom on the pillow. It tugs my attention toward it, and suddenly I'm moving without thinking. It wasn't there when I left, and I haven't seen a lotus blossom in the South . . . ever. It's practically glowing where it rests on my discarded bed coverings. My fingers tremble as I reach for it, remembering the lotus blossoms in my room every day, decorating the entire palace, really. I'm not sure where anyone here in Louisiana would have found it—I doubt there's much demand for exotic flowers here in the middle of nowhere.

The fresh scent floods the room and I inhale it slowly, savoring the tangy sweet smell, laden with memories. It's as large as my palm and looks like it was just picked moments ago. Only once I've taken several breaths with it right underneath my nose do I realize there's a slip of paper on the pillow that must have been underneath it all along. It's thick, made of pressed fibers, and folded simply in half. I use my free hand to flip it open and then I freeze.

Don't starve yourself, cub. Lions can't eat grass.

Footsteps sound behind me.

I drop the lotus blossom and the paper and spin around to see who's there.

"We didn't manage to bring anything with us." John cringes. "We were in a hurry, and it didn't even occur—"

"It's fine," I say. "I'm sure that wherever the clothes I'm wearing now came from, we can find more. I don't care much about soap or clothing or personal belongings."

I expect him to comment on the flower or the note, but he merely shrugs. "If you make me a list of what you need, I'll make sure we have it on the plane." He turns back toward the door. "We really ought to leave soon, though."

"Right," I say. "Absolutely." I walk toward him, and he heads out. I spin around, ready to scoop up the flower and the note . . . but they're both gone.

Some part of Dad's magic? Or am I losing my mind? I can't get on that plane soon enough. I really hope I can find some answers when we find that reservoir of power. I'm sick of having no idea what's possible and fumbling around like an idiot all the time.

"You alright?" Jesse's waiting in the foyer. "You're really pale."

"I'm fine," I say. "I'm not the one who's leaking bits of my soul."

He rolls his eyes. "Please. Not my soul. Just my soul *energy*."

"You sound more like yourself than you did when I went under for the last prison break."

"I manage to knock more dreams loose every time I go to sleep these days." He grins at me. "Like, I remember what you gave me for Christmas last year."

"But do you recall how I *got* that fat stack of movie ticket vouchers?"

His grin widens, becoming even more crooked than usual, his eyes squinting up until I almost can't see how blue they are. "You dressed up as *Sponge Bob* to welcome people to that new movie theater." He laughs then. "And had them pay you in movie tickets."

"They paid me double," I say, "which is what made it worth it, but it was really frigging hot in that suit, even in October and November."

"And we got double our money again by sticking around for a second show after each one," he says.

I try not to think about how our last movie ended. "I miss those days," I say. "When our biggest fear was that a social worker might drag us back to a group home."

Jesse steps toward me and wraps an arm around my shoulder. "I always knew you were amazing, even if no one else realized it yet. And I don't wish we were there again. I'm proud of you now."

It's eerily close to the message Ra somehow sent me. "Have you had any other memories?"

His brows draw together. "Sure. Not all of them have been good. Too many of Aunt Trina, and even a few with Mom and Dad before they died."

I shake my head. "I don't mean memories as Jesse."

"Huh?"

"I've been remembering my time as Sekhmet, daughter of Ra, and you're there too. You're Shu, my older brother, son of Ra and Hathor."

He shakes his head. "Nothing like that. Not so far, anyway, but I'll tell you if I do remember any of it."

"It's weird," I say.

"Luckily, you're an expert on weird."

"I need to figure out what to do before I go to sleep." I can't help yawning just thinking about it.

"We'll probably all fall asleep on the plane," he says. "It's a long flight. But we'll have a lot of Healers on board, so I think you can do what you did the last two times and cut or burn a message to yourself that'll help you remember Earth when you're on Rra. Right?"

"Yeah, but first I have to think what to say."

"How about 'This world isn't real. It's a bizarre shifter world that's actually a prison for people with the ability to turn into animals. Remember your awesome brother Jesse, and free your mind.'"

"That would be perfect, but I'd need to carve it from my neck to my ankle," I say. "And also, that many words would really hurt."

He rolls his eyes, and we start brainstorming actual ideas.

I take a break to scrawl down a list of items I'll need, including clothing, toiletries, etcetera, for John. Then Jesse and I climb into a big black suburban bound for a private airstrip. Mehen insists on being next to us both. Kahn and John do as well, but surprisingly they don't argue in the vehicle, which is a relief.

"We need to refine your Lifting," Mehen says. "We may as well work on it now."

Oh, goodie.

He literally pulls a handful of sand from his pocket and dumps it on the floor of the suburban. "Lift those."

So I do, easily. The entire handful of sand flies into the air, hovering in front of us.

"No." Mehen snatches the sand from me easily.

"How did you do that?" I ask.

"You're like a child fumbling with thick, clumsy hands to put a bite of something in her mouth." His lips are a hard line. "You must learn to control your abilities." He begins to weave the sand in an intricate pattern of tiny lines, all flowing at once, so confusing and multilayered that

I can't even follow it. "Replicate that." He drops the sand again, only this time it scatters all over the vehicle as if blown by invisible wind.

I reach out with my senses and feel for the sand grains and pull . . . and they stream toward me slowly. I'm kind of proud of that, but Mehen looks entirely unimpressed. "I don't recall what pattern you were following," I say.

He yanks the sand away again, in spite of my efforts to retain it, and rolls his eyes. Rolls his eyes, like he's a teenage girl at the mall. "Pay attention, little one. I don't know how much time we have. You need to learn to Lift with purpose."

The rest of the ride continues in much the same way, with Mehen schooling me over and over. By the time we reach the airstrip, my eyes are exhausted, and my mind is fuzzy.

"If it makes you feel better," Kahn says, "I couldn't have done any of that either. That guy's the best Lifter I've ever seen."

Mehen glares at Kahn like he'd relish gutting him slowly.

"Why does he hate me so much?" Kahn asks.

"Could be that you're Alexander the Great, reborn," John says casually.

Kahn laughs. So does Jesse.

I ought to correct them, but for some reason I don't. It feels like the kind of thing Kahn ought to remember for himself.

After what feels like an hour of inspecting it, Mehen's finally satisfied that the plane is safe, at least as far as outside enemies go. "This thing, it flies up into the air like a great bird?" He frowns. "And you sit inside its belly voluntarily?"

"What's the holdup now?" John asks.

"He's worried about the logistics of air travel," I say.

"He thinks it sounds insane to climb inside the plane's 'belly.' I can't even really argue. If I hadn't seen it on television so many times, I'd be a lot more nervous myself."

"Wait, you've never been on a plane?" John asks.

I shake my head. "Nope. We rode a bus from the Pacific Northwest to the South. Never been glamorous enough for air travel."

"I will not climb in there," Mehen says. "I do not let creatures put me in their bellies."

I translate again.

"Tell him that we all sit inside its belly," Jesse says. "It's the whole reason it was created."

Even after I explain to him that Shu's fine with it, Mehen won't budge. "It's an abomination. A boat is better. With a Wind Called soldier and my Lifting powers, we could make quick time."

"He says a boat would be just as fast." I groan.

"Quicker than a few hours?" Kahn asks.

After arguing every angle I can imagine unsuccessfully, I'm stuck ordering him to board. It's the first time I've been grateful that Mehen swore an oath to serve, because there's no way that Jesse will last the duration of a boating trip to *Europe*. A few moments later, I have to order him again, but this time, it's to stand calmly while I let John carve some words into my arm with a dagger. If I'm going to fall asleep and likely slip into Rra, I'm not doing it with no message at all like I did on Erra.

Mehen is furious, but he finally relents. John carves the words: *Remember Jesse. His soul is leaking. He needs you.*

It's not elegant, but hopefully it will get the job done. Luckily, I've gotten pretty good at falling asleep with injuries. After the plane takes off and levels out, I close my eyes and lean my chair back as far as it will go. With Mehen on my right and Jesse on my left, I close my eyes and go to sleep.

$\maltese$ 6 $\maltese$

ANCIENT EGYPT

Dad's pacing. It's never a good sign when he paces.

"What's wrong?" I drop my fork. It's not like I'm going to eat anything while he's this upset. "And where's Shu?"

Dad finally stops, his hands clasped behind his back, his eyes troubled. "Your brother's securing our border. We suffered a significant loss yesterday, and I'm not sure what to do about it."

I pull out the chair next to me. "Come tell me."

He swallows, looking me over from head to toe as if he hasn't seen me every single day of my eighteen years of life. "Fine. You're old enough to become more involved." He strides quickly around the table and slides into the seat next to me. He doesn't eat a bite, but it's a start.

"Okay, so tell me what happened, and what Shu's doing about it today." I really hope he's not in danger. Dad hardly ever worries about him, probably because he's capable of taking care of himself, but it still makes me nervous when he's away. Especially when Dad's pacing.

"You've heard me talk about the Sacred Band of Thebes."

"Not often."

"I don't go into many specifics about warfare—you don't seem drawn to it, for one thing. But also, it's exhausting for me. I imagine for you, it's even worse."

Irritation pulses through me. I'm sick of being sheltered from what's really happening. "You can tell me the truth. I want to know."

"One of my advisors, a man I respected named Plato, who died around the time you were born, had an idea many years ago. He suggested that an army would hold together much better if they were bound by more than honor or duty."

Huh?

"He suggested that if we were to select soldiers who—"

"Were in love?" I raise my eyebrows.

Dad laughs. "I appreciate your youthful exuberance more than you know. That was his suggestion, yes. Of course, that failed abysmally. The first army we assembled was so worried about their lovers that they couldn't focus. They crumpled like a rotten gourd."

"That's too bad."

Dad shrugs. "So we moved on to another idea. A better one."

I sit up a little straighter. "Which was?"

"We stuck a supra alpha at the head of a band of elite warriors."

I swallow. "A supra? Why not just a regular alpha?"

"Using alphas in battle has been standard for years. They can keep their troops fighting, and often force them to maintain their animal forms, which are usually more savage. But as you already know, supras are rare. Typically we don't risk them in battle. If one is killed, there's no telling how long it might be before we find and train another."

"But this sacred band?"

Dad sighs. "You know that shifter alphas all make me uncomfortable. Supra alphas are the worst of the lot, as no one can challenge them. But even among them, there's a pecking order." He stands up and circles around behind the chair. He really is agitated, his hands gripping the back of the chair so hard his knuckles have gone white. "My friend Pelopidas has been with me since shortly after I vanquished my father." Dad's voice is low. He still hates talking about Amun. "I only send his soldiers in when I want something *finished*."

"What did you want to end?" I look into his eyes, searching for his emotions. Is he angry? Scared? Remorseful? "Who did you send him after?"

He shoves the chair forward and resumes his pacing. "The Macedonians are snatching up my land. They're encroaching on all sides, and they're gobbling up any governments not specifically under my protection."

"Do you care about the other countries? You haven't even claimed them, right? Are the Macedonians cruel or unjust?"

Dad shakes his head. "It's not that. I doubt their rule is worse than the chaos that reigned before they took over. It's the person behind their movements that concerns me."

I frown.

"Isis," he says. "She took her son and fled many years ago." He sighs. "I knew it wasn't the end, but now it appears she's finally ready to confront me. I find, now that the day is here, I'm exhausted."

"Who is she?" I stand up and circle the table. "Didn't Mother leave to join her?"

Dad stops pacing to stare out the open window, which is almost as disconcerting. "Hathor was convinced by her lies, yes."

"Convinced that I'm a monster," I whisper.

Dad spins around so quickly that it startles me. "You're nothing of the kind."

"What really happened, Dad? That's the reason you don't involve me. Everything you do, everything you task Shu to handle, it always comes back around to Mother leaving. Just tell me—what about me is so awful that it forced Mother to flee?"

Tears well in Dad's eyes. I've never seen that in all my years. It terrifies me in a way I can't quite explain. If it's something this bad . . . do I really want to know? My hands tremble, but I grasp the sides of my tunic tightly to still them. "Please just tell me."

He points at the bench by the window. "Alright."

I nearly stumble in my shock. He's going to tell me the truth, after all this time? I practically sprint to the bench.

He follows me over, his eyes heavy, his mouth twisted. "You know about my father. You know that I didn't have an excellent entry into this world. But from the second we eliminated his stranglehold on Egypt, I did my best to erase the damage he did and to brighten the world around me in the same way he dimmed it."

"Okay," I say.

"It worked, largely. I eliminated villains. I learned to use my powers, and I developed a code, which I followed religiously. I accumulated loyal followers, beginning with Mehen."

"Like Am-Heh," I say. "Anat and Aha."

Dad nods. "I now have many supporters I trust. Some have stayed with me always, whereas some have left, changing until their paths diverged from mine. I've allowed them to leave me and follow their own paths. I believe people must go where ma'at dictates, and I believe that when things are out of alignment, balance will return, however much blood is required to bring it. In those early years, I made mistakes, but I did some things right. I tried to learn when I did things wrong and never repeat my errors."

That all sounds good.

"I fell in love. I had children. Many, many children."

For some reason, that upsets me. "*Many* others?" Then I remember the old stories Shu would tell me. "Do you mean the past Pharaohs, like Hatshepsut and Thutmose?"

He places a hand over mine. "They are two of them, yes. But I've had over a hundred children in my lifetime, cub."

Tefnut was always reserved around me, aloof even, but I hadn't considered why. I wonder how much older than me she is, and how many other brothers and sisters we have that I've never even met. The number he threw out so casually finally registers in my brain. "Wait, you have more than *a hundred?*"

He laughs. "I've been alive for a very long time, remember?"

It's still hard for me to believe that he's been alive more than twenty-four hundred years. And although I understand the number, comprehending what a life that long would be like is difficult.

"I've met many powerful people in my life," he says. "And I've had many children, one hundred and eighteen to be precise, as far as I know, anyway."

I'm still barely able to comprehend it. "And what powers have they had?"

"Every power out there," he says.

It's hard to imagine that I have so many siblings I've never even heard of before, much less met. "Where are they?" I glance around, as if they might suddenly parade through the palace.

"People often become greedy," he says, "and the more power you give them . . . "

"What are you saying?"

"I've watched my children love me, hate me, and leave me. I've even had to—" He coughs. "Eliminate a few of them." His eyes are profoundly sad, but his voice. The stark pain in it shreds my insides.

"Your own children?"

He closes his eyes. "It has been the single greatest horror of my life."

"Will you kill me one day?"

His eyes spring open. "Of course not. I couldn't, in any case. You're stronger than I am."

"Your other children weren't?"

He shakes his head. "In all the years I've been alive, I've never had a child like me, a child who could do what I can do."

"Why not?"

"You know that children take their power from their mother," he says, "and mine were no exception to that. I fathered quite a few Assimilators over the years, but none who could pull power as we can, from a distance. All of them had to be in physical contact with someone or something before they could siphon its energy."

"Like Anat," I say.

"Like every other Assimilator alive."

"But where are they, the ones you didn't have to destroy? Wouldn't you have kept your other children alive as you do your followers?"

"I do," he says. "And you've met quite a few of your siblings over the years without knowing it. But eventually, they all want to create their own courts and establish their own space. They don't want to live in my shadow forever."

"So I have siblings living elsewhere? Is that what was wrong today? Did one of the Assimilators—"

Dad shakes his head. "None of my children who could assimilate are yet living. Assimilators take power, cub. They take it whenever they want, and they do whatever they'd like with it. Most Assimilators eventually become power-crazed."

The word is new, but it's terrifying. "I don't understand." Is that hovering on the horizon for me, too?

"It's a poor name, probably, but it existed long before me. It's what they call Assims who can't ever get enough. They have to be put down, for the good of the world around us. They never stop *taking*."

"And your children—"

"Those are the children I had to destroy, yes."

"But you never became power-crazed, right?"

"I didn't, no. I did begin to wonder whether I'd ever meet another person like me." His shoulders slump. "I was pretty desperate, in fact."

"What did you do?" This is all leading somewhere, which means something went wrong. Something other than his children making poor choices or becoming power-crazed or leaving him.

"You know that Isis is our enemy." The words feel ripped from him.

I nod mutely.

His hands clench. "What you may not know is that she was my lover for a time."

I can see why he didn't want to share this story with me when I was young.

"She's an Assim, you know."

"Did you love her?" For some reason, that thought of him with someone specific who isn't Mother makes me angry—or sad?

He shakes his head. "Not at all, and she didn't love me either. She craved my power, but she didn't love me. What we had was . . . casual." He looks pained, as if he's being tortured.

I suppose this isn't exactly the easiest thing to talk about with your teenage daughter. "Okay."

"We were on and then off, and on and off. Whenever it was convenient for both of us." He waves his hand dismissively. "It was fine with me. But during a time when we were . . . off . . . she became pregnant from a man who was a Lifter." He doesn't meet my eyes.

"Were you angry?" I wonder what Dad would do if he got angry or jealous.

He shakes his head. "Not at all, and the father, well, he wasn't someone who . . . "

"The baby's an Assim, too?" Why haven't I heard about another male Assim?

Dad looks upward, as if asking for patience. "He should have been an Assimilator, yes."

Should have been? Oh no. "What did you do?"

He swallows. "Something I shouldn't have done. I channeled power into him. I thought that if I could only modify—"

I stand up and begin walking away from him.

He flies after me, grabbing my arm. "You have to listen, cub. You owe me that, at least."

My hands ball into tight fists as I spin around, shaking his hands off my arm. "Mother was right." My voice is tight. I don't even sound like myself, but I can't believe that what Mother said so long ago . . . that it has been true this whole time. I'm exactly what she said.

"Sekhmet." Dad's eyes flash. "I order you to sit and listen until I'm done. You don't need to jump to conclusions when I'm telling you everything."

Everything.

For eight years I've been desperate to understand why Mother left. What *really* went wrong? Why does she think I'm a monster when Dad insists that I'm not? But I've been too afraid, terrified that Dad was wrong and Mother was right.

Terrified that I must be a monster after all.

And it turns out, Dad has been lying to me all this time. Which means. . .he probably lied to me about how I came to be. Why else would Mother leave?

I stumble back to the wooden bench near the window and collapse onto it. "Fine." I'll listen, but I don't have to like it. I don't have to look at him, either.

"What I did was wrong—I should not have tried to change a baby in the womb. I know that now. I tried to change him, and the baby . . . he took that energy, as an Assim, and he did *something* with it."

"What did he do?" In spite of myself, I'm desperate to know what happened.

"No one's quite sure. I used energy from a variety of places, but much of it came from a group of elementals that had formed in Cyprus. They had—it doesn't matter. What does matter is that I pulled power from them, and chan-neled it into Isis—and she had no idea that I was doing it."

The egregious violation floors me. How could this man I love so much have done something so terrible? "What happened?"

"The delivery was . . . difficult. The babe had been given power far too soon, you see. I believe his resistance to it caused the . . . complications. That was my fault. I accept that."

"And?"

"He was not an Assimilator at birth. The gift he should have received from Isis had somehow transformed. In taking the magic I wove, he changed it. Or he changed himself, perhaps. I'm not quite sure. I'd have to investigate further to know, and I vowed never to do anything like that ever again."

"What powers does he have?"

"Isis named her son Apophis, and as soon as she real-ized he could Lift as well as manipulate all four elements, she confronted me. When I confessed what I had done and apologized for the gross miscalculation I had made, she left in a rage."

"You let her leave?" I hate the doubt in my voice, but I can't suppress it.

"I did, Sekhmet, I swear it."

"And you haven't tried to kill her? Not once in all these years?"

Dad shakes his head. "Never, but you should know that I have fought her every time she's attacked me. She has never relented, not in the past fifty plus years."

"Fifty . . . " I count in my head. "Wait, you met Mother—"

His smile is wry. "You never miss a beat. Yes, I met your mother very shortly after she left, only a year or so." He drops his face into his hands. "I'd given up by then. After so many children turned against me, left me, or began to destroy the world around them, and after my attempts to bring a child like myself into the world failed, I wearied of this life." He drops his head into his hands. "I was ready to surrender."

"Surrender?"

"I knew in my heart that Isis' anger was justified, and that what I did to Apophis was unforgivable . . . I was done, exhausted. Mentally, spiritually, and physically."

"What does that mean?"

"When Isis gathered troops and attacked me, I walked out to surrender. I went out peacefully, hands extended, no effort made to defend myself."

He went to die. I can't quite suppress my gasp.

"Your mother saved me. Hathor was Isis' chosen weapon, a miracle above all miracles. The first and only person I'd ever heard of who was like Apophis—called of all four elements—but naturally. She was utterly unique, just as I was the only Assimilator ever born who could siphon from a distance. We were inexplicable anomalies, both of us. Miracles or curses, depending on your view."

"And then what?" My anger and disgust with him has already begun to dissipate.

"Hathor couldn't do it; she couldn't murder someone who wasn't even resisting. Instead of killing me, she captured me and locked me up. Her men tortured me to find out what I'd done. It was then that I began to wonder whether Isis was more jealous of what I could do than angry that I'd done it."

I don't want to think about that.

"The pain felt fitting, like it was exactly what I deserved. Did I really think I should simply be killed without pain, without punishment? I deserved to pay, so I didn't fight back. The torture went on for quite some time. They got pretty creative, and I took it all without resistance. In my selfishness, I had ruined another person's life. Apophis would forever be something other than he ought, and it was my fault. He was a Lifter and also able to control all four elements. For the first time in the world, there was a human who fit into more than one box."

"But Mother could call all the elements, you said, and no one did that." I shrug. "Maybe you didn't do it after all."

Dad's chuckle isn't happy. "I did it. I know I did."

"But Mother didn't kill you or let anyone else do it either," I say, "because you're here."

"She didn't kill me," he agrees. "In fact, something strange happened. As she watched me endure, as she watched me surrender moment by moment, day by day, she fell in love with me. It didn't happen in a single instant, nothing so clear or memorable as that, but when we got word that Isis was coming to finish me herself, Hathor couldn't accept it. She begged me to fight back. And for the first time in my twenty-four hundred years, I felt like I wasn't totally alone."

Something sparks inside my chest, and it takes a moment, but I recognize it: hope. I want my dad to find joy. I want him not to be alone. I want joy for him—for both of us.

"I loved Hathor as I'd never loved another. As I've never loved anyone . . . until you."

"What about Shu?"

Dad smiles. "You loyal little thing. I love Shu, of course I do."

"He was born after you and Hathor married?"

"Married." He chuckles. "Of course he was."

"But why is he telekinetic, when Mother calls the elements?"

"You can thank Isis for that," Dad says. "She snuck into the palace when she discovered that not only had I turned her strongest Lieutenant, but that we were expecting a child."

It's easy to sneak in as an Assimilator. Disguises are a snap. "What did she do?"

Dad shrugs. "I'm not quite sure what I told Hathor in my misery about what I did to Apophis, or how Isis misinterpreted it. I know that your mother was furious with Isis for tampering with her child. In fact, Hathor vowed to kill Isis. Only my insistence that the debt was repaid kept her from it—and Shu was fine. He wasn't an elemental like his mother, but he could Lift, and he was happy. He was healthy. He was loved."

"And then?"

Dad shrugs. "When Hathor became pregnant with you, I became a little paranoid. I checked and double-checked every single person allowed near her. I was vigilant. I wouldn't allow a single thing to happen to you."

"Then why did Mother think—"

"I'm getting there." Dad's tone is tense. Something bad is still coming. "Something I forgot to mention before—I told you that I channeled power into Isis when she was expecting, but it wasn't the first time I'd tried something similar." He looks down at his hands.

I'm angry with him, but my love and sympathy for what he went through overwhelms it.

"I was very careful to always pull power only from bad people and from evil things."

I close my eyes. He is always very careful to do that. Ma'at.

"So the first time I tried to influence the powers in an unborn child . . . " He shudders. "I did it because in my attempt to have an Assimilator child, I'd managed to have four children who were power-crazed from birth. I couldn't take another. I resolved to try something new. I channeled my power into the child, hoping to create . . . what I am. In my defense, I had the idea when Mehen told me that my mother was essentially siphoning non-stop while I was in utero. I thought perhaps her use of magic had . . . But it doesn't matter." His voice is utterly flat. "It backfired. The child was born insatiable—far, far worse than the prior four. She did all the worst things power-crazed Assimilators did, from the very first moment. I tried for months to feed her, to suppress—" He chokes. "It was a thousand years before I tried again with Apophis, and when I did, I made sure that all the power I funneled into him derived from light sources."

"What does that mean?"

"I assimilated power from raging infernos set by Fire Called to cleanse old, cluttered forests. I assimilated power from tumultuous winds sent by the Wind Called. And I siphoned power from cities blanketed in ice."

That doesn't sound so bad.

"And at the end, to get the power I needed, I leveled an entire forest, every cedar in Lebanon."

I can hardly believe it. I wouldn't even know where to begin.

"It worked," he whispers. "Apophis wasn't an Assimilator as he would have been, but he's not evil. He's not dark. And he's not power-crazed."

"But when Mother was pregnant with me?" I don't want to, but I force myself to stare into his eyes. "What did you do?" I know it in my bones—I know why Mother left.

Because I'm like Apophis.

Or, possibly, like the first child Dad created.

"What did you do to me?" My words emerge as the barest of whispers.

Dad slowly circles both my wrists with his hands. His eyes practically burn with fervor when he says, "Sekhmet, if you never believe another single thing I say, know this. You are pure. You are a shining light in a world of darkness. You are my miracle. I did not siphon trees or fire or anything like that. I didn't channel dark light into you either. If there is a god in heaven, that's who gave you to me. You're the one thing I've always wanted, and the one thing I never deserved."

"You didn't make me what I am?"

Dad shakes his head. "I could never have created anything as magical as you."

"Did someone else do it for you?"

He laughs then, and it's loud and long. "You are your mother's child in the most delightful ways. No, darling little cub. I didn't force anyone else to do anything either."

"Then why did Mother leave?"

"She spent more and more time with Isis," he says, "and eventually, Isis struck upon a coincidence that your mother could not ignore. That coincidence burned in her brain until she couldn't believe anything I said anymore. I blame my past mistakes for the chink in her armor that allowed the concern to fester. I don't blame her."

"What was it Isis told her?"

"I was growing more trees." Dad grunts. "To build a navy, which we badly needed if we wanted to expand our borders at all."

"And?"

"I had the teak forest I'd grown harvested, and afterward I ordered the field burned and replanted."

Now I see. "Isis showed her the forest or the site of it," I say, "and how it had been burned."

"By the time Isis stumbled upon it, there were saplings of four or five years growing there," he says, "but Isis had witnesses testify, I presume. That would have been enough."

"Why didn't Mother trust you?" I ask.

"That's entirely my fault," he says. "It's the reason I'll never speak against your mother. She had good reason not to trust me. I had tried to alter a child in the womb, not once, but twice. After Shu was born with mismatched powers . . . I initially mistrusted her. I thought perhaps she'd been unfaithful."

"But the child always follows the mother," I say.

He nods. "Almost always, yes. It's quite uncommon, but not unheard of, for the child to follow the father. It happens once or twice every few hundred years. Usually when the mother is quite powerful and the child can't seem to handle that kind of power. I was this close—" he narrows his thumb and forefinger until they're almost touching "—to accusing her of infidelity when our spies revealed that Isis had been present."

I swallow. "But after Shu and Apophis, she didn't believe you." My mother really did leave because she thought I was a monster.

In spite of Dad's explanation, I wonder whether she's right. I'm not like anyone else on Earth. Even Dad can't do what I can do.

But I do trust him. He's told me so many other things—why would he lie about this? "What happened with the Sacred Band of Thebes today?"

"Apophis managed, a year or two ago, to win over the friendship of a very bizarre individual."

"Who?"

"Most alphas are Renders. There's one per eight or ten thousand Renders, but only one per twenty or thirty thousand Reapers. They exist in much lower numbers, and the theory is that Renders need an alpha more desperately, to control their ferocious and violent natures. As you might imagine, supra alphas who are also Reapers are much rarer as well. In fact, I've never heard of one. It's not in the Reaper nature to dominate others. But Apophis met one, a horse-shifter named Bucephalus, and instead of destroying him as most powerful men would—no one wants to be controlled, as you can understand—he befriended him. This particular man, Bucephalus, allows Apophis to *ride him* into battle, as if he's a normal horse. My armies didn't even suspect his true nature, but it allowed his supra alpha close enough to wrest control from Pelopidas, and after that, the destruction of my soldiers was a simple task. He killed every last one." Dad's voice is grim. "It's said that Apophis' adoptive father, Philip of Macedonia, wept when he saw the state of the bodies of the fallen, such was the fury Bucephalus inspired in his men and the languor in the Band."

"He killed them all?" I ask. "Why didn't he spare them, once he had won?"

"Isis wants you dead," Dad says. "And me as well. She wants her revenge, and she's using her powerful son, the one who engendered the fury in her heart to begin with, to attain it."

"I thought Shu said the man who defeated our troops was named Alexander."

Dad shrugs. "Isis is now calling herself Olympias. She's married a man who's a powerful Lifter—Philip, King of Macedonia. She did always know how to manipulate others. He thinks Apophis is his, and named him Alexander.'"

"I don't get it. If Isis thinks, and has convinced Mother, that Apophis and I are monsters, why would she have Apophis work for her?"

Dad shrugs. "Isis isn't always very consistent. In fact, if you abandoned me, she'd likely welcome you with open arms. For her, it's always been fair game to do anything at all to take me down. Her son is now her greatest weapon." He shrugs. "Not that it'll be enough." The lines around his eyes are deeper than they've been in a long time. The set of his shoulders is utterly dejected. It tears at my heart.

"Why do you do it?" I ask.

"Why do I do what?"

"Why do you bother?" I stand up and begin to pace, the lion inside of me tense and searching for action. Maybe Dad has more of his father in him than he realizes, with his constant pacing, if that's where my desire to pace originates. "You're constantly fighting these battles against her. Isis clearly only wants you to lose. Why not just surrender and be done? We don't need countries and thrones and armies. Let's leave all of this behind and see the world together. There must be more than what we've already seen. Anat, Mehen, Shu, and Am-Heh, they would come with us. They all would."

"She won't buy it," Dad says. "She'd never let us walk away. She'll hound us forever. I've been thinking that as much as I shrink from the idea, my only reprieve may be in actually killing her."

"That would eat at your conscience even more than what you did to Apophis already does. No, I have a better idea."

Dad's mouth curls into a half smile. "You do?"

"Let her finally defeat you," I say. "We'd have to be very cunning and very careful, but you said yourself that Apophis defeated your best soldiers. If we let him keep winning—each time after a struggle, with a believable cost —we can convince her. And if we do that, we can walk away from all this and be free from those demons that plague you."

"Free," Dad says. "I'm not sure I even know what that means anymore."

But he doesn't contradict me, and for the first time in a very long time, I have hope for the future.

7

RRA

The smell of terror wakes me. Something delicious is close, its heart racing, its blood pulsing hot and quick in its veins. I don't think —I react. My muscles bunch, and as they do, a surge of pain in my left front leg rolls through me. The pain clears the fogginess from my mind, but when I examine that area, all I see is bloody fur. Nothing I can do about that, so I roll from my back to my stomach, my claws dislodging chunks of dirt and other detritus from the forest floor. The sharp smell of pine trees and the tang of decaying forest undergrowth flood my nostrils and I sneeze.

Others, predators like me, approach from behind, also chasing the terrified deer that must have woken me— fleeing from these pursuers, surely. I haven't seen them yet, but I hear them, and I can sense their movements some- how. They're like me. Large, stealthy, and dangerous.

And I'm not about to let them have my meal, because I'm desperately hungry.

My belly rumbles, and I spring into action, legs pump- ing, nose guiding me surely and swiftly through the unfamiliar surroundings. Where am I? Why don't I remember anything about where I was before or who I am?

A rustling sound ahead sends adrenaline spiking through me, and I shoot forward even faster. Something thrills inside of me, and I roar from the depths of my soul, the sound ringing through the bright morning air. I know without being sure how that I ought not to roar—it alerts my meal to my presence.

But part of me doesn't care.

It does serve as a warning to those behind me that this food is *mine.* I can sense them falter in their pursuit, and my lips curl upward, baring my incisors. Saliva flows in my mouth and my sides heave as I draw nearer. The deer crashes into the massive trunk of a fallen tree up ahead and scrambles to get moving again. Its hooves finally find purchase and it springs over the blockage, mere feet away from me, now.

But the forest ends abruptly in front of us, the obstacles blocking our route and allowing it to duck and dodge my pursuit disappearing.

It's not sure where to go.

Which means that it's mine for the taking.

Elation pulses through me as power builds in my hind end . . . and I pounce. My massive right paw connects with the rump of the deer, slicing easily through its hide and crippling it. But the other predators have reached us, and now they circle around my flanks.

The deer drags its injured leg toward the open field ahead. Anything I do now merely prolongs its misery, and that's cruel. I leap again, my teeth coming down around its jugular, severing it quickly and efficiently. The blood rushes into my mouth, delicious and hot.

But I'm not alone, free to revel in my success. I can't celebrate—I need to defend my meal from interlopers. I drop the carcass and swivel my head to identify the creatures who are threatening me, shifting naturally to form a semicircle, their eyes gleaming in the lower light on the edge of the forest.

"Mraow," I roar again. Back away, dummies, or I'll rend you, too. Find your own dinner.

A half dozen roars counter mine, and they advance . . . seven lions against one lone creature. The two males are more aggressive, more sure of themselves. The five females hang back a bit, their eyes unsure and shifty. A rumble in my throat is their last warning before I'm forced to act. Where did they come from? Why can't they move along and find their own kills?

The male at the front steps inside my personal circle, encroaching, his eyes steady on the bloody carcass. Intent, even, as if he assumes I'll simply step aside and pass it to him.

Entitled.

But he can't have it. It's not his.

Mine.

The thought rips out of me and rolls over them like a wave. They crumple to the ground, their heads lowered, whimpers escaping their throats.

Inexplicably, they don't flee. They freeze in place, still posing a threat. Still a problem to be dealt with. *MINE.* My command is clearer this time, my desire blatantly obvious. Leave me alone!

But they don't leave. They shift sideways, each of them together in some kind of bizarre synchronized movement, baring their necks and closing their eyes. What do they expect me to do now? I stare at them, annoyed, for a few moments. And then I lose interest. The smell of the deer, its carcass cooling behind me, draws my attention and I turn to eat. They can leave or not. What do I care? If they're not threatening me, they're of no interest.

I tear muscle, skin, and sinew, and I gulp bite after bite

until the pulsing rumble in my stomach wanes. It's only then that I begin to contemplate what's happening inside my mouth. I'm chewing and swallowing chunks of a dead animal. A mutilated body. Blood. Skin. Muscle. Tendons. The half-chewed chunks in my mouth fall to the ground as revulsion rolls through me. I back away from the poor deer, disgusted.

What am I doing? Why would I kill a living creature and then tear apart chunks of its body and consume them? I shudder then, suddenly cold. And another shiver, this one stronger, ripples through me, and suddenly I'm not a lion.

I'm standing upright on two feet.

Thankfully, I'm not covered in blood and I'm not naked. I'm wearing a simple pair of black pants and a black shirt that are both quite soft. I stare at my hands—completely smooth and clean—and blink. The other lions are shifting now, moving out of their submissive positions, and creeping forward, their noses sniffing the air, their eyes trained on me.

The wind shifts, and even with my weaker human senses, the smell of the dismembered carcass next to me blows clear and strong into my face, turning my stomach. I bend over double and vomit onto the bushy grass to my left. Turns out, the only thing nastier than chunks of half-chewed deer carcass is regurgitated chunks of half-chewed deer carcass.

The smell is beyond revolting.

The male lion closest to me rumbles, and then mraows. It's a querulous sound, clearly inviting some kind of explanation from me. I step even further away from the deer I killed and my puke, desperate to put some space between me and everything I don't understand. My head spins a bit, and I struggle to stay upright.

Who am I? A lion? A woman? What am I doing here?

And what will those lions do now that I'm no longer one of them?

I point at the remains of the deer and wave my hand. "Please. Eat."

Otherwise, it's a terrible waste. My stomach complains again, and I sidestep an approaching lioness. She bends down to lick up my puke, and I almost throw up again. As they set to work cleaning the meat off the dead deer, I quietly and quickly move toward the cover of the forest, hoping they won't pay attention to my departure.

It works, mostly, until my left foot snaps a twig and the larger of the two male lions snaps to attention, his head spinning until his deep golden eyes are once again focused on me. He narrows his eyes, almost like a human might. Though how I know what expressions humans make, I'm not sure. I can't quite think of any interactions with others. And I'm not sure how I know this form is called 'human.'

I am aware that I should know how I know these things.

It's all very confusing.

My heart hammers in my chest, and I imagine he can hear it, based on my senses when I was a lion chasing that deer. I will it to slow, but my heart's unimpressed by my suggestions. The male lion licks his front paw clean and then slowly, purposefully, circles around the other members of his pack and rounds on me.

Who are you?

The words explode inside my skull, like the most egregious of all violations. My hands fly to my head, clutching at my ears. I hate the feel of someone else's question in the inner sanctum of my mind, and rage pulses through me.

All the lions freeze, and the large male who was walking toward me crouches down, his head nearly pressed to the ground. Is he reacting to my anger? I force myself to relax.

His movements and messages weren't hostile. Maybe he's not an enemy.

Who are you? I think the words forcefully, but nothing happens. The lions don't move, still frozen in place, and the male remains pressed against the ground.

I try again, pushing harder this time. *Who are you?*

This time, his head snaps up, his eyes widening. *Do you know where you are?*

I still dislike the feeling of his words inside my head, but I was expecting it this time, so it's not as jarring. I shake my head. "No."

I hope he can understand my words when I vocalize. It's so much easier, and it feels far more natural, less invasive.

"I awoke here, and I was hungry. The deer ran. I attacked on instinct, but I'm not sure I'm supposed to be here. Something's wrong."

She Who Gathers.

It's She Who Gathers.

She Who Gathers?

She Who Gathers.

She Who Gathers!

The words explode into my mind from at least six distinct voices. All the lions are now moving toward me, not in a threatening way, but with their heads down, their eyes toward the ground.

"What does that mean, She Who Gathers?"

We were told you would come, the first male voice says. *When the change wouldn't come. We were told you would save us, or if you deemed us unworthy, that we would perish.*

They all seem so sure, but I have no idea what they're talking about. I lean against the nearest tree and bang myself against it, probably bruising my head, which doesn't help at all.

Why can't I remember anything? Who I am? Where I am and why?

Gathering is when you bring things together—that much I know. I know enough to be sure I ought to have memories of the past, but it's nothing but blank space. Which means I have no idea what they're talking about.

She Who Gathers . . . what? They think that's supposed to be me? Why?

The lions have me entirely circled now, but I'm surprisingly unafraid. They seem to think I'm important to them. They all look . . . deferential. Almost desperate.

"What's wrong? Why would you perish?"

It's easier to speak. Or at least, I think it is, if they can understand me. No one seems to acknowledge that I've spoken.

"Can any of you become human? Can you change into a shape like mine?" That would be a lot easier, or at least, it feels like a much simpler way to communicate.

We could, the male conveys with a sorrowful tone. *But we can't now.*

They could turn into humans, but now they can't? Why not? "What's keeping you from doing it?"

The male growls this time, noticeably agitated. The others reposition, several of them hissing and spitting. It doesn't seem to be directed at me, but they're clearly upset. I imagine if they were stuck in animal forms, it would be upsetting, especially if, like me, they're more comfortable in a human form. "Okay, well, I don't remember who I am or why I'm here. I'm not this person you seem to be seeking . . . She Who Gathers. I don't even know what that means."

Come with us. The male entreats me this time. The other lions calm immediately, dropping down in front of me and pressing their faces to the ground. Why are they so desperate? What do they think I can do?

"What do you believe I'm supposed to do?"

You will save us. His tone is so sure, so faithful.

So confused.

But my only other option is staying here with the bones of a deer skeleton, so I don't argue. "Move slowly. I'm not very speedy in this shape."

Shift back. It will be much faster.

I sigh. I worried that he might ask that. I'm probably a lot faster as a lion, but I'm also prone to attacking living animals and gorging myself on their raw innards. Another wave of disgust rolls through me, but I shake it off.

That's when I realize I have no idea *how* to shift.

"Um, so. I don't know how to shift back." I think about having paws. About shrinking down and growing fur.

Nothing happens.

The large male's lips curl up, and he coughs. The other lions sniff and whuffle, and I'm practically positive they're laughing at me.

Close your eyes and imagine the wind on your face. The ground beneath your paws. And then roar.

That can't be right. That sounds moronic. Roar? Is he kidding?

But no matter how much time I spend imagining my body reshaping, nothing happens. I'm about to have to walk, barefoot, from here to wherever they're headed. The few steps I've taken have shown me that I'm not equipped for travel in this form, at least, not in a forest strewn with needles, acorns, sticks, and pinecones. I groan, and then I do what he said.

I close my eyes.

I imagine the wind blowing through the fur on my face. I imagine the bright, clear, crisp lines of the world as I saw it in my lion form. And then I flex my hands, imagining the thick new undergrowth and the springy, dry loam of the ground. And finally, I reach deep down inside.

And I roar.

In the blink of an eye, I *melt* downward until I'm standing on four enormous paws. I didn't think lions could frolic, but I was wrong. When I shift, all eight of them bound around me with glee, tossing up chunks of needles and pinecones and dry clumps of dirt.

In this form, it occurs to me that the larger of the two males is much younger than the smaller one—and he's kind of hot, too, for a lion. His mane is full and shiny. His eyes are bright, almost a molten gold. And his coat sleekly covers what's clearly well-developed muscle underneath. He roars even more loudly than I did, and then he takes off at a bounding lope, his legs moving with easy grace.

I scramble to catch up, pulling up alongside him, my lungs working hard to support the exertion. *Is it far?* I'm kind of proud of myself for mentally communicating.

Not far, Supra, no. It's good to move after eating, or you become sluggish.

Speak for yourself, handsome. I'm never sluggish. *What's supra?*

You are supra.

I can't grumble in this form, but if I could, I totally would. *But what does it mean?*

I am alpha. You can control even me.

Alpha. The word rolls around in my head, conjuring up an image of a boss with followers gathered around, listening, obeying. I can *control* him? I don't want to control anyone. Ugh. I don't want to eat raw animals, and I don't want to order people around. I don't want to gather anyone. I want to go home.

A vague memory flits past me—home. A place where someone I love is present. He has dark hair and cerulean eyes. Eyes that squint up when he smiles.

Then the memory's gone and I'm left grasping. What was it? A man? A place? What word did I react to? My brain feels as foggy and unsure as it did when I first awoke. Frustration floods every cell of my body and I speed up. The male next to me reacts to my energy and accelerates as well. At least I can't fault him for slowing me down.

Why are you in charge? I ask.

I am alpha.

None of them are alpha? *That's all it takes?*

Until a few days ago, the females could not shift forms. They were human. Always. Most of the males couldn't shift. Now everyone is an animal. Men. Women. Children. All of us.

I try to process what he's telling me. *Most of you couldn't change forms. Women and most children and even most men couldn't?*

I sense his affirmation of that.

But now you are all *lions all the time?*

Again, he agrees.

Why?

That's what we want to know. You must fix things.

Anger seems to be a prevalent emotion for me. *I can't help anyone. You've got the wrong idea.*

She Who Gathers is a Supra Lioness.

The person who can control the people who can control other people. Fabulous. *You're saying I am this Supra Lion thing, and there aren't any others?*

There are only a dozen supras of any species on Rra right now — none of them are lions, either male or female. But no females have been alpha or supra in our lifetime, not of any species. You must be She Who Gathers. You can save us. Only you.

I growl, low and deep, and Mr. Handsome next to me doesn't even miss a beat. *I'm taking groups out to teach them how to move, how to hide, and how to hunt.*

Great. I intercepted a kindergarten class.

Kindergarten? What the heck is that? It's an odd word, that's for sure. It felt familiar, and then any meaning slipped away as soon as it appeared in my mind. The forest drops away in favor of rocky ground. The air thins and cools, and I breathe it down greedily. I'm not used to running this hard or this long. Even my powerful lion body is starting to tire.

Finally, we begin to slow, and I could almost cry with gratitude. Or meow? Either way, I'm glad. *Is there some kind of instructor prepared to teach She Who Gathers? Someone who will tell me exactly what you expect me to do?*

I take his silence as a 'no.'

Seeing as he had to walk me through how to shift, I really doubt that I'm their golden ticket. And, now I've thought of another phrase that makes no sense. A golden . . . what? Ticket? Something that allows entry. But entry to what? My own thoughts are insane. How can I possibly help them sort their problems?

I can barely shift.

You are the only person who can shift at all. *You will figure it out.*

What if I can't? This is starting to feel like a lot of pressure.

Mr. Handsome stops and drops into a squat, his bum on the rocks, his front paws resting in front of him calmly. And then he roars so loudly, I worry I'll never hear properly again. *She Who Gathers has come. Summon the Pride.*

Whoa. What's the Pride? I feel like clawing his perfect face. He could have prepared me for this. *Where are we, and what did you just do?*

He couldn't possibly look any more smug. *I've called a meeting of alphas. They'll know what to do.*

I did ask for someone to tell me what to do, but this feels like a betrayal somehow. *Thanks for running that past me.* A deep rumble starts in my chest, and it conveys my deep displeasure adequately.

We're out of time.

What does that mean? I look around, noticing we're on

the top of a high cliff overlooking a vast plain below us. It's empty now, but I can see why animals might gather here for the view of the valley.

The full moon is only three days away.

Everything you tell me confuses me more. Why does the moon matter?

The moon triggers the hunt. His tone is definitely annoyed, as if he's sick of answering my stupid questions. Or as if he doesn't believe I don't know the answers.

I grit my teeth. *What is the hunt? Why does any of this matter? How is time running out?*

His enormous head swivels toward me, and I swear one of his eyes is cocked in frustration. *On a full moon, every Render on Rra hunts. Usually the alpha Reapers can keep their kind indoors so we hunt only animals. Right now, every human on Rra is in animal form. When the moon comes, none of us will be able to stop the hunt. There will be many bellies to fill, and no way to know which meal is human, and which is animal.*

The taste of blood in my mouth, the surge of delight with which I ripped into that deer. . . *The deer I killed earlier?* My lip curls.

Animal.

Relief overcomes me.

But if you can't gather us in . . . or if you can't shift us back . . . many, many humans will be eaten.

8

EARTH

It's probably in my head, but I swear instead of morning breath, when I wake up, I can taste the metallic tang of blood in my mouth. I try to stand up, but I'm held back by my seatbelt. It takes me a moment to realize I'm still on a plane, the buzzing sound coming from the heavy engines holding us aloft in the sky.

People have been living in a world without magic for millennia thanks to Terra, but it feels like magic still surrounds us. Even without our powers, humans have been able to do amazing things.

Microwaves.

Airplanes.

Refrigeration.

Heart transplants.

Even the Internet is pretty mind blowing.

Which is probably why Mehen's pressing his nose to the glass, just as he was when we took off. His hands are still clenched around the armrests, too.

"You alright?" I whisper, so I don't wake up Jesse, who's snoring lightly across the aisle from me.

Mehen's head whips around so fast I'm worried that

Martin will have to Heal his whiplash. "You're awake." His eyes dart to my arm. "You healed several hours ago."

I sigh. "The message was useless. I woke up as a lion." My lips twist. For once, my tried and true plan failed. "When I shifted—"

"Your body healed it, of course."

I nod. "I should have thought of that."

"You remember being a lion before?" His eyebrows rise.

"Not a lot about it," I admit, "but some things, yeah. Including a conversation I had with Dad, when he told me about his father."

The set of Mehen's mouth is bleak. "Amun was an evil man."

"How can you be sure Ra isn't?" I want to believe him. I want to fling off the prison bars and release everyone. It seems like the right thing to do, but why would I have locked him up—or allowed someone else to—in the first place, if he was guiltless?

"I can't be sure." Mehen presses his right hand to the left side of his chest. "But I have faith inside. I have followed your father for a very, very long time, and I have watched him make terribly hard decisions. No matter how desperate the circumstances, no matter how difficult the choice, he has always vanquished darkness. He has always ushered in light."

I wish I had that same faith, that same undying confidence in my own hunches. But Mehen has seen things with his own eyes. He has memories to back up that faith. I'm regaining things in tiny, bite-size chunks, but even things from my own childhood are sometimes hazy. My memories of my time as Sekhmet are like a crocheted blanket— unfaithful and unreliable because they're full of so many holes.

The captain's voice crackles through the loud speaker above our heads, announcing that we'll be landing soon. It doesn't wake Jesse, but I notice that Kahn and John on the row ahead of us, and Martin and Roland on the row behind us, are all stretching and groaning. We must all have gone to sleep at some point, which is probably good.

We have no idea what we'll face when we do reach the ground in the United Kingdom.

I lean across Mehen's knee so I can see out the window he was peering through with rapt attention, and I realize why he was so transfixed.

London is burning.

I watched briefly while we lifted into the air in Houston, as the subdivisions and streets, the cars and the people, all shrunk at an alarming rate. But below me now, as we lower toward the earth again, lit by the early morning rays from the rising sun, it's plain to see that whole swaths of the city, entire neighborhoods and blocks, are blackened. Some places are actively burning, flames licking up the side of buildings and racing through dry vegetation.

"Why is no one putting those out?"

Mehen grunts.

"What does that mean?"

"No offense meant," he says, "but firebugs are the worst, especially new ones. All the women you released likely had their powers restored and have no idea what to do with them. I was informed that something similar happened for the Lifters. Newly Fire Called will be erratic, possibly angry, and unable to control their actions or emotions now that they finally have a way to pay the world back for the wrongs done to them."

I hadn't even thought about all the women—so many women—who have been belittled, pushed around, and abused over the years. They were unable to stop the men on Terra and Erra—but now? What would they do now that they have powers they're unaccustomed to using? "It could just as easily be angry members of the Followers of Isis or Amun."

"Ah, but they would have put the fires out once their purposes were served," Mehen says. "From what I've seen, neither group senselessly destroys or damages things. No, this is part of the chaos of restoring powers to the people of Earth. It was inevitable. It will eventually settle as people gain control of their lives and their abilities."

"They need to be taught," I say.

He smiles then. "And will you teach them?"

"I barely know how to control my own abilities, but John—"

Mehen's laugh is short and sharp. "That child knows so little it's frightening."

"It's hardly helpful for you to be dismissive of everyone else," I say.

"I'm not dismissive," Mehen says. "I'm honest, and in this case, I'm correct. You need better teachers."

"Until someone you deem worthy appears, I may have to make do with what I have."

At least as the plane descends, I notice that the airstrip outside of London that Martin found seems free of fire and ice. The plane lands smoothly, in spite of Mehen's misgivings about our flight.

"You got a good nap, it seems." Jesse yawns. "Did you go to Rra, then?"

I nod.

"And?"

"Our message failed miserably." I explain how I shifted, and how that apparently heals me.

"That's an irritation."

"Not nearly as big a problem as the other wrinkle I discovered," I say.

Kahn's head pops up ahead of me, which means now that I'm speaking in English, he's clearly listening.

"What wrinkle?" John asks, his eyes appearing in the space between the two seats in front of me. "What's wrong on Rra?"

I raise my voice. "Can everyone hear me?"

Martin, Oliver, Roland, Thomas, Henry, Rosalinde, John, the men Devlin insisted on sending, and Kahn are all so close that there seems no point in delaying. I explain that I appeared on Rra as a lion . . . and that I communicated with the other lions there. Two male . . . and seven female.

"But females can't shift," John says. "There must have been some mistake. Perhaps they were male cougars. They'd look similar to a female lion."

I explain the rest. How they're stuck—and they're looking to me as the one person who might be able to keep them from eating all the people who are stuck as Reapers in a few days' time.

A loud boom outside the plane has me scrambling for the window—but Mehen beats me to the one that's closest. I head for the aisle, looking for a place to get eyes on what's happening.

Which is why I have a clear line of sight when a bullet explodes through the far window and the right side of Oliver's face, blood spattering my legs. I scream without meaning to, clamping down on the sound as quickly as I can.

Martin moves quickly and efficiently, taking Oliver by the shoulders and immediately taking the injury on himself. I have to turn away as his face seems to, well, to melt. Even a fraction of a wound like that is grisly. Luckily, Roland doesn't miss a beat taking it from Martin, and even Rosalinde steps up. By the time she takes the injury from Roland, it's no more than a scratch and a black eye.

My attention reverts to Oliver, who's still not moving.

"Is he alright?"

Martin's smile looks forced. "You can't Heal a dead person, so yes. He'll be alright. He's just stunned. It'll take a moment for his mind to catch up to what we did."

A grinding sound next to me shifts our attention to the metal door on our left.

Someone's trying to get inside. Judging by their opening foray, it's not anyone with good intentions.

"This is bad." John lifts both hands and flames burst to life above them.

"Limited oxygen in here, sparky," Kahn says. "Maybe chill."

"We won't be in here much longer," John says. "And they're waiting right outside."

"More than thirty men," Mehen says.

Kahn's eyes are closed. "Thirty-four men."

They're both counting. If they spoke the same language, we could save a lot of time.

I can't be bothered to translate right now. "Why all men?" I wonder aloud, anxiety making me say dumb things.

"It's either Isis or Amun," John says. "The only people they'd have trained right now and ready for combat are the men."

Duh.

"What do we do?" I ask.

"You need to choose one of us to lead this defense," Mehen says.

"Everyone get back." Kahn strides toward the door.

It whines—someone is clearly pulling on it, bending the metal exterior.

Jesse follows right behind him, and they look like the soldiers I knew on Terra—no fear, shoulders broad, hands clenched. "You take the first wave. I'll be right behind you," Jesse says.

"You should fall back with the Healers," John says. "And then—"

"These idiots have no idea what they're doing." Mehen closes his eyes and begins to hum.

What's going on?

For the first time—way late, admittedly—I reach out with my telekinetic senses and *feel* for what's out there.

Three men are hunched over the door with a blowtorch and a sledgehammer. That explains the whamming and humming/grinding sounds. A semicircle of eight surround them. And beyond that, a much larger semicircle of another twenty-two stand watch.

And one man stands behind all the rest, his arms folded, his mouth moving slightly. He's probably issuing orders. I'm trying to assess what weapons they each have when . . .

The men's own guns Lift up and away, and then fire on them. Grunts. Cries of pain. Shouting. Four or five more shots. And then it's quiet.

"What just happened?" Kahn asks.

Mehen shrugs. "You modern people rely too much on your technical magic."

I had to explain the word to him before, in English. The word technology didn't exist in his time, not the way it does now. "It's pronounced technology," I say. "Not technical." I can't decide whether I like the idea of him learning English.

"I used their own weapons against them, and they were too poorly trained to realize I'd do it." He's not even smug about it. He's legitimately appalled by our own faith in firearms.

"Did that old weirdo just kill every single person who was out there, trying to take us out?" John asks.

I nod. "Pretty sure that's exactly what just happened."

"Wait, so they're . . . dead?" Jesse asks.

That's when it hits me, the reality of it all. Thirty-four men just *died* because they wanted to attack me. Or take me? I'm not even sure what they wanted, and now they can never tell me.

But they did put a bullet through the side of Oliver's head, which we only healed with quick thinking and an abundance of talented and brave Healers. I collapse into my seat. "Why?" I shake my head. "Why would they attack us? Why would they shoot at Oliver? What did they hope to gain?"

Kahn wrenches the mangled door from its frame, his eyes shining like blue fire. I doubt Devlin's pal is going to be pleased with the state of the jet he loaned us. "Let's find out."

With a little more investigation, and possibly some luck, John manages to figure some of it out. "I know this guy." He prods one of the men with his boot. "His name was Nolan—he's Isis. I'm pretty sure they all are."

At least we know which side they were on. They weren't carrying stun guns or tranquilizers. They had fully loaded weapons—powerful handguns and rifles. They were shooting to kill.

They're likely here to keep me from collapsing Rra. I wrap my arms around my own waist and rock slightly back and forth. It's still warm in Texas, but outside of London, it's already brisk.

"You're not just cold." Jesse slings an arm around my shoulders. "You're scared."

A shiver runs through me at his words, and I realize he's right. "They want to kill me, J. And I guess that's not really anything new, but—" I drop my head against his shoulder. "I'm tired of it. So tired."

He ruffles my hair with his free hand. "I know. Everyone wants something, right? Rra is full of animals that want you to gather them—they don't even know what that means, but they know you're their only hope, Obi-wan."

"And here, Isis thinks if they can kill me, things will, what? Go back to normal? They think they can keep control over the world and the things around them? Obviously the status quo is gone. The prison world is cracked. It's going down. What will killing me accomplish?"

"It'll ensure that everyone who hasn't already been gathered dies," John says, "but they're too stupid to comprehend that."

I close my eyes and breathe in the smell of my brother.

Rra.

Earth.

Total chaos, and people swearing to me, and people shooting at me. The world is bonkers. The only thing that makes sense has its arm around me.

Which is why, right now, I have got to get to that museum and find Ra's reservoirs, and *then* we can talk about what my options are to save all those poor fuzzy humans who are stuck as who knows what kinds of animals. Because if something happens to Jesse, I'm not sure I'll care whether they live or die.

"We can't sit around here and wait for them to take another shot at us," Oliver says from the top of the steps on the plane.

He may have been willing to sell me down the river for his sister, but can I really blame him? I'm kind of glad he's still with me, that someone here gets it. People are what matter—not vague stakes and the unfounded generalities of ethics.

"How's the face?" I ask.

Oliver shrugs. "Can't complain."

"Then I think you're right," I say. "We've got a museum to visit."

It takes a few minutes, but we manage to locate a few working vehicles and appropriate them for our own use. As we drive from the rural area where we landed toward town, we pass a lot of things that would have terrified me down to my toes a few weeks ago.

Buildings covered in ice.

Wind, whipping cars through the air wildly.

Men and women with glowing eyes, shouting at one another and hurling objects.

Trees, sprouting from the center of buildings, and in the middle of roads.

And so many, many blackened and charred buildings, cars, and patches of ground that I lose track of the number. If this is what the world looks like with only the reunification of Terra and Erra . . .

I wonder how terrified the vast majority of the earth's citizens are—the ones who still have no powers.

How much worse will things yet become?

We spend the next twenty minutes in a long white delivery van, driving past people in the middle of bizarre arguments. Eventually I stop staring at things I can't control and begin assembling the basics of a plan to infiltrate the museum and locate what I want—namely, any artifacts they have from around 300 B.C., but especially the reservoirs and any documents or records they kept.

"We're turning onto Great Russell Street," Martin says. He's driving, since he's the only one of my group who's really familiar with London. Not that anything around us looks familiar or right.

"When we arrive, you'll all listen to Kahn," I say. "He's got the most combat experience on Earth and on Terra, and he's—"

The van rolls to a stop, and I realize why. We're here— the enormous black gate punctuated by large, concrete block sections, presumably guard houses. Massive, weathered columns rise up along the facade of the building set back from the black fencing, but the black gate hangs askew, and no guards man the towers.

I open the van door and scramble out, much to the dismay of Mehen, Kahn, Henry, and John. Maybe Jesse and the others too—I'm not paying a lot of attention to their shouts and general displeasure. Because all my attention is riveted on the scene in front of me. I've never been to London, and all of this is a little overwhelming. Unlike Houston, it's an old city. The stonework, the brick, the streets and the buildings, they all show their age—but not only in cracks or weathering. No, they're nothing like Houston or Washington State, because of the materials used in building. The distinctive decor clearly developed over many centuries, laying one style over another, adapting the existing terrain to the newest fads and developments. The weight of it all presses on me . . .

But that's not what demands my attention either.

We expected to have to overpower guards. We planned to deal with angry followers of Isis or even possibly Amun. After all, Devlin only runs the North American region. We're not entirely certain what sort of welcome we'll be met with here, in Europe.

But one thing I hadn't planned for, although clearly I should have, is what I would do if we arrived at the British Museum . . . and found it had already been looted.

By common vandals, judging from the tagging on the stone walls.

A tear rolls down my cheek. Another follows.

"Don't cry, please." Mehen's words sounds strangled almost, like something is terribly wrong. It grabs my attention, but when I focus on him, I realize that what's wrong . . . is me.

I wipe my face and try to adopt an expression of nonchalance. "So a few people arrived before we did. It's hardly surprising. No big deal. They won't know what things are valuable."

Mehen frowns. "I know you want Ra's reservoir, but perhaps this is for the best. He needs that energy, whereas you have access to literally the entire world—"

"No." I shake my head. "No. I won't talk about this right now." I can't just start siphoning whomever I need for whatever I want. It's a slippery slope, and beyond that, Jesse would never allow it.

My big brother's already eyeing us strangely, and I know he'll want to know why I'm so upset. He's too intuitive. He'll realize that it wasn't just about gaining access to old records—speaking of which, we do still have to investigate.

Maybe some old documents with important information were left behind.

But there's no chance they'd have left a golden neck cuff set with sparkly red gems. No looters are that moronic.

"I can teach you all about Lifting," Mehen says, "and once we locate Am-Heh, who must be awake now that you've collapsed Erra, he can teach you things these modern day Fire Called never knew." He sniffs at John.

"There's a group of men staring at us about a block down the way," Kahn says.

One thing we can't do is stand around on the street. It's bound to attract unwanted attention. It's not like many people are wandering around sightseeing today.

"Clearly the museum has been breached," I say. "But we still need to see what may be left. The information we're looking for wouldn't be immediately valuable." I try to sound convincing.

John pulls out his phone and holds it to his ear, murmuring quietly.

"Who's that?"

He pauses. "My dad. Would you be willing to talk to him?"

I toss my head at the front of the museum. "We need to go inside, but I can talk to him while we walk."

John passes me the phone, and Oliver, Martin, Roland, Thomas, and Rosalinde form a kind of five-pointed star around me and Mehen as we walk. Kahn and John walk on either side of the group, with Jesse behind and Henry out front.

"Hello?"

"Alora? You're alright. When you didn't land where John said—"

"We changed our destination to avoid unwanted attention. We're all fine, but someone, probably Isis, did send a team to the airstrip—so they must have known to watch for planes landing in the general vicinity. It was a lot of soldiers to send to a tiny, remote airport."

"We identified a leak." He sounds frustrated—I don't blame him. "I'm sure they told them you were headed for the London area. I didn't tell anyone else where, but you changed that detail anyway."

"I knew anything we told you was subject to being shared. Amun's too big for that not to happen."

"I'm still sorry it did. I also wanted you to know that here in North America, Isis was previously split. Although the main directors wanted you dead, your father led a large contingent that argued for your capture and training."

"He told me that." Although, I had thought the split was quite even. Apparently he was in the minority. I hate that I'm worried about him, but I hope that didn't leave him in any danger. "Is he alright?"

"Have you talked to him recently?"

My pulse picks up, which is stupid. It's not like I actually care about Duncan. "No."

"Isis caught all the leaders of that contingent, including your father."

I catch myself before asking whether he's alright for a second time.

"They didn't kill him . . . because he agreed that they were right." Devlin's voice is flat. He's taking no pleasure in delivering this news, which surprises me.

"You're saying that my father now wants me dead."

"I'm saying that all of Isis is now united in their desire to end the threat of the Warden."

"But Erra was unstable," I say. "Your wife was proof of that."

"They didn't believe me," he says. "I wasn't even sure that you did."

"Rra is just as unstable. Worse, actually," I say. "When I

was there a few hours ago, every single person on Rra was stuck in an animal form."

"Most of them can't even shift," Devlin says. "And of course the women—"

"I didn't stutter, Devlin. And I wasn't exaggerating. *All* of them are shifted, and all of them are stuck. And I'm not sure what you know about Rra, but according to the man I spoke to, on the full moon, which is in three days—"

"The hunt."

He knows. He must have had dreamers, women who occasionally visit Rra in their sleep, explain how life on Rra works. I suppose I'd have done the same if I were in his situation, and I knew that Rra was the next prison in sequence, but it's disconcerting that he always seems to know everything as soon as I do. "And if they're all animals . . ."

"The alphas will keep the Renders from hunting." He doesn't sound very sure.

"They don't believe they can control so many individuals," I say. "Their powers aren't working right, and the women and men who don't typically shift as well as all the children are animals for the first time."

"You have to stop the hunt from happening," Devlin says. "Or force them all to change back. They'll kill actual people. A lot of people."

"They will," I say. "Let the top brass in Isis know that if they kill me before I figure out some kind of fix, they're dooming countless humans. They can verify that with whatever dreamers they have who happen to visit Rra. My guess is that they already know there's an issue, or they've been ignoring any alarming reports for the last day or so. Because, Devlin? You weren't wrong. There's something amiss with the prison, and I don't know how to even go about fixing it."

"You need to prepare to gather all those souls," he says.

"It took you three days to gather the seven million on Erra."

I don't even want to think about gathering seven *billion* souls. If I can't figure something out before this next full moon, there won't be nearly as many to deal with. I try not to think about that.

We've reached the entrance to the museum. "I've got to go. But Devlin?"

"Yes?"

"Don't tell anyone where I am, please?"

"How could I?" he asks. "John won't tell me. He wouldn't even tell me why you insisted on going—only that you needed to find some information about the prison when it was first created."

"We've been on this call long enough for you to trace my location, I'm sure. Do the right thing for once, and keep it a secret. I know you think it would help to send an army of your people after me, but if Isis and Amun really are at war here, like you said, drawing attention from either side would be bad."

Luckily, the museum isn't currently full of people—apparently once the things that were of clear value had been stolen, there wasn't much to draw crowds.

Unfortunately, most of the things kept in the Egyptian exhibit appeared, at least to looters, to be of some significant value. Or perhaps the looters had heard the words Isis and Amun in the past few days and inferred that anything from ancient Egypt would be powerful.

Either way, nothing helpful remains.

I sit down on the dais that formerly held the Rosetta stone and drop my face in my hands.

"That dumb rock wasn't even from the right time period." John leans against a faux marble column. "And it was basically just Egyptian propaganda a teenager could have seen through."

I laugh. "The Pharaoh was only thirteen, and even so, he had better PR than I do."

"Yeah, among the general population, your stock isn't very high right now." John slides down until he's sitting on the floor, looking up at me. "Dad told me Isis has everyone here, back at home, and pretty much all over trying to kill you."

"I know." I shake my head. "Compared to me, Pol Pot was a saint. Hitler was Mother Teresa. Stalin was . . . "

"Santa Claus."

"Santa what?" Jesse shoves me over a bit and sits down.

"Nothing." I can't quite bring myself to explain, but his lack of memory about Santa Claus isn't helping.

"You're learning things every time you sleep," Jesse says. "So even if this wasn't quite the vault of information you were hoping to find . . . you shouldn't be too upset."

"It's not even—" I shake my head. "The world is a mess."

"Everyone hates her," John says.

"And I'm worried I've risked all of us and wasted our time, too." I shouldn't care that no one likes me, but I do anyway.

"What did you really come here to get?" Jesse asks. "You may as well just tell me."

My mouth drops open.

"We came for the Egyptian artifacts," John says. "This is the largest, er, this *was* the largest collection that dates to the period of time just before Terra was created—"

"Yeah, yeah. I know what you told everyone else." He dips his head to catch my eye and holds my gaze. "I'm wondering why we're really here. I figure if you can tell John, you can go ahead and tell me, too. It's not like I haven't figured out that it has something to do with my soul hole."

I hate how well he knows me sometimes. But I'm

delighted he's remembering enough to puzzle this kind of thing out. "Ra told me I could come use his reservoir," I say, "if I could find it on Earth."

"Reservoir of what?" Jesse frowns.

"Magic or energy or whatever we siphon as Assims." I shrug. "I know I can't go around killing people, even bad people, to save you. But I figured if I had that as a failsafe when things got rough, you couldn't complain. It's just a battery, and I had nothing to do with charging it."

Jesse sighs. "You've spent the better part of a day and a half, planned an around-the-world trip, and flown into a war zone . . . all so that you'd have magic that I'd approve of to save me when I wilt again?"

I swallow. "Are you saying it was unnecessary? That you'll let me siphon, I don't know, bad guys? Villains? People on death row? Because I can see people's souls, you know. I'm not sure if it's an Assim thing, or like, an Heir of Ra type of deal, but the state of people's souls are plain as day when I focus on them."

Jesse wraps an arm around my shoulders. "I'm saying that you should be worrying about things that are far more important than this. I'm saying that I died already, Alora. I've been living on borrowed time since you yanked me back from Terra, and that whenever I fade again . . . you need to let me go."

My mouth dries out.

My knees tremble.

A terrible ache forms at the base of my skull.

"I can't let that happen," I whisper.

His smile is terribly sad. "I know. I love you, too. More than you will ever know. And I'm never, ever going to be the reason that your soul darkens. Do you understand?"

Tears well up in my eyes. I knew if he found out, this is exactly what he'd say. "It's not like that. As long as I only take energy from people who aren't worthy, people who are dark—"

"You can't just keep taking energy from bad guys and killing trees forever, Alora. Sometimes, you can't put everything back in Pandora's box."

"I'm not Pandora," I say. "She was a moron. We didn't cause your death. This was done to us."

Jesse nods. "Sometimes life really sucks. Sometimes we aren't dealt a fair hand. Sometimes the other side cheats, and that doesn't change one thing: we still have to play fair. We still have to do the right thing—or we become the bad guys ourselves."

"But if I had found that battery?"

He sighs. "It would have been fine to use that—it's not like you made it—but it would have been like every other little Band-Aid you've found. Temporary." He squeezes me tightly, and drops his voice until only I can hear it. "You need to start to wrap your brain around the fact that I'm not going to be with you much longer. But you're not alone anymore. You have family and friends. You have people who love and care for you who aren't only me."

I shake my head. "Maybe I fixed the hole. Maybe you're fine now."

"You might be right. Maybe it's repaired. Maybe I'm fine." But I can tell he doesn't believe it.

Kahn and Roland turn the corner and stop in front of us.

"If there's nothing helpful here," Kahn says, "we should try and find a relatively safe place to stay until we work out our next move."

"You know, if the artifacts you wanted were here," Roland says, "and someone local saw an opportunity to snatch them and took some things—"

"They wouldn't be too far away," Martin says. "It's too

bad we don't have a way to track them down." His eyes scan the ceiling.

"What are you doing?" I ask.

"Looking for cameras," Martin says. "The police surely have better things to do right now, more urgent tasks, but if we can access the security feed and figure out who took them . . ."

We might be able to find the battery yet.

"What are the idiots saying now?" Mehen asks.

"They're trying to help me use the technology of the modern world—magic you don't understand—to find the missing collar."

"Magic I don't understand?" Mehen smirks. "A pale imitation of the magic that existed before Terra. There is no real magic that I don't understand."

"Even so," I say. "Their idea is the only real hope we have of tracking down where Ra's golden collar may have gone."

Mehen lifts his hand and I notice a ring on his pinkie finger. A deep golden band with a dimly glinting red stone.

"Whoa." I leap to my feet. "Are you telling me you had a battery all this time? Why didn't you tell me before?"

He holds up both hands, palms out.

Kahn and John both move toward him, their hands raised threateningly, like they're going to attack the man who killed thirty-something guys in a flash. They can't understand what I'm saying, but they can surely interpret my tone.

"Let's all calm down," I say in English. "I'm just having a little talk with Mehen. I'll let you know when I need backup."

"I don't have a battery, not as you mean it," Mehen says slowly. "You're looking for a way to draw power. All I have is a receptacle—an instrument through which Ra can feed me energy if I'm ever in trouble."

"So it's useless? That's what you're saying?" I arch one eyebrow. "Hand it over. Sorry to be rude, but I don't trust you."

"I'll gladly pass it to you, but I am revealing it now to mention that with it, I believe I might be able to track the collar to which it's linked. It wouldn't have worked from another continent, but it might work here, if the collar is quite close."

Hope sparks again in my heart, and I nod. "Yes. Let's try that. We'll follow your lead."

It takes a moment for me to catch everyone else up—Kahn especially isn't super excited about any part of my plan—but eventually, everyone agrees that since we're here, if we can use Mehen's weird ring to find the looters and recover any artifacts from the time period just before the creation of Terra, including hopefully Ra's collar, we should do it.

I'm a little nervous we'll stumble onto his perfectly preserved body, but not enough to put this off. I'm way more worried about Jesse's soul hole than seeing my dad's almost five-thousand-year-old body.

"Alright, everyone's on board," I say. "So how will this work, exactly? How can you track it?"

"When I suffer an injury or illness, Ra can feel it and he'll send a surge of power my direction. When that happens, if he's close enough, I can sense where it's coming from. In this case, he's not here, but the physical manifestation of his power is present, so I should feel that."

"What does that mean?" I ask.

"Someone needs to injure me in some way." Mehen folds his arms.

"What's he saying?" John asks.

"He says if someone harms him," I say, "then Ra will use his energy to heal him, and that pulse of energy will lead him to the anchor for the reservoir here on Earth."

Kahn throws the dagger so quickly I barely realize he's done it before it's sinking into Mehen's chest.

"Whoa," I say.

The smile that spreads across Kahn's face is unapologetic. "Don't have to tell me twice."

Mehen snarls.

Kahn leans toward him. "I was doing you a favor, you madman."

Before Mehen can do anything else, he freezes, his body spasming a bit, and then the dagger drops to the ground. The blood seeping from the hole disappears.

"Did it work?" I ask.

Mehen stumbles forward, walking quickly toward the exit to the museum, and we all scramble after him. By the time we leave, my little circle of Healers has fallen into formation around me and Jesse, with Kahn and John on opposite sides, my bristly electrons maintaining an orbit around the nucleus of protection.

We must look pretty ridiculous.

Also, our van is totally gone. Probably jacked by the same people who nabbed the Rosetta stone, may they burn miserably. Dirty little thieves. So we're stuck chasing Mehen on foot as he bobs and weaves up Montague Street, past the entire footprint of the British Museum and then beyond. It's almost eerie how quiet it is. It's the middle of the day and *no one* is out or about. No pedestrians, no cyclists, no automobiles.

Mehen doesn't even seem to notice the eerie, unsettling quiet of the place; he just keeps struggling along in fits and starts until he comes to a dead standstill in the center of Russell Square. "It's gone," he says, "the pull from the energy."

"Well, this has been super helpful," Kahn says. "We're now exactly where we want to be." He circles around, arms wide. "Completely exposed out in the open, where anyone and everyone can see us, without any cover, and no closer to Ra's magic necklace of purloined power."

Mehen narrows his eyes. "What's he saying?"

"He's not pleased to be in the middle of a park like sitting ducks." I shrug. "He has a point."

"Ducks don't sit." Mehen frowns. "They fly. They swim. They walk. They don't often sit."

I roll my eyes. "Can we focus? What do we do now?"

"If he's lost his magical cell reception, I volunteer to stab him again," Kahn says. "Actually, for the guy who collapsed my windpipe, I'll do it whether he asks for it or not."

Jesse yawns.

"Maybe we should try and find somewhere to set up camp around here," I say. "And then—"

This time the dagger doesn't hit Mehen. It hits me—in the center of my chest, and it hurts. Oh, sweet Ra, does it hurt.

EARTH

The moment when my parents died felt surreal. The world around me changed, profoundly, and it felt like I didn't recognize where I was, or who I was, or where I was going. My future exploded and suddenly I stared into the future as someone else, unsure what might happen next year, next week, or even in the next moment. But when I tried to look back at the exact moment they died, it was fuzzy and insubstantial. Maybe my mind blocked it out. Maybe I rejected what happened. I'm not sure.

The moment Jesse died was completely different.

Time froze and then only moved ahead at a crawl. It allowed me to recall each second individually, so that I can relive those critical few seconds over and over. It was like I stepped out of my own body to witness the horror of the world around me from all sides.

Being stabbed myself is nothing like either scenario.

If anything, the world speeds up. Warm, wet blood gushes from the place where the knife hilt protrudes from my chest, but I don't freeze. My senses expand in a way Mehen has probably always experienced. The ground under my feet has a weight to it. The trees shift and creak and tremble, the benches in a large circle at the center of the square vibrate, the walkways thrum, the grass quivers, the walkways and the buildings around me exist in a way they didn't before. Birds fly overhead. Bugs teem in the ground at our feet, some meandering, some racing, and some sleeping.

And I feel people, too. People I'd been trying hard to ignore, as they clearly wanted nothing to do with me. People quietly watching us from their homes, hiding inside closed bookstores, apartments, bars, and who knew where else. They pulse in a way that's distinctly different than my senses that allow me to Lift.

I realize that even Mehen can't feel the world in quite the way that I can. I can sense the objects all around me, things I could Lift or Bind. I sense the inanimate things of the world . . . but I can also feel the life humming and whispering and effervescing around me. It *beckons*, it calls to me, and I *yearn* to take it. A gaping hole opens up inside of me, begging me to pull on the life force of the grass, the trees, and the people. My body, in this injured state, seeks to prolong its existence. Like a greedy little beggar, it *wants* that which will make it whole again.

Like a hound salivating over someone else's sandwich, I ache to snap up the energy from those huddled people. I long to reach out and *pull* what I need from anyone else who has it. The agony in my chest demands attention. The heat soaking the front of my shirt demands repair. The rapid beat of my heart tells me that the injury's significant, and that something has to be done quickly, before it's too late.

Luckily, before I can do anything I'd eternally regret, my healing circle closes in, their hands clamping down on my shoulders, my neck, and my waist. Martin Heals me first, forcing the knife from my body. It drops to the ground, the pain receding as quickly as it came, the hole in my chest simply . . . closing up. A grunt is the only sound Martin makes, but before I can even say thank you, Roland takes the injury from him. By the time Oliver Heals Roland, the wound is so small that he doesn't even flinch.

The power of Healing when the burden's shared has always amazed me. Its only danger comes from a lack of adequate numbers to prevent the pain from being diffused. Which means that with a community of Healers who are willing to selflessly give, there's not much they can't fix.

It's kind of the opposite of my power. I would have taken and taken and taken to save myself.

But I did learn one thing in my energy-desperate state, something vital. "We're under attack," I say. "That knife wasn't thrown by a scared person or an uninterested bystander." It was no mistake that it hit me. I move past my healing circle, Lifting them behind me and away from the threat. "They're hiding up and down the West side. Stay back."

Mehen's eyes are lit up, as are Kahn's, and Jesse's, too. They're all three focused on the buildings that compose the University of London, according to the signage.

"Who's here?" John asks. "Is it Isis? Can anyone tell?"

"There are more than a hundred men," Mehen says. "Many of them Lifters."

"It must be Isis," I say.

Kahn doesn't even bother to argue. They're the group that wants me dead. Objects begin to fly toward us in earnest—more knives. Bullets. Shards of glass. But this time, I'm ready.

I shove them back, my eyes shining like tiny suns as I deflect, shatter, twist, and block. But we're not the only people in this area of London. Children and their mothers, men with portly bellies, they stupidly step out of doors and peer out of windows up and down the street, smart enough to hide initially, but curious enough to risk a peek now. The more distracted I become by the civilians at risk, the more things penetrate my defenses. A sharp rock grazes my arm, opening up a painful scrape. A long, pointed screw lodges in my upper thigh.

One glance shows me Jesse and Kahn and Mehen aren't doing much better.

And then another wave arrives, this one from the East.

Not predominantly Lifters.

Elementals.

Fire licks the base of the trees near where we're standing. Wind whips my hair, blowing the heat from the flames in our direction.

John immediately douses the fire, thankfully, since I'm too busy blocking projectiles, but they're not done, not by a long shot. I reach out with my Lifting senses, needing to know how many people we're facing from the East, and my knees weaken. It's at least another hundred. There may even be more beyond the ones I sense. And then someone zooms above my head. A Wind Called warrior, clearly, hurling a spear that barely misses my shoulder, embedding itself into the soft soil just to my right.

Mehen moves toward me, clearly the one who deflected that blow. "You need to get out of here," he says. "Right now."

"They'll follow me," I say. "I can't simply run."

"We should have brought more men," Mehen says. "Let that stupid human's dad send his troops. There are too many people and you're in danger."

My senses reach out instinctively and take hold of each threat, their energy pulsing and thrumming inside of their bodies. Without being sure quite how, I know exactly what I could do . . . siphon them. It would be like slurping down a milkshake. Like zooming down a slide. Like inhaling a mouthful of bracing winter air, I could steal their energy all at once. I could end this attack . . . and be flush with power, all at the same time. They are, after all, trying to kill me. They're hurling knives, and spears, and screws, and shards of glass at me and my friends.

I probably should siphon them all. It's the smart move.

With that much energy funneled into Jesse, maybe I could seal the hole.

Or I could build a wall around us, keeping us safe right here in the center of London.

But at what cost?

I can't start stealing people's lives from them. I can't suck people down like a Slurpee whenever they threaten me. That would make me no better than Ra—who's probably currently stuck in a prison for doing just what I'm considering—taking what wasn't his.

Jesse's cry distracts me from my greedy desires, and I watch as he slumps to the ground. My arm burns, my thigh screams at me, and a million tiny cuts howl for my attention, but I don't care about any of that. I Lift my Healing circle and fling them at Jesse, focusing all my efforts on keeping him shielded while they fix whatever injured him. "Heal him!"

And in that moment, all my qualms about stealing from other people, all my fears about robbing humans of their lives unfairly evaporate. Because it's not about me. It's about my Healers. About John, and Kahn, and Mehen, and it's about Jesse. He didn't ask for this. He doesn't deserve this.

And I won't let him die.

I reach out with the eager, desperately angry part of myself and I'm about to yank it away, to *pull* that energy to myself, when a wall of fire erupts along the West side of the Russell Square Gardens.

The heat that rolls toward me from the barrier of flames is scorching.

John throws his hands up and his arms shake, but he successfully blocks the heat rolling toward us. He either doesn't try or fails miserably in putting out the source of the heat—the inferno that rages along the entirety of the University of London building where the Lifters are hiding. At least there aren't residents in that building, because it *melts* in front of our eyes.

Seconds later, with a terrible groaning sound, the entire thing collapses. My Lifting senses tell me that every single one of the hundred people hiding inside is gone. Incinerated to ash.

Before I can even look for an explanation, a group of people move toward us from the North end of the Square. I can barely make them out through the trees—but one man walks at the front of them, his hands raised, his face familiar.

From my dreams.

Before I can shout or wave or do anything at all, Am-Heh flings a wall of fire toward the elementals on the East as well, molten flame billowing away from him. I can see why the people of Egypt thought he lived in an ocean of fire. I can see why Ra's enemies called him the Devourer of Millions.

Mehen's shouting at my side, his face split into a wide grin. "Am-Heh! You're alive! You're here! Praise and glory be to Ra himself for reuniting us!"

But nothing distracts my father's General from his work —he doesn't stop incinerating the buildings around us until there's nothing but smoke and cinder left where the elementals were formerly attacking. I ought to be horrified. I ought to be upset. I should berate him for destroying what amounts to nearly a full city block.

Only, if he hadn't shown up, I'm pretty sure I'd have killed the same number of people, and Jesse would be looking at me like he's currently looking at Am-Heh, the strongest fire elemental who has ever lived.

"Sekhmet!" He finally reaches us, his usual silver vambraces in place, etched with symbols I didn't understand even in my past life. His skin is a deep olive, his complexion smooth but for a few freckles across his broad nose. His eyes are as dark as the depths of the ocean, a foggy grey so rich that they're nearly black. His smile reveals huge, bright white teeth. His voice rumbles when he speaks, like the idling engine of an enormous truck. "I've longed to see you." He plows into me, his arms wrapping around me and squeezing me tightly.

I should be repulsed by an embrace from someone who just killed at least two hundred people and leveled two buildings—someone who then cut off the fire as quickly as he had created it, leaving nothing but smoking slag. But instead, I'm relieved. He kept me from killing those people in a much less obvious and probably more terrifying way. And no one is looking at me like they're looking at him.

"Do you know this man?" John asks, his eyes suspicious.

Am-Heh finally releases me, and then he drops into a low, practiced bow. "I forgot myself in my joy. Pardon me, Your Most Divine. It's a pleasure to be restored to your presence."

"Stand up," I say. "I can't tell you how grateful I am that you found me." Which reminds me. "How *did* you find us?"

"The power released by that group of incompetent elementals was staggering." His lip curls. "I knew that something big was going on, but not what."

"You just wander around the city now, searching for anything 'big' that might be happening?" My brow is cocked, but my mouth curls into a smile, undercutting the skepticism in my tone.

"When the half-trained children running the Followers of Amun informed me that the Warden was coming to the big city, I began sweeping the city. I evaluated the players in every large-scale skirmish in the hopes of locating this woman who created Terra."

"The idiots running the world right now could speak to you, when you woke?" Mehen asks.

Am-Heh rolls his eyes. "You were always so dismissive of anyone with less power than yourself. They boast several scholars, and although their pronunciation is not quite right, we're able to communicate reasonably well. With Sekhmet here to help them along, I imagine many of them will catch on in no time."

"I doubt the world is going to learn your language," I say. "You need to start learning English."

Mehen frowns. "The world will do as Ra commands."

"Ra is still stuck on Ā," I say, "and I haven't decided whether to free him. I still don't know why he was locked up in the first place. He either really doesn't know, or he won't tell me."

Am-Heh's eyes are wide, and he exchanges a glance with Mehen. "Your father would want us to support your decision, whatever it is."

Mehen grunts.

"But for now," Am-Heh says, "I'd feel much better if you'd accompany us back to our current accommodations. There's more than enough space for your small group."

Jesse! I spin around to make sure that the Healers were able to repair him, and I breathe a heavy sigh of relief when I see that they have.

"Shu's here?" Am-Heh strides past me and offers Jesse his hand.

Jesse takes it, their hands grasping one another's forearms.

"You look so young, like a man barely needing a razor." Am-Heh's broad smile is back.

Jesse looks at me for guidance.

"He can't understand you," I say. "In fact, other than a memory or two, I should probably warn you that I don't recall much of my life as Sekhmet and Jesse doesn't recall any of his life as Shu."

"That's a terrible travesty," Am-Heh says. "Especially since Shu was a—" He freezes, his entire body going utterly rigid. And then his hand reaches for his belt and he draws a terribly long, terribly shiny sword and shifts until he looks ready to jam it into someone . . .

Not someone. A very particular someone.

Kahn. Of course. His reaction is even more dramatic than Mehen's.

Only this time, Kahn's prepared for it. He extends both hands, flinging Am-Heh backward two dozen feet. The three men and four women who accompanied him into the square assume warrior position as well, hands extended, eyes flashing.

"Stop," I shout. "Stop!" I repeat in ancient Egyptian. "No one will do a single thing." I turn toward where Am-Heh is slowly standing back up, brushing the dirt and twigs from his linen pants, his eyes flashing. "Do not burn him. That's an order."

"You shelter your greatest enemy?" His words are clipped, his anger barely contained.

"I know it's confusing, but we have all been reborn, and none of us remember what happened before."

"She didn't believe me when I told her how evil he was," Mehen says. "Maybe you'll have better luck convincing her that he's the worst of enemies."

"Kahn is not Alexander," I say. "He is not my enemy."

There is no world in which we are enemies.

I feel the truth of that statement in my bones. "I'm not sure he ever was my enemy." I recall the conversation I had with Ra, where we worked up a plan to escape the tedium and never-ending conflict of our past lives. Twenty-four hundred years of mediating people's issues must have been truly overwhelming. "In fact, in one of the memories that has resurfaced, Dad and I worked out a plan in which we'd allow Alexander or Apophis, or whatever you want to call him, to defeat us, one incremental attack at a time."

Am-Heh narrows his eyes. "Not because of *him*, but because it was a convenient way to escape."

Mehen frowns.

"So you both knew that already?"

"Isis is your father's greatest enemy, and he is her son." Mehen crosses his arms and glares at Kahn. "I never thought it was a great plan."

"It was my idea." I grit my teeth.

Am-Heh isn't glaring, but he's staring at Kahn intently. Luckily Kahn seems uninterested in escalating anything, even if he's the one constantly being accused of things he never actually did.

"We will accompany you to your shelter." I glance around, uncomfortable with being out in the open. "If the offer still stands."

"Of course." Am-Heh straightens. "All but Apophis are welcome."

I shake my head. "*Kahn* comes with me wherever I go until I say otherwise."

The muscles in Am-Heh's throat work and his hands clench, but finally he swallows and nods stiffly. "Fine."

I smile. "Wonderful."

"But what were you doing out here in the open like this?" Am-Heh glares at Mehen. "We were both asleep for a long time, but I didn't wake up stupid."

Mehen scowls. "I was trying to locate the reservoirs. Ra offered their use to Sekhmet, but we aren't sure where any of them are at present."

"If you were following the tug," Am-Heh says, "you must have suffered an injury first?"

Mehen says, "The trail went cold. It was too far away."

Am-Heh smiles. "That's alright."

"I really need it," I say. "Once we've had a chance to catch our breath, I'd like Mehen to try again."

"I'm not sure why you would need it," Am-Heh says, "of all people. But you don't need to worry. The collar is in our possession."

I practically choke. "You have it?"

"The Followers of Amun were the first ones through the door of several museums when Erra collapsed," Am-Heh says. "Many of the ancient Egyptian collections were privately owned by members of the organization, obviously, and they were protective of their treasures being lost."

Why didn't I think about that? Of course they'd have a compelling interest in studying Egyptian history, just like I do. They'd know it was the last time that powers didn't need to be Awoken, and that people walked the earth freely with their abilities. That thought leaves me greedy to see what else they have. Could some of the texts explain how Terra was created? With all the other Assimilators locked in $\bar{A}$, anything about that particular skillset would be useless to everyone else.

Assuming that Devlin and Duncan are right and no Assimilators have Woken. I'm not sure I trust either of them, and that mistrust began long before my dad hopped on the "Kill Alora" bandwagon. Not that it sounds like he had much choice.

The streets are mostly empty as we walk north, and if it weren't for a few doors that slam shut and a few blinds yanked closed as we pass, I'd assume the humans living here had gone. I could use my Lifter senses, and maybe I should, but it feels like such an invasion of privacy in the absence of hostility from any possible threats.

"I only brought seven million over from Erra," I whisper. "How did it change the world this much?"

"They all had memories that went along with those powers," Jesse says. "And the women who had been oppressed for thousands of years on Erra, and presumably also on Terra, are probably angry. I doubt that helped them settle in peacefully now that they can do something about whoever harmed them."

I think about how it feels to know that you have zero control over what happens to you. As a woman, I've always known on some level, but as a foster kid, it became second nature for me to hide, to prepare, and to create an escape plan. I'd scan every room I entered for threats and position myself accordingly. I learned to take hits, literal and figurative, and keep on moving. I learned when to stand up for myself, and much more often, when to run or hide.

But if I'd been hiding my entire life and someone handed me a magical wand that allowed me to take revenge on anyone who had wronged me?

"What's the situation here?" I ask Am-Heh. "Who's in charge in London?"

He snorts. "No one, as far as I can tell. The leadership here has made a real mess of things. The Followers of Amun, as they call themselves, have been so brutal that everyone hates them. And the Followers of Isis have vowed to kill you, so I can't support them either, in spite of their more measured policies."

"What's he saying?" John asks.

I fill him in—all of them, really.

"The Followers of Amun have been tending to them all these years," John says. "Aren't they a little grateful? That we've stayed loyal and true to Ra and his Lieutenants?"

I find his use of 'we' a little surprising, since last I checked John was on the fence with me. That appears to have shifted.

When I convey his question to Am-Heh, John's query is met with an incredulous exhalation. "They've tended to me? Ra's power has kept me alive and hale." He shakes his head. "They've done nothing other than watch us, preserved perfectly, while we rested in a protective stasis. They're no more than voyeurs who will now seek acclaim and rewards for their non-actions."

I don't share that part with everyone else. "Uh, yeah. He's grateful." I force a smile.

Am-Heh was never scary—not to me—but in the modern world? He's a lot more frightening than he was, even in ancient Egypt. His sword looks odd, contrasted with the carefully manufactured clay pots and brittle ornamentation on cars, houses, and buildings. His hair, worn long but shaved on the sides and pulled back into a high ponytail, should look idiotic. Instead it looks *right*, and the world around us looks somehow *wrong*. He has a ring that looks quite similar to Mehen's, but it's on the middle finger of his left hand.

Neither of them boast stones that shine nearly as bright as the stones in Ra's collar when I saw him last. I hope that doesn't reflect the speed with which the power in the reservoirs is declining.

Kahn drops into step beside me, sliding past my Healer circle and taking up a position on the opposite side from Jesse. "Are you joining Amun?"

I shake my head.

"But we're following this old fire guy to their base."

"They have something I need—something that technically belongs to me, I think. I mean, it was my father's, and he basically told me to find it." Plus, I need it so I don't start snatching up the life force of everyone around me to keep Jesse alive.

Kahn doesn't argue with me, but he's not pleased.

I'm not sure what I'm expecting, but after walking for what feels like miles, we pass through a very unimpressive park sort of area with a few nice big trees, and a few iron benches, marked 'Wilmington Square,' and then we turn onto a small road labeled 'Merlin Street.' That sounds promisingly magical and amazing, but I don't see any swords, and the only stones are the uneven man-formed concrete variety laid into the sidewalks that flank the street itself. On one side of the road, there's a rather cute sort of building. The bottom third is whitewashed and the top portion is a tired old yellowish brick.

On the other side of the road, there's a large red brick building that probably looked quite stately fifty years ago. And that's where Am-Heh stops. "Let me go in first and explain—"

"Do we have to tell them who I am?" If the leaders of Amun discover I've shown up here, I have no idea how they'll react, but I'm pretty sure they'll let Isis know, and then any hope I have of making peace between the two of them will be gone forever.

"I doubt they'd allow you to examine the artifacts without knowing who you are." Am-Heh grunts.

"Can't you order it?"

He shrugs.

Which means he can, but he doesn't want to—he's pleased I'm with him. "You must understand that I don't *want* to pick sides, not yet. Not until I know more."

"You aren't picking sides," he says. "They will flock to you, once you have proclaimed who you are. Once you've shown them what you can do."

"I don't want anyone to flock to me. I don't want to be in charge of anything."

"Then who do you suggest I tell them you are?"

I shrug, "One of Ra's other Lieutenants, maybe?"

"When I ran out of here, I told them I'd felt the resonance in my ring of the pull of another Lieutenant—close. Do you truly wish to conceal who you are?"

Would I like to hide the truth from the world? Do I want to duck in, grab what I need to keep Jesse safe, and waltz back out?

Yes.

That's what I want.

But the note of censure in Am-Heh's voice tells me that would be a huge disappointment. I don't remember enough about our past to really feel awful about letting him down, but I do feel a twinge of unease. Probably because letting him down feels like letting Ra down.

How bad would it be if Isis thinks I've sided with Amun? They already want me dead, including my own birth father, apparently. And what are the odds that whoever is inside will press, and someone will give me away? Then I'll look like a liar. For no real reason, other than my own wish to avoid attention. I sigh heavily. "It's fine. You can tell them who I am."

Mehen grins. "Good. Because as soon as you've examined whatever they have that might be of use, we really need to train you. Your power is as great as ever, but your control is appallingly bad. And once you start Lifting and Calling Fire, they'll know who you are right away."

I try not to let his assessment bother me, but it does, a little at least.

Not that I can dwell on it. The second Am-Heh identifies me as Sekhmet, daughter of Ra, the reaction from the people inside this nondescript red brick building is borderline obnoxious. It's tiring, asking everyone to stop bowing.

And calling me Most Divine, which apparently Am-Heh was able to relay as the proper title. But most of the people in charge aren't in residence, as this is apparently the barracks for the low-level flunkies.

"Why do they have you staying here?" I ask. "I'd have thought the Followers of Amun would want you in some kind of position of great power and glory." I can't quite suppress my smile. This all seems so ridiculous, somehow.

Am-Heh glares at me.

"What?"

"My top priority was locating you, of course," he says. "Once we heard from the North American leadership that you'd been found. But I actually do have rooms in their main office."

"And we came here . . . "

"Because it's where most of their ancient Egyptian relics are stored—in the basement." Am-Heh folds his arms, the muscles in his powerful torso rippling. "I assume you still want to see them?"

"I do," I say. "I very much do."

"Wait," Mehen says. "I have an idea."

Am-Heh turns toward his old friend.

"I mentioned that Sekhmet needs to train, but when I've tried to make her, her focus has been quite poor. I suggest that, in order to motivate her, she be required to spend time training before searching for Ra's collar." His smile is positively smug.

"You're saying she can't skillfully Call Fire?" Am-Heh arches one eyebrow and spins on me. "Is he correct?"

"I can Call Fire," I say. "I'm just not very familiar with how to use it yet."

"I did wonder why you were standing in the center of that melee, suffering injury." Am-Heh frowns.

"I've never been able to rival you in a battle situation,"

Mehen says. "You've always had the better ability for military applications."

"But Sekhmet should have been able to best both you and I," Am-Heh says, "and you're implying that she can't."

"I'm standing right here," I say. "Stop talking about me like I'm a child."

They both laugh.

"What's so humorous?"

"You are a child," Am-Heh says. "A miraculous, talented, well-loved one, but still a child."

"I may not remember everything about my time in Egypt, but I hardly—"

"You were a child when Terra was formed, and you're even younger now," Am-Heh says. "It's the reason you need our guidance and support."

"And training." Mehen presses his lips into a tight line. "Remedial training."

I'm all set to argue when Jesse asks, "Are they saying you need to learn to use your abilities?"

I blink. "Why do you think that?" Is he remembering things?

"I figure that's their next step. Keep you safe, then educate you so you can protect yourself. Am I right?"

I huff.

"If that's what they want, can I come along? I'd really love to learn some of those things Mehen can do."

If it were anyone else—but I have trouble telling Jesse no. "Fine," I say. "But once I've worked with you for one hour, we go to check out whatever is in the supply closet downstairs."

Am-Heh grunts. "One hour each."

"You'll show me everything in storage, including the red stones that power your batteries."

"Deal," Mehen says.

"And you have the Followers of Amun show my people somewhere they can settle in and rest."

Except, apparently, no one wants to rest.

"I'm not leaving you," Martin says.

"I hardly think I should go take a nap while you take a pounding," Rosalinde says.

"If you're learning how to Call Fire, I'd like to tag along," John says.

"Me too," Kahn says, "even if they only let me watch."

"I can always work with you later," Jesse says.

I don't really want him to use any more energy than he absolutely must, but I can hardly say that. At least the stupid battery is supposed to be close. And even if the energy in the reservoir is low, Jesse won't know how much power it has. Maybe I can siphon a bit here and there from trees and bushes and birds or something, and he won't notice. That will be much easier if I can find any records that explain how to Assimilate and how to use the energy once I have . . .

"Let's get this training done," I say.

Of course, Mehen and Am-Heh insist on feeding me something before we start. But finally, I follow them back out of the building and into the little park area we passed through before. "Wilmington Square is a funny name for a park," I say. "Although, I suppose it is a square park."

"I'll go first," Mehen says. "Because I'm worried that after Am-Heh's done there won't be much left in this depressingly small forest to work with." He smirks.

Am-Heh shrugs and leans against the trunk of a large tree. "Go ahead."

Mehen points at a black metal bench. "We need to talk first."

"I want to know what he's saying," Kahn says.

"Learn Egyptian," I say.

He rolls his eyes. "Me too," Jesse says.

"And me," Henry says.

"I'll translate," I promise.

"It might help you understand the lesson if you have to teach the others." Mehen smiles. "It appears, based on what I've seen and what you've told me, that your focus in the past has been ascertaining how much power you have and learning to augment it."

I think about Kahn's training and shrug. "Sure. That's probably right."

"But that's far less important than how much *control* you have over your power."

"I don't understand."

"I know you don't." He stands up and turns his palms face up. "You don't need to use your hands to Lift. You don't need to move at all. That's the point, after all. But it often helps new Lifters to focus when we add motions." He gestures around the square, where broken limbs and leaves litter the ground. "The area is a mess—full of things that should have been tidied."

I'm sure that landscaping hasn't been a priority since telekinetics and then elementals started popping up around every corner. "It is."

"You can do more with one pebble well used than you can with a boulder." Mehen's eyes blaze with aqua light and the bench behind us screeches as it's ripped up from where it was secured to the ground with bolts set in concrete. "It took a lot of power to do that." He sets it back down and points at another bench, a dozen yards further down the paved path. "Or I could have simply done this." His eyes light up softly, and without any screeching, the bench a few feet away Lifts. "I removed the constraints, and now it Lifts easily."

Work smart, not hard. "I get that," I say. "I think that may be the American motto." I take a moment and explain to Jesse, Henry, and Kahn. John and Am-Heh exchange a glance, as if they already knew all of this and we're truly remedial.

"But when you have great power *and* you work with intelligence, if you can learn extensive control, limited only by your capacity to split your focus, you can do most anything." Mehen lifts both hands, like a chorister telling her choir to stand up, and every leaf, every pebble, and every bit of detritus in the entire park lifts into the air. After a single breath, a mere heartbeat, they begin to move. They weave in and out, up and down. I can't even follow the movements, there are so many, and they're complicated in a way my brain can't grasp.

It feels like it's been years since Kahn trained me on Terra, but he had me doing something like this with sand. Only it's like the drawings I made as a toddler, compared to the paintings of Van Gogh. He's not spelling letters. He's not merely holding things aloft. He's carefully and precisely controlling the interconnected motion of a hundred thousand objects at once.

And then, as if it was his end goal all along, the leaves all fall into a single pile. The pebbles into another. The twigs into yet another. I can't help myself—I jog over and look at each one, Jesse, Kahn, and Henry on my heels. They're not just piles, I realize, but the leaves are actually organized into many stacks based on type and size. The pebbles are organized by type of stone. The twigs are in groupings based on general size and shape.

"You didn't need to physically move over to look at them," Mehen says. "Just as I could organize them by sensing the objects I controlled, you too could sense that they were in like groupings from where you were sitting. That is the type of control we must develop."

More than two hours later, sweat is pouring down my forehead, and I've created my own piles, much smaller than Mehen's, but organized by *me*. Jesse has made a few tiny stacks, and Kahn and Henry have done the same. "This guy's a freaking genius," Jesse says. "I can't decide whether I love or hate him."

"I hate him," I say. "He's demonic."

"You've made enough progress for today." Am-Heh shoves away from the tree he's been resting on for the better part of the afternoon. "It's time for you to learn a bit of control with fire as well."

I hold out my hand, palm up, thumb extended from my other fingers, forming a square, and I think about the burst of heat and fury I created on Erra and wham. A tiny flame bursts into existence. "Look at that! Agnes followed me to Earth."

"Agnes?" Am-Heh cocks his head sideways. "You named your fire?"

"You bet your britches I did."

"Why would I bet my—never mind. It doesn't matter. Our goal today isn't to create flame. That's the simplest of objectives for Fire Called. In fact, most of us can do it while wearing diapers."

Agnes blinks out. I thought Mehen was rude, but this is just mean. "It took me an entire day to figure that out. You're kind of a jerk."

Am-Heh laughs. "It's my job to be hard on you. The meaner I am, the more able you are to defeat your foes."

"I don't want to defeat any foes," I say.

"But you will need to," he says. "And you'll thank me when you do."

I doubt it.

"The hardest part of being Fire Called is controlling exactly where your fire goes, and how hot it burns while it's there."

"How hot?" I don't even understand what he's saying.

"Let's see what your little friend can do." Am-Heh

motions for John to join us. "Ask him to create a blue flame."

"A what?" I ask.

"Tell him you want him to make a flame that is blue." Am-Heh folds his arms, all the muscles in his chest and arms bunching up around the metal arm bands and leather vest he's wearing.

I'm pretty sure he knows it makes him look twice as tough as usual. "Fine." I explain it to John.

His eyebrows come together. "Blue, huh?"

"I think he wants it to be really hot."

"Don't explain anything further," Am-Heh says. "This is a test for him. Tell him blue, nothing more."

Good grief. "Blue, he says. That's all he wants me to share."

John doesn't hold up a hand, or anything else like that to help him focus. He merely looks at a place a few feet in front of him, and a flame bursts to life. It's whitish blue. And it's so hot, the heat rolls off it like a slap to the face. I take a step back.

"Extinguish his flame," Am-Heh says to me.

"He wants you to—"

Am-Heh tsks. "Not him. You."

"Uh. What?"

"I want you to make his flame go out," Am-Heh says. "This is still quite basic." He clasps his hands behind his back.

I remember what John taught me on Erra. This flame isn't large, but it's hot. Far hotter than anything I've ever created. Far brighter, too. It takes me several tries, but I finally put it out.

"He sustained that for much longer than I thought he could." Am-Heh sounds pleased, and I realize it wasn't a test for me. It was for John—he knew I would fumble around trying to extinguish it and he was wondering whether John could hold out that long.

"You like him," Mehen says in an accusatory tone.

"He has raw talent," Am-Heh says. "Not many Fire Called could create a flame that hot, much less sustain it for so long."

"He's been kissing Sekhmet."

Am-Heh's eyes widen slightly and his mouth twists.

"Which is none of your business." I scowl at Mehen. Then I shift my irritation to Am-Heh. "Not for either of you."

Judging by the glint in Am-Heh's eye as he puts John through his paces, he doesn't agree. John's forced to extinguish fire after fire, of increasing intensity and size. Then he's forced to shrink fires, lots of them, and finally, Am-Heh makes him hurl fire right at me. Repeatedly.

"No," John finally says, when I almost fail to put out a fireball before it hits my chest.

"Is he declining to participate further?" Am-Heh arches an imperious brow.

"He is," I say. "I think he's unimpressed with your methods."

"We're not sure how much time we have," Am-Heh says. "We don't know what threats may come your way, and I need you and your *boyfriend* to be ready."

"He's not my boyfriend." I put my hands on my hips.

"Then why are you kissing him?" Am-Heh scowls at John.

I'm kind of impressed when John scowls right back.

"None of your business," I say. "Does that phrase translate? It means that you aren't the boss of whom I kiss or don't kiss."

Am-Heh steps closer to me, heat rolling off of him. "I don't want you to date someone who's not worthy of you."

"Does this guy have a crush on you?" John clenches his fists.

"What's he asking?" Am-Heh demands.

"You don't even want to know."

He laughs then. "He thinks I'm a threat to him, romantically?" His laughter redoubles. "Young people are cute."

"Excuse me," I say. "But why is that so funny?"

Am-Heh leans close to me, his breath like that of a dragon. Ash and flame. "You must not remember this, but I'm your uncle. I'm Ra's older half-brother. And I'm *delighted* that you seem to be drawn to a Fire Called, but I'll never allow someone *lesser* to court my niece. Ra would string me up by my toes if I did."

That's awkward. He's my uncle and I didn't even remember that.

He wraps a beefy arm around my shoulder. "And for what it's worth, I actually do like him. His control is pathetic, but he can improve that. The raw ability isn't lacking."

"I thought you were training me." I hate the petulant tone in my voice.

Am-Heh's laugh is like the bark of a seal this time. "You may not remember your life before, but you are *exactly* the same." He presses a kiss to my forehead. "It has eased my heart tremendously to see you again—healthy, strong, and as beautiful as ever."

"I swear, if that creepy old guy is trying to put the moves on you," Jesse says, "I will—"

"That creepy old guy," I say, "is our uncle. He's Ra's half-brother."

That shuts them all up.

"So have I done well enough to look at Dad's old junk yet?"

Am-Heh has a much better sense of humor than Mehen. He laughs and laughs. He may despise Kahn as much as Mehen does, but that's where their similarities end. "Yes, I think you have. Let's go."

He keeps his arm around my shoulders as we return to the red brick building and head down to the storage rooms.

Before I even see it, I can *feel* it—the power held inside it calling to me. Am-Heh reaches into a large black box, and lifts a golden collar out of it slowly, carefully. Hammered gold forms the wide collar I saw on Ra, set with twenty red cabochon-cut stones that look like rubies, pulsing intently.

And then, as I reach for them, my greedy hands eager to see whether I can siphon from them, they spark brightly for one enormous flash . . . and go dark. Black. Dead.

Empty.

Every last one of them.

"What was that?" My hands close over the collar. I've pinned all my hopes on this dumb thing—it was my method of preserving Jesse the next time he dims. How, right in front of my eyes, could they all have gone dark? Maybe it's cyclical. "Does it just do that sometimes? Will they spark back to life?"

Mehen frowns. "No. Ra had to draw a significant amount of power for some reason—I've never seen him pull so much at once—outside of a major spell."

I could scream. But instead, I realize that it's time for me to look for answers somewhere else. Ra has some explaining to do. "I am going to need a knife," I say. "A big one this time." There's no way that the Rra version of me is going to miss the message this time.

And once I've figured out where and who I am, I'm going to see Ra to give him a piece of my mind.

12

ANCIENT EGYPT

"We have a problem," Dad says.

"I thought things were going exactly as they should?" I can't help my bad attitude. It seems like every time things are going well, *bam*, something comes up.

"They're going *too* well." Dad finishes the parchment he was working on, signs it, and blows on it. He folds it, dumps wax on the back and stamps it with his solid gold ring. "Isis is suspicious."

"What can we do about that?" I cross the room to stare at the enormous map Dad painted onto the center of the table in the antechamber to his bedroom. "The Lycians were too easy to defeat? Is that the problem?"

Dad nods. "It's a delicate balance, you see, letting Isis and young Apophis believe they're taking my subordinate countries. If we put up too big of a fight, innocent people will die."

I cringe. "Maybe we should give up," I say. "I hadn't considered the cost to innocent bystanders."

Dad shakes his head. "It's not your fault. Whether we

allow Isis to take over, or whether we continue to repel her never-ending attacks, innocents will perish along with trained military forces. We haven't planned or executed a single attack—we've only defended from hers."

"But we could finish her," I say. "Decisively. Put this to rest forever."

"And you and I would be doomed to rule over these lands and their people, arbitrating disputes, maintaining peace, repairing the world after natural disasters. All the things you find tedious, never-ending, and thankless. More Isis-like characters would arise, possibly those who couldn't actually keep hold of the lands and maintain a real peace. More wars would need to be fought."

"It never ends," I say. "And I can't decide whether it's more noble to hide away and let the world rule itself, or to stay and bear up under the onslaught of injustice and greed and suffering."

Dad's smile is kind. "You've been here for the ruling and weighing and suffering part. Let's see this through and we can decide whether we like living a quiet life. In all the years I've been alive, that's one thing I've never attempted."

"If we can even pull it off," I grumble. "What exactly makes you think Isis is suspicious?"

"You know that I have spies everywhere," Dad says. "They report that Isis is looking for ulterior motives for my allowing Apophis to advance. She's searching for a trap."

"Well, there isn't one," I say. "So she can search as much as she'd like."

"You and I know that," Dad says, "but often, you find what you're looking for. You remember all the people who died after she finally assassinated her husband." He shakes his head. "Landing Philip was quite the prize, but he wasn't a very faithful or engaging spouse. And after he died, with rumors that Alexander wasn't really Philip's heir . . . "

"How could he possibly have believed that a full-grown man whom Isis brought with her was his heir?" I shake my head. "It makes no sense."

Dad laughs. "In this instance, it was actually true. He was her lover when she wound up pregnant. He was a powerful Lifter, and quite handsome. It has been some time since they were together, although I hear they're on again and off again, but she made up with him, convinced him to take them back, and used her powers to make Apophis much younger, an early teenager, so that his people would accept Apophis too. It helped that she boosted her brother to the rank of king of Epirus. That's also where she got the name Alexander."

"She re-named Apophis after her own brother?" I shake my head. "The more I learn about her, the crazier this woman sounds."

Dad laughs. "I hope you never have cause to learn for yourself."

Which reminds me that Isis convinced Mother to join her. She must be quite smooth-tongued. "What can we do to allay her suspicions?"

"She puts great weight in signs from heaven, in omens, if you will," Dad says. "Our best bet would be to convince her that something points toward Apophis' greatness and power only growing. She needs to believe that his great success is somehow foreordained. Then she'll stop worrying that we're trying to lure him toward us and believe what she's wanted to believe all along—that she's destined to defeat me."

It takes about three hours, but Dad and I manage to come up with an existing legend that lies mostly in the path Apophis' army is headed that we could use to our advantage. "That means that someone needs to lure him to Gordion," Dad says. "I'll summon Ptah—"

I shake my head. "That's a terrible idea. You said that Isis and Apophis know your Lieutenants by sight. You can't send one of them. It'll never work. Besides, if we bring one of them in on it, then our plan will spread. You said I can't even tell Shu—we can't tell anyone else without telling him first."

"What would you have me do, then?" Dad asks. "Perhaps I could write—"

"I'll go." It's simple, it's clean, it's efficient. "No one knows my face."

"Your mother does." Dad shoves away from the table. "It's too dangerous, and you're the one person whose safety I won't risk."

A roar rips itself out of my throat, so loud that part of me must have shifted. "You think everything is too dangerous. But I'm a supra alpha who can Call Fire, who Lifts, and who can siphon from a distance. Who exactly is going to harm me?"

"I don't want your identity to become public knowledge."

"Good," I say. "Neither do I. I'm not planning to go as myself, or wear a shirt that says, 'Princess of Egypt.'"

Dad laughs. "But—"

"No buts. I'm perfect for this one small thing—to lure Alexander's army to Gordion and make sure he can untie the impossible knot, foreordaining him to become king of all Asia."

"How will you do it?"

"By spreading the tiny, little-known fable until he hears it from all sides, of course." I smile. I've always loved telling stories, and this might be the most exciting one I've ever told. And for once, I'll be out in the world, helping. It's the reason I'm most excited about a small life—a life where I'm not confined to a palace or followed incessantly by guards.

"You'll take Am-Heh," he says.

I roll my eyes. "I may as well take a group of fifty heralds, all proclaiming my identity."

"Fine, who do you want to take?" Dad pins me with a glare. "You can't go alone. Everyone needs someone to watch their back."

"I'll take Shu."

Dad's mouth drops open in a very satisfying way. "Apophis would recognize him. He accompanied your mother on several trips to Macedonia. How about Anat?"

She could probably go alone. She can make herself look like most anyone. Although, she's taught me that trick, so I suppose I can, too. But if she goes, I won't need to do anything. Dad will think of that in about three seconds and I'll be stuck here, listening to reports and sitting on my hands again.

"I could go with Ptah."

"You could," Dad says. "Sure."

He agreed to that far too quickly.

I just *knew* he was behind Ptah proposing.

Ever since I turned him down, Dad's been very cagey about the whole thing. I'm not actually excited about the prospect of dragging him along with me, but I know he's the least conspicuous companion Dad might accept. If only because he's still hoping I'll change my mind and decide Ptah makes my heart race. Blech.

"We'll leave in the morning," I say.

"You can stop in outlying areas, starting rumors and reminding them of the old legends and stories—but you'll need to start no closer than Phoenicia or someone might recognize you."

"I'd better prepare my trunks," I say. "I'll need a convincing disguise." I can't stop myself from poking fun at Ptah and Dad for thinking we'd be a good match. "I know exactly what our story should be!"

Dad sighs.

Clearly I tipped him off—he must have heard something in my tone. "We could tell everyone that we're a father and daughter—no one will question our traveling in close quarters, and that makes the most sense given our age gap, don't you think?"

He rolls his eyes. If he hadn't recently magicked Ptah to be so young that he looked my age, it would have worked perfectly. As if I'd suddenly believe that he actually was *my* age just because he looks younger. "That won't work."

"Alright, I suppose we can tell people he's my brother."

"I suppose you can at that," Dad agrees. "But what will we tell Ptah, so that he doesn't suspect our real purpose?"

"We tell him that we're planning to ensure that Apophis *fails* at untying the knot." I'm rather proud of that lie. "Then when he *does* it, even we can seem shocked and concerned."

"You grow cleverer every day." Dad hugs me.

"I'm going to miss you." I mean it.

"We've never been apart for quite so long." When he releases me and steps back, his eyes are sad.

"Are you going to cry?" I'm teasing him to keep from bawling myself.

His voice is thick. "Would you be embarrassed if I did?"

"You've spent the last twenty-four years training me in everything—one day you'll have to actually send me to do *something* on my own."

"You can't blame a father for being protective of his most precious miracle."

No, he's right. I can't. I love him for it. "I'll plant the seeds that draw Apophis to Gordion, and then I'll make sure the dolt actually solves the infernal knot, so that his mother will believe he's foreordained to destroy us. I'll do it in a way that ensures no one knows who I am or what I can do." I smirk. "I'll be so sneaky and so devious that I'll make you proud, I swear it."

"You make me proud every single moment of every single day." When he hugs me, I almost cave and suggest that Anat can go in my place. But one day I have to leave and do something on my own—one day, I'll have to be useful.

That day may as well be tomorrow.

13

ANCIENT EGYPT

I think the most annoying thing about Ptah is his beard.

Mehen told me that when Dad grew a beard, most everyone in Egypt copied him, growing it long and curved. Ptah, perhaps in a bid to be different, grew his long . . . and straight. It dangles down from his chin like dripping wax.

Not a day has passed that I haven't considered chopping it off while he sleeps.

But the second most annoying thing about him is how obsessed he is with architecture and stonework. "Yes," I say. "That building sure is unique."

"It's also—"

"And it's beautiful, yes," I say. I can't understand why he needs me to agree with him, that every single new building is a treasure.

It's also a complete lie. This temple looks exactly like the twenty-five other stone temples we've passed in Phrygia.

"The lines are so clean." He runs his hand down the side once we're close enough. "They clearly had a gifted Lifter, to slice the stone like that, right along an existing fault line. Look—they didn't even need mortar on this joint."

"You appreciate stonework?" A tall man with a heavy bag slung over his shoulder peeks his head around the corner of the temple.

Ptah straightens his broad shoulders. "I do. It may be my favorite branch of study."

"There's to be a conference of stonemasons this afternoon." The man drops his bag. "It's not far from here, actually. I'm planning on going with a friend of mine. You'd be welcome to join us. I hear there's to be a presentation on the benefits of the various stone types, including those brought on great barges from the other side of the Black Sea."

Of course that puts a glint in Ptah's eye. "You don't say."

"No," I whisper. Not another side trip. Not another single one, especially not to debate the merits of *rocks*.

"Where will the conference be meeting?" He glances toward me. "It would be a diverse group of people from several places, I'm sure." He raises his eyebrows, as if I don't already get his point.

We've disseminated the story to enough places. Apophis' army is already on the move. "We're in a hurry," I say. "We probably shouldn't delay."

"Your wife is quite a fiery one," the tall man says. "I hope you can manage her."

"Oh, I can," Ptah says, just as I say, "I'm not his wife. I'm his sister." My nostrils flare. I've regretted agreeing to take Ptah with me since the very day we left.

"It would be a pity to miss the conference." Ptah looks back at me. "I think we can spare one day."

I grit my teeth. No woman in this region would gainsay her brother, but I'm considering all the ways I could tie him up in a bag and drag him the rest of the way to

Gordion. I could tell other travelers I pass that he's a side of lamb . . .

"Why don't you go to your little meeting of builders or whatever," a deep voice says, "and I'll keep our *sister* safe." Shu's voice carries from where our horses are tied across the courtyard.

My mouth curls up into a smile.

"You're not supposed to be here," Ptah says.

"Did you want to learn about new kinds of rocks?" Shu lifts both eyebrows. "Or did I misunderstand? Maybe you weren't giddy with joy at the mere mention."

I've missed Shu's smirk more than anything else. "Yes, do stay for the meeting," I say. "My other brother will take great care of me, and we can all leave together when you're finished."

Ptah's eyes narrow and I worry he'll beg off, or order us both to go with him, but his excitement over new building supplies wins out over his sense of duty.

"I can't tell you how delighted I am to see the back of him," I say, as soon as Ptah's stupid long beard is out of sight. "He's even worse away from the palace."

"Why in the world would Father support him as a good match for you?" Shu whistles. "You'd kill him inside of a year."

I laugh. "Maybe inside of a month. I was thinking of ways to tie him up and stuff him in a bag when you showed up."

"Why don't we ditch him and head for Gordion without him?" Shu tosses his head at the horses. "I brought Killian, so we can even race there. I hear it's less than a day's ride. Surely at this point, all you need to do is make sure that the knot can't be solved. Put some magic spell on it or some-thing? The last thing we need right now is for Apophis to get *more* confidence, after all."

"The next part is simple," I say, "but Dad didn't want to

risk having you anywhere near Apophis, in case Mother or Isis were around and recognized you."

Shu rolls his eyes. "So change my appearance a bit. Anat does it all the time. I'm sure she's taught you the basics."

I freeze. "The simplest forms, sure, but what if I can't get your nose right again afterward? It's complicated—you put the energy on like a mask, but the longer it sits in place, the harder it is to remove."

He shrugs. "I've never loved my nose. It's a little on the beaky side. I'm okay with the risk."

I shove him. "I love your nose just as it is." But I can't take him with me. Not to Gordion. He'd be sure to notice that I'm helping Apophis *solve* the knot, not making it harder.

"Oh, come on." Shu spreads his arms and spins in a circle. "We're out in the *world*, doing something, together for once. Don't you love it?" He beams at me. "I didn't think Dad would ever let you out of his sight."

"He's not that bad, and I like being with him. I like being at home."

"You do?" He purses his lips.

"Of course I do. You don't?"

Shu shrugs. "I do, yeah. I love you, and I love him, but it's kind of boring, just handling all the administrative stuff and putting down rebellions. Give it a few decades and you'll probably feel the same."

I can't ditch him, and I can't keep lying to him. Not anymore. Not when he just wants to be with me. I have to tell him the truth. "So . . . I'm actually not here to make sure Apophis can't solve the dumb Gordian knot."

Jesse blinks. "Then why are you here?"

"Well, the reason we chose this legend—"

"Remind me what the legend even says? Dad said Isis will never give up if Apophis unties some knot?"

"It's actually a small story, native only to Phrygia, but

Dad and I are using it because, well, there was this oracle in the capital of Lycia, right? Their king had died without leaving an heir. No one could agree who should ascend the throne—in fact, there were about five warring factions. They had gathered outside the city and were supposed to be fighting to the death. Until the oracle predicted that the next person to pass through the city gates on wheels would be their new king, an epic king, bringing blessings to all the citizens of Phrygia. Everyone was sick of fighting, and they were expecting one of the five main warriors, probably in a chariot."

Shu sits on the bench outside the temple. "But it wasn't one of them?"

I shake my head. "No, it was a relatively weak guy, not even a soldier. He was Earth Called, in fact. But apparently the heads of each of the warring divisions had killed one another—the last one dying from blood loss. No Healers deemed them worthy of their time and expertise, they were so bloodthirsty."

"You're kidding. So a random farmer became their new king?"

"The people trusted the oracle, who had promised anointing him king would end the fighting and bring them prosperity."

"That's wild." Shu shakes his head.

"Well, that farmer's name was Gordias, and he ended up being a wonderful king. They named their capital city after him. He adjudicated disputes, tended and nurtured, and figured out how to make sure they always had enough food for every one of the subjects. They adored him. His son was a pretty decent king too—also Earth Called, but you'll probably remember his name. Midas."

"Everything he touched turned to gold?" Shu frowns. "Is that right?"

"Not exactly. He had an affinity for heavy metal detection, though, and they found quite a few gold mines within their national boundaries, increasing the wealth of the nation quite substantially."

"What does that have to do with—"

"I'm getting there. Geez."

"Get there faster," Shu says. "Or I'll change my mind and decide you're perfect for boring old Ptah."

I swat his arm. "You'd have to shut your mouth for me to do any better. As I was saying, Gordias came on a wagon. And the people loved that about him. Years after he became king, after he was a beloved figure, that old wagon that he rode in on, the one that landed him the throne, was wheeled out into the central square of the city and tied to a huge post he had erected there, next to a statue."

"A statue of the farmer?"

I shake my head. "No, a pillar that had the values of their entire country carved into it. At the base, it had images of life itself—crops, the sun, the rain. As the carvings wrapped their way up the pillar, there were images of the boundaries of the nation, and at the top, it had scales for justice, and bowls of figs and dates and bread, to symbolize their bounty. He said that as he had conquered by cultivating, so too would another come one day. Instead of rolling in on a chariot, someone intelligent, someone strong, and someone clever would come. Gordias said that person, the one who could untie the knot that he had employed all his smartest advisors to create, would go on to rule Asia in the same way he had ruled Phrygia. Surprisingly, adeptly, and with great success and prosperity for all the citizens."

"But why are you here? What does that legend have to do with us?"

I come clean then, explaining that I'm tired of the tedium of ruling and the ongoing fighting. Isis won't ever let go of her anger, and she has the ability to extend her rule, or that of her son, indefinitely. Assuming they're fair and just, they could be excellent replacements. They could rule in a way I don't even want to.

Shu places his hand on mine. "Hathor's wrong, you know. You're not a monster. You'd be an excellent empress."

I look at my feet. "It doesn't even matter."

"You're a huge blessing—Mother was confused and made a tremendous mistake. I wonder sometimes whether she'd take it back if she could. You can't make life decisions based on someone else's wrongful assessment of who you are."

I can barely talk over the lump in my throat. "That's not even why—look, the point is that we're going to escape all of it, and we'll be free of Isis' pursuit, too."

"How?"

"By convincing her that we've all died. Then we can leave—go somewhere very far away—and live a quiet life. We can paint, or sing, or I don't know what. But all this civilization development and being worshipped as gods?" I shake my head. "I don't like it. Not a single bit of it."

"Dad loves it," Shu says. "He'll be miserable if you leave."

"He said he wanted to leave."

"Where does he get his power?" Shu crosses his arms.

"He's an Assimilat—"

"No, that's not what I'm asking. From whom does he siphon?"

I think about it for a moment. "From the bad people—the ones who can't be rehabilitated."

"Right," Shu says. "He siphons their life force and uses it for what?"

"To heal the broken things, to fix the wrongs in the world."

Shu snorts. "Sure. And he also wants to end world hunger. He's a saint. But he also loves being the supreme being. He loves that people come to him, begging for his help. It's the one part of his life that brought him joy all these years." His face softens. "Until you, I suppose."

I hope he's not right. I hope I'm not asking Dad to give up everything he cares about—other than me. Because I don't want to make him miserable. "He said he'd be happy to walk away from all of it."

"He'd do anything you asked," Shu says. "But I doubt his contentment with it will last."

"We're here because my plan to let Apophis conquer us and everyone else Dad rules is going well. Too well."

"Ah, so you told Ptah and the rest of us that you're here to ensure he *doesn't* untie this knot, but really you're here to make sure he gets it done?"

"Exactly," I say. "When we set out, I made sure to embellish the story a bit here and there, to remind people of its significance. And we also mentioned that the oracle spoke of how this king of Phrygia would be a type of the king to come."

"Did the oracle actually say that?" Shu's forehead crinkles.

I laugh. "Of course not. But what matters is that it's a compelling story. A conquering warrior, fated to take down the supreme commander—the grand master for thousands of years—a feat prophesied by the same oracle who confirmed the elevation of a farmer to a king? That's something people will repeat to their friends."

"I assume they have, and that the great Alexander is now making a detour to come through Gordion? A land of relative insignificance to the surrounding areas, a place guaranteed to put up no real military opposition to his rule?"

I nod.

"And you just need to go and make sure he can work it out."

"He's a Lifter," I say. "So I imagine he can figure it out, but yeah, that's what I need to do."

"I hear he's a Lifter *and* an elemental."

"Yeah, I've heard that as well." I shrug. "But I'm pretty sure I can ensure his success."

"Alter my appearance," Shu says. "Just do it. I want to watch, and maybe I can even help you."

"Help me how?" I frown. "I don't need you picking a fight with—"

"Oh, please. I'm not that dumb."

"I'm seriously worried that your face will—"

"Anat or Dad can fix anything you screw up," he says with total confidence. "I'm positive."

"But if they have to, they'll be furious with you for ignoring Dad and coming all the way out here."

"I'll risk it."

"You just want to see Apophis," I say. "To see if all the legends about him are true."

"So do you." He smirks.

And I hate that he's right. After telling this stupid story so many times, part of me is desperate to see this dumb knot and make sure it's hard enough that he'll struggle to untie it. "If there really is a knot, why hasn't it already been untied?" I shake my head. "Any Lifter should be able to do it, no matter how weak. We can sense the bands we can't see, and shift them easily enough."

"Which means there must be more to it," Shu says.

"I guess so," I say. "Or maybe there's no knot at all. Maybe it's an illusion—a trick somehow."

Shu points at his nose. "I've always wanted a stately nose. Sharper, thinner." He lifts his eyebrows expectantly. "And perhaps lighter hair. Glowing golden locks?"

I laugh. "You would look stupid with blond hair."

"Alright, then, ebony instead. Dark brown is boring. Everyone has it."

He acts like he's younger than I am, I swear. "Fine." My heart accelerates, just thinking about doing something like this. Anat said I was proficient enough, but I've never done it without her standing over my shoulder, directing, watching, and correcting. "But if I totally screw up, you can't be mad."

"I won't be," Shu says. "But unless you want Ptah to locate you posthaste, you should change a few things about yourself as well."

He's right. Why didn't I think of it? If I change my appearance and Shu's, we could evade him here, and then head home without him. It would be *glorious* to skip out on all the boring, pedantic treatises on architecture and proper technique. And if he talks any more about the legacy of pyramids, I might scream.

I lift my right hand toward Shu's face. It doesn't matter how close it is, not for this, but it's kind of a habit. The red stone on my ring finger flashes and pulses as I tug on the power inside it.

"What kind of magic are we working with here?" Shu eyes the ring as if it might bite him. "Scorpion? Plant life? A prisoner doomed for death?"

I shrug. "Dad filled it. I have no idea."

"Prisoner, then. Dad doesn't mess around with the tiny junk."

"Only I do that." I suppress my annoyance at everyone's judgment. "But if you had to siphon a person—even a bad person—you'd get it. It gives me the willies every time."

"You misunderstand. I think I'd be right where you are, if it were me. But Dad had to do it for almost a hundred and fifty years—he had no choice. Willies or not, he siphoned." When he was under the control of his father, the supra alpha—the one who's like me.

The genesis of my Render power. "I wish I wasn't an alpha."

"It's a blessing, and you never abuse it, so you're nothing like everyone says Grandpa was. Now get to the appearance changing stuff before Ptah gets bored or offends someone and catches us."

I dip gingerly into the well of power and spin out a thread of energy, and then I funnel it into a shape—a mask of sorts. Jesse's eyes become a dark, deep brown. His hair lengthens, darkens to a black so deep it's nearly purple, and is pulled back in a tight leather-bound queue. I add bulk to his spare frame, and heft to his arms. His nose sharpens, and his cheeks become much more angular, almost hollow. And to torment him a bit, I give him a huge scar that runs up the side of his face. "See how the ladies like that."

"Oh come on, what did you do?"

I walk toward our horses and pull a small mirror from my saddlebag. "See for yourself."

"Really? That scar is terrible. What kind of person has no Healer friends and can't afford to pay one?"

"I suppose you can tell people you got it in the war. Not enough Healers to go around, then."

"What war?" He asks. "Oh, fine. It gives me personality, I suppose."

"It sure does."

"Now, fair is fair. No pulling an Anat and turning yourself into the most beautiful woman alive when you've given me this gnarly scar."

"I wouldn't dream of it." Besides. I think classic beauty is almost boring. Instead, I reach for the things that I haven't experienced. I was born with a wide smile, brown hair with streaks of gold, full, round cheeks, and bright hazel eyes. I'm of average height, with a slight build.

When I dip into the energy this time, and pull out about the same amount of magic as before, I spin it into something new. Something exciting. I darken my hair to match Jesse's rich ebony shade, and then plait it in a complicated knot on the back of my neck. I broaden my face even further, sharpening my nose to match my brothers, and leave my cheeks quite hollow indeed. I make my eyes almost comically large, and change the irises to a bright, piercing yellow that resembles a tiger's. I drop a large mole onto the bottom of my right cheek, but I can't quite bring myself to sprout a hair. For my final change, I add height and strength, but no curves. Gaunt, that's how I'd describe myself—like someone who has missed too many meals and can't quite afford to make them up.

"There," I say. "I don't think anyone could accuse me of coming too close to perfection."

Shu shakes his head. "No, and yet, even with all the differences . . . there's something compelling about you, yet. The set of your jaw, maybe? The way you hold your chin? You're not beautiful—but you're not plain either. You're striking in the same way a falcon or a lion commands attention."

I ignore him. "Keep yammering like that. I'll beat you there for sure."

He mounts his huge white horse, Killian, a few seconds after I swing up onto Charger. "See if you can keep up."

Whoever said Gordion was a day's ride away didn't have mounts like us. We drop to a trot pretty often to let them recover, but they like to run.

"After we reach that tumulus, we run again?" Shu asks.

"I'm not sure it's respectful to race past burial mounds," I say.

"The inhabitants are dead. They don't care what we do." Shu urges Killian forward, and I don't even have to ask Charger. It's like they can tell that the sooner we reach Gordion, the sooner they can graze again.

The sun has barely passed the midpoint when we reach the outskirts of the town. "I think we find a farmer and pay him to watch them for us," Shu says. "Otherwise, Ptah might spot them."

"Plus, they've earned some grass," I say. "They were champs."

Less than an hour later, after splashing water on our faces and for me, changing clothes and stowing most of my belongings in a shed, Shu and I walk briskly down the main lane that leads to the center of the city. The farmer assured us the knot was impossible to miss. For some reason, when the gate to the city looms before us, my hands begin to tremble, like something important has been set in motion. I pause for a moment.

"You alright?" Shu turns around to face me. "Even with your golden skin, you look pale."

"I'm fine." I inhale and exhale. "Just trying to figure out what could be so special about this wad of rope."

"It's probably not even a knot," Shu says. "A knot is something tied in on itself."

"How could it not be a knot?" I'm confused. "Everyone calls it that."

"You said it connects the wagon owned by the first king to the pole that symbolizes the city."

"Right."

"Well, something that ties one thing to another is actually called a hitch. A knot is different."

"Oh, come on. There's no way they're as obnoxious as you about the semantics of language." I pick up the pace, eager to see whether I've made up all these stories for no reason at all. Will Apophis just laugh when he finally reaches it? If Isis doesn't buy this as a sign, an omen, then this has all been a waste of time.

Gordion is nicer than I expected. Clearly the history of most of the inhabitants being Earth Called has continued. The homes lining the streets aren't lavish or ostentatious, but they're surrounded by profusely blooming flowers in an otherwise arid location. And they're all nicely whitewashed and maintained. Hallmarks of Earth Called care.

As we turn on to the main street, larger buildings rise up ahead of us. The location of the temple built to Apollo is clear, but there's a modest palace up ahead, too. It clearly descends below ground, as well as above, and beautiful paintings, mostly featuring women, adorn all sides of the stone walls.

If I were a conqueror, this city would be well worth a stop. And finally, I see it. The farmer didn't lie. In the very center of town, the main road splits to go around a large square—and in the middle of that there's a huge pillar carved into marble—beautiful, richly veined marble. Ptah would be composing wordy, impressive descriptions of its beauty and unicity in multiple languages, I'm sure. What strikes me is the union of the pink veins and the dark golden ones, both of which stand out in the deep, dark russet tones of the rest of the column.

Near the bottom, there's a wagon that's shockingly well preserved for something that should be several hundred years old at this point. And the rope that ties it to the base of the column looks just as fresh—spun from camel hair, perhaps, judging from the color and the texture of the fibers used. There are dozens of separate threads, all inter-twined—it's clear to see, but when I reach for it with my Lifter senses . . . I come up blank. It's like there's nothing there at all.

"That looks simple enough." Shu must be sensing the same thing as me, because his brow furrows. "I wonder why I can't feel it."

"Wait." Out of the corner of my eye, I notice a sign. It's not large, but the paint is bold, and the handwritten shape of the Persian words is crisp. I point.

Shu squints. "What does that say? Dad made you learn Persian, didn't he?"

"Of course he did. The entire Achaemenid Empire uses it." I huff. "Why you wanted to avoid learning the building blocks of solid communication with the world around you, I'll never understand."

"Dad knew I'd never be a statesman." Shu shrugs. "What does it say?"

"It says: Knots bring us together. Knots pull us apart. But this knot will only be undone by those bound both together and apart. He who unties it unworthily will unbind the moorings of his very soul. Once it has been loosed, the one who released it will unite all of Asia. And from there, all the world."

"Why did you stop me?" Shu asks. "Maybe *I'm* supposed to do it."

"It's a gimmick," I say. "Remember? I'm the one pushing this whole thing, so that we can convince Isis to relax. It's not real."

"Right," Shu says. "Forgot for a moment."

"Besides," I say. "That line about unbinding the moorings of your soul?" I shiver. "Combined with the fact that I can't sense it?" I shake my head. "Something's not right."

A woman's hustling past us, her eyes down, her shoulders slumped. She's in a hurry, but it's more than that. She doesn't want to see us touch the knot.

"Ma'am," I call as respectfully as I know how in Persian. Dad made me learn, but some of the nuances still escape me.

She stops, but doesn't meet my eye.

"What would happen if I reached over and touched that knot?"

Why is it so pristine after five hundred years? Why hasn't the wagon deteriorated by now, exposed to the elements as it is? And although it's complicated, it's not so complicated that someone shouldn't have untied it, with a prize like ruling all of Asia hanging in the balance.

The woman shrugs.

I soften my voice and pull a few gold coins from the purse on my belt. "I'm not asking for information for nothing," I say. "I'm happy to pay."

She shakes her head. "I don't require payment, but you won't believe me, and I don't wish to be here to witness it."

Witness it? In a world full of magic, why wouldn't I believe whatever she tells me? "Please?"

As if she's given up any hope of escape, she shuffles around slowly, her eyes still trained on the ground. "If you touch it, it'll steal your soul."

Okay, she's right. I don't believe that. "What exactly happens?"

"Anyone who has tried to untie it dies straight away. They wither right there, in front of our eyes. I'm pretty sure that curse has something to do with keeping the wagon and knot pristine."

And . . . that's a real problem. Shu groans, because he gets it too.

I've created all this buzz so that Apophis will come here and untie this knot—and instead of helping him to take over the world as Dad and I planned—I'm pretty sure I've signed his death warrant.

"What are you going to do?" Shu asks. "Because if he touches that knot and dies . . . "

"I'll be stuck ruling in Memphis forever." My voice is flat. "Not to mention, if Isis is mad now, and she figures out that me or Ptah had anything to do with luring her son here, and he dies . . . " I shake my head.

"She's only going to double down on her obsession with attacking Dad." Shu's not laughing now.

"Here's what we'll need to do," I say. "I'm going to have to figure out what's going on and solve this thing before he gets here and croaks trying."

"If anyone can figure it out, it's you," Shu says.

"Did you meet Apophis on your trips with Mother?" I ask. "Is he clever? Or will he barge in here and kill himself double quick?"

"I've seen him from a distance—we were leaving as he arrived—but I didn't spend much time around him." Shu shrugs. "His mother made him so young to convince Philip to take them in—let's just say, I doubt he'll remember me, especially with the way I look right now."

"But was he clever?"

Shu shrugs. "I didn't care then, so I don't remember. I'm sorry."

"You're useless." I walk as close to the knot as I dare, peering at it from every angle I can easily reach. It's large—clearly the work of at least four ropes. It's intricate. I can't quite figure out what the basic knot form is—or where it might have started. And no matter how hard I press with my telekinetic sense, I can't feel anything at all, which means I'm limited to what I can see with my eyes. That's not a typical situation for me.

I Lift a branch off a wild maple at the edge of the square and fling it at the knot, wondering whether, without touching it, I can use a tool to dislodge some part of it.

"Surely someone has tried that," Shu says.

The second the recently snapped end of the branch makes contact with the edge of the knot, it blackens, and then it spreads all the way up the entire branch until the leaves shrivel and fall to the ground near my feet. Shu groans. "That could have been you. You can't just go around—"

"I'm not the one who almost wandered up and grabbed it," I say. "And look." I'm not sure whether it's because I'm an Assim that it's obvious, but the energy from the branch has been absorbed by the knot, and the colors of the wagon and the knot themselves have *brightened*.

"What am I looking at?"

"Did you see it?" I narrow my eyes. "It's . . . more beautiful now. It's more vibrant. The people it consumes power the spell." I can't quite keep from smiling. "It's actually quite elegant."

"Are you saying an Assim is responsible for this disaster?" Shu frowns.

"I'm not positive it was created *only* by an Assimilator, but one of them certainly had a hand in setting it up, yeah."

The sound of hooves pounding on hard-packed dirt thrums in the distance, and I freeze, extending my senses to their utmost limits. Shu's as still as I am, presumably doing the same thing, at least, until he turns to meet my eye. "Let's hope Alexander *is* quite clever, because . . ."

"Unless there's another army close by, the Macedonians have arrived."

And I'm out of time to figure this dumb thing out.

14

ANCIENT EGYPT

"We need to go." Shu grabs my arm. "Right now."

Except as we turn away, mounted cavalry comes into view, thundering toward us, an enormous black beast with a brilliant white star on his forehead leading the charge. I know we need to escape, but I can't help thinking that if I do, if Apophis is so stupid that he waltzes right up and touches the knot, then all our planning over the past two years will be wasted. Dad and I will never be able to leave someone else powerful enough to maintain order in his place so that we can live free and simple lives.

Isis and Apophis may both be awful to deal with, but I need them alive.

"Now," Shu hisses. "Come on."

I shake my head. "There's no way he'll recognize us, and someone needs to warn him like that woman warned us."

"From what I've heard, he's not going to listen to you." Shu tosses his head again. "Besides. His General, Parmenion, has had possession of this region for quite some time. Surely he'll warn him that the knot is treacherous. You've done what you can."

I finally let him tug me away.

"You there, girl." A deep voice barks at me, completely sure of his own ability to command.

I look upward, and it's a strange feeling knowing that I'm not looking with my own face. A tiny part of me wishes that, since I'm actually meeting Apophis, that I look nice while doing it. But that's idiotic. It doesn't matter one whit how I look. He's my father's enemy, and a man we are using to accomplish a necessary task.

It would be nice to be completely positive that if our plan works, he'll be fair and just while ruling. "Yes?"

"You speak Greek?"

"Of course." I duck my head, as a typical girl of my age and supposed station would do.

"Is this the knot—the famous Gordian knot?"

I swallow, as if he's overwhelmed me, and then nod.

He swings off his horse smoothly, without Binding or Lifting at all, in spite of the lack of a saddle or straps of any kind, and when I steal a glance, I realize he's smiling. "Excellent."

Shu clears his throat. "You shouldn't—"

Alexander glares at him. "I shouldn't what?"

My older brother isn't typically intimidated by anyone, but this tall, broad-shouldered man is not like anyone I've ever met. His hair curls slightly around his temples, and it shines like the midday sun. His eyes are so light blue they're nearly white. In typical Greek fashion, his loose chiton covers his chest and shoulders, leaving his arms free, is bound at his trim waist, and falls only to his knees, allowing him to ride. The trim is quite fine, and it's dyed bright red, which is quite uncommon, but looks great with his golden hair. His chlamys is thrown back, leaving both shoulders bare and showcasing his large, muscular forearms. "My name is Alexander, and in case you haven't heard of me, I'll explain. I've come here to untie the

Gordian knot, and I won't leave until I've accomplished the task."

Shu may be nervous around him, but I'm not. In fact, I can't quite resist baiting him. "You've never failed at anything, good sir? That's quite a surprise, indeed."

He spins on me so quickly that I nearly step backward. "It's a surprise? Why? Do I look like someone who often fails to you?" He straightens his already impressive shoulders, reminding me of a rooster, strutting.

I suppress a laugh.

"You only truly fail when you quit trying, so no. I've never failed in my life." He tilts his head sideways. "Your companion looks like a warrior, but you . . . you look half starved, like you've missed too many meals. Your clothing, however, is quite fine—who are you, and why are you here?"

I've told the same lie with Ptah for so long, the words should roll off my tongue automatically, but this time, for some reason, they don't. Maybe I'm irritated that he thinks he has the right to question me. Or perhaps I'm not very good at acting. "Well, Alexander-who-fails-all-the-time, but keeps trying until he can lie and say he didn't, it's not any of your business what my name is. I don't care to share it with you, no matter how much you strut, or how many times you try to obtain it."

His eyes brighten and the corner of his mouth turns up. "Is that so?"

"You're certainly not entitled to know where I'm from or where I live."

"Really?" His lips curve more sharply and he's almost smiling.

"My brother and I planned to warn you about the knot, but since you *never* fail, it's clear you don't need our wisdom. Carry on." I lift the fabric of my cloak so it doesn't drag and walk away, leaving Shu to follow. My heart hammers against my chest—hoping against hope that my non-warning will still give him pause.

"Ignore her," one of his men says. "She's clearly insane."

"What would she have warned me about, do you think?" The irritation in Alexander's voice is plain.

I don't stop walking, and I don't turn around.

"Why are you in such a rush?" Alexander's voice is strong and carries quite clearly.

I don't answer him. He's not my master.

"Madam, please. Give me the warning you think I didn't earn."

I can't help my answering smile. Officially I despise him, of course. His mother is my father's greatest enemy. But his youthful enthusiasm and confidence are more charming than I expected them to be. I sigh, heavily, so I'm sure he will hear it. "Why don't you Lift a branch and shove it against the knot? That should show you what you need to know."

"I don't understand."

"Because you don't listen very well." I resume my walking.

A groaning sound behind me demands my attention and, in spite of my better judgment, I look over my shoulder.

Instead of yanking a branch off the tree, he Lifts the entire thing, uprooting it entirely. Pale blue light bathes the ground, the wagon, and the knot as he shoves the poor tree at the knot. The second the outermost branch touches the strands, it blackens, the darkness spreading through the tree like flame through dry kindling. Alexander lurches backward, startling his enormous black horse, who spooks.

His men struggle with their mounts, and one of them is thrown off. I muffle my laugh against the sleeve of my cloak.

"We should go, right now," Shu says. "You may not be

able to help him solve it, but at least thanks to your warning, he won't die."

"I don't think he *can* solve it without an Assimilator," I say.

"His mother is one, in case you forgot," Shu says. "Our work here is clearly done."

"Do you see her around?" I whisper. "Because I don't."

Shu groans. "This is going to be like trying to force you to eat your breakfast, isn't it? Long, exhausting, pointless."

I haven't eaten leeks since the week after Mother left. I don't even bother covering up my smirk, not at this point.

"You may not like Ptah," Shu says, "and I don't blame you. He's a blockhead—I have no idea why Father thought you might go for him. But there's no world in which you and *that guy* have a future."

I roll my eyes. "Please. I don't want to stay because I like him—the knot fascinates me. That's all."

"Really?" Shu scoffs.

I start walking again. "Of course." It's not like I'm *interested* in Dad's enemy. In my enemy. I only want to make sure he's capable of providing peace and justice for our people before I help him 'defeat' us and bow out. That's all. "You can calm down."

"Alright, if you're positive."

We're nearly to the edge of the main road out of Gordion. I can see the largest tumulus up ahead, the Midas Mound, as the locals call it. I didn't hear any shouts or exclamations, which must mean that Apophis—er, I should probably try to remember to think of him as Alexander while we're close to their armies—Alexander didn't get fried. How would *I* create a spell like that, one that would prevent people from sensing something and also steal any life forces shoved at it? I consider the fact that I can't sense it. I reach out for Shu's face with my telekinetic senses . . . and it feels the same. So an overlay made of pure energy works the same as a real face. There's no way to detect that his appearance has been altered.

Which means it's more than just an overlay.

Very loud hoof falls behind us distract me, and Shu and I both spin around. Alexander's horse halts dramatically, flinging clods of dirt and spraying dust all over me.

"You are the most boorish man I've ever met." I brush the detritus off my arms and scowl at him. "What do you want now?"

Alexander blinks. "I'm so sorry. I didn't even think—"

"No, you did not. It's hard enough keeping my clothes clean while I'm traveling without careless idiots spraying me with the contents of half the road surface."

"I didn't want to lose you," he says. "I wasn't contemplating how my stop might—" He straightens. "We did not get off to a great start. My name is Alexander of Macedonia, son of Philip the Second."

He's expecting me to be shocked, or maybe amazed and impressed. "I already told you that I don't feel like sharing my name." I scowl. "Even if you're sharing yours, which anyone with half a brain likely already knows."

His brows draw together, and I force myself to look behind him. Because if I keep staring at his face, I will soon be staying here because I like him. He may be the most handsome man I've ever seen, especially when he's flummoxed.

"I haven't earned your name yet," he murmurs.

"Oh for goodness' sake," I say. "Don't turn me into one of your challenges—letting me walk away is not a failure."

The grin on his face actually sends a shiver up my spine. I don't look attractive. My facial features are far too strong and not aesthetically pleasing. I'm practically emaciated. I've harangued him up one side and down the other . . . and he's fascinated? What an idiot.

"We should go," Shu says. "Good luck with the knot."

"You're not from here," Alexander says. "So how did you know touching that knot would kill me, and somehow power the magic that keeps it strong?"

"Why do you think we're not from here?" My plain robes and cloak are something a local Phrygian might wear. I darkened my skin a bit, and adopted features not out of line with the area.

He lifts both eyebrows. "Were you not both speaking in Egyptian?"

Stupid. Why didn't we keep to Greek? "Uh, right."

"I'm no expert, but you sounded fluent to me."

At least we know he's clever enough. I realize I'm pressing my lips together in frustration and force them into a simper. "You caught us. Our father's a merchant, looking to establish trade with further flung locations. He sent us to find out who might be interested."

"What does your father want to export?" A shrewd look steals over Alexander's face. "Perhaps I might be able to help."

"He's a talented glass maker," Shu says. "Have you heard of it? It's a clear substance that allows light into rooms, and keeps bugs and other pests out. He also makes beautiful beads, bowls, and other decorative items with it."

As if Apophis might not have heard of glass. I almost laugh.

"Glass?" he asks.

"Our father is Fire Called," Shu says, "and he can turn sand, of which we have an ample supply, into many beautiful and amazing things."

"I'd like to invite you both to dine with me this evening," Alexander says. "I'm sure many of my Diadochi will have contacts that could help you."

"I'm sure we don't need the help of Alexander the Great's most terrifying generals to firm up some additional avenues of lucrative trade. Our family has no grand ambition, like conquering all of Asia. We're small people with small goals." I pick up my hem again. "Besides. We're expected elsewhere."

"You knew the knot would cause me harm," Alexander says, "and instead of letting me walk up and grab it, you warned me. You can act like you dislike me, but your actions belie your words."

Clever indeed. But of course, "I can want you to go on living without liking you."

"Give me a chance to change your mind," he says.

"I rather like the idea of you failing at something," I say, "even if it's only charming the homely daughter of a merchant."

"Homely?" Alexander sounds shocked. "If anyone else said that about you, I'd—" His hands clench at his sides.

He can't possibly find me attractive, not like this. It's only because I walked away and then when he pursued me, I declined his offer. It finally occurs to me how I can escape without being an ongoing object of his attention. It's all a matter of picking something for him to fail at that matters *more*. "If you'll admit that you failed at untying the Gordian knot, then I'll eat dinner with you."

"Alright," he says. "I admit it. For the time being, I've failed. I can't work out how to touch it without dying, so, like every single person on Earth for the past four hundred years, the solution to the Gordian knot has so far eluded me."

Shu laughs. Now who's being charmed, the idiot? "Please tell me you have decent food," my traitorous brother says. "I don't think I can choke down dried meat and gruel."

Alexander snorts. "No gruel for us. My warriors mostly carry their own provisions—wagons slow the army down far too much. And troops won't fight well if they're poorly fed, but I do afford myself the luxury of a few supply carts that keep up relatively well in most cases."

"What does that mean?" Shu asks.

"I have fresh lemons from India," Alexander says. "They make a remarkable—"

"I'm familiar with lemons." He sounds so condescending, I'd like to slap him.

"Your father must be doing quite well if he's importing fruit from India." Alexander's eyes narrow. "Now I insist that you join us."

"How about this?" I ask. "You and your men can go and prepare food, and I'll spend an hour or so studying the knot. If I figure anything out, I'll let you know."

"Over dinner?" he asks.

I roll my eyes. "Yes, over dinner."

"Sure." He's smiling as he mounts his enormous horse again. "I'll be back for both of you when the sun has sunk to here." He points to a spot rather low on the horizon.

"What do you think you're going to figure out?" Shu asks me, as he watches Alexander and his men leave.

"I have to figure out how he can solve it," I say. "Or the last ten days of my life have been a complete waste."

"It's a sunk cost at this point," Shu says. "Worry about the next ten."

"It's more like the last few years, really," I say. "If we can't bolster Isis' belief that her son is *anointed* to win, she'll never buy it when he defeats Ra."

Shu stops arguing with me, which I appreciate, but he looks skeptical. At least he follows me quietly as I approach the confounded knot again.

I waste a few moments hurling different things at it, trying to figure out what exactly triggers it to start siphoning. The only thing I really feel bad about chucking at it is the bird.

"It squawked as it died," Shu says. "That was . . . horrific."

"I'm sorry, but I learned that even if something passes above it, without touching any part of the knot, it's sucked in."

"And that helps us, how?" Shu sinks onto the ground and leans back against one of the trees that Alexander didn't yank out of the ground. "He was showing off for your benefit, you know."

"What?"

"You told him to use a limb, and he uprooted an entire tree. Someone clearly likes you."

"Stop. It's just that he doesn't like anyone telling him no."

"Maybe you should stop telling him no, then."

"Hush."

This time, I Lift a delicate purple flower I found at the edge of the clearing toward the knot. I hold it just outside of the power-sucking zone and I wait.

"What are you doing now?"

"Be patient."

Shu isn't patient. He starts tapping his foot and humming.

That's alright—I'm used to it. I shift the flower closer, but only incrementally. One tiny fraction of a measure closer at a time . . . until. Bam. It's sucked the rest of the way toward the knot and destroyed.

"It actually has a pull to it," I say.

"What does that mean?"

"I'm not sure." I sit down next to him. "At its heart, it must be a basic siphon trap, which Dad says are really complicated and very few Assimilators can manage, but it's been inverted somehow, so I can't see it to defuse it."

"What exactly is a siphon trap?" Shu's brow furrows. "Do I want to know?"

"It's a simple concept. Most Assimilators must touch something in order to pull energy from it. So once someone knows they're an Assimilator . . . it becomes much harder to actually get close enough to siphon someone. They generally flame you, or Lift and fling you, or hurl an ice spear at you before you can approach."

"Right, sure. Sounds reasonable."

"So how would Anat collect energy, if no one would let her get close?"

"I hadn't really thought about it."

"I mean, by now, she siphons from the same sources as Ra, people condemned to die. They're brought before her in chains as payment for their crimes. But when she wasn't established, when she had no irredeemable prisoners to siphon at will, what could she do?"

Shu shrugs.

"I'm not sure how long ago, but an Assimilator discovered that he could take energy and fashion it into a, well, let's call it a tube with a pouch at the bottom. It would essentially grab whatever it touched and slurp it down, like a trap would capture a wild animal, and then the pouch, or one of dad's cabochon stones, could store it until the Assimilator returned. As an added benefit, you could place them in locations with clearly posted warnings that people should not enter. Around your valuables, outside of prisons, that sort of thing. So anyone who is violating those rules—"

"Deserves what he or she gets."

"Exactly," I say. "Well, this is like that, only normally, another Assim would be able to see the trap."

"Which is a pretty big limitation," Shu says. "Because if another Assim sees it, they can avoid it, or disarm and take it for themselves."

I shrug. "This siphon tube, however, was inverted, and I think it has to do with the storage mechanism. There's no stone or any kind of container that could gather power—in fact, the power is being funneled into another spell, a preservation and protection spell. I think the inversion, the hiding of the spell, might have been inadvertent."

"You think whoever made this . . . screwed up?"

I laugh. "Basically, yeah. I think they set up the protection spell, and then created this siphon trap to feed it . . . and then somehow, it got flipped upside down so no one could see it, making it impossible to solve."

"Unless?"

"Unless someone with enough power, another Assim, came along and was willing to gamble that she could pull back on the trap hard enough to invert it again."

"That does not sound like a solid plan," Shu says.

I glance at the sun. We're nearly out of time. And the fact that I want to stay for dinner tells me that I really can't. "It's the only one I have," I say. "And I think if anyone can do it, it's me. Plus, I've got a full reservoir." I tap my ring. "And an extra, because Dad is paranoid." I brush my fingers against the pulsing stone set into my belt. "I'm almost certain my plan will work."

Shu shakes his head. "No way Dad would allow you to—"

"What else should we do?" I put both hands on my hips. "What's your suggestion?"

"We have some lemon—"

"You're the one who was saying I can't spend time with Alexander."

Shu frowns. "I never said that. I said you can't *like* him."

"It's not like Dad's here to fix this himself," I say.

"That's what we should do. Go home, get Father to come here and fix it, and then lure Alexander back."

"No. That's stupid." And if we do that, Dad will never trust me again, not with anything, not if I have to race home and drag him back here to do this little thing. That's all the encouragement I need, the thought of how I'd explain my failure to Dad if I *don't* figure this out. Without another thought, I reach for the knot with my hand.

And a great, twisting vortex of hunger *pulls* at me, shredding my very soul. I scream. But I also remember what I need to do.

I yank back with everything I have, digging into the well of magic in both stones at once. At first, the siphon trap feels insatiable, like it will never stop. I tremble, I gasp, and I cry out again . . . and then finally, I reach down deep and drag back on it as hard as I can. And it flips, suddenly, like a starling wheeling, mid-dive. Like a burst of lightning arcing through the sky.

Power surges into me and I funnel it into both stones, but it keeps coming. It crashes over me like a salty sea wave, waking me up, buoying my flagging energy, and flooding me with immeasurable joy. I can't contain all this energy—not without becoming something I don't want to be. *Power-starved.* I fling the energy outward, sinking it into the farmer's fields around us, into the animals tucked into modest barns and shelters.

And then I sink to my feet, exhausted.

"What did you do?" Shu asks.

"I solved it." I beam at him. "I solved that confounded knot."

He turns sideways. "I hate to say this, but . . . it actually looks exactly like it did before."

I roll my eyes. "Tell me you can't sense the rope, now. Tell me you can't *feel* right where it starts."

Shu's eyes widen and he swears under his breath. "You did it. Was that why I felt that shiver of giddy joy? Was that you?"

My smile broadens. "Exactly. Yes. I busted that stupid trap wide open."

"Which means the conceited conqueror can now fulfill his phony destiny," he says.

"Exactly."

A few moments later, Alexander shows up. To my surprise, his columns of men aren't present. He's flanked by only four other soldiers. "I came." He points to the skyline. "As promised."

"I think you should try the knot again," I say.

He tenses. "Why?"

"Isn't that why you're here?" The corner of my mouth twists into a wry grin. "To untie it? As part of your path to take over the world?"

"You make that sound like a fool's errand," he says.

I shrug.

"Earlier you warned me, but what? Now you want me dead?" He slides from his black horse again, two ground-eating strides from him putting us much closer together. "Do I annoy you that much?"

"If you're afraid, you can test it like you did the last time," I say.

He scowls. "I'm not afraid. Being prudent and being afraid aren't the same thing."

"I'd be afraid of something that roasts living things into black char," Shu says. "I think that's a reasonable fear."

"After I try it again, will you make me admit I failed again, too?" Alexander takes a step toward me, his sky blue eyes intent on mine, his posture purposeful.

"Of course I will."

He tilts his head. "I don't understand you."

"Good."

He Lifts a scraggly weed out of the ground and flings it casually at the knot. It knocks against it and drops to the ground, unharmed. Other than being yanked from the dirt, of course. Alexander's gaze pivots immediately and he *looks* at the knot. He's finally taking note of the fact that he can sense it. He turns back toward me, his mouth gaping open. "What did you do?"

I shrug. "I studied it. Suddenly, I could sense it. I did the same as you—flung a plant against it."

He frowns. "I don't see any other plants anywhere near it."

His cleverness now annoys me. "I already disposed of it."

One of his eyebrows quirks upward. "Why the change?"

I point at the sun. "Probably the time of day."

"Wouldn't dinner time be the most common time for someone to try to untie it?"

"Do you want to grill me about it all day, or untie it yourself?"

"Why didn't you already do it?" His nostrils flare and he looks around, as if he's scenting a lie.

"I have no interest in ruling Asia."

"That simple," he says. "You just don't *want* all that power."

"I don't."

He steps toward me, not the knot. "You knew I wouldn't be able to say it again—you did this to get out of eating dinner with me."

I laugh. "You think I solved the problem preventing people—for the last four hundred years—from untying this knot . . . to avoid eating with you?" I shake my head. "I'm not sure if that indicates an overinflated ego, or a terrible sense of inadequacy. Care to clarify?"

He pivots on his heel and crosses to the knot. Then he focuses on it, clearly extending his senses as I am. I know just when he *tugs* on it, because his eyes flash with ice-blue light. Only, nothing happens.

"It's been like that for quite some time." I start to walk down the road again, waving for Shu to follow. "I imagine it'll take you quite some time to work those strands of rope loose, even though you can Lift."

He grunts.

"Tearing a tree out by the roots doesn't require much finesse," I say over my shoulder. "Maybe you need to work on fine tuning your control."

"What about dinner?" he asks. "You promised."

"I said that if you admit that you failed at untying the knot, I'd eat dinner with you." I look pointedly at the knot. "But have you failed? You can't really expect me to go back on my word, can you?"

He whips his sword from its sheath across his back, and before I can say another word, takes it in a powerful two-handed grip and slices the entire mass of rope clean in half. "There. History will remember me as the man who couldn't untie the knot and cleaved it in half instead. Someone who failed at that task, utterly and completely." He doesn't look like someone who lost. He's smiling like the cat who just got all the cream.

That teaches me something about him that I missed before. I miscalculated what matters to him. Knowing that he'd give up laying claim to the prophesy of conquering Asia . . . to eat dinner with me? It's disconcerting.

A glowy feeling suffuses me from head to toe. Something I've never felt before in my entire life. And it's all caused by this man with the blond hair and the broad shoulders and the easy, confident smile. The smile that's turned on me, along with eyes that stare intently into mine.

"He did hold up his end," Shu whispers.

"I can't stay for dinner, I'm afraid," I say. "I have urgent business to attend. Perhaps another time."

The confident smile wavers, just a hair, and I see firm resolve underneath. "You owe me a meal, which means I'll need your name, so I can collect."

"He has you there," Shu says.

"My name is Neser," I say.

"Careful," Shu hisses. "That's dangerously close—"

"And your father is a wealthy and successful Fire Called

glass merchant." Alexander grins as if there's no way he won't be able to find me with that information. "I plan to collect on our meal soon."

Shu and I turn and walk away, knowing Alexander can't actually walk away from his army and his military plans to pursue me, even if he wanted to—homely nobody that he thinks I am.

But for the first time in a very long time, I'm scared. Not at the prospect of Alexander tracking me down or collecting on the dinner he's due, but because I actually *want* him to do it.

The outrageous pain in my front leg wakes me, and I want to roar so loud that it knocks the roof off the hut I'm lying underneath.

Only the press of tiny, furry bodies against mine keeps me from doing it.

Where am I? Why are tiny lion cubs pressed against me in front and behind? I move carefully, the memory of where I am and what's happening today finally surfacing as I ease myself away from the sleeping cubs.

Billions of humans are currently stuck in animal form—the vast majority of which couldn't shift at all until a week ago, when every single Reaper and every single Render on Rra shifted into an animal form. Permanently, it seems. Including all the females, none of whom could shift previously.

They're all convinced that I'm the only one who can save them.

And I can't even remember my own name.

She Who Gathers.

The same lion who brought me here is standing in the

doorway. I move toward him, whimpering when I'm forced to put pressure on my front right leg. The last time I woke up, I had blood on the inside of my leg as well. I lift it up to examine it, and sure enough, there's fresh blood dripping from my fur.

What happened? You're bleeding?

The cubs stir, their tiny noses sniffing as they awaken. Fresh blood isn't exactly a wonderful smell to present around lions—it draws them like honey calls to bears.

Honey calls to bears? Does it? How do I even know that? I don't know any bears. Or at least, I don't think I do.

I shake my head and keep moving toward the door. It's hard to communicate when I'm like this—I have to really focus. *When I woke, I was bleeding. There doesn't seem to be any danger.*

Self-inflicted? His lips pull back to show his enormous teeth—clearly a look of distaste.

No. I have no idea what happened, but I'd never injure myself like this.

Shift and it will heal. None of us have that option, but you can take advantage of it.

Wait. I want to make sure I understand. *Shifting heals me? Correct.*

I imagine myself standing on two feet, my shoulders out, my hands by my sides, fingers forming from furry paws. And then, in a blink, I am. And the pain in my front arm is gone. The skin is smooth. Like magic. I suppose shifting from an animal to a human is already magic, but somehow, this feels stranger, injuries disappearing with a shift.

The Pride is gathered.

"I thought I'm the one who's supposed to gather people."

The lion makes a rumbling sound—not quite a purr, not

that content. He's annoyed, I realize. He didn't like my joke, or he didn't get it.

"I'm ready to talk to them," I say. "Or, you know, listen to them yell in my mind."

No one will yell. We need your help.

I wish I knew what to do—how to help them. Perhaps once they've explained things more, an answer will become obvious. I follow him down a sloping path and then up a very steep one. We climb steadily for so long that my thighs burn and my lungs complain. We're going much higher than the point where I looked over the valley last night. Higher, probably, than I've ever been. The air is thin by the time we finally stop climbing and step from a carved stone stair onto a narrow, flat ledge that curves sharply to the left.

I follow the young alpha lion blithely, unconcerned, until I glance to the right and realize that we're walking along the ledge of a very steep, very high mountain path. One misstep and I'll plunge over the edge to my death. I'm pretty sure that even shifting can't heal the type of dismemberment that would ensue from going splat all the way down there. I shimmy as close to the rocky outcropping on my left side as I can, and in the process drift away from the lion . . . and come around the bend. Suddenly I see the Pride that's gathered. The narrow ledge opens onto a vast plateau that overlooks the entire region below. Clouds float next to us, but none of that commands my attention.

What does draw my eye is the sight of so many animals, most of whom had to reach this place the same way that we just did, all crowded in next to one another. A rooster fluffs his feathers and crows. Behind him, a hippo clears his nostrils gustily. An eagle perches on a rock jutting out of the side of the far mountain wall, his head cocked to the side. A wolf rests his head on his paws as if he's bored, his eyes nearly closed, the slits tracking our slightest movement.

A hyena paces in front of an angry white goose, and a tiny brown monkey chatters with a larger, white-faced black one. Horses. A skunk. Giraffes. A zebra. Small wrens. A rhino. Even, near the back, an elephant. I can't catalogue all the animals in front of me, but the Renders vastly outnumber the Reapers. Maybe that's a good thing.

All the alphas have gathered to represent their herds.

"What about the supras?" I ask. "You said there aren't as many of those."

My guess was slightly inaccurate. There are almost three dozen supras.

Three dozen, out of seven billion. It seems an impossible task. Only three dozen people who can manipulate the people who can control the others. I suppose it's good there aren't too many in the normal course of events—people who can compel others to think and act as they wish—but just now I wish there were more. "I'm not convinced I'm even a supra," I say. "But even if I am . . . " I turn to face the gathered crowd, hoping they can understand me. "What exactly are you hoping I'll do?"

Change us back.

Help us shift.

Keep us safe.

Gather us.

Protect us.

Shelter us.

Strengthen us.

Altogether too many thoughts crowd into my brain, and I shake my head and lift my hands. "I'm not sure what I *can* do. I'm new. This lion here . . . " I realize I don't even know his name.

Christopher.

"Christopher had to teach me how to shift at all."

But you can *shift. You're human now. You must save us.* I'm not sure how this could possibly be the case, but I can clearly hear from the tone of the thought that it's coming from the eagle. It sounds like an eagle, and it feels thrown from above me, somehow.

"I don't know what it means, to Gather any of you. I don't know why I can shift when you can't, and I don't even know who I am. I woke up here yesterday, without knowing my own name or what I had for breakfast the morning before. Eating animal flesh . . . raw . . . " My stomach churns at the thought. "It's not something I do very often, I don't think. It made me sick, once I thought about what I was doing."

Growling, yapping, screeching, howling, chittering, and shrieking flood the open air. I don't see how I can possibly accomplish what they want—how can I restore things here to normal? I don't even recall my life before the odd happenings. Besides which, no one even knows what exactly they want me to do, much less how. 'Protect them' is so vague—especially when what they want protection from is seemingly themselves.

"You're all here because you're concerned about the Hunt. Is that right?"

Heads bob all around. Even the snake near my feet bobs its triangular head up and down.

"Alphas usually keep you in check, holding the Reapers indoors while the Renders hunt. Right?"

More agreement.

"I'm not sure how to be a proper alpha, and I certainly don't know how to be a supra alpha, but I will do my best."

You must Gather us, a sheep bleats. *It's the only way to keep us all safe.*

"What does that even mean?" Gather them where? "Do you want me to drive the Reapers behind a wall or something? Somewhere they'll be safe?"

There are too many, an enormous brown bear rumbles. *She can't keep them all away from us.*

"I don't understand what Gathering means." Can't someone be clearer? I feel like I'm sprinting to catch up, desperate to understand, but I can't quite reach the place where they explain who and what I am.

Gathering us keeps us safe, a rabbit says. *It takes us away from here, from Rra, and the moon and the hunt and the danger.*

That is totally unhelpful. I take them away? To where? How? Looking down at the rabbit in my frustrated confusion, something occurs to me. "Where are the water creatures? Aren't there water shifters?"

They can't meet us up here, Christopher says. *They're waiting below.*

Fabulous. "Look, I want to help, but seeing as I know basically nothing about shifting, about being a Render or an alpha, much less a supra, perhaps we ought to start with some kind of crash course in basic Shifter rules. Maybe learning some things you all know will help jog my memory."

They take my plea to heart. The next two hours consist of a series of confusing and exhausting attempts by various groups to teach me what it means to be a shifter. I do learn a few things, but nothing helps me remember who I am, why I'm here, or how I might help prevent this approaching calamity.

"You can't all take shelter. Your alphas can't keep you from shifting, as you can't shift into human form at all." I pause. "But what triggered this massive shift in the first place? Children, women, and all the men who were previously unable to shift must have suddenly shifted as the result of something, right? When did it happen exactly, and what caused it?"

Christopher growls. *The moon turned red, and then the agony began.*

"The agony?" I want to sit down and cry. Why can't one of them—an individual who knows all of this already—be the one who gathers?

The females, the children, the men who couldn't shift, they all fell on the floor, writhing. They shouted and yelled and cried. And finally, after what felt like hours, they shifted. It was agonizingly slow the first time, like they were waking from a terrible nightmare. One claw, one fang, one patch of hair at a time. Christopher shudders. *It was horrible, but we couldn't comfort them, because all of us were shifting too, in the same, slow, forced way. No one knows why it happened or what caused it.*

"You're all here, together, just fine. Why will the hunt be so different?"

We are human, with the body of an animal in many ways. But during a full moon, on that night, the animal surges inside of us. Even when we are in human form, we are more primal, more desperate, more impulsive. Christopher scratches his claws against the stone, making a terrible screeching sound. *More first kills take place, more blood feuds begin, and more mating bonds form during the Hunt than the rest of the month altogether.*

Fantastic.

A koala walks around the back of a cow and waves at me to get my attention. *It is no coincidence you arrived just after the forced shift. You may be confused, but to me it is clear.*

It's hard to take anything seriously with ears that fluffy and a big, adorable black nose.

You can end this never-ending shift. You can gather us back to ourselves—into our human forms. That is your purpose. The koala stares at me with his brown, button eyes.

It's the first thing anyone has said that makes sense. I consider how I shift into my lioness form. I imagine the wind in my fur, the strength in my snapping jaw, and I embrace the roar that builds inside me until, bam. I transform.

Moving from lioness to human is simpler in every way. I

simply imagine myself as a human. That's the shift we need —back to the form they are more familiar with. It should be easy to force, right?

I straighten my shoulders and scan every critter on this ledge. "I think we can do this. I can help you do what I do. First, close your eyes and imagine yourself in your human form. Imagine standing straight and tall. Imagine your hands at your side, your heart beating in your chest, your legs strong and solid beneath you. Now, push toward that. Reach out and take that form instead of the one you presently occupy."

I look around expectantly, but nothing happens.

"Okay, let's do that again, but when you push to become human, I'm going to give you a little shove too." Just like yesterday when I said 'MINE' and forced the other lions to back off. If I'm a supra, I may as well own it. I look around at them again, slowly, meeting each animal's gaze in turn. "Alright. Your head is held high. Your hair is short or long or loose or pulled back, however you usually wear it. Your lungs expand and contract, as your chest rises and falls. You clench your hands into fists and release them. And now, with your legs firmly beneath you—" I push. "*BECOME HUMAN.*"

Nothing.

A terrible sorrow, a feeling of overwhelming inadequacy and incomprehensible fatigue swells inside of me. I am not She Who Gathers. I'm nobody. An anomaly, not a savior. I can't even change one single . . . I look at the snake, still watching me with his beady, dead eyes.

I crouch down in front of him. "How about we try it with just one creature?"

He nods.

"I'm going to have you envision the same thing, alright? Your hair. Your—"

I'm bald.

I laugh. I needed that. "Alright. Your shiny round head. Your strong legs. Your squared shoulders. The sun on your face, your mouth open, breathing deeply."

He sends me an image mentally—which I didn't realize could be done.

He's bald, with broad shoulders and a dark beard. A few freckles cover his nose and cheeks, and his eyes are a bright hazel.

"Alright, thanks. That helps." I meet his eyes again to make sure he's with me, and clearly, he is. "And now we will both imagine you turning back to your human form, only, I'm going to push too, alright?"

His head nods up and down.

"Alright. You're thinking of your human form, and so am I." I inhale and then exhale. "Now, *SHIFT*." I push, with every ounce of resolve that's coiled inside of me. Every single bit of reserved energy, every speck of my fury and my fear and my hope.

And the snake actually shifts, his skin shifting and twisting, his eyes widening and contorting. The ground around me begins to shudder and shake, and then . . .

He explodes.

Sticky pinkish goo covers my face, and chunks of it land in my hair. It's a snake, but he's also a human. I know exactly how he looked, thanks to the image he sent me, and now I can't stop shuddering. The animals around me scurry backward in fear and disgust. They chitter. They cluck. They coo. They growl.

"I'm so sorry." I'm not sure who I'm apologizing to— it's not like there are any other snakes here. His wife or daughter or mother isn't present to hiss at me. But I failed at my most basic task: helping them return to human form. Instead of gathering him, I disintegrated him.

I turn around and run down the ledge that led me here.

I'm clearly not She Who Gathers. I'm She Who Ruins. Or perhaps, She Who Runs.

The only good thing is that, even after I shift into my lion form and return to the shed I vacated, even after I curl up into a ball, no one follows me. No one badgers me. No one asks anything of me. They're all as upset as I am. They're all as disappointed. They wanted a savior.

They got a disaster instead.

❧ 16 ❧

EARTH

The second I wake, I bolt upright in bed, searching my arms and legs for snake guts. I'm clean—totally unmarked by my murder.

Other than my soul. It feels pretty black.

"You look shaken." Jesse's sitting in the corner of the small room, hunched over in a small wingback chair. "I'm guessing it's not good news from Rra?"

"I can't go back there." It sounds almost like a sob, and I don't even try to hide it. Not from Jesse. "It's so broken, J. The whole prison is malfunctioning. And I want to fix it, but—"

"Do you?" He stares at me. "Want to fix it?"

"What does that mean?"

He shifts forward, perching on the edge of the chair. "You and I never had good parents. Our birth parents left us. Our adoptive parents weren't very affectionate and now we know why. Aunt Trina was a joke." He purses his lips and huffs. "I don't have all my memories yet, but I'm regaining more each night, and I think you are too."

"I didn't forget our life together." My tone is soft, and I

197

can't quite eliminate the note of sorrow, because he doesn't even recall most of the details.

His smile is sad. "I meant about your past life. Or, our past life, if you're right and I'm there too. You said my name was Shu?"

"Yeah. I'm remembering more and more about that, and you are there. It's definitely you—in every single way. It's disconcerting, being there, remembering things that took place in a totally different *lifetime*." Which is probably how he feels as he regains his Earth memories.

"I get it."

"But you love Duncan," I say. "And I know he wants me to fix everything." I sigh. "The animals on Rra, they want me to fix everything too." Tears well in my eyes. "Everyone wants me to do something, and it feels like I can't make anyone happy, no matter what I do. The harder I try, the worse I screw up. I killed someone on Rra."

"Oh, no. You did?"

A single tear streaks down my cheek. "I don't even know how I did it. I was doing what they asked me to do—I was trying to force one of them to shift back into a human form, and I pressed, harder, harder, and then." I choke. "He exploded, J."

Jesse crosses the feet separating us and perches on the edge of the bed. "That sounds horrifying." He touches my arm and sits with me, letting me relive it and then try and put it behind me.

"You should know that I'll support you, no matter what you do. Try to rebuild Rra, tear it down, whatever."

I know it's true—he will. In everything but the one thing that matters most to me. "Except you won't let me siphon someone to keep you with me." This time, tears roll down my cheeks. Should I feel awful that I'm more upset about the possibility of Jesse dying than about my actions in murdering someone? "You think I'm a better person than I am. If walking away from Rra and letting them burn would save you—permanently fix you—I'd probably do it."

Jesse laughs. Not a bark. Not a nervous release of uncomfortable energy. A big, bold, beautiful, throw-your-face-to-the-sky laugh. He laughs so long and so hard that tears roll down his cheeks. Finally he stops, slowly, and wipes his face. "You want to be this fierce, strong conqueror, but you're not." He places his hand on top of mine and squeezes. "We're the same, you and I. You wouldn't do that at all—you'd do the right thing every single time, no matter the cost to yourself."

I don't have the strength to argue with him. "Alright." It's touching, the faith he has in my moral compass. I'm not convinced I even have a moral compass anymore.

Or maybe I do, and it's right in front of me. Which means I'm stuck in a real Joseph Heller-inspired Catch-22. If I do the 'right thing' and let him die, then I'll literally be off the chain. I could do anything at that point.

So I need to do whatever it takes to keep him.

But he's saying that it's the one thing I can't do.

"It doesn't matter anyway," Jesse says. "I feel fine."

Which is good, because now that I've found Ra's dumb battery-powered necklace, the magic in it is drained. It's useless—which means I'm out of luck if Jesse's soul hole becomes too large again. Or whatever is actually happening.

"What are you going to do when you go back?" he asks. "I imagine you were pretty shaken up."

"Understatement. I doubt they'll even want my help after what happened. I think it's safe to say that I can't *make* them shift back."

"And your messages to yourself won't work—you always seem to wake up as a lion, and when you shift, the message disappears."

"Exactly," I say. "So how do I remember who I really am and what the stakes are?"

"Did you see anything odd there? Something that might clue you in that the world isn't quite right there?"

I shrug. "I've seen it in every prison. On Terra, during the Ascension. On Erra, after I almost drowned myself. It didn't matter—I never put the pieces together until I managed to send myself a message."

He frowns, his brow furrowed in thought, but like me, he's clearly drawing a blank.

"Am-Heh brought some stuff up for you while you were asleep." Jesse stands up and crosses to the door. He pivots around and lugs a box over to the bed.

"What is it?"

"We couldn't really fit all the artifacts up here in your room and they're spread out in this building and a dozen others, so Am-Heh asked the Amun lackeys to make photos and print them up." He picks up a stack of papers and hands them to me. The empty golden collar is resting on top of the stack. On a whim, I buckle it around my own neck. It clears the way for me to dig out the papers resting beneath it—that's the reason I put it on. It's heavy, but I'll probably get used to wearing it within a few hours.

The photos show a bunch of old Egyptian stuff— statutes with words on them. Carvings. Even images of scrolls in varying stages of repair. I squint and focus and blur my eyes and refocus, but it's a waste of time. I can only make out a few words from the images.

A knock at the door distracts me *just* when I'm about ready to chuck the whole box against the wall. "Yeah?"

And Mehen's face isn't exactly one I've been longing to see. "Most Divine."

I suppress a groan. It's an old habit for him, I'm sure, but if he doesn't stop calling me that I may explode. "What's wrong?" There's no way he'd be here, pushing through to where I was sleeping, if there wasn't a problem.

"Isis has discovered you're here."

"What does that mean?"

He sniffs loudly. "They've brought an army, of sorts."

For the love. I slide out of bed and cast around for something I can wear other than a shirt with a bloody sleeve and biker shorts. "How urgent is this?"

He grimaces. "Fairly urgent. They've brought . . . non-magical people."

What's he talking about? "I'll change clothes and be right out."

Jesse glares at the now-closed door, as if he can wish away the bad news. "That guy never has anything helpful to share. He's like a harbinger of misery or a little stormcloud."

I snort. "He can't help it. It's not his fault Isis wants me dead." I'm not even sure they're wrong. "Do you think there's any chance that if I died, Rra would go back to normal?"

Jesse shrugs. "I suppose there's no way to know, but I don't think you can be blamed for Terra falling apart. Your birth, or mine, or Kahn's might have accelerated things, but Terra started crumbling before you knew anything at all."

So many things we don't know. So many things I'm learning every time I close my eyes. And still so many things I can't do anything about.

"I do wonder whether the world would be better off without me." I stare at my feet. Plain old regular toes, badly in need of a clip and polish, and regular legs that need to be shaved—nothing special here.

Why me? Why can't someone else be stuck with this mess?

Jesse hugs me to his chest, unconcerned about my bloody shirt or my unshaved legs. "The world would be a much, much darker place without you in it. Not just for me. It's funny to me that the people who bring the most light can't even see it themselves. Trust me. Nothing would be better without you. I'm sorry all of this has fallen to you —none of the great people of the world had things easy. Poring over old stuff piqued my interest and I've been reading up on ancient history a bit. Alexander the Great tamed a wild, unridable horse at the age of thirteen. He studied with some famous philosopher named Aristotle. And Julius Caesar was a famous politician, but he only got where he was by being a brilliant general. Nothing in life worth doing is simple."

Suddenly, I can't not tell him for another second. "Kahn was Alexander the Great in his past life—John wasn't kidding when he said that."

Jesse's eyes widen. "What?"

"Mehen's the one who told me first. Terra was created just after Alexander the Great died."

"That's bizarre. I mean, Kahn died before Terra was created? How could that be?"

"None of this makes any sense to me. The only thing that does seem logical is Isis sending an army to follow up on the advance troops they sent to kill me in that park by the London University, or whatever. I'm actually surprised it took them this long." There are clothes draped over the top of a table in the corner, and a pair of black boots underneath. No time for a shower, sadly, but at least I should change clothes. Biker shorts and a ripped t-shirt don't feel like army-confronting clothes. "Turn around."

He does.

I change quickly, my pulse already racing as I ponder what *an army of sorts* might actually mean. I may be willing to do most anything for Jesse, but if Isis is right, I'd be a horrible monster not to trade my own life for seven billion plus people. "I wish we understood more about the rules. I wish someone had answers."

"Other than sleeping again, I don't have any brilliant ideas. And that'll put you one day closer to the deadline on

Rra." He scratches his chin where stubble now mars his jawline. "Do we have an idea of just how many people might die during this full moon hunt? I mean, is it like a half dozen? Or, like thousands? Or millions?"

I shake my head. "I bet Amun knows—I'm not sure the ratio of Reapers to Renders, but in the natural earth population, I think it's around thirty to one. So assume that it's a few million, if every Render kills someone."

I open the door, but Kahn's already standing in the hall outside, his eyes intent. I stare into his eyes, frozen.

"What are you doing?" Jesse asks.

"You should stay in your room," Kahn says.

"Mehen says I'm needed urgently," I say. "He said Isis is here."

"They are," Kahn says. "The morons think you need to die. They think you're going to free Ra. They don't get that you're trying to figure out how to reinforce the whole thing and fix what's wrong. They think you're *causing* the issues."

I make eye contact with Jesse and toss my head, sending him down nonverbally to suss out how bad things really are. He goes, understanding in his eyes. I try reaching out with my telekinetic senses to see what I can discover, but the lead-lined walls of this building block me from feeling anything beyond them. It means no Lifters outside can sense me, but it's obnoxious when I want to know what's going on.

"What do you want me to do?" I ask. "Hide forever?"

"Not forever," he says. "But Am-Heh and Mehen and I can handle this. There's no need to confirm that you're here."

"What's really going on?" He didn't stop Jesse.

"They'll try and kill you," he says simply.

"And you think I'll be safer inside than out there?" Something doesn't compute. He didn't come in here broadcasting a protective vibe. He seemed borderline hostile.

"I'm worried about what you'll do if you go out there."
He shrugs. "Send me instead. I'll talk to them."

"How do you know I won't free Ra?"

His chin lifts just half an inch, his perfectly chiseled face tense. "Are you considering it?"

"I don't know what choices I have." I explain what happened on Rra. "I don't even know who I am there, and the way I broke through the veil over my mind the last times won't work."

"And you think that means you need to free the man whom people worshipped as God of the Sun?" His contempt is clear.

"Why do you hate him so much?" What does he remember about his past life? Has he had any memories resurface? I think about the smile on his face, the absolute confidence in his posture as he sliced that knot. I wonder whether he even knows he met me in his past life. Alexander certainly had no idea. I doubt Kahn does either —he laughed not long ago at the notion of even *being* who he is.

That was unfair of me. I'd be furious if someone knew about me and didn't share.

"Kahn, there's something you need to know." I force myself to meet his eyes.

"It's not that I hate him," he says. "It's that I hate what he represents."

Huh?

"He was the most powerful person who had ever lived. He could snatch the life force away from literally anyone in existence. No one stood a chance opposing him, and he didn't just rule." Kahn shakes his head. "He conquered and subjugated millions—and he made them or let them, either way is bad, worship him like he was a god. Like his power wasn't some fluke of fate."

The irony of this accusation isn't lost on me. According

to the history I've studied of the time, Alexander actually had his face cast on coins in the same manner of the Greek Gods at the time. "So. That thing I need to tell you—it might shift your perspective."

His half smile is familiar. Endearing, even. It's the Kahn I know.

"You were Alexander the Great," I say. "I know that Mehen called you Apophis—and to him that was the name that mattered. Apophis was the son of Isis—who called herself Olympias and married Philip of Macedonia."

Kahn grunts.

"It's not a joke. I'm deadly serious, and I can attest that it's true. My memories of my time in Egypt have been coming back." My voice has dropped until it's barely above a whisper. "And I met you, back then."

His eyes widen. His words are slow, measured, almost as if they're being dragged out of him. "There's no world in which we're enemies."

The hairs on my arms rise. A chill runs through my entire body. This time, it really is a whisper. "Yes."

His head lowers slowly—giving me plenty of time to step away. But unlike that old memory, Kahn's not a stranger to me. He's not the enemy I know he was back then. His mouth is soft, yet firm. His arms are strong and sure and they wrap around me just as his lips meet mine.

And that chill disappears in favor of heat like I've never experienced. My hands clench on his shirt, dragging him closer, so much closer. He gasps against my mouth and deepens the kiss, and I can't tell where I stop and he starts. I don't even want that distinction anymore of me and him. I want *us* in every single way—kissing, breathing, thinking, living. Our kiss is remaking me into something else, someone else.

"Alora." Jesse's voice is urgent, raw.

It drags me back to myself. It reminds me who and

where I am. It's the slap across the face that I need. We may not be enemies, Kahn and I, but I have a lot of other things that are much more important right now than sucking his face until he turns inside out. "Yeah." I lean my forehead against Kahn's chest. "What?"

"You need to come. Right now."

"Send me," Kahn whispers. "Stay here."

"You need to come yourself," Jesse insists.

"Why?"

"They're threatening to kill women and children and—" Jesse's voice cracks. "Isis says they'll start killing them in five minutes, and they'll keep killing them until you surrender."

The ice is back. Every part of me is cold. Is Jesse kidding? "They're supposed to be the good guys." I'm nearly yelling, but I don't even care. "They're going to kill *children?*"

Jesse swallows. "They're broadcasting on every channel in Europe right now. They claim that you're about to kill far, far more people and that the ends justify the means. They say their only hope is if your followers see you for who you really are and turn you over to them in time for them to stop you. I think they're trying to put enough pressure on the population that they'll turn against you."

"That's a terrorist tactic if ever I heard one," Kahn says. "I can't believe it's come to that."

I push past Kahn, but he doesn't argue. Not again. Not now that I've heard what they're planning.

"They'll kill you," Kahn says.

"I don't care," I say. "I can't be the reason they kill kids."

"It's an excuse," Jesse says. "You're not doing anything evil—they are."

I duck out the door, ready to break into a sprint as soon as I've got a straight path.

"Alora!" Kahn's voice is ragged.

"What?" I turn back.

"I'm not worried they'll kill you." His eyes are sad. "I'm not sure anyone *can* kill you anymore."

He's worried that I'll kill them.

His fears might be right.

EARTH

No one is standing in the doorways I pass. No one is lined up in the hall. No one is lining the stairs, or standing at attention as I approach the doors. In fact, inside these lead-lined walls, I don't sense anyone at all. That should have been my first sign there was a problem. Where did they all go . . . and why?

I pause and push my senses past the lead with a significant effort—the stuff I need is stuff Mehen can't train me to do, it seems.

And I sense more people—many, many more. Lined up in Wilmington Square. Running along Wilmington Street, Merlin Street, and covering all the sidewalks and every space in between.

I race to the front door, where two men stand with their hands on semi-automatic machine guns, braced at an angle against their chests.

"I need to leave."

The men look at one another, and I prepare for them to argue. But before I have to become more forceful, they straighten and turn sideways, allowing me through.

Kahn and Jesse catch up, both of them breathing heavily.

"I'm going to talk to Isis myself."

"They won't talk to you." Kahn's eyes are sad. This time, he does look protective. "Let me go. Stay here. I might know a few of them. They might listen to me." He doesn't sound very hopeful.

"If my own father couldn't do anything to protect me, they won't listen to you." I put my hand on the handle of the door. "But you two can come, as long as you stay behind me."

"Behind you?" Jesse's fuming. "If you think—"

I ignore him and shove my way through.

The sun's rays are just rising—early morning, then. The air is brisk here, in a way it's not this time of year in Houston. That's all I have time to notice before the cries of the children reach my ears.

My eyes quickly scan the lines of innocent people and the soldiers standing behind them. Now that I'm outside of the lead lining, I easily expand my reach until I sense all of them, every last one. And from the top of the steps, I can even see most everyone.

Seven hundred and thirty-one soldiers face off against us.

Two hundred and eleven of the Followers of Amun, plus John, Am-Heh, and Mehen have spread out in front of the building, blocking their advance. Martin, Rosalinde, Thomas, Oliver, and Roland are thankfully bunched close to the building on my right, as far from the front of this standoff as they can reasonably be. So far, no one seems to have noticed that I've emerged.

"We won't turn her over to you," John says. "Kill as many innocents as you feel you must. Their deaths will be on your heads."

"You're badly outnumbered." A short man with a very

full head of reddish hair stands in the front, his eyes shining brightly. His British accent is thick, almost as thick as his arrogance. "And you're wrong. Any innocent people we're forced to kill will be entirely her fault, every last one. We've only gathered people who are already stuck on Rra, which is a tiny sample of the number of people who are at risk right now."

"You're threatening to kill people who have done nothing wrong, people who have no ability to defend them-selves." John spits on the ground. "You're disgusting."

"We're doing it to make a point," a deep voice says. An American voice. A familiar voice.

"Dad?" Jesse's voice is unsure, and that splits a crack in the edge of my poor, bruised heart. My expectations for our father have never been high, but my brother loves him.

I spot Duncan right away, standing a little behind the redheaded man. Unfortunately, Jesse's voice clued them in that we had emerged and Duncan and the red-haired man immediately focus on us.

"Duncan isn't our father." My lip may have curled, but my voice is steady and calm. "He legally separated himself from both of us long ago, and I'm glad of it. It's the only good thing he's ever done for me."

In that moment, I have an epiphany—we are what we do. Anyone who would threaten this—even disguised as a symbolic act to showcase the risk I'm exposing the world to —isn't a good guy.

What have I seen of Ra, the father of mine who is locked up in a prison? He's been honest, kind, compassion-ate, and just. He's shown mercy as well. And he's trapped, patiently waiting, while these men chivy, threaten, and harm innocent people—all because of their own ignorance. Maybe whoever set up Terra locked up the wrong people. Maybe it was all a big mistake.

Or maybe I still don't know enough.

Isis hasn't actually harmed anyone so far. At least, not that I've seen.

"Let them go," I say. "Do it in the next two minutes—release every single man, woman, and child, and send them home. If you do that, I'll hear your demands."

"They're simple," Duncan says. "Surrender. Come with us to stand trial for your actions on Terra and Erra, and we'll free them. Every last one of them."

"Don't do it," Kahn says. "It won't be a fair trial. They'll just execute you, and you know that won't fix anything. You're the only one who can fix things."

"She's not going with you," John says. "No matter what evil things you threaten."

"They're liars," Mehen says. "Believe nothing they say. They will harm you in any way they can."

Even the guy who can't understand a word doesn't believe them.

I can barely see them from this far back—sensing them isn't quite the same. Dozens of Amun troops have lined up in front of me to protect me, but they're also blocking my path. I Lift them gently, shifting them to either side so that I can walk close enough to see what's going on with my physical eyes. Most importantly, I need to see my own father. Is it possible he's trying to send me a different message? A week ago he was trying to make amends, and now he's advocating for me to surrender . . . so they can kill me?

The men and women I shift turn shocked faces toward me, but they don't object. I walk up the pathway I've cleared, and I finally set eyes on Duncan, hoping against hope that he'll wink, or maybe widen his eyes to tell me that he's got another plan in mind. But his eyes are hard and steady. His breathing is consistent. If anything, he looks more determined than the other man, the red-haired one.

I'm still more than a dozen paces from Duncan when there's a cracking sound, followed by a bullet striking my right shoulder from above. It jerks me backward, and I nearly fall to the ground, blood pouring down my back.

I crouch, allowing the troops I shifted to close back in around me, blocking the clear view the snipers on the rooftop had to take me out again. Before I issue any orders at all, four different people on that rooftop cry out, loudly.

I assume it was Mehen who took them out.

I'm wrong.

Jesse's eyes are alight, and he's scowling. "You hadn't even threatened them."

Mehen's eyes flare next and six more shout. He's beaming. This is definitely his element.

Rosalinde's hands reach me first, and she grimaces, but the sharp pain in my shoulder is immediately gone. I push up to standing. "How can this solve anything?" I ask, peering around the mass of shoulders in front of me at my father's face. "You really want to *kill* me? Rra is coming down—and that's not even my doing."

"You've destabilized everything," Duncan says, "by collapsing both Terra and Erra."

I shake my head. "Terra and Erra were already fracturing."

"Why aren't you shoring up Rra?" The red-haired man sneers. "You haven't even tried."

"I don't know how," I say.

"Which means the only play for us," Duncan says, "is elimination of the cause of the problem."

"Every single person on Rra is locked in a shifted form," I say. "*I* didn't do that, but if I can't solve that in the next thirty-six hours, they'll be hunting one another."

"We're aware of the situation," Duncan says. "That's why we're here, threatening innocent lives. You've left us no other options. Release them from this forced shift."

"I can't believe you think I'd *want* that to happen. I have no control over—"

"They won't listen." Jesse's voice is fraught with terrible sorrow. "They're clinging to a desperate hope, too afraid to accept the truth."

We can't even discuss the reality of it until they've released their hostages. These poor people must be absolutely terrified. I scan the front line, noting that it's a mixture of men, women, and children, but there are more children than anything else. My blood boils in my veins. "Tell your troops—"

More gunfire—I'm not sure from which side—and then a shout. A tiny, pained cry. "Mother!"

My eyes find the source at the same time as another gunshot fires—this one from close range. The little boy with the dark, dark hair collapses next to his mother, his arms still outstretched, his eyes painfully wide. His hopelessness, his dark hair, it shouldn't remind me of Jesse, but it does. The helpless terror I felt in that moment is the same, as is my inability to do anything to stop the senseless violence . . .

Something inside of me snaps. I'm tired of being helpless. I'm tired of watching as bad people ruin things. I need to do something.

"Surrender," the short red-haired man shouts. "Or you leave us no choice."

"You've already left me no choice," I growl.

"Let's all take a step back. That was an accident." Duncan turns toward the red-haired man and shakes his head. "We had an agreement."

"You have no authority here."

A tiny corner of my heart swells, knowing that my father hadn't agreed to this—not to actually killing them. He probably just assumed that I'd surrender for the innocents, and a part of me wants to do just that. But he doesn't know me well enough. He hasn't spent enough time with me.

And he has no idea what I'm capable of.

"Do it." The British leader of Isis waves his hand through the air, and his men all fire at once, hundreds of innocent people suddenly crying out and slumping all around the square.

Rosalinde screams next to me, equal parts terror and fury. No matter how quickly my Healers work, they can't save them all. They can't save more than a handful of these poor people. People whom I'm desperate to save on Rra. People I want to protect.

Fury, hot, quick, and consuming floods my body, for all the times I've been unable to stop the injustices in my life. For all the blows I took as a child, curling inward helplessly. For each time I was called a name—excluded, insulted, and ignored. For the way my parents, and then my aunt, and then the system let me down. For the brutal murder of my brother Jesse who had never done anything but help other people. For the rage inside of me that, even with all my power, I'm unable to repair the damage that was dealt to him and all of these people trapped against their wills and used by those more powerful.

For my helpless rage at the thought of watching Jesse die again—any day, any moment, any second—from an injury I created in my desperation to save him. And now for this horrible travesty that they're blaming me for. I'm sick to death of running. I'm finished with curling inward. I'm about done being calm and level-headed and talking things through.

Instead, I reach outward, sensing each and every pulsing light facing me.

Shots fire again, this time at the troops blocking me, the ones waiting for my command. My eyes flare to life, halting every single bullet in mid-air. I spread my hands in front of me and flip my palms down, dropping the inert bullets. The square is filled with the sound of bullets clinking against the pavement. And the sound of moans and whimpers as innocent people suffer and die from violence done against them in my name. I should have stopped them before. I should have been better, stronger, faster.

I failed many of them just as I failed Jesse.

Never again.

I don't try to weigh and measure the weight or goodness in each soul—there's not enough time for that. No, I reach for *all* the soldiers who were willing to use innocent people to stand against me, for every last one—except my own father. I can't quite bring myself to take him, not yet. Once I sense them all, the life force of every last one, I *pull*. Hard. Long. Desperate.

It's as easy as riding a bike. It's as simple as swimming across a pool. It's as refreshing as splashing water against my face. Their life forces evacuate their bodies and flood into mine—swirling around without much purpose other than buoying me up, lifting me to the power of an actual god. As the hundreds of soldiers around me wither and die, their blackened bodies collapsing in the same moment, I understand why Ra was worshipped as a deity.

They weren't entirely wrong.

This power is too great for anyone to wield, control over life and death. Unlimited magic at the expense of others.

I extend my senses again, reaching for the innocent people, the children, the women, their fathers and brothers and uncles, and I focus on those who aren't yet gone. One hundred. A hundred and forty. A hundred and sixty-five. A hundred and sixty-seven. And then I can't identify any more. I shove the power I've taken into them, mending and repairing, shoring up major damage. It's not elegant. It's not efficient. It's not clean. But I restore the parts of their bodies that don't work, that are injured, that are broken, and I make them as whole as I can.

Even still, a vast well of power remains, and it beats against me. It clouds my mind, it floods my soul with light and heat and pleasure, and I hate it. Reaching back to my memories, I focus on what I did with the well on my belt, and the one in my ring and I shove all the energy into a bucket—first one, and then another, until the stones inside Ra's collar pulse with bright white magic—magic ripped from the bodies of men who would shoot children.

And then, once it's done, I sink to my knees and begin to sob.

I can't seem to stop.

"It's over." Jesse wraps me in his arms and carries me away. I'm not sure where. I don't even care. I just can't see it anymore—the slumped bodies of the bad men I withered and the innocent people I couldn't save. The sounds of their cries reverberate in my skull until it feels like my brain has turned to mush. Jesse never releases me—he holds me against him, rubbing my back softly until I finally drift into darkness.

Every single time I go to sleep, I dream of icy blue eyes and shining golden hair. I dream of broad shoulders and a commanding voice. Savage movements and powerful strokes . . . Alexander. Even when I daydream, my mind drifts to him.

It's become a real distraction.

"—don't think we should wait until he arrives," Am-Heh is saying. "We should take the fight to him."

"I'm tired of fighting," Dad says, just as we rehearsed.

"Then let Sekhmet lead the army," Anat says. "She can give you the break you need, but easily keep our people and lands safe."

"Or if she has no taste for it, send me." Am-Hch flexes his muscles and they push at the leather vest and vambraces he wears. He's always so eager to destroy things. Impatient. Brash. Eager. So typically Fire Called.

"Agreed," Mehen says. "It's time we stop letting him roll over the country around us. We have to stop this madness. They're calling him Alexander *the Great*, as if he is *anything* to Ra!"

"As if Ra didn't make him who he is," Ptah says.

"Without Ra, he'd just be another Assimilator, like his mother. He'd be nothing."

"Maybe not nothing." Anat arches one perfectly manicured eyebrow.

"They're calling him the All-Called," Aha says. "The *All-Called*, as if he was somehow endowed with these powers as a gift from heaven, as if he's the embodiment of all that is good, sent here to free them all from your unjust rule. It's infuriating. Especially when his only real claim to fame is being the child of the worst woman ever to live."

"Lifting powerfully *and* wielding all four elements is no small feat. He's a force to be reckoned with, and Isis has valid grievances against me," Dad says. "Just complaints, even. As you know, what I did to her and her child was unthinkable. I won't stand in their way if expanding their borders will finally bring her a feeling of security or comfort. And if they come here, we'll see what happens."

None of Dad's Lieutenants will argue with him, but they don't agree. It's clear in the set of their twisted mouths, in the way they clench their hands on their tables and plates, and in the glint in their eyes.

"What I don't understand," Dad says, "is who is this Fire Called woman 'Neser,' whom Alexander is doggedly searching for? He's offering more and more as a reward for any information and no one seems to know a single thing about her. Does he love her or hate her? And why won't he say what he wants with her?"

I can't let him think about that much more. Either Dad or Am-Heh is sure to recall that when I first began my training to Call Fire, I razed an entire geographical region to the ground, and the people of Nubia called me Neser for miles and miles around. It means 'flame,' and they didn't mean it as a compliment. Shu arranged for a group of Earth Called to go and repair the damage I'd caused, but I still feel guilty.

"I think it's time we tell them," I say softly, in part to distract Dad and in part because it's time. The Lieutenants are asking too many questions.

"Tell us what?" Anubis nearly growls. He's maintaining his human shape, which is rare, frankly, but his canines look far too long. I'm a little concerned he's spent too much time as a wolf and he'll be unable to maintain human form for more than brief periods. I hear that can happen with Renders who too heavily embrace their animal form.

"Dad?"

His head snaps toward me.

"They won't let it go," I say, "and we should offer to take them with us in any case."

Normally I'd have brought this up with him in private, but I can't have him connecting the dots with Alexander and Neser. The best way to deflect is to attack. He taught me that.

"You're still set on this course?" Dad's eyes are steady on my face.

I nod. "Aren't you?"

He shrugs. "I'll do whatever will bring you joy."

Whatever will bring me joy? What if that's spending time with the son of his worst enemy? I don't even dare ask for that. Besides, it's not like dreaming about someone means that they'd bring me happiness in real life. I'm sure the version of Alexander who lives in my head is nothing like the real Apophis, son of Isis.

Horus stands up. "If you're going to tell us something, then do it." A brisk wind whips through my hair. He always loses control when he's agitated.

I look around the room slowly, taking in all the familiar faces of my childhood, the faces of those who have trained me, protected me, and revered me. Dad trusts them all, and that confidence and faith has been passed along to me—not just because he feels it, but because like Dad, I've seen it.

These people love him and would do anything to keep us safe.

Anat, Dad's strongest and most gifted Assimilator, and my dear friend. She has taught me everything that Dad couldn't, and when Mother left, she stepped right into that void. She held my hand and braided my hair. Her features have changed slightly over the years with her own personal opinions of beauty, her nose becoming more prominent, and her hair changing color with her whims, her body shape shifting with changing fashion, but her eyes have remained constant. Liquid, dark, caring, and completely confident.

Ammit, with his snapping eyes, jutting jaw, and dark, thick skin may not be super reliable with times and meetings, but he's fiercely loyal. Even if I didn't know he turned into a crocodile, I'd know he was a Render by his sharp, almost feral movements. But in all the time I've known him, I've never once felt the *push* from him that gives away a supra trying to force my actions. Not one single time. He possesses great strength, amazing power, and he never tries to assert it without Dad's go-ahead.

Mehen's always quiet, always calm, and always watching. He's been beside my father in almost every situation as long as I can recall. He's unassuming, he's tough, and he's doggedly true. His arms rest patiently on the table, fingers not tapping, hands not gripping anything. No matter what I tell them, he'll be behind us, utterly and completely.

Imhotep, with his nearly black skin, the strongest Healer ever to live. Like Dad and me with our assimilation, he can Heal from a distance, making him an invaluable personal physician. He's worked tirelessly to perfect his skill, and he has even transformed the day-to-day practices that keep our people healthy and strong.

Aha, now using the name Bastet again, has rejoined Dad's Lieutenants with a vengeance. I've never seen someone so delighted to rejoin military applications in my life. Acting as my nursemaid and my personal guard was probably the hardest thing Dad could ever have asked of her, and yet she trained and guarded me perfectly, constantly, without any complaint. She taught me to control my inner animal, releasing my lion only when I'm scared or need the extra speed, agility, or more powerful senses. She taught me to find peace through being more closely aligned with ma'at, with the purpose and call of nature itself.

Am-Heh's the most volatile, which I should expect given that he's Fire Called. His eyes smolder, his hands smoke where they grip the table. He hates not knowing all the things that can be known, but he also surrenders to Dad and to me at all times. In all places. In all ways. He told me once that it was freeing to him, knowing that in the end, he's accountable to someone else. It helps him douse the fire that rages inside of him, threatening to melt the whole earth.

Ptah didn't take my refusal of his proposal very well, and he asked for my hand in marriage a dozen more times, even inscribing proposals into temples, pyramids, and the newly constructed walls of the palace. I realized, finally, that Dad favored him because he's not destructive like the others. He's stable. He's steady, and he looks to the future while honoring the past. He's angry only when threatened, and that makes him someone Dad would trust to be with his daughter at all times. But he's also boring. He's predictable, and thankfully, he finally let his dreams for our never-going-to-happen future go.

Tefnut, who I didn't realize was my own half-sister until a few years ago, is quiet, reserved, and unpredictable. But she's always there when we need her, and she has never once resented the time or attention Dad pays me. In some ways, I wonder whether she pities me. True to her Ice Called powers, she's cold and calculating, but time and time again she's used that quality to protect and serve.

And of course, there's Horus, the friendliest of Dad's men, the most amicable, and the Lieutenant who played with me most as a child. He would whisk me up into the air and then drop me, buoying me back up at the very last minute. He's exciting and fun and he leads a horrifying band of shock troops just like him. They've hacked other, much larger battalions, to bits just for fun. I struggle sometimes to reconcile the part of him that plays with a toddler with total abandon, and the part of him that turns humans into chunks.

Anubis leads the largest single force of soldiers in our entire land. It took time for Dad to win over the Prince of Nubia, but his wolf pack is the most terrifying force in all of Asia, and he would turn them on anyone who challenged us in a hot second.

They have very little in common, these warriors, other than a love for my father, and I suppose their love for me by extension.

Except for Shu, who knows more than Dad, but has kept quiet about it to keep Dad from knowing he joined me in Gordion and that I met Alexander. In many ways, he's the only member of Dad's inner circle who loves me more, who cares for me more, who would turn on even my father, if it was what I needed.

He's the only person here who is *mine*.

"Dad and I have decided it's time to move on, at least for now. We're tired of ruling, tired of judging and weighing and measuring, and protecting, and mostly, tired of fighting. Isis has grievances against my father that are, as you know, legitimate. She was wronged, and her son Alexander—"

"Apophis," Dad says softly.

I clear my throat. "Her son Apophis has been gathering troops and amassing allies to come and take us down. It has been his mother's greatest wish ever since she left."

"She's not even mad about what Ra did," Anat says. "She's angry he didn't love her. She's angry he cast her out. If that wasn't true, she'd never have tried so hard to separate him from Hathor."

Which she only accomplished by convincing my own mother that I'm an abomination. I try not to dwell on that part. "Regardless of her motivations or her feelings," I say, "we have decided to let them conquer us and take everything."

Jaws drop. Eyes widen. They gasp. They murmur. I expected all of this and more, including the blackening of the wooden table under Am-Heh's hands and the whipping wind in my hair that reveals Horus' shock.

"Sekhmet is tired of ruling and she's only just begun," Dad says. "It's no way to start a life, exhausted with your role from the outset. I promised her that we could see the world together. It has always been her greatest joy, to see new places and meet new people. We can travel, we can live as we choose, once we've parted from this region, and we can return here if or when she ever desires to resume her rightful place as queen."

Am-Heh's eyes snap. "But you fought so hard to create—"

"I wanted to make something for my family." Dad gestures at Shu, and then at me. "A family who doesn't care about having an empire. A family that wants the freedom not to be worshipped and watched at all times. It's a desire I understand entirely."

"What will you do with us?" Horus asks. "Are we to be disbanded?"

"Not at all," Dad says. "You may choose your own future. You're welcome to accompany us—after all, even once we've vacated the palace, once our ruse has been completed, we'll want friends, allies, and supporters."

He doesn't say it, but he'll want bodyguards. Everyone sleeps sometimes.

"But if you love what you do, if you love keeping the peace and fighting off threats, I'm sure Apophis will find a place for you here, aiding him in subduing those who will not welcome his rule. He has ambitions, that one. He'll spread his control far and wide, and I think he'll do an admirable job governing. His mother can keep you young in the same way that I do."

"She's nothing like you." Tefnut's eyes are intense, but there's no anger in them, no reproach when she looks at me. She understands—of course she does. She's kept it quiet that she's Ra's daughter for a reason, distancing herself from his legacy of her own volition. Either to avoid the shadow he casts, or because, like me, she finds it tiring.

"What if he won't accept us?" Am-Heh asks.

I'm surprised he's considering staying, but perhaps I shouldn't be. He's not built for traipsing around the world or living a quiet life in seclusion. He's made to raze enemy forces to the ground.

"Unlike me, Alexander *wants* to govern. He wants to rule. He wants to judge and weigh and provide peace and prosperity." Sometimes I wonder whether my failure to have that drive disappoints Dad. He's never said, but . . .

"I'm relieved at the prospect of leaving too," Shu says, his unfailing support unsurprising. "I didn't want to complain, but if I have to listen to one more person's complaint about how their neighbor stole their goat, I might lose my mind."

"What about your people?" Anat's voice is barely above a whisper, as if it pains her to question anything Ra does.

"What about them?" Dad asks.

"Will Isis care for them as you have?" Her question is a legitimate one.

"I believe she will," I say. "But I think we should confirm that, before making a final decision."

Dad's eyebrows rise. "What do you mean?" Is it hope in his tone? Is he hoping I'll rethink our plan?

"We should ensure that the countries Apophis has overtaken are being justly ruled, and that the people will not suffer from our absence." What in the world am I saying? I've met Alexander, and I know he would never . . . I realize then what I was doing without even consciously realizing it.

I want to see him again.

I've been searching for an excuse to see him again ever since Gordion. Each time reports of his search for Neser surface, my heart contracts, wishing . . . what? That I could somehow spend more time with Dad's enemy?

No. I would never betray my father. Obviously.

But it is true that our people's lives and wellbeing matter. It would be foolish of us to leave, only to discover we'd harmed everyone whom we'd left.

"How do you propose we find out whether he's a good ruler?" Dad asks.

"I think the best way is to investigate for ourselves—pretend to be the subjects he's recently conquered." I can't help glancing at Shu. He's frowning. That's not good.

"You think you and I should simply traipse in?" Dad asks. "Don't you think we might be noticed?"

"I can convincingly act like someone else," I say. "Fire Called, a Lifter, or a Render. Whichever you suggest. Then I can decide whether we can, in good conscience, follow through with the rest of our plan."

No one says a word for an uncomfortable length of time. Dad sighs heavily, and I realize he's going to shoot me down. Maybe he's finally realized that I've met Alexander.

Maybe Shu and I didn't really surprise Ptah—maybe he knew all along. Or worst of all, he's going to tell me this entire thing is insane, and it's time for me to accompany Am-Heh and Anubis to destroy Apophis once and for all.

"It's as good a plan as any, but you must take at least two others with you." He crosses his arms over his chest. "I can't have you head out on your own."

"They're all too recognizable," I say.

"You'll modify their appearance," Anat says. "Or you'll take me with you and I'll do it."

"Shu," I say.

"I'll go as well," Tefnut says.

Every face in the room swivels her direction. No one in the world expected her to offer that, least of all me.

"A Lifter, an Ice Called, and . . . what will you be pretending to be?" Dad's voice doesn't change, but I can sense his uncertainty—his discomfort. "It sounds like a pretty conspicuous group to me."

"If Shu and I are both Lifters," I say, "then—"

"A wealthy ice merchant and her two body guards," Tefnut says. "It makes as compelling a story as any other. Besides, no one will be examining people sneaking in too closely. It's the citizens attempting to escape and share intelligence that will be scrutinized."

"You won't be returning, then?" Dad asks, his expression bemused.

"I doubt they'll be able to stop us when we decide to do that," she says.

I'd have preferred to take Ptah again—he was easy to ditch—but I'm actually excited to get to know my enigmatic sister a bit more.

"You'd better leave quickly, then," Dad says. "I hear he's readying for yet another campaign."

He doesn't have to tell me twice. I work hard to

disguise it, but my heartbeat picks up at just the thought of seeing Alexander again. I can't quite believe it's happening.

The second we're free of the council chamber, Shu hisses at me. "I know what you're up to."

"Oh?"

"You picked the wrong person to accompany you. I'm the only one who knows why you really want to go—and I'm going to be on you like beetles on a fig."

19

ANCIENT EGYPT

"I can't believe we're headed back to Gordion," Shu whispers. "This is messed up."

"It's not like I'm going back as Neser." I snatch my bag out of his hand and Lift it, securing it in place over the broad withers of my favorite horse. "He'll never even know who I am. I just want to be sure that we're doing the right thing."

"For what it's worth," Tefnut says from the steps of the palace, "I think you're being prudent."

Shu glares at me, but doesn't dig any further. After all, he can't—not without giving me away. I'm actually grateful Dad insisted on sending a second companion along.

"How does this work?" Tefnut eyes the horse tied next to mine and Shu's warily. I didn't realize she wasn't a fan of horses. I suppose if I couldn't Lift, giving me a lot more control over my own balance, I might be nervous too.

"Have you ridden a horse before?" Shu asks.

She laughs, then. "I was riding a horse before you were a gleam in Father's eye."

I'm confused. "Then what—"

"I prefer mares, but I'll be fine to handle this guy." She

pats the dapple grey on his rounded rump. "I'm asking about the disguises you're making for us. Surely Apophis would recognize three of Ra's children on sight."

Oh. Right. "Well, if you tell me how you'd like to look, I'll make it happen. If you don't care, I'll be creative."

"Sekhmet prefers to look quite homely, herself," Shu says. "It ensures she doesn't get too much undesirable male attention." Shu is such a brat. As if I needed his hint—I'm not going because I think Alexander and I will . . . whatever. I'm fine with having an unattractive disguise.

Tefnut's smile is almost sultry. "I'll go the opposite direction, thanks." I take in her pale hair, so blonde it's nearly white, and her startlingly green eyes. Her coloring is distinctive, but her body is so slender, she could almost pass for a young boy. "In fact, I'd like to be much more . . . " Her hands shape a fuller figure. "Curvy."

I don't argue, with either of them. I merely pull a bit of energy from my ring, and shape it into the proper threads —I've been practicing since my last clumsy efforts. I think even Anat would be impressed with me this time. By the time I'm done with Tefnut, even Anat wouldn't be able to pull male attention away. Her figure is as curvy as an hourglass, with lips of bright red, set inside a uniquely heart-shaped face. Raven hair curves around her high cheekbones and spills over her pale, almost white shoulders. According to the style of our era, she couldn't look more fetching.

Shu whistles. "Nicely done. Now, make sure I'm just as handsome."

I chuckle. "Nice try. You and I are the bodyguards." My brother's already pretty strong, but I bulk up his mass significantly, and for fun, I give him a burn from his jaw down his neck. "There. I think that looks like a guard who's willing to do some real damage, even against a Fire Called."

Shu pulls a mirror out of his bag, which almost makes me laugh again. When he's finally done grumbling and huff-ing, Tefnut borrows it. The smile that spreads across her exquisite face is quite pleased. "Do you have to remove this when we return?" She turns to face me. "How long will it last?"

I shrug. "It's permanent, until I intentionally change you back. That's the danger, really. It relies on an Assimilator to repair it."

She coos. "This is amazing. I can't believe I've never asked Father to do anything like this before."

"Eternal youth isn't enough?" Shu asks. "You're bummed you never thought to ask for ungodly beauty as well?"

"Shut up," she says easily. "You're just jealous." She snickers, eying his terrible burn.

I snort. "It's not as if it hurts him, and our appearance won't matter for the short time we maintain it."

"Well, go on, then," Tefnut says. "I can't wait to see what you have ready for yourself."

I did have something planned, but it wasn't hideous. And if I use it, Shu will not shut up about it. The idea of meeting Alexander as another unattractive . . . but it can't be helped. I didn't have any plans to flirt with him again— just to see him. I pull a bit more energy and shape it carefully. First, I fashion an untamed mane of epic proportions, tangled and a bit dirty. Then I pour power into my skin, shaping blotchy freckles and moles, and finally, I give myself two different-colored eyes—one brown, one green, set too far apart. Thin lips, ears that stick out just a bit too far, and shoulders that hunch from my excessive height.

That should satisfy Shu, and if it makes me cringe a bit, well, that's probably for the best. He's only trying to save me from myself. Someone should.

What I really want is to capture an image in my mind of Alexander—someone human and fallible to replace the iconic memory that I've inexplicably painted of him. I'm sure my memories are out of alignment with reality. The way he reacts to someone who looks as unattractive as I do will likely more accurately convey his true personality anyway. That should be just what I need to stop thinking about him incessantly.

I Bind air and use it to swing up onto Charger's back—my massive roan—and cluck so he'll get going already. When I look over my shoulder to make sure Shu and Tefnut are following, I notice movement in the window of the third floor. Dad's room. He's standing in the window, watching us leave. I wave, and he presses his hand to his mouth and blows me a kiss. He must have watched my transformation, to know who I am—I hope he found it sufficient.

I will miss him—and I feel terrible about covering up my real reason for going. But it's not like it will cause him any harm. I'm going to rid myself of whatever bizarre dreams I've been having over the child of his enemy. It's really a good thing, the loyal thing for me to do. I smile up at him, and he smiles back.

My second time away from home is a little less exhilarating, but a little less sorrowful, too. It feels almost as if I'm learning to rely upon myself and not on Dad's confidence and power and protection. We cover ground so much faster this time, without Ptah making me stop to ooh and aah over every stupid temple, palace, and shrine, and without trying to plant the seeds of rumor and legend. Tefnut and Shu are hilarious—they've apparently known one another for years and years, long before I was born, and they have a lot of inside jokes, but we make a few of our own as well.

When it grows unbearably hot, Tefnut cools us both down. She chills our water, drops the temperature of the air around us, and refreshes the horses. Far, far sooner than I expected, we're sitting outside of Gordion again, and this time it won't be as simple as wandering around and bumping into him.

If I want a peek at Alexander, I'm going to have to be resourceful. Unlike last time I was here, there's now a wall surrounding the perimeter of the main town. There are guards standing on duty—likely to be Renders, based on the way they sniff the air. Tefnut takes over when we reach the outpost, explaining that she's here to negotiate contracts for ice supplies to local inns and taverns.

"I assume that with the arrival and apparent residence of a new ruler, you've had a dramatic increase in visitors," Tefnut says in flawless Persian. "Many of your visitors are likely accustomed to a more refined palate, and I can offer more than simply cold beverages or chilled cellar space for your meats. I can provide sugared creams that your merchants will fight to secure and the means with which to keep them fresh for as long as necessary."

The guard can barely form a coherent sentence while looking at her, which I suppose is helpful. He doesn't spare me a second glance, which is what I want as a bodyguard, of course.

Once we're inside, Tefnut heads directly for the closest inn.

"Don't you think we should talk to a variety of people?" I ask. "Innkeepers, yes, but also soldiers, officers, and the poorer, less prosperous farmers?"

Tefnut frowns. "I suppose that's the thorough way to handle things. I imagine we'll find quite a few of each category at the various inns around town."

A groom meets us at the barn outside the inn. I toss him my reins. "I need to walk after all that time in the saddle. My legs barely work." I Bind air and swing down. "I'll circle back momentarily."

"I don't think you should be alone," Tefnut says.

I arch one eyebrow. "I'd never even contemplate leaving

you alone, milady. That's why my brother will be sure to stay by your side every second."

Shu's eyes narrow at me, but he can't very well argue that a servant can't be left unsupervised, not with the innkeeper approaching and the grooms waiting for them to surrender their horses. I'm sure Shu will be quick to track me down, so I waste no time slipping away and mixing into the throngs of people in the much busier marketplace than we saw a few months back.

Alexander has been busy.

If Gordion is any indication of how he'll rule, it'll be a good transition. The roads have all been improved—widened and fortified. The townsfolk appear happy and prosperous. Soldiers stride through the streets, yes, but so do more foreigners. No one seems terrified when a soldier looks their way, which bodes well for the order Alexander commands. A quiet conversation in Greek draws my attention. Two soldiers are standing near a street vendor.

"—on toward Egypt next instead, thank Zeus himself." The soldier stuffs an overly large bite in his mouth and chews, his mouth entirely open, food rolling around alarmingly.

"We'll have to push past Issus and Tyre first," a grey-haired soldier next to him says.

"But at least we're moving south. If we had to keep pressing forward through Asia, slogging through the miserable farming towns toward Nineveh, I'd desert." He spits and wipes his chin with his hand. "I can barely stand to be camped in this provincial backwoods town any longer."

"Backwoods? This is a lovely capital," the other soldier says. He shakes a head covered with thinning grey hair. "I would retire here, if I thought that possible, but I'm sure he'll need all his troops to have any chance against Ra, and he's clearly moving toward that, idiotic though it may be."

The open-mouthed chewer scoffs, bits of chicken

spraying from his mouth. "Ra's old," he says. His grin has the signature overconfidence that alcohol brings. "They say he's scared of Alexander, and it must be true. These were all his lands, and what has he done about Alexander's conquests? Nothing. No, we have nothing to fear, other than winning so many spoils that we can't transport them all home."

"We're not allowed to take spoils, or have you forgotten?" The grey-haired man clucks. "Alexander wants peaceful transitions. He wants the local population to be happier under his rule than they were before. That's why he pays us so well."

"He won't stop us," the first man says. "Not once we've won him Egypt. Not from there."

The men think he's headed for Egypt next, not pressing onward toward Nineveh and Babylon as we'd heard. I'm sure Tefnut and Shu are furious with me for leaving, but seeing as I already have . . . I might as well discover what more I can learn. I duck behind a woman carrying a basketful of bread and sashay along in the same way that she is, actually happy about my unimpressive appearance in this moment.

Once her path veers off to the side, I tag along with a group of scholars, caught up in a debate about the best way to shift injuries and the reason that Healers can repair flesh when Lifters can only move things. It makes me wonder why all the best scholars are always found among Healers. What is it about repairing peoples' bodies that makes men and women pay closer attention to the abstract principles of right and wrong and moral ethics?

But when they turn to head for the temple of Apollo, I'm standing alone in the middle of the street . . . just in front of the painted palace, where rumor has it Alexander has taken up residence. And where else would he live in Gordion? It's the finest, the most lavish, and the most central building in town. It makes sense he would move in here. As it's set into the earth, at least two levels of the residence set below ground level, it only rises three floors into the air. I glance around to make sure no one has taken note of me, but as a slender, unattractive woman, no one's paying me much attention.

I duck around the corner and jog toward the side of the palace, hopping the low wall that separates the palace garden from the street. Then I drop into a crouch and move more quietly. That's when it hits me, the horror. *What am I doing?* If someone finds me here, what possible reason could I give for my presence? What excuse could I make?

As if my thoughts summoned her, a woman wrapped in a very finely woven robe and fine hose steps through a door on a balcony and scowls. "Who are you, and why are you in the royal gardens?"

Ugh. The royal garden? I'm on the side where Alexander's rooms are located? I hate that a shiver of anticipation, of delight, runs through me. I'm so close, and yet, I'm also unequivocally caught. Except . . . I've never used this ability, but I don't see another way to avoid things becoming quite messy.

"You invited me," I say. "Remember?" I send a little *push* with the words, just as Aha taught me, and then I hold my breath.

A tiny wrinkle appears between the woman's eyebrows, and she inhales sharply. "Of course I did. I must have forgotten. What did you say your name was?"

"Artunis," I say. "You brought me here to loan me a robe and sandals. You said it was the least you could do after I did your family such a service." I push again, this time with a little more force.

"Right. How could I have forgotten?" She beams at me this time, and I realize she's quite lovely. "Come in, come in." She waves her hand toward the door she just exited, and I follow the path she indicated, around several potted trees and flowering shrubs. I've almost followed her inside when it occurs to me that I'll likely encounter even more people. The likelihood of meeting an alpha who might recognize what I've done will only increase, and Alexander, if he is inside, is likely not far from Bucephalus—a rare supra Reaper. He would most certainly notice if I tried to *convince* anyone else that they knew me. "Actually, I'd better come back later and borrow your robe another time."

The woman blinks.

"You're tired and need to go and lie down and take a long nap."

She presses her hand against her forehead. "Yes, I am quite exhausted. You're right." She no sooner ducks through the door and pulls it shut than my heart races in my chest and a surge of adrenaline shoots through my veins —as well as a huge, wildly deserved surge of guilt.

I should not have used that ability.

But that was a close call. I'm such an idiot. I can't just march in and look at Alexander, not without risking exposing myself. And there's no way Shu or Tefnut would allow us to petition for an audience, either. What was I thinking, hoping to simply bump into him? The last time was a colossal fluke. I shouldn't have come at all. I could have sent anyone at all to report back on how he treats the people he rules.

What is wrong with me?

I walk toward the front of the garden, prepared to hop the fence again and sprint back to the inn where Shu and Tefnut are probably either fuming or working out a plan to recover me even now, when I hear it.

A familiar laugh.

Brash. Confident. Eager.

My heart stops dead in my chest.

The skin on my hands becomes clammy, and that never happens.

My mouth goes dry.

I should keep going the way I was headed. I should march back to my brother and sister and make a half-hearted effort to confirm that Alexander will be a fine substitute for Dad's leadership. But . . . I can't turn away. I'm drawn to the laughter like a moth to an inferno. My feet move without even thinking about them, and suddenly I'm standing just beneath the source of the sound. There's only one problem.

The laughter's coming from three floors up.

I should turn around now that I know reaching it from here is impossible. I should head back the way I always intended to go. I didn't see him, but I heard him one last time, and that should be more than I had any right to expect. Why I've been curious about someone who was predestined to be my enemy, I have no idea. It makes no sense.

I eye the balcony one last time, and realize that I could Bind air and hop from one place to the next until I reach it. I could climb, hand over hand, until I'm standing on his balcony.

But if anyone sees me, that would be bad. Really bad.

They might even see my ascent as an attack—and then things could get really, really nasty.

If I were in the shape of a lion, I could more easily bend people to my story, and I would bound easily from one balcony to the next. I'd move so fast and so quietly that they'd hardly notice I was there. And I could crouch more readily as well. Move more softly and stealthily. And hear with even better acuity.

Without thinking about it any further, I shift, my body flowing easily into the form of a lioness, my limbs shifting to four paws, my face melting forward into a snout and sprouting whiskers.

It's the most magical part of my everyday life, the shift, and it's beautiful in a way I can't even describe, much less explain. And again, without dwelling on the why, I leap from the ground to the second floor balcony, and then from there, to the third, my claws digging into the heavy stone and anchoring me, and then I pelt over the rail and softly approach the room where I still hear Alexander speaking. He's softer now, gentler, and I stop, just before the open doorway.

"Are you sure?" The voice is female and it practically purrs. I should know. I've done a lot of purring in my lifetime.

A low rumble starts in my own throat, less purr and more warning, but I quickly cut it off. I freeze, unsure whether either of them noticed the noise. Or whether anyone else might be present—a third party I haven't yet heard or seen.

"I asked the kitchen to send a flagon of wine and a platter of food so I could review my plans for our next campaign. I didn't ask you to come at all, Thermusa. In fact, I thought I was quite adamant last week when you tried to . . ." He clears his throat. "Leave the food and go."

I can't help making a tiny whuffle of air as she leaves. Once the door inside his room closes soundly, I wait for one beat, then two. I hear him eating for a few moments, and then he crosses the room and there's a soft rustle, like the sound of someone climbing onto a bedroll. I decide to wait a bit longer, since I don't hear any sounds coming from the room at all, other than the soft noises of his breathing.

If I'm lucky, he could go to sleep and I could take a peek at the plans he mentioned. Then I'd be able to return to Dad with a real coup—knowledge of all his upcoming movements and goals. We could use them to chart our retreat, Dad's fake defeat, and then our disappearance.

Once he's been quiet for a long while, long enough I'm fairly certain he's asleep or preoccupied, I creep around the corner of the open door, eager to take one little look before escaping forever.

Only, when my head peeks around the corner, Alexander's not on his bed. He's standing in front of me, his eyes lit up, his hands spread wide. "Got you."

20

ANCIENT EGYPT

His bright, ice blue eyes light up, flooding the room with light, and he Binds me in place. I have a split second to decide what to do. Do I try to break the binding? Do I Bind him?

I could also compel him to release me, and he'd never even know he didn't choose to do that.

Dad and Shu and probably every single person I know and love would order me to do just that. Free myself and run. Escape while I can, and never look back. My very presence endangers the freedom I've longed for, the goal we've worked toward.

But something tugged me here, and that same curiosity, that same odd compulsion, combined with my ingrained discomfort in ordering anyone to do anything, keeps me from doing the one thing I ought to do . . . That's when I finally admit to myself what I've probably known all along. What Shu must have already realized.

I like Alexander. Like, *like*, like him.

Which is moronic. He's an adult. I am too, technically, but I've been so sheltered, so closely guarded, that I may as well be a child. If he discovered who I really was, if he had any idea . . . he'd laugh in my face. Probably right before running me through with his blade.

As if he can read my mind, he draws his sword, with a cautious gleam in his eyes.

I mean you no harm, I finally say.

"Oh good," he says. "The alpha in my bedchamber means me no harm. Usually friendly Renders sneak into my room and wait until I'm alone to pounce."

I didn't pounce. I can't quite keep the irritation out of my tone. *And I wasn't even the first female in your bedchamber when I arrived.*

This isn't a disaster. Yet. People in the know are aware that I'm a lioness shifter, but I'm hardly the only one around. He knows I'm an alpha now, since only alphas can project telepathically, but there's no way for him to know I'm supra . . . unless he summons his horse friend, Bucephalus. The prideful part of me wonders whether I could overcome him—I hear he's quite strong.

Alexander's mouth curls upward into a smile. "So you don't mean me harm." The light blinks out of his eyes, and I'm free to move. "Go ahead, then. Who are you?"

He does welcome women into his bedroom, then? It annoys me, badly, actually. I shouldn't be surprised—he's a grown man who rules an increasingly large empire. Of course women flock to him. It would be much stranger if he did turn them away. But I feel what I feel.

I'm not here to seduce you.

"That's a little confusing, and also disappointing." His eyes run over my leonine body, from the tip of my tail, which is lashing back and forth, to the whiskers on my face. "Judging by your animal form, I'll be *quite* disappointed when you shift." He frowns. "Is that an offensive stereo-type? Assuming that a gorgeous animal form makes for an excellent human one?" His lips twist in a sardonic way.

I hadn't planned to shift at all.

Alexander drops into a chair next to him as if he's suddenly bored. "Enough with the banter. I'm tired. What do you want, if it's not pleasure?"

If I were human, my face would be bright red. I want to tell him that I'm very interested in pleasure—but I'm pretty sure saying that is what Anat would call flirting, and I have no idea how to do it, much less where exactly it would lead. *I'm the daughter of a powerful warrior who has grown tired of fighting. I was sent to evaluate whether you're someone to whom he can surrender. Whether you're a ruler to be trusted.*

He straightens immediately. Perhaps that was too close to the truth—not that anyone would imagine Ra surrendering to anyone, ever. "My interest is again piqued. Bravo."

I wasn't supposed to break into your chambers. I heard your laugh and was, well, sort of drawn to it. I'm only in Gordion to observe how you lead, how you rule, and how the common people fare under your reign.

His smile is back in full force. "Drawn to it, you say?" He leans toward me, bracing his powerful forearms on his knees. "Now I'm desperate for you to shift. Surely you won't deny me."

Then you might know who I am and where I'm from? Sorry.

"If you shift here and now, assuming you don't threaten me, I vow that you'll have safe passage out of my palace and my lands. If I do puzzle out who your father is, I'll even promise not to tell him that we ever spoke."

How did he know I'd care about my actions being revealed? I pace in a small circle, thinking this through. I could leap from the balcony right now. He might Bind me, but I'm fairly sure that I could break it and leave. He might puzzle together enough to know who I am—but if I shift into my human form, I'll still be altered into the homely shape I crafted. If he's seen any portraits or renderings of me, he'll never suspect that I'm Sekhmet.

Except that his mother's an Assim. Who knows what he knows about our abilities?

I should force him to release me and forget this interchange ever happened. The one thing I've *never, ever* done, not in all my years of life, is wipe another person's mind. Aha insisted on showing me how, something that only alphas can do, but the idea is so repugnant to me that I've shied away from it uniformly. Could I do it now? To save my own hide?

In the end, it was probably really never a question of what I'd do. The same desire that brought me here still burns in my breast—to see . . . and be seen. By someone who matters. By someone I admire.

By someone I want. Someone I've dreamed of now, over and over.

So I shift.

His eyes widen.

He was expecting someone beautiful, clearly.

But he doesn't express disappointment or displeasure. He gestures for me to take the seat next to him. "I'm a man of my word. I won't reveal you to your father, or even to my advisors. I won't even press you for more information on where you're from. Instead, for the woman brash enough to scale the wall in order to break into my room, I'll grant you three questions. Ask me what I'd do, or what I've done, and I'll answer honestly."

"What do you want from me in exchange?" I ask.

His head tilts when I speak, his eyes intent upon mine. "Your voice . . . it's familiar. Have we met before?"

I swallow and shake my head.

"If I answer your three questions, you must tell me, truthfully, where you're from."

"Then you'll know just where to conserve your army and strike a deal." I exhale. "You're asking me to betray my own people."

"Not at all." He leans back in his chair, stretching his long, lean legs in front of me. "You said yourself that your father's weary of fighting. You were sent to see whether I'd be doing him a favor. Make the decision for yourself. If you think, based on my honest answers, that I'd be a poor substitute for him, then knowing your location won't harm your people. They can always meet me on the field of battle instead."

That much is true. It would simply give them the chance to sue for peace. But if he's totally honest with me, how can I lie to him by way of payment?

Since I can see men's hearts, I suppose I can judge for myself whether he's lying. And if he is, which I imagine is the case, I won't need to fret about lying back.

"Alright." I cross my arms. "Question number one. How do you improve the lives of the people you rule when you take control?"

"You ask that as though you think the life of the common person matters," he says.

I clench my fists at my side. "Of course it matters. The job of a sovereign isn't to be catered to—it's not to aggrandize oneself. It's to improve the lives of the nation, to afford better education, cleaner water, consistent nutrition. If you aren't doing those things, then I have my answer with just one question." I stand up.

He whistles. "Sit down, firebrand. You sound like a Fire Called, not a Render." He freezes then and looks up toward my face. "You remind me of someone, actually."

I relax my hands slowly, letting them rest at my side. "It may be a radical concept to some people, but being a sovereign shouldn't be about glory or power. It should be about peace and stability. It enrages me at times that such a concept is rare."

"I agree."

"You can't simply—" His words finally register. "You do?"

He shrugs.

I sit back down. "Then answer the question instead of provoking me."

His sideways grin reminds me of an incorrigible little boy. "When you're angry, your eyes light up like torches."

"You still haven't answered." I quirk one eyebrow. "Scrambling for time?"

"Not at all. The answer's a long one. As you probably know, no single nation effectively produces everything. Almost every country I've conquered has brought something new to the table. Education, political structure, goods, clothing, art. My answer won't be as simple as, 'I am fair and establish peace and prosperity.' That would be a pat answer you'd never fully believe or take comfort in."

I grunt.

"When I take over a new nation, time and weather and strategy permitting, I learn about the new place. I meet the people. I encourage my own men and women to form bonds there, and I do my best to integrate the new country with my other holdings. Macedonians, in general, have long believed themselves superior to everyone, including other Greek city-states. It's time for them to learn and acknowledge the good in the new areas we're encountering, and I hope to improve all my holdings by embracing the good and casting out the bad, much as I've cultivated olive orchards back home."

He's eloquent. I'll give him that much, but he's also passionate and convincing. I actually believe him. A quick perusal of his room supports his claim. Dishes from Crete. Linens from Thrace. His style of dress is clearly Persian. A sword of Rhodes. Sandals from Epirus. And books from all over.

"Fine. My second question. Why do you want to conquer the world?"

"How do you know that I do?"

"You need to stop asking me questions," I say. "That wasn't the deal. If you don't want to conquer the world, then why did you slice the Gordian knot in half?"

He freezes.

And I realize my mistake. I know he sliced it in half, but the story that circulated was that he solved it—that he finally untied it. It was the exact story I had hoped his mother would hear, but I kept waiting for Dad to ask me about the truth. An unknown princess from some far-flung land shouldn't—couldn't—know what really happened.

Alexander stands and grabs my wrists, pulling me upward. "What's your name?"

My voice is unbearably breathy and horribly unsteady. "It doesn't matter."

His eyes study mine. His breath is so close that it fans over my face, warm and not at all comforting. In fact, every nerve in my body throbs uncomfortably with his proximity, my heart thundering along in my chest. I almost feel ill—I should want to flee. But instead, I lean imperceptibly closer, craving this moment for some reason, desperate to prolong the exquisite pain of *feeling* too much.

"It matters to me."

My heart lurches.

I've always mattered. Ra, the man worshipped as a God in most of the world, is my father. My brother adores me. Our people love me. Dad's powerful Lieutenants follow and protect. But that was a given from the day I was born. Because of my parents. Not because of *me, of who I am.*

This—whatever this is—Alexander's attention, his wry smile, his focus, it has nothing to do with being Sekhmet, with being an Assimilator who can siphon without touching. Or a supra alpha. Or a Lifter. Or a Fire Called. He knows nothing about me, or even about Neser, for that matter. His interest is on my responses, my opinions, not my power or even my appearance.

"Why?"

He releases me, backing up until the backs of his legs bump into his seat. The Adam's apple in his throat shifts up and down slightly. "I'm not sure."

That makes two of us. "I'm not beautiful."

"Aren't you?" He lifts his chin. "Physical beauty is commonplace. It's boring."

"I'm certainly not physically beautiful."

"Your mind is what interests me."

But his touch burned.

His breath excited.

The tilt of his head sent my heart racing.

"Who's your father?" He narrows his eyes. "Don't tell me he's a wealthy glass merchant." His lips purse. "Neser."

He has figured out that I'm her, and that I lied to him by the knot.

"I don't know what you're talking about."

He steps toward me again, his broad shoulders and bulky frame blocking my view of the rest of the room when he's this close. Not that I could look anywhere but his face. "Don't lie. It's boring. I've put forth enough effort over the past months. And now you're here, so you felt something too." He reaches for me.

I don't stop him, his hands closing around my upper arms. I breathe deeply, inhaling the smell I never forgot.

"You told me your father was Fire Called and that you could Lift," he says. "But you're a Render. No wonder I couldn't find you."

I shrug. "I couldn't figure out why you tried."

"I'm not sure either." He licks his lips. "But I can't stop thinking about you—however you look—you pull me toward you, like a magnet. Like a panther to fresh meat. Like a beetle to the light."

"How attractive."

"Tell me you don't feel it." His eyes are intense, focused entirely on my face.

"I don't feel it."

He grins then, different than his smile, more mischievous, and then he laughs. The laugh that drew me to his room in the first place. It's bold, it's confident, it's totally free. The laugh of a conqueror. "You're such a bad liar."

"Only around you," I say. "And to my father," I admit. "He would be furious if he knew I was here."

He pulls me so close that his lips nearly hover over mine. "Then we won't tell him."

I swallow. "I'm not sure why I came. It was stupid. You could have killed me."

He shakes his head. "I knew the second I saw you."

"Now who's the liar?" I ask. "You saw a lion."

"I saw a gorgeous, tawny creature, and it captivated me from the first second. It didn't attack or growl or bare its teeth. It didn't try to force me into anything—it merely stared, all grace and confidence and curiosity."

"Why did you look for me before?"

"Who are you?" His head drops a hair. "Why were you in Gordion at all?"

"I'm your enemy," I say. "My father is your enemy. You should kill me."

"Why won't you show me your real face?" His hand releases my right arm and lifts up slowly, so slowly it's agony. It's torture.

And then his fingers brush my cheek, gently, so at odds with his other movements. Not bold or brash or confident. Unsure, nervous, and tentative. All the things Alexander never is.

"I'll give you Gordion," he whispers. "For a glance at your true visage."

"It's not stunning," I say. "I'm not gorgeous. I'm plain."

He laughs. "You're not plain now. You're so unattractive that you're striking in your unicity."

"I can't show myself," I say.

"I don't want to *conquer* the world," Alexander whispers. "My mother does, but I don't."

My heart stops. "What do *you* want?"

"I want to make her happy."

"Is she often happy?" My voice is soft—as soft as his.

"Never."

"So it's an impossible task."

He shrugs. "If I conquer all the world, maybe that will be enough."

"What about the toll? How many people will die to make her happy?"

He closes his eyes. "People fight without a conqueror threatening. They kill themselves for nothing at all. But as for my mother, a great wrong was done to her, and she never forgets it."

"What was it?" I almost don't want to hear. It's too close to what my mother believes of me.

"She fell deeply in love—she trusted someone with her whole heart, with the key to her soul, and he betrayed her."

Is he talking about Ra? That's not what I expected to hear. "What?"

Alexander releases me. "You know something of my mother?" His eyebrows rise. "What did you think the great wrong done to her was?"

I shake my head. "I have no idea."

"You do know something." He frowns. "My heart tells me to trust you. My head tells me you're lying and I should run. Or behead you. One or the other."

I laugh this time. "What if they're both right?"

"I should behead you and then trust you?" He smirks. "Or maybe trust you . . . and then behead you?"

"Perhaps a promise from me will help," I say. "I press my hand to my heart. I vow, on my real name, that I mean you no harm. I'm no threat to you."

"You said we were enemies."

I shake my head. "I said I'm *your* enemy. You're taking over the whole world, after all. But you're not mine. I wasn't lying when I said we might just surrender."

"Who? Tell me."

"I'm nothing more than a puzzle to you." I step backward. "Once you've solved it, you'll be bored."

"I doubt you could ever bore me."

"Nothing lasts forever. The only constant in the world is change."

"Heraclitus said that first, I believe. My teacher would love you," he says.

"Who's that?"

"Aristotle," he says. "And if you share your identity, I could arrange a meeting."

"Nice try," I say. "I have one more question."

"I've been honest," he says. "I hope you're prepared to honor your end of our bargain."

The thought of telling him where I'm from—there aren't *that* many lion shifters . . . and a father who's a warrior? He'd figure it out. But the idea of lying to him makes me sick to my stomach. Which means I need to ask him something he can't answer.

"Your entire life has been dedicated to doing what your mother wants." I move toward the balcony, preparing my escape if necessary. If he somehow answers this satisfactorily, and I'm stuck—I can't lie to him now—running may be my best option. As if I could ever run fast enough to escape Alexander and his many, many troops in a capital he's taken. "If you ever fell in love—" I almost cringe at the word, but I push through "—would that person always take second place to making your mother happy? Will she always govern your life?"

"Love?" Alexander laughs. "If my mother's taught me one thing, it's never to fall prey to *love*. It makes you weak. You can't win—it's a terrible vulnerability. For now, I serve my mother in my own way, improving the world while also fulfilling her desires. I can't tell whether it brings her joy, or whether it will, but I think I'm doing more good than evil."

"If you think love makes you weak, you don't know anything about it." I think about my father. About my brother. Even about my mother—and the pain she caused when she renounced me and left. Is that what he means? But if I hadn't cared for her, if I didn't care for Shu and for Dad, what would my life be? "Love is the one true source of strength in life." For the first time since we met, I actually feel sorry for him. "You're wrong if you think you don't love —you care for your subjects. I saw that on your face. You want the world to be better, richer, and fairer. That's love for humanity, if not any particular person. And to serve your mother as you do, you love her as well. Eschewing romantic love is like avoiding figs because they might not always be in season. You're the one who loses."

Alexander goes unnaturally still, eyeing me intently.

"What?"

"You're not going to tell me where you're from, are you?"

"Why do you say that?" My pulse pounds in my ears.

"You have a look—the same one you had back in Gordion. Like you're about to bolt. For someone who makes speeches on love, you sure frighten easily."

"Those speeches weren't about you," I say.

"Weren't they?" He's striding toward me then, his long legs eating up the tile. "Because for the first time you had me wondering whether I've been missing out." He doesn't pause. He doesn't falter. He never veers off course. Seconds later, his hands reach for my waist, yanking me closer, and I don't resist.

Why am I not pulling away?

I ought to press my palms flat against his chiseled chest and shove.

Or protest that I want nothing to do with him.

But that would be a lie of epic proportions.

For months, I've been dreaming every night that he would say my name. That he would press his mouth to mine. That our breaths would mix together until I couldn't differentiate one from the other.

I've thought about him while awake. I've imagined seeing him again over and over and over. And no matter how many times I thought about it, no matter how many times I sighed like a dreamy teenager over mention of Alexander the Great's search for a woman named Neser, none of those imaginings come close to the reality.

His sheer presence can't be imagined properly. His eyes consume me. His hands possess me. His lips mock me, and at the same time, draw me in, compelling my gaze.

This time, when his head lowers toward mine, I don't change the subject. I don't pull away. I don't even look away. Because ever since he said the word, my curiosity has eaten me alive. Pleasure. That's what I feel when I think about him. When I dream about him. Pleasure in a way I've never before experienced.

So I lean in.

And he crushes his mouth against mine. The world shifts underneath my feet. The sound of the ocean, a million miles away, roars in my ears. Heat invades my entire body, but I embrace it. I moan into his mouth, and his hands tighten around my hips, yanking me closer, pulling me into him in a way I've never experienced to any degree.

It's everything. It's passion. It's desire. It's possession.

But it's not enough. I want more. So much more.

My hands trail from his sides upward, my fingers tracing the line of his abdominal muscles, caressing each hard plane, splaying across the place where his chest meets his midsection, and shifting further upward. His breath catches and he freezes.

And terror rips through me.

He's the key to my salvation—he will allow Ra and me to leave. His rule will be just, it will be good, and we can step away with a good conscience.

But now that I've ascertained that truth . . . I'm not sure I want to disappear at all. My heart yearns for more of *this,* for more time with him. Only, there's no way for him to make his mother happy without destroying my father. My father would never accept me being with someone like Alexander. Someone explosive and dangerous and wild. Someone strong and possessive and insightful.

He's as opposite of Ptah as exists in the world.

What have I done?

I stumble backward, dangerously close to the edge of the balcony, pulling away from Alexander even though it's the last thing I want to do. I tap the tiniest bit of power from my ring and I release the façade covering my real face, deforming my actual body. "You held up your end." My words are soft, barely audible. "So here's me, holding up mine."

Alexander reaches for me, his mouth dangling open, his eyes soft but intense.

One more step backward and my calves make contact with the stone of the balcony railing. "My name is Sekhmet, and I am from Egypt. And I am your enemy. Forever."

It takes me less than a single second to shift into a lioness. But in that moment, Alexander lunges for me.

I pivot and leap from the balcony, Binding Air to bound

from place to place until I reach the ground. I pause for only a second and look back over my shoulder.

"There's no world in which you and I are enemies," Alexander shouts.

And then I lope away at a dead run. If I were human, I'd be sobbing right now. But I'm not, so it's all I can do to suppress the epic, heart-rending roar that's trying to claw its way free.

Apparently, even *exploding* one of their alphas isn't enough to dissuade them from the idea that I'm their savior.

"Perhaps the alphas will still be able to control their packs," I say. "Maybe all of this fear is unfounded."

Christopher closes his eyes and covers his face with a paw. *Not this many. The pack is usually one one-hundredth as large as it is right now. Too many to control.*

"But they're weaker, right?" I ask. "Maybe all the people who couldn't shift until this weird change took place will be easy to control."

They previously had much weaker animal forms, yes. Some could shift their ears only, or sprout a tail. But none of the females could shift at all, and now every single one of us is locked into the body of an animal.

"You have no idea what it means, though," I say. "For all we know, the moon won't even do what it usually does. Maybe there won't be a Hunt at all."

I hope you're right.

But he fears I'm not. Hope for the best and plan for the

worst; I imagine that's the sentiment. But our last attempt at planning resulted in the obliteration of a snake person.

Another petitioner is here. The hyena alpha's voice manages to be shrill, even though it's telepathic. I'm not sure how that works, but I wish I could tone adjust the receivers in my head or something. Every time he communicates, I cringe. Although, every time I hear from him, it's about someone else here to plead with me, like I'm just a selfish or fickle overlord, disinclined to put myself out by helping.

"Tell them there's nothing I can do."

They're begging to see you. Please.

I want to shout and cry and pull out all my hair. These people think I'm She Who Gathers, some prophesied savior, about whom no one really had any preconceived notions, until this weird thing happened, and now I'm the only one unaffected. Plus, I'm a lioness, just like She Who Gathers was supposed to be. But nothing I do helps, and every single time I agree to meet with another hopeful alpha, I'm forced to explain that over and over again.

"Fine," I say. "Fine." Because if I don't agree, I'm really a monster. All they want is for me to save the world. All they want is for me to have a magical solution. All they want is for me to try and force them to shift again, but this time, do it right.

They all want what I already have—the ability to be human. How can I deny them that? How can I refuse to listen and try and try again?

I sit down on the rather finely carved chair someone must have dragged into the room with their teeth. It was probably Christopher. How do I know? The bite marks on the front right leg would be obvious to anyone, but they're certainly recognizable to someone who's had to drag things with her teeth a few times now.

The kangaroo who bounds into the room has a sweet

face and gentle eyes. She hardly looks like an alpha, and from what they tell me, she wouldn't even have had powers a week and a half ago. But if she can project telepathically, she is an alpha now. I suppose they'd know.

"How can I help you?" Like I don't know.

I'm here to beg you to protect our family. Tiny ears poke out of the top of her pouch, and the most precious face ever follows.

This is a new low.

They're bringing babies to plead with me? Gather them. Restore their world to balance. They're reasonable requests, but I don't know how! "I want to help you. Of course I do."

Her eyes brighten. She hops a bit closer. *What a relief.*

My tone is hard. "But there's nothing I can do. I've tried, and it did not go well."

Try again. Try harder.

I imagine her beautiful baby, exploding into bits, and I shudder. "I'm not this person you all believe me to be. I don't even know my own name. I can't help you, even though I'm desperate to do it. Your best bet is to go home. Hide. Keep as far away from the Renders as you can and stay as hidden as you can."

It's like they're not hearing me.

We can't hide, not in this form. We can't lock doors. We can't mask our scent. We're helpless. We need you.

Fury mixes with helplessness and fear until it bursts inside of me. "Prey have hidden from predators since the beginning of time. Figure it out!"

The joey ducks down inside its mothers pouch, disappearing in the same way I wish I could disappear. The chittering of a bird outside the door, combined with the whine of some kind of dog, tells me there are more of them waiting to badger me. All day long I've been meeting with supplicants, Reapers begging me to do something. Renders asking me to keep them from harming others. They all want me to save them.

Save them.

Save them.

Save them.

I can't even save myself. Every time I close my eyes I see the snake exploding. *I* did that. I destroyed that alpha —when I was trying to help.

Without speaking another word, I close my eyes and imagine fur and claws and massive, bunching muscles, and I shift into a lioness, and I leap over the top of the kangaroo and push through the doorway, scattering what I think is a gathering of a dingo, a crow, a rabbit, and two porcupines, and picking up speed as I lope down the hallway. By the time I reach the freedom of the outdoors, I'm moving too quickly for anyone to stop me.

I startle a flock of geese, terrify a herd of deer, and upend a stack of baskets when I turn away from the rows of houses toward the open savannah that yawns ahead of me. Finally, finally, I'm free. Mice dart away as I pass. A large, dark bird wheels overhead, but it doesn't seem to be following me.

I still don't slow down.

I'm not sure how long I run.

My lungs burn.

My muscles ache.

My paw pads complain.

Only when the sun's rays cause my entire body to feel like it's being baked do I finally slow, moving toward the lee of a large boulder where I might be able to rest for a bit.

You can't run from them. You can't escape this task.

Now I'm the one startled. Christopher's cursed voice is in my head, still. I pivot on my back paw and round on him, my lips curled to reveal a mouth full of sharp teeth. *I can't save them. I can't do anything. You saw what I did yesterday when I tried.*

Christopher's mouth is open wide, and he's panting. His sides heave. I have no idea how he kept up with me. *The first time I tried to leap into a tree, I broke the branch and fell to the ground, landing on my face.*

I thought cats always landed on their feet.

Why would you think that? His internal voice is mocking. *I certainly haven't.*

I didn't land on my face or fall on the ground or break a branch, Christopher. I murdered someone.

Christopher sits, his face serene. *You did. I saw.* His eyes flutter and his nose scrunches. *I smelled. It was a very bad fall.*

You're saying I can't quit. Is that it?

His head bobs.

You're telling me there are more than millions. More than a billion shifters on Rra. You think me, one single person, who doesn't even know her own name or where she came from, can save them all? I want to bawl. *There's nothing I can do. You got a defective 'chosen one.'*

I don't believe that.

I roar then, louder and longer than I've ever roared before. The ground around me shudders and I pause. I crouch down lower, my eyes trained on the boulder next to us and the grass at my paws. Then I roar again. And again, the loudest, harshest roar I've ever made.

And the ground around us *wobbles.*

I blink.

That was new.

He saw it too.

But what does it mean?

It means that I don't understand what I can do or who I am, and that he's right. If I run, I'm a coward. Everyone who dies tonight will be my fault.

We don't even have time to rest—not if I'm going to

keep working to figure this out. I can't run though—not after my epic attempt at running away. So I start walking back, wincing whenever the edge of my sore paw hits something sharp. I could shift to human and back, erasing my aches and pains and the tiny scrapes on the bottoms of my paws, but Christopher can't. It feels like cheating to do what he should be able to and can't.

When we finally reach the pride headquarters again, there are four times as many supplicants gathered, but this time, I hear them all out. I shift and sit on the makeshift throne they've set up for me. They come in droves to beg me for aid. Birds, burrow creatures, jungle animals, forest dwellers, and savannah grazers. They all plead with me to try again.

Perhaps the problem was with whom you tried to help, Christopher says.

"I don't understand."

You tried to force a shift on a supra. He shrugs, his mane shifting slightly. *Maybe you should try to shift someone who isn't accustomed to resisting. Who welcomes the orders and commands from those above them.*

The image of that snake exploding . . . I suppress it. Dwelling on my failures won't help. "Alright. It's worth a try, I suppose." But how do we choose a volunteer? "You need to inform anyone I may experiment on of exactly what happened the last time I tried this."

He nods and disappears.

In the end, volunteers aren't the problem. Plenty of Reapers are eager to sacrifice themselves to save their families. At least loyalty and dedication aren't in short supply.

They're insisting that you select several of each animal type. They're hopeful that perhaps something that might not work with a reptile or amphibian might work for a mammal or an avian.

Oh good. I can explode dozens at once. My stomach turns, and the palms of my hands begin to sweat. I can't believe I'm going to try this again. "Maybe instead, I try to prevent Renders from attacking."

Christopher lifts one skeptical eyebrow. *You can't possibly prevent all the animals on Rra from attacking. There are too many.*

"Then obviously I can't force a shift on all of them, either." He must see how impossible it is for them to pin all their hopes on me.

That can be done over a period of time, whereas the urge to hunt will be persistent, all night long. It takes the combined efforts of all alphas to suppress it.

"Fine." I follow him to the clearing just outside where there are several dozen creatures gathered. A vulture. A hawk. A sparrow. A cardinal. A parrot. A zebra. A kangaroo. A frog. An iguana. A turtle. A rabbit. A platypus. A koala. A tiger. A ferret. A goat. A deer. A hippopotamus. A guinea pig. A sheep. A monkey. More creatures that I don't recognize and can't name.

"Maybe we should start with half this many," I say.

So that if you fail, you can flatly refuse to try again?

Or so that I don't massacre this many creatures in my unskilled, confused, terrifying efforts. "Because I'd like to mitigate the damage if I land on my face."

He purrs. Honest to goodness, purrs and rubs his head against my hand. *We know you're trying. That's enough.*

Of course they think that—because I haven't killed anyone yet. Last time, I tried as a human. This time, I shift back to a lioness, and I circle the gathered animals.

In this form, they're frightened. I can sense it clearly, so I send a command, my first. *You will not fear me.* It works. Their shoulders straighten. Their faces lift. They shift less and stare more as I circle.

Close your eyes and imagine your human forms. Imagine your fingers. Imagine your toes. Imagine your face, and the sun beating down on it. Imagine the joy you feel when you hug your mother, your father, or your friend. Now, shift. Shift!

But not a single one does.

I roar this time, *Shift!* The force of the command tears through me and crashes into them, forcing them to submit.

They don't shift, but they do writhe, painfully, their teeth bared, their beaks open, shrieking and whining and squawking and screaming and bleating. They contort their bodies in ways they shouldn't be able to do . . . until I release the command. Until I back away from them, my head down, my eyes closed. This was a mistake. Landing on my face? I'm shoving them to the ground with me, only it's not hurting them at all.

But Christopher won't let me quit. Neither will the volunteers. They insist I try again.

And again.

And again.

Until, when I close my eyes, all I see is agony, pain, fear, terror, and death.

On the fourth try, the sparrow dies. Its heart simply stops.

On the seventh, the hedgehog passes.

On the tenth, the zebra and the turtle collapse, never again to rise.

I stop counting after that. Attempts. Deaths. More volunteers come to replace those we lose and I keep trying. Roaring. Commanding. Circling. I try encouraging them. I try begging them. I try forcing them to surrender. I try encouraging them to push the shift themselves. I do it as a lion. I do it as a human. I do it while I'm shifting. It doesn't matter. No matter what we try, the result is always the same.

They die.

They die.

They all die.

"I can't," I say. "I can't do it anymore." Tears leak down my human cheeks. "Please don't make me."

Even Christopher doesn't argue this time.

I collapse into a boneless heap and cry for the poor people I killed. I cry for the people I can't save. I cry for the failure that I am, and for the savior they deserve. I cry for the fall after fall after fall on my face that feels utterly pointless and totally unfair.

"Why is this happening?"

Christopher, through it all, remains stoic by my side. *I don't know.*

"What was the timeline on all this?" How have I not asked this before?

Weeks ago, a few who could not shift began to shift. And then two weeks ago, several in our pride couldn't shift back to human. And as I already explained, several days ago, all our members, female, male, everyone shifted, and none of us could shift back. That was a single day before you arrived.

Why? Why did I simply show up? Why don't I recall anything before that? Who am I? "No one recognizes me? Has anyone said anything else?"

Christopher shakes his head slowly, despairingly.

"Is there a way to communicate with the entire population of Rra? How did you disseminate the message that I'm here? How did people find out that I had even been located?"

Alphas can send messages to other alphas from some distance, he says. *We can communicate within a few hours' radius in that way. It still takes substantial time for news to travel —I have never seen the vast majority of the surface of Rra.*

Which means entire swaths of the population may have no idea what's going on. The total number of people with whom we've communicated may represent only a fraction of the population. And even if I work up a strategy to mitigate the death toll, it's too late to enact it.

Which means I've already failed.

I'm not She Who Gathers.

I'm She Who Ruins.

The futility of it all overwhelms me, and I roar. Not at anything in particular, not at anyone specifically, just at the world around us. It thrust me here, gave people hope that I could help, and then gave me no knowledge with which to do it. I think about the injuries I've felt each morning when I woke. "Every day, I've had bloody arms—but when I shift, the injury is healed. Is that common?"

No.

I wish there had been a way to shift without healing— so I could see what kind of injury it was. "Have I been attacked at all? While I slept, I mean?"

Never.

Could it be something else? Could it have been a message of some kind? Maybe I'm supposed to sacrifice myself. Maybe the injury itself *was* the message. The only way to fix things is my blood. A lot of it.

All of it.

That makes sense, somehow. Perhaps my ability is inversely related to their inability. Maybe if I kill myself . . . it will free the others. "What if . . . "

Christopher's ears swivel toward me.

"What if I was always meant to be a sacrifice? What if we've been doing this all wrong? Perhaps my very existence is what prevents you from shifting?"

A rumble deep in his chest surprises me.

"No?"

None shall harm you.

"That's just the protective alpha in you coming out."

He growls, louder this time. *It feels* wrong.

Why won't he even consider it? He'll let me kill dozens of them trying to solve the problem, yet he won't even consider that *I* might be the problem. The timing of my arrival, my lack of any memories, they're all suspect. They all point toward this being my fault, don't they? Is it possible that the deep, abiding belief that I'm the solution that Christopher seems to have is there for a reason? Could their desire to protect me and everyone else be dooming them all?

How could I even go about sacrificing myself, if that's what it takes?

If there were enough Renders in one place . . . and if I didn't use my supra ability to stop them from attacking me, that might work. I think I can keep it in check. My self-loathing is nearly as overpowering as my own fear. "I need to be there—in the midst of the largest group of Renders we can find tonight."

Christopher studies me slowly, calmly. *You will not harm yourself.*

"Of course not," I lie.

Renders do not attack others of their kind.

Unless provoked. "I know that."

And this is my last idea. The only thing I haven't already tried and failed to do. My only hope of saving all these people who think I'm supposed to protect them.

He stares at me for a long moment before he nods. I follow him as the sun sets in the sky. I shift a mile or two down the road, and as the moon begins to rise, I'm loping behind him. Other predators fall in alongside us. Wolves. Caracals. Panthers. Tigers. Bobcats. Hawks swoop overhead, as restless as the lot of us.

A rumble in my stomach makes me nervous. I wonder how many of the Renders around me are also starving. And then it hits me—a wave of desperation and anger. My heart thunders in my chest. My claws dig into the ground underneath my feet, and my mouth floods with saliva.

I must hunt.

I'm dying to sink my teeth into something.

My stomach clenches and I accelerate.

So does every animal near me. The wolves veer off,

heading toward the forest to my left. The big cats head for the rocky mountains to our right. Christopher and his pack continue onward, and I move with them, forgetting my purpose, forgetting my plan entirely. Nothing remains in my brain other than my desperation to *feed*. My urge to *destroy*. A gripping need to *rend*.

A scent up ahead floods my nostrils and everything amplifies beyond what I previously fathomed. My muscles bunch and contract, my claws retract and extend. My lips curl away from my teeth and I *roar*. The pack surges forward with me. *Gazelle*.

They follow my lead perfectly, as we near the herd up ahead. Our burst of speed put them right in our sights, and a large one near the back stumbles, its sharply pointed horns dipping, its black tail flicking upward, its white haunches scrambling in the scree. I lunge without thought, my teeth sinking into its back leg as my paws sink into the thick flesh of its flank.

Blood floods my mouth, hot and fresh, and the gazelle struggles. Its hooves scratch and thud against me, and I release it, only to pounce forward and sink my teeth into its throat and *tear*. It's caught between glorious and terribly pathetic, the struggle of the pitiful creature against the apex predator on Rra—it never had a chance. But as it dies, its eyes shift somehow, widening and changing shape, and it *transforms*.

Into a human.

I scramble backward, looking around in horror, as all around me, slaughtered gazelle *shift* into their human forms. Something deep down inside awakens, and horror wells up from places I didn't know it existed. The roar that tears its way free from me in that moment is darker, stronger, and more desperate than any I've ever voiced in my life.

Every single creature in the clearing freezes, bows their

heads, and cries out at once. Horror. Terror. Anger. Fear. They're all the same—a desperate feeling borne of failure, of lack of control, of fury at the futility of it all. Of the knowledge of our own mortality.

The rage inside of me continues to pour outward, and my roar amplifies, until the ground beneath our feet and the sky above shatters from the vibrations. Every single animal, every single human, they *vibrate* and *shake*, filaments that compose their entire forms shuddering and writhing uncontrollably.

I turn to my left, my eyes falling on Christopher, so familiar, and yet a complete stranger. The filaments that compose his body settle back into place, making sense once more. His mane shrinks, his claws and paws flex and stretch, fingers emerging, and his eyes are thrown wide, his body bowed outward as the change is forced upon him.

But no one is attacking.

No one is consuming.

There's not a single Reaper being chewed or chomped or eaten.

In fact, many of the prone beasts are re-shifting into their human forms, their damaged flesh reforming and flowing into a perfect shape—devoid of the damage we just caused. Christopher stands up, sobs wracking his entire body, and walks toward me, arms outstretched. "You did it," he says.

But what exactly did I do? I wish I knew.

I hope it's enough.

The dead body at my feet, its throat ripped out by my teeth, seems like pretty solid evidence to the contrary.

❧ 22 ❧

EARTH

"You survived the hunt." Jesse rubs his eyes blearily, the TV reporter shrieking in the background.

"You need sleep." I shove up in the bed, stretching my neck side to side. I expect to see blood all over my hands. I should be covered in it. I was, back on Rra.

"What happened?" Jesse presses, unwilling to acknowledge that he's not strong enough to be watching over me like this.

"Why aren't you sleeping right now?" I place my hand over his where it's resting on the edge of my bed.

"Kahn and John were fighting about who got to stay with you." Jesse sighs. "I kicked them out, and that felt good." His half smile lifts my spirits in a way nothing else can. In a way I probably don't deserve.

I choke on a sob and Jesse stands up and slides onto the bed next to me. His arm wraps around my shoulders. "What's going on?"

"I killed someone," I say. "Actually." I think about all the Reapers I tried to force into shifting. "I killed a lot of people." Tears stream freely down my face. Sobs wrack my body, but I manage to describe what happened and how. "But I did it, in the end. After that gazelle turned into—" I cut off. I can't say it again. "Afterward, I roared, and it was unlike anything before. I *saw* the filaments that made up Rra, and I forced them all to shift to human."

"The seven *billion* people there?" Jesse asks. "You forced them all?"

I shrug. "I guess there's no way to know, but I think so. It was like I reached out and grabbed the entire fabric of the prison and shook it out like a tablecloth, flipping it over to the other side."

"Like flipping and straightening a comforter?" Jesse's eyes sparkle.

"I guess," I say. "Or like flipping a pancake."

"Seven billion pancakes."

I shudder then, the enormity of the night washing over me. "And I had another memory. I really, really liked Alexander back in my past life, as Sekhmet. Or, Apophis—Kahn. He was there then, like you're there." I shake my head. "It's so strange, knowing him as all these different people. He's different in Egypt than he was on Terra and than he is now, but in some ways he's the same."

"You call him Apophis? Or Alexander?" he asks.

"When I'm talking to Dad—er, to Ra, I call him Apophis. That's how he knows him. But to me, when I'm there, he's Alexander. I wonder if that's how I justify my feelings—like telling myself that Dad doesn't really know him. That he's different than Ra thinks he is." I shrug. "But none of it matters. It doesn't change how I feel here."

"You're sure?"

I drop my face in my hands. "I'm not sure of anything. On Rra, I don't even know my own name."

"But the world survived the hunt. The news isn't even reporting anything terrible, like thousands and thousands dying at once. Seems like, however ghastly it may have been for you, you were in the right place at the right time and that moon rose near you before anywhere else."

I hadn't even thought of the moon—when it would rise, when it would cause the hunt to take hold. Or maybe the moon doesn't actually control it. I know so very little about the world I'm supposed to be able to control. "Remind me. The next time we're reborn," I say, "I want it to come with a manual."

Jesse laughs, and I lean against his shoulder.

"Remember when we thought things sucked because our parents died and Aunt Trina didn't love us?" I look up at him.

This time, he doesn't laugh. "Don't do that," he says.

"What?"

"The pain we feel, the difficulty everyone experiences, it's no less real because we've now endured worse. The child who cuts her finger, the boy whose parents die." He swallows. "Both things are hard for them when they endure them. Our trials are hard for us, but they aren't greater or lesser because other people have experienced something else. Comparing your past to your present, or comparing our lives to others', either way, comparison like that is the thief of joy."

"You think so?" My brow furrows. "What brings us joy, then?"

"Living life as well as we can in the time we have to live it." His arm loosens where it's clasping my shoulder.

"No." I straighten, and he leans back against the wall. "I know where this is going." I examine him closely. His skin is pale. His eyes are dull.

He's fading. How could I have missed that?

"How bad is it?" I cast around for the collar we found—the one I refueled when I killed those Followers of Isis. "Your time isn't up, not yet. Not by a long shot."

His smile is half-hearted. "My time has been up for a

long time, Alora." A tear rolls down his cheek. "I've been grateful for the time you stole. I'd be lying if I said I wasn't."

I shake my head. "No. No!" I scramble off the bed and stand up, realizing that I'm in the same dirty clothes I was wearing when I went down to face Isis. "Your time isn't gone." I shake my head again. "It was *stolen* from us. They had no right." My voice cracks and tears well in my eyes. "Devlin killed you, murdered you."

The image of a gazelle, broken and bloody, shifting to a person, a snake exploding, a sparrow's heart giving out, hundreds of people withering and collapsing in the street, all of the misery we've endured crowds into my mind. How many people's lives have I stolen since Jesse's was taken?

How many will I continue to take?

"You know it's true." Jesse coughs, his entire body shaking. "My soul isn't quite whole, Alora, and it's not something that can be fixed, not even by you."

"Ra can fix it." I imagine collapsing Rra, and then Ā. I can do that if it's what it takes. I will do it. It might even have been the right thing to do all along.

It might have always been inevitable.

"Our father can save you. Ra can do anything."

Jesse's smile is sad, so desperately sad. "He's not our father. You know that much."

Do I? The more I recall, the more memories that resurface, the more confusing it becomes. And that's when the thought hits me. Jesse may be missing his Earth life, those shards of his soul, but he's already the reborn version of Shu. His soul existed in Egypt with me, and those memories are coming back piece by piece. If they could come back to him too—could they be enough? Could his soul be restored by what he lost in Egypt? Surely the combined shards of two lifetimes' worth of memory can stitch him back together. Surely there's some kind of magic that can repair what was stolen from me.

"You can't keep dumping the life out of others and pouring it into me forever," Jesse says. "We both know it. And the more you pretend, the more danger you're in of losing who you really are and becoming something neither of us want."

A pulse of energy in the corner beckons me. I back toward it, turning at the last moment from my brother and snatching the golden collar he clearly tossed aside when he laid me in the bed to begin with. "I have this," I say. "It's not stolen from anyone—it was taken to spare the innocent people they threatened. You can't possibly argue with me using this." And with as many lives as I took, this could sustain him for a year or more.

Jesse's expression is grim. "And when that's gone?"

"Look, I just woke from a horrible nightmare in which there was no possible solution—until there was."

My big brother stares at me for a moment, his resolve wavering. I think about the years we've shared, and the time we've been forced apart—all that time on Terra we missed.

"I'm not saying you're wrong. I know that I can't be stealing the life force from people right and left. It's not sustainable, and clearly that would be evil. Maybe not the first time, or the second, especially if their death served a greater good, but it's a slippery slope. I get it."

"Do you?" Jesse swings off the bed, stumbling a bit as he hits the ground. But he rights himself and walks toward me, feebly, as if he's eighty-five, not almost twenty. I hate this—watching how weak he grows, day by day.

"I do, I swear."

He frowns. "As long as you understand."

I nod vehemently. "I do. I really, really do." I slowly lift the collar until it's in place around my throat, the red stones winking at me. "And I've learned, from my memories, how to better use the magic, how not to waste it. I swear, this reserve will last a long time."

"Fine." Jesse's smile is genuine, warm even.

I beam back at him, and then I reach for the stones.

And in that very same second, in a bright flash, something drains them, pulling out every last speck of energy until they're solid black. Black as death.

"No!" My shout is loud, angry, and desperate. "What—who?"

Jesse's smile twists into a forced, broken laugh. "You know who."

Ra.

Rage floods every part of my body. Every speck of my soul. Fury and despair and helplessness battle inside of me. Why would Ra offer me the use of these reservoirs, only to drain them the second I'm about to use them? Not once, but twice?

Why?

Jesse coughs again, this time sinking to the ground, hunched over.

"This isn't the end," I say. "There are plenty of awful people out there who need to be dispatched."

Jesse shakes his head. "You said you understood."

I drop to the floor. "You're the one who doesn't understand." I can't help the bawling now, my vision blurring with tears, my hands finding his. "I can't do this without you. I can't do any of it. I can't." I shake my head. "If you die, I swear, I will burn the world to the ground and I won't even regret it."

He just keeps shaking his head. "You will not. You're so much stronger than you know. You'll honor my memory as you honor the memory of our mother. You'll live as you've always lived—bravely, fiercely, championing those who can't protect themselves."

Jesse has always seen bravery and goodness in me that isn't there. "You're my heart. You're my good. I can't lose you. Think of the harm that will be caused by your absence."

I ignore a knock at the door.

"Alora." Jesse's arms are weak when they wrap around me. "Don't ruin our remaining time."

Our remaining time?

His words are a slap in the face. Cold water over my head. A stab in my stomach.

The knocking returns, much louder and much more insistent. "What!?"

"Uh, it's John." He clears his throat. "I'm sorry to interrupt, but there's an army gathering—much larger than the last one. They're about four blocks away, thousands strong, and they all seem to be elementals or telekinetics."

Isis hasn't given up.

I should be devastated. I should be concerned about the people they might kill. I should be terrified at what I may need to do, but I'm not. A smile spreads across my face. Because I'll be justified in siphoning power—someone will do something terrible. Someone will force my hand . . . and I'll save Jesse. I don't even need these stupid siphons. So what if Ra has betrayed me? So what if he tricked me so I'd funnel energy to him?

I don't need him.

I don't need anyone.

Only Jesse, and I can save him myself.

I'm a lion, not a lamb.

I stand up.

"I won't accept it," Jesse whispers. "I'll never forgive you. It's time for you to stop focusing on saving me, and direct your attention toward fulfilling your purpose. I'm causing you to head down the wrong path. You're making decisions for the wrong reasons and you know it as well as I do. I can see it."

I Lift Jesse and set him in the bed I recently vacated. "Sleep. I'll be back soon." I press a kiss to his forehead.

He's too weak to argue or protest. He's not quite unconscious yet, but he's close.

I open the door, and I step through.

John and Kahn are both standing on the other side, glaring at one another. I look first at Kahn, his brilliantly golden hair. His sharp cheekbones, his icy blue eyes. The confidence is the same. His bold insistence on what is right hasn't changed either.

But when I glance at John, he's just as gorgeous. Dark hair, flashing amber eyes, and a scruff covered jaw that could practically cut glass. Kahn's bulkier, his muscles more obvious, but John's lean strength is just as compelling.

"What do you think I should do?"

"Talk to your father before you approach them," Kahn says. "He clearly didn't mean to attack any innocents, and indeed, it seemed like he'd negotiated to accompany those soldiers who attacked. I think he wanted to talk to you. I think he's still on your side."

Of course he thinks that. "What do you say?" I meet John's gaze.

"I say roll over them. Don't wait, don't hesitate, and don't feel guilty. You're doing the very best you can do, and you've done it in every circumstance. They've attacked. They've ignored. They've damaged. You don't owe Duncan anything—you don't owe anyone anything. I have no idea how you did it, but you kept the shifters from tearing one another apart last night. And here you are, still trying to do the right thing. Stop listening to what everyone else thinks and twisting yourself into an ethical pretzel and just *act*." He shrugs. "Your majesty." His lips curl up into a half smile.

"I'm not majestic in any form," I say.

"I find lions quite majestic." John winks. "But if you insist, I'll call you your very esteemed and amazing Assimilator instead." He drops his voice. "What you did earlier was straight up amazing. That's why they're attacking. It's not because they need to prevent the threat you pose. That's over. You saved them. Now the truth is clear: they're attacking because they're scared of you. They can't allow a power shift in which they won't be ruling the world, and you're a seismic shift. No, you're a freaking tsunami."

Kahn doesn't argue. He doesn't say another word. But his eyes flash angrily and he presses his lips together as if he's sorely tempted.

"They're still a few blocks away, assembling?" I lift my eyebrows.

John nods.

"I have time to stop by Duncan's cell. Send Mehen and Am-Heh."

Neither of them argue. John marches off to convey my orders, and I head for the stairs.

"I assume you know where Duncan's being held?"

Kahn nods.

"What do you think he'll be able to tell me?" I sigh. "I'm sick of the fighting. I'm sick of people trying to kill me. I'm sick of the world being in jeopardy."

He laughs then. "I imagine you are. What happened on Rra?"

I tell him, as quickly and as unemotionally as possible. I still choke up when I describe my efforts to force shifts, and again when I describe the gazelle, but it's a much smoother explanation than poor Jesse had to endure.

"That sounds awful. I'm sorry, but no one could fault you for failing to do any of that before. It's an impossible task you were set—making decisions blind."

His mouth is still moving, and he's saying all the right things, but I keep getting distracted. His haircut and style are different. His clothes aren't the same, but his voice, his eyes, his jaw, it's all the same.

"Are you alright?" He peers at me as though he's worried for my health.

"I'm fine."

"What else is going on? You're in a daze."

I can't talk to him about my memories from before. I just can't. Not right now. "Jesse's fading again." It's easy to convince him that's my issue, since I can barely get words out. "He wants me to let him go. He says I can't keep pouring energy into him forever." As I say the words, I realize that focusing on my connection to Kahn was just masking what really matters, what's really tearing me up —Jesse.

"You've got a fully charged battery or two though, surely, after what happened yesterday."

I look at my feet as we walk down what feels like an interminable hallway. "I did."

"What does that mean?" He ducks his head a bit, trying to catch my eye again. "Did you already use all of that and it wasn't enough?"

For some reason, I can't bring myself to tell him that Ra must have taken it. He doesn't need any more reasons to hate him, and the betrayal feels . . . sore somehow. Like anything he says would only upset me more. How could my own father have tricked me? How could he have told me to use his batteries, just so I'd power them up and he could steal from me? Is he taking advantage of the fact that I'll keep recharging it for Jesse? Did he really set me up so I'd keep sending him power?

I feel taken advantage of.

Duped.

It's not a good feeling. My frustration and betrayal battles with my deep-seated belief that he loves me, that he'd do anything for me. I was even starting to believe he didn't belong in Ā, that somehow his incarceration must have been a mistake.

How stupid would I feel if I'd already freed him?

Kahn finally stops in front of a solid wooden door. "This is the holding cell. They won't let me come and go, since John told them I'm with Isis."

"Are you?" I ask.

He looks confused.

"With Isis, I mean."

His lips compress.

"I thought you were with me." My words sound more pathetic than I intended.

His hand takes mine gently. "I am. With you, I mean, of course I am. But I happen to think that the real principles of Isis, not what the leaders have contorted it into, are still correct. I think the formation of Terra in the first place was to prevent any one person from being so powerful they could completely dominate another."

This sounds nothing like my Alexander.

My Alexander? Have I lost my mind? Kahn sounds nothing like the Alexander the Great from my memories. That's what I mean. He sounds like he stands for something completely opposite of what Alexander wanted. He desired control of everyone to keep them safe.

Although, now that I consider it—is that really so different? If he can't rule everyone forever, what better way to create peace and safety than to declaw the cats, so to speak. If people don't have powers, they can't inflict nearly the same damage.

It still rubs me dramatically the wrong way that all the women sacrificed their powers, leaving them helpless on Terra and on Earth, but that's still not something that makes sense. Maybe someday the explanation for that will surface.

"I'll see if they'll let me in."

Kahn snorts. "Your Royal Divine Majesty? You can do whatever you want, I'm quite sure."

But the men whose faces appear when I knock aren't impressed. They aren't in awe or full of respect.

No, they nearly crap their pants trying to get out of my way.

Looks like word has spread. The Harvester of Souls is here. At least they let me in without a fight, and when he stands, Duncan doesn't look terrified. He looks . . . expectant. Like he knew I'd come.

"You're being fed?" I ask.

He nods.

"Isis is assembling again not far from here. Looks like your dear friends weren't the only ones intent on killing me."

"You can't let Rra collapse," Duncan says. "The cost to create the prison must be tied to the number of people it contains. Think about it. You freed a few hundred thousand, and then a few million, but Rra." He inhales slowly and shakes his head as if warning me. "It's *everyone else.*"

"That's a very astute observation," I say. "And I'd counter with this. All those are people who can die, easily, if I can't evacuate the sinking ship fast enough. Have you thought of that?"

"Why haven't you already done it, then?" he asks.

I don't want to admit that I can't—that I don't have the knowledge there of who I am, and my method for breaking through to myself the last two times isn't working. "I'm not actually the harbinger of doom," I say. "Rra was broken before I ever showed up there. I didn't cause them to lock into animal forms."

"You collapsed Terra and then Erra. It's unfair for you now to claim that you had nothing to do with the total collapse of the network."

"Terra was already unraveling when I brought people over," I say.

"Was it?" Duncan asks. "Before you ripped Jesse's soul free and dragged him here?"

I freeze.

"You started the entire collapse, and you're standing in the same building as the solution."

"What are you saying?" My hands tremble at my sides.

"You think it's a matter of feeding him some energy here and there," Duncan says. "But what if Jesse's very existence is *causing* the prison world you created to break down? What if your selfishness—your refusal to let reality, to let balance exist—is causing it? Have you considered that you might be the reason all those people are at risk in the first place? Let Jesse go, and turn your attention to rebuilding the prison, and you'll be on the right path to undoing the damage you've done."

He's wrong. John's father—Devlin—said his wife Wasted on Earth. He said the prison was already crumbling.

But he also killed Jesse.

He's wanted it to come down all along. Would he have lied to hurry it along? Even he was shocked—terrified, really—when he saw Jesse alive. He was horrified that I'd brought him to Earth.

It's awfully close to my thoughts on Rra, thoughts that weren't clouded by Jesse or what I'd lost. Thoughts that weren't confused by my own desires. Jesse just told me that I'm not able to think straight because of him. Is he right? Is Duncan?

No.

This is insane.

I haven't caused any of these problems. I've done all that I could to fix things. Kahn was just telling me that. I turn toward where he's standing in the doorway, his eyes wide, his hands balled up so tightly at his sides that his knuckles are white.

"Do you believe him?" I ask.

His eyes are tortured, but he doesn't look away. He shrugs.

I can barely form the words. "You think I should let Jesse die?"

"I don't want to lose him." His voice is barely a whisper, too. "I love your brother, but he's asking for the same thing himself."

I can't listen to anymore. I can't think, not with everyone expressing so much certainty about things they know nothing about. I shove past Kahn and sprint down the hall, running anywhere, just so that I can escape. I finally almost knock someone over, someone whose arms are spread wide, someone whose concerned look nearly shreds the last of my defenses.

John.

"What's wrong?" He opens his arms up and I step into them, letting him wrap me up.

Letting my troubles evacuate my body as tearful sobs against his chest. "Duncan and Kahn think I did this. They say that Terra's collapsing because of me—because I brought Jesse to Earth after he'd already died."

His mouth drops open, and my heart stops dead in my chest. It feels as if my entire world rests on the next words spoken. If John agrees with them, I don't know what I'll do. I'll shatter, and I might take this entire building with me.

"That's the most ridiculous, delusional thing I've ever heard." He whistles. "And I'll be damned if it doesn't serve their narrative perfectly. I just can't believe Duncan would be that cold about his own son."

"You don't think it's true?" I ask, desperate for him to tell me it's all absurd.

John grabs me and pulls me against him, his breath

against my ear. "Not even a little bit. Did you pulling him home cause you to be reborn? Did he cause you to start having dreams of Terra? Is he the reason you're Fire Called? And a Render? Did he give you the powers of assimilation?" His laugh is bitter. "They're clutching at straws, spouting any kind of fairy tale that they can conjure up to keep their world view in place, but it's small, Alora. So small. Don't let them force you down that path. That way leads to madness. Can you imagine if you listened, if you let Jesse die, and then, once Ra is free, if he told you that he could have saved him?" He clears his throat. "You'd never be able to forgive yourself. Never."

"I may never be able to recover from everything I've seen and done as it is. If I had normal dreams, I'm sure they'd be riddled with nightmares—I've killed so many people. I've burned, and siphoned, and *exploded*—"

His arms tighten around me. "You've done what you had to do. You're the brightest soul I know. The kindest, the strongest, and the most compassionate." He shifts so that my face can turn, so that my gaze meets his. "You are *epic,* Alora. A shining, blazing, stunning shooting star. No one can comprehend what you've endured, or what you will yet do. Don't let them douse your flame."

Spoken like a true Fire Called.

But it's also what I wanted to hear, so I let him convince me that he's right. And I march out the door with him, prepared to face the army gathering against us.

But.

More and more, I'm not sure there's any way out of this for me that doesn't involve freeing Ra—the person I'm pretty sure was the reason the entire prison was created in the first place.

And that scares me far less than it probably should.

23

EARTH

The second we reach the front door of the red brick building, Am-Heh and Mehen fall into place on either side of us. "You shouldn't approach the army yourself," Am-Heh says. "Send me and I'll end this before it starts."

And how many buildings will be melted? How many innocents burned? "I appreciate your support," I say, more sincerely than I expected. "But this situation calls for a surgical knife, not a hatchet."

Am-Heh's brow furrows. "A what?"

That might not have translated as well as I'd hoped. "I don't want to burn everything down."

"You don't even deserve to be Fire Called." He smirks. "But seriously, there are thousands of men out there, according to the Amun leader. He says they—"

"You can keep me from being hit with bullets?" I stare at Mehen. "Right?"

"The small exploding things?" He waits for confirmation.

I nod.

"Yes. I can keep those away from you. I can't do the same for all your men, though."

"We aren't taking any," I say.

Mehen and Am-Heh smile. "Ra's daughter is ready to play." Am-Heh's smile is so broad that I can see two gold molars in the back of his mouth. I had no idea they did such sophisticated dental work back then.

"You have gold crowns?"

Am-Heh looks at Mehen and they both look confused.

"Your teeth are gold," I say.

"Ah. Yes. It was a reward from Ra," he says. "A badge of success. Each time we conquered a nation for him." He leans closer. "Mehen doesn't have a single one."

"I thought it was a replacement for a rotten tooth," I say. "That's what they're for now."

Am-Heh frowns. "Ra would simply repair that problem," he says. "The gold was reserved for a badge of honor."

Of course it was. "Alright, look, here's the plan. We're going to sneak around to the front of the army. Me, you, and Mehen."

"I'm going too," John says.

"Can you understand us?" I glance at the men standing behind him and lining the halls.

He shakes his head. "But I know you well enough to know you won't risk anyone else. And I'm telling you that Kahn may not have your back. Your dad may be a moron, but I won't let you go alone with just Dumb and Dumber here to watch you. They may be able to Lift and flame circles around me, but they know nothing of the world today, and they know nothing of technology."

I smile.

John's whole face relaxes. "Oh, good. I was worried I'd have to argue with you."

"We're coming too," Martin says.

Before I can protest, Rosalinde puts her hands on her hips. "You needed us last time."

I don't deserve them—and I don't want to put them at risk.

"It's non-negotiable," Thomas says. "You can leave Oliver and Roland here, but the three of us are your family, and we're coming."

When my eyes well with tears this time, it's not from sorrow. It's because I'm not alone. I've been so focused on saving Jesse that I forgot that he's not the only person who cares about me.

"I'd like to come too," Henry says, from a half dozen people away. "They shoved me into this stupid uniform, and they're insisting that I answer to someone named James, but I want to help."

"That's fine," I say, "but I don't have much time."

"Jesse's weak again," Martin says.

I don't argue.

"We'd better hurry, then," John says. "Are you all ready to go?"

They are, and it takes quite a few hardline orders to dissuade the others from following us, but I won't win by trotting out more and more people whom I'll need to protect. Finally, we break away. John, Mehen, Am-Heh, Henry, and my circle of three Healers.

We don't have to travel very far, Mehen Lifting and Am-Heh flaming anyone who looks threatening, before we round the corner on Rosoman Street, pass a pizza place, and the street opens up. Soldiers flood the walkways, the park ahead, and the trail behind into every passable walkway, street, and park area. My heart skips a beat at the hatred in each face, in every glaring eye. At the anger in the line of each jaw, and the force with which they grip guns and hold knives and even heft the occasional sword.

"Do you really mean to kill me, then?" I ask no one in particular.

No one comes forward to negotiate. No one says anything at all. Someone shouts, and shots begin to fire. Bullets rain down, but they stop at an invisible wall a few dozen feet in front of us, falling to the ground, exploding in mid-air, and some of them even stopping in place. Henry's and Mehen's eyes flood the entire area.

And I wait.

After a few moments, the men with guns who are in range have run through their ammunition, and they stop. Either to reload, or . . .

Another row of soldiers rush forward, their weapons raised.

I've had about enough.

I Lift them all up in the air. "I don't want to harm you. I don't want to harm anyone. I only ask that you leave me alone while I try and repair the damage to Rra. I'm trying to figure out the best course with which to proceed, but threatening me isn't helping you. It's not helping me. It's not helping anyone."

"Nothing you do will help," a man in the front shouts. "You've ruined everything. The only hope we have is to contain the damage."

Ice spears form in front of us, and fires blaze to life.

I'm reminded of the futility of everything I did on Rra. I tried, and I tried, and I tried, and with each attempt, more innocent people died. No matter how much I talk, no matter how much I plead, I can't change their minds. I can't stop them from throwing themselves against me over and over.

A rock from above us pelts a Fire Called in the head, and he spins and lashes out, flames arcing from his hand upward, toward the open window.

At a little boy.

Afraid for his home, probably. Afraid for the future. Afraid of me.

The collateral damage is unacceptable.

The soldiers standing here chose this—they're here because they believe in a cause. I wish I knew all the answers, but I don't. The one thing I know for sure is that I can't simply watch as little boys burn up.

Without another thought, I reach for the Fire Called man and I *pull*. It's faster than before, and easier too. Like I've snapped my fingers, his flame cuts off, mere feet before it would have roasted the rock-throwing child. And the Fire Called collapses, his body shrinking, blackening, and his power floods into me. Luckily I'm still wearing Ra's stupid collar. I funnel the power into the stone set on the very bottom.

"Who else will flame or Bind or freeze innocent bystanders merely to get at me?" I step forward slowly, Lifting my own supporters back and behind me. "Who?" My nostrils flare, as the acrid smell of fire from the Fire Called man's flames reach me. "Who else thinks I'm such a hideous monster I must be stopped *at all costs?*"

I sense the guns before I see them, raised and aimed at me. I take aim myself, siphoning the shooters before their fingers have compressed the trigger. The men and women who raise their hands, their eyes flooding with light, they're next.

I'm not sure how many people I siphon—I lose track. Every hand that aims a gun. Every person who throws a knife. Every Lifter who hurls a projectile. Every elemental who shapes a spear. In pairs. By the dozen. In waves. Several hundred, at least, but before very long, they realize what's happening and begin to flee. It starts around the edges of the gathered force, but within a few more moments, the entire army has turned tail.

"I may be the monster they say I am," I shout. "But you

should remember that monsters have fangs and claws and they don't lie down when you attack them. They fight back."

The people in windows above, and the families standing in doorways up and down the street cheer as the army melts away. The fear on the faces of the soldiers I faced isn't reflected in the eyes of the residents of this area. It's not much of a relief, but it helps some.

By the time we turn to head home, my shoulders ache. My head throbs. But my reservoirs are once again full, flickering bright red where they're set in the solid gold.

Martin bumps me with his hip as we walk. "That was hard."

I nod.

"But you did the right thing."

My head snaps to the side, and I meet his gaze. "What?"

"You may worry you're a monster, but you're not. Monsters don't care about harm to children. They only feed. Those soldiers are acting on fear, but you're not. You're doing what's right."

His words are like a salve, but unfortunately, I can't trust them. I can't believe what he's saying, because I know something he doesn't. I wanted to save that little boy, and I wanted to disperse the army, but more than anything else, I was looking for an excuse to siphon the energy I needed to refill the reservoirs. Which means I did it all for the wrong reasons. And if I hadn't needed the magic for Jesse, I might have found a better way. A way I didn't even look for . . .

When I reach the red brick building again, Amun's barracks, I race up the stairs to the room I was in. To the place I left Jesse. I expect him to be unconscious.

"I hear you defeated the army—alone," he rasps.

I wish he'd been asleep. "Not exactly," I say. "John and Martin, Henry, and Am-Heh and Mehen, they all came too."

"But you did it—you siphoned the aggressive soldiers who were attacking until they all ran."

"How could you have heard that already?"

He points at the television, and I realize that someone was videotaping it—someone sent the footage to the news crews and voila. Now everyone knows. "Everyone saw it, live."

"I have the energy to save you."

Jesse struggles up to a seated position. "Kahn came by while you were gone. He watched it on the television with me."

My heart stops beating in my chest. He wouldn't dare . .
.

"He told me what Dad thinks. Kahn agrees with him."

I shake my head. "They're wrong."

Jesse's smile is sad. "I think they're right. I'm not sure that my death will fix things, not now, not after you've already collapsed Terra and Erra. That's done, I think, but my ongoing existence can't be helping." He pats the bed.

I climb up next to him and take his hand. It's cold. Clammy. Weak.

"Can you honestly tell me that you did everything you did only because it's what was needful? You did it all to save the civilians living in the area?"

I open my mouth to lie, but I can't do it. Not to him. I shake my head instead. "I don't know."

"I do." His voice is weak—so weak. "Let me go, Alora. It's time."

He's wrong. It's not time. I can't take it. Not now, maybe not ever. It's all so monstrously unfair.

"Promise," he whispers. His lips are whitish, cracked. He looks like he's aged ten years in the last half hour.

I shake my head.

"Promise me."

So I do. The words feel ripped from deep, deep down in

my soul. "I won't funnel more energy into you. Not this time."

He smiles then, a sweet, genuine smile. "It has been my life's greatest gift," he whispers, "having you as my sister. You're brilliant. You're kind. You're generous. You're brave. Be brave now." He squeezes my hand, but it's so slight it's like he's done nothing at all. "I wish we'd taken more photos."

Me too. Why didn't we?

His eyes close. His body stills. And his chest stops rising and falling. And I realize he's finally slipping away. For good.

I know I promised.

Some part of me fears that he's right. That it's all my fault that the world is falling apart. That I've caused all this misery, all these dangers.

But.

Even so.

I still can't let it happen. I just can't. The power is right here, pulsing around my neck. And no matter whether it was all our fault or not, it's done at this point. Self-sacrifice and regrets won't help, and there's no evidence that allowing him to die will help anything.

Myself, I would gladly sacrifice.

But not Jesse.

Never Jesse.

The thought of him dying is a million times worse than when the snake exploded. A million times worse than when the Reapers died. So much worse, even, than when I ripped out the throat of that gazelle, who wasn't really a gazelle.

I wonder what it says about me, that I'd lay down and die myself a thousand times before I'd let my brother go. I'd sacrifice myself—but I can't give him up.

Before Jesse can take his last gasp, I tap into the power stored in the glowing red stones, and I spin it into pure energy and funnel it into my brother, filling up his leaking soul, powering up his cracked mortal vessel until he's practically shining with light.

When his eyes open, my heartache eases. My spirits lift.

But his eyes, they're not thankful or delighted or joyful. They're full of disappointment. They're full of sorrow.

And they're full of something else, something I've never seen from Jesse before.

Reproach.

"You promised me," he says. "You said you would let me go. You said you'd do the right thing, and you *lied* to me."

The pain in his eyes, the hurt from my betrayal, it's the worst thing I've ever seen.

It might hurt more than the pain of losing him—because this is a loss from which I might never recover. Except . . . an idea occurs to me. Something so dark, so hideous, that I ought to shove it away immediately. I ought not to even consider it.

But once I have the idea, I can't seem to shake it.

I try.

I really do.

But it's like a weed. It grows and it grows and it grows.

And I pull it out.

And it sprouts up again.

Alphas can erase memories.

Supra alphas can reset things—make it like they never happened at all.

And if anything on Earth, if anyone on Earth, deserves a reset, it's Jesse. So I reach tentatively for his mind, the bright, shining cords of it, and I run a metaphysical finger down the length of them, searching, searching, for the last few moments, for our conversation, for the promise I made to Jesse, the promise that I betrayed, and I *Lift* it up and away. I fling it out into space where it whirls and disappears.

I replace that shining conviction that he should have died, that he ought not to be here at all, with a desire to stay with me. I take the strongest, brightest cord in his soul, his love for me, and I stretch it into the place of the one I Lifted, the one I excavated, and I twist them all back together.

And it works.

Jesse beams up at me. "You survived the invading army?"

I swallow and nod.

"I'm so glad. Thank goodness." He hugs me, and it feels *almost* right.

I wonder whether anything will ever feel exactly right again.

But the pain of losing him, the absolute pulverization of my innards, the destruction of all that I am—I can't face that. I shouldn't have done what I did, but I did it because it wasn't *fair,* what we've endured. It wasn't *just,* the hand we were dealt.

Now if only I could prune my own doubts, my own memories, and my own guilt.

But that's not within the ability of a supra alpha. I'm stuck with all the regret, and the memory of Jesse's reproach . . .

Forever.

24

RRA

"Yesterday you were begging me to shift you all back to human," I say. "You said if I didn't, many, many people would die."

"That's true." Christopher paces in his human form almost exactly the same way as he did in his lion form, only there's no lashing tail. "But you have to understand why they're worried."

If I couldn't shift into a lion form . . . I'd be alright, but I'd probably be agitated, yes. I lean back in my chair and massage my temples. One crisis averted, another complaint shoved right in my face.

"Quite a few people have gathered and asked to speak with you."

"They couldn't wait a few days?" I ask. "Maybe they can throw a party to celebrate that we fixed things in time."

Christopher drags a chair across the room and sits down directly across from me. "They're still scared— they're still unsure what's going on." His voice drops to a whisper. "I'm right there with them. What's going on? Why were we locked as animals, and now still stuck, but as humans?"

I drag a hand through my tangled hair. "I'm sorry, I must have forgotten my Book of Answers in my other pants. Let me go see if I can find it."

"Just talk to them," he says.

"And try not to explode anyone into goo," I mutter.

He doesn't smile, which is good. It wasn't funny.

"*Fine*, I'll see a few of them. Not a whole herd, you hear me?"

He's darting for the door the second I agree. Moments later, people pour through the doors. Mostly men, but a few women, too. They don't speak as they form into a loose semi-circle. I'm not quite sure what I expect. I'm waiting for one of them to say something—clearly I'm not good at public speaking—when they all drop down to their knees and bow their faces down on the ground.

"What are you doing?" I stand up.

They shuffle around, rising to their knees, their eyes confused.

"Stand up, for heaven's sake."

They do, but still, no one speaks. Tall. Short. Round. Bony. Pale. Dark skinned. They look as different from one another in human form as the animals that gathered previously. "You've all come to beg me to restore your ability to shift. Right?"

They nod.

"Can you not speak?"

Murmurs. "We can talk," the tall, dark-skinned woman in the front says. "But we can't shift. You're right about that."

"You couldn't shift at all a few weeks ago," I say. "And now you're desperate to get the ability back?"

She shrugs. "If it's possible. Mostly, we want to know what's going on."

Get in line. "I wasn't even here a few weeks ago, or if I was, I don't remember it and no one else remembers me either. I don't know my own name, but for some reason everyone thinks I should fix this." I shake my head and sigh.

Christopher leans against the doorframe, his eyes sad.

"I'm not sure what you think I can do," I say. "I can't tell which of you might have been present yesterday, before the hunt, when I tried everything I could think of to force you to shift into your human forms." I shake my head. "I couldn't do it. It wasn't until things were desperate that I could do anything at all."

"Perhaps we need to force you into it," a short man in the corner says. "Create some kind of deadline."

Are they kidding? "Or maybe you could try being happy with what you have—which is safety, and some semblance of normalcy. It's been less than six hours since the sun rose. Perhaps you're all too exhausted from being in animal forms for so long—"

"Can you shift?" the dark-skinned woman asks.

I pause. Can I? When I woke this morning I was a lion, like always. I shifted not too many hours ago, but can I now? I close my eyes and imagine my paws pounding on the soft ground, my claws digging into the soil, my whiskers being blown in the wind. And I melt downward.

I guess so.

More murmurs, which are easier to parse out in this form than they were as a human.

"We just want what you have," the woman says. "To have our abilities returned."

She never could shift back and forth at will, but how quickly our expectations are reset. Give someone wealth and ease for a day and he'll be spoiled forever. *What exactly are you asking me to do?*

"Try it," the woman says. "Force us to shift."

Has anyone informed you of how my attempts at that went before?

"It worked last night." She crosses her arms.

Are you volunteering? I'm not even sure whether the woman's ability can be restored at all or whether her former shape was a bizarre fluke.

"I am." She steps forward two steps, away from the others. "I'll bear the risk. I have no children, no husband, and no family I'd be abandoning."

"But you might not even be able to shift at all," Christopher says. "You should start with me."

He's trying to be noble, but the woman's eyes flash. "All the more reason to start with me. If she can shift me, then everything has changed. If she can't force me to shift, she can test a male next."

Yes, who cares about little old me and the trauma I endure when I *murder* someone. Let's start with the hardest option first. The one most likely not to work . . . *Maybe we should start with a male.*

"If you forced him successfully," the woman says, "can you honestly promise me you'd be willing to risk trying to force a female?" She puts her hands on her hips. "Or would you give up, write us off, and assume things have gone back to the status quo?"

She might be right. It won't be any easier for me to try and force her if it works on Christopher.

The problem is that I sincerely doubt whether any of this is going to work. I don't bother arguing, though. I'm sick of arguing. I'm sick of people begging and cajoling and badgering and guilting me all day, every day. I circle the woman, examining her, and wondering what her animal form might be. Her eyes track me easily, and I don't seem to make her uncomfortable. Her eyes are calculating, and she's clearly brave. A leader.

Panther? No, leopard. I guess.

"A goose," she says.

If lions could laugh, I'd be laughing. That's what I get

for assuming anyone is a Render, or that I have any idea what kind of animal lives inside someone based on what I see on the outside. Now that I think about it, geese are pretty fierce. A memory of one charging me while I was traveling in a bizarre box thing with seats swims through my mind, evaporating as soon as I try to focus on it.

"I miss flying." Her chin lifts like she feels the need to defend her form.

Of course you do. I imagine her with feathers, wings, a beak. *What color feathers?*

"Grey."

I keep on thinking it through until I have an image fixed in my mind, and then I focus on her human body. I imagine her melting downward and I *push*. She doesn't shift, but she pulses, and it's like her body *unravels* somehow, strands fraying and waving in nonexistent wind. I shake my head and she falls back into place as if nothing happened.

"Did you try it?" She frowns. "I didn't feel anything."

I focus again, this time pushing harder. *Shift.*

Her entire body ripples, from her head to her toes, but not in a shifting way—as if she's been plucked by a giant hand—and she vibrates. This time she feels it, her body bowing outward, and the filaments this time come completely unwound. Her hands writhe, spreading unnaturally, and they sparkle, almost, as if they're full of too much light.

When I release her, she collapses inward, sinking to the floor and curling in a fetal position.

I shift back into my human form and look around the room. "Something's wrong. That's nothing like the last few times I tried. Could any of you see the energy leaking out of her?"

The people gathered look at one another and back and me, and then shake their heads.

"She went taut," Christopher says. "Like all her muscles contracted at once."

"And she shuddered," another man says.

"Maybe you can't shift her," another man says, "because she's female."

None of them can see what I saw, that she was unraveling, that her energy was unspooling as I tried to force the change on her body. It happened last night too, the world around me buckling and warping.

The woman finally sits up and then stands. She doesn't beg me to try again, but she doesn't leave either. I can tell she still wants her ability to shift into a goose.

Boy, is that not a thought I expected to be having this morning when I woke up.

"Perhaps the problem is that she's female." Or maybe this whole thing was always doomed.

"Try with me." Christopher weaves his way through the people between us and stands at the front, in the spot the woman just left.

I close my eyes and think about what more I can do. What did I do that worked last night? Nothing. I killed someone—a person—and he changed back to torment me. Was that really it? And the vibrations, the susurrations of the world around me, didn't happen until after I roared.

Is that it? My roar? Or was it killing someone? I exploded a snake. I killed several Reapers, and nothing expansive happened then. Maybe it was the way I killed the man—by tearing out his throat. I want to scream and yell and cry and bawl and laugh at the same time. Who am I? Why am I here? What am I supposed to do? How should I proceed?

"Fine," I say, weary to my bones. "Fine. I'll try killing you. I mean, shifting you. Into the animal you didn't want to be last night."

He flinches.

"I don't want any of this," I say. "But I'll try again, to do something I don't know how to do, something I'm not even sure I can do." The same helpless fury rises inside of me that I felt last night. The anger at the futility of all of it. At my inability to do anything right. And I shout the words, this time, as my hands clench at my sides. *"Shift!"*

He collapses on the floor and thrashes, his fingers curling inward, his eyes bulging, his muscles taut. And just like before, the filaments that compose his body come unwound and energy sparks from his fingertips, from his elbows, and from the tips of his shaggy blond hair.

Eventually, he calms down, because I don't push it further.

Because I don't keep trying.

I knew I would fail before I began.

Only, Christopher isn't the only one who needs convincing. I'm forced to try the same thing dozens of times before the sun finally drops low in the sky, before even Christopher and the goose woman have lost all hope of my ability to restore their powers. Each time, all I manage to do is rattle their forms loose—releasing whatever lives inside the human body, I suppose. But finally, I've had enough.

"Try me one last time," Christopher says, his jaw set, his eyes hard. "And this time, keep on pushing. Don't quit to spare me."

The image of the snake exploding floods my brain, and I shake my head.

"Do it," he says. "None of us can ever quit without knowing whether we didn't push hard enough. Whether the solution might be there, just past where we endured."

The people in the room nod and murmur and I want to maul them all, one at a time, like they're shredding my heart into pieces. How dare they ask that of me? They're not at risk. It's only Christopher whom I might have to remember destroying for the rest of my life. It's only Christopher whose body could be turned into pink mist.

"You don't understand," I say.

"You're the only one who does," he says. "You're She Who Gathers."

I hate my stupid title. "Fine, but everyone needs to remember that you begged me for this."

He walks to the front of the room again, his eyes certain, his shoulders relaxed. He's prepared to die, I realize. He's ready to sacrifice himself. Maybe he's always wanted this—to feel like his life means something. I hate that about him. Dying for a cause is idiotic. It's better to live for the cause.

It's harder, but it's always better to *live* for something.

I imagine my fangs, my claws, my paws, my pelt, and I melt down into lion form. I haven't tried this in my animal form since the goose experiment. Maybe roaring will help. This time, before I try to force his change, I dig down deep for all my anger, my fury, and my pent up despair, and I channel it all into the biggest roar I've ever released. And when I do, Christopher drops to his hands and knees, as do all the other people gathered in front of me. The men, the women, the Reapers, the Renders, they all bow.

And they all shudder.

And then they all unspool somehow, like their bodies are made up of individual threads. They wobble, and they waver, and they sparkle, and they flash.

Shift, I command. *SHIFT!*

They don't shift into animal forms, but they do unspool further, until they're less people and more a mass of strings of light. I can see their hearts, their souls, their goals and hopes and dreams.

And then I yank back, as fast as I can, pulling away all the pressure I've exerted, and they all snap back into place. I breathe a sigh of relief that no one has exploded, and then

I stumble to the back of the room and shift back into human form. "I'm done," I say. "No more. Not a single attempt more." I open the door and duck out, escaping into the night.

She Who Gathers? That's definitely not right.

I'm She Who Unravels.

She Who Dooms.

25

EARTH

Jesse's still sleeping when I wake up, but his cheeks are rosy and his pulse is strong. He's still doing great. And I have someone I need to find.

When I try to sneak out, Am-Heh's waiting outside my door. "Most Divine," he says. "There's an envoy waiting for you downstairs. They've been waiting quite some time."

"Oh my goodness," I say. "Didn't we discuss this? Most Divine?" I make a puking sound. "Just call me Alora, okay?"

"Alora." It looks like he's swallowing a lemon again. "Right. Sorry for the confusion, Most Di—" He coughs. "I'm happy you're awake."

"I need to see Kahn." I purse my lips to keep from ranting in the hallway.

"You look unhappy." Am-Heh crosses his arms, his pecs rippling under the leather vest he never changes. Mehen immediately updated to era-appropriate clothing, but Am-Heh appears to be unwilling to shift into the twentieth century.

I suppose that's understandable.

"I am not unhappy," I say. "I'm furious. I'm livid. I'm irate."

His eyes light up and he gestures with animation. "Right this way, then." He's muttering under his breath as we walk down the hallway, and it's hard to make out his exact wording, but it sounds something like, "—hope he gets tossed out on his ear."

I suppress my laugh.

The thought of throwing Kahn out for interfering with Jesse is quite satisfying. And the idea of watching him leave makes me feel sucker punched at the same time.

Am-Heh doesn't tap on the door. He doesn't even pause. He simply flings the solid wooden door open and steps aside so I can enter. I'm just ticked enough that I don't care about the tremendous violation of privacy, and I stalk inside, my anger brimming to the very top.

Kahn's standing in the center of the room wearing nothing but a towel. Water drips from his shaggy hair and runs down the plane between his pectoral muscles. My eyes follow the drips as they zigzag between perfectly sculpted abdominal muscles, finally dead-ending into the towel. Which is why I'm staring somewhere I shouldn't.

I cough and yank my eyes back to his slightly bemused face. His gorgeous skin, his angelic eyes, and his chiseled jawline never fail to distract me.

"Did you need something?"

But I can't be distracted, not today. I stalk across the room, my footfalls not nearly heavy enough to satisfy me. "Yes, I do." I clench my hands at my side and freeze a few feet away. The smell of sage and leather hits my nostrils, and it's a surprisingly good combination.

I ignore it.

"You had no right to talk to Jesse. You had *no right* to tell him that it's his fault that Terra collapsed. You don't even have any idea whether it's true."

"And you have no proof that it's not," Kahn says. "I merely told him it was Duncan's theory."

"If no one had murdered my brother, and if I hadn't saved him, and if Terra had still collapsed, as it was already on its way to doing, then what would Duncan have used to blame me?" An overwhelming urge to set something on fire, or tear into something with my teeth grips me. "I'm sick of everyone telling me what I can and can't do. I'm utterly exhausted from people trying to force my hand. I spend every single day trying my best to do a million things I don't know how to do. I try to save people I don't know. I try to reassemble a jumble of mess I didn't make, and not one single person ever thanks me."

Kahn steps toward me. His voice is soft—unbelievably soft. I have to strain just to make out his words. "Thank you."

"It doesn't count now."

"Even so, I am grateful. I know what you're doing is hard, but Jesse deserves to know the truth."

Which he now won't remember at all—but if Kahn just tells him again . . . I can't face that. "Luckily, after I recharged him, he forgot all the nonsense you told him just before he passed out."

Kahn frowns. "He forgot? As in, all recollection of our conversation was gone?"

"Everything from just before, yeah. I think maybe he was too exhausted for any of it to process." Lie, lie, lie.

Kahn's eyes meet mine and he inhales sharply. "He *forgot*? Or you helped him forget?"

How could he know that?

"I know you, Alora. We haven't spent much time together, but it feels like I've known you my entire life, somehow. It's not just the stupid glowing whatever, either." He waves his hands through the air. "It's more than that. I can't explain it."

I force myself to step backward, since that dumb glowing effervescence appears to be clouding my judgment. Again. "You never apologized for interfering with me and Jesse."

"Interfering?" He shakes his head. "Is that what we call the truth these days? Really? I hope it hasn't come to that."

I swear under my breath. "Kahn, I can't lose him. You may not understand, but I'd rather die than lose him. Okay?"

"That's not your decision to make," he says. "That's always been the problem with Ra, at its most basic. He doesn't think the rules of this world apply to him. He was told he was a god for so long that he started to believe his own press. Even gods have to follow the laws of right and wrong, or the universe will cease to exist."

"The world is black and white to you," I say. "It's like you're living in a fairy tale, like you're a child. Everywhere I look, the world is grey. So very grey."

"That's the saddest thing I've heard all day," Kahn says. "Step into the light. Blink until you've cleared your vision. The world *isn't* grey. That's what people tell themselves when they're doing the wrong things—they try and explain that they're justified in them by saying that right and wrong don't really exist."

"So I should just let Jesse die? That's what you think?"

"I think the world is full of things that aren't fair and aren't good, and they're usually the consequences of either our actions or those of other people. But just like my mom taught me as a child, two wrongs never make a right."

"When evil people like Devlin do terrible things, you're saying that we can't take action to repair them? We can't set them right?"

"If our efforts don't harm the rest of the world, if they don't have far-reaching ramifications, then sure. Go ahead. If I steal someone's car, and the insurance company has to buy a new one, you're within your rights to find me and make me purchase you a new one. You could even make me pay damages for the stress, harm, or emotional distress I caused. But you can't cut off my foot to make me suffer. That's not justice. That's grey. It's black added to white."

"Will you swear not to tell Jesse again? Will you keep your mouth shut, at least?"

When Kahn's eyes meet mine, they're brimming with pain, with sorrow, with regret. "I can't do that."

"What do you mean?"

He shakes his head. "I think I love you, as idiotic as that sounds. I would cut off my foot if it would make you happy. I'd do worse to keep you alive, and I'm worried what morally grey things I'd allow to creep up on me if you asked. But right now, I've got enough white inside to know that what you're asking is wrong."

"So you'll tell him again." Thinking of losing Kahn does feel like losing a limb, but losing Jesse feels worse. I can't do it. I won't risk it. "I'm not asking you to lie to him. I don't even believe what Duncan thinks is true. I think Terra has been unstable for a long time. Maybe since I was reborn. Maybe before that, even. But I'm not asking you to tell Jesse something you don't believe. All you have to do is keep your mouth shut about Duncan's accusations."

Tiny wrinkles appear at the corners of his eyes. That's my only sign that he can't do it.

"I can't trust you. You don't have my back." My heart feels like it's been speared. "You're not my friend or my ally."

"What are you saying?"

"Am-Heh," I say. "Please escort Kahn out of the facility. He'll be leaving to join Isis."

There is no world in which we are enemies.

Except this one.

"Alora, I'm trying to help you."

"I don't need your brand of *help,* thanks." I don't cry. I don't collapse to my knees. I don't even frown while Kahn ducks into the bathroom to put on clothing, grabs his bag, and follows Am-Heh out the door.

But the second they're gone, I sink to the bed and press my face to his sheets. They still smell like him. For some reason that wrecks me more than anything he said or did. I bawl like a sad little child for far too long.

"Most Divine?"

My head snaps up, and I wipe at my eyes. "Mehen?"

He's wearing a plaid shirt and khaki pants with a braided belt. He's clearly decided to embrace the modern world, but he's just as obviously not entirely sure how things work together yet. "An envoy has been waiting to speak to you for quite some time."

Right. Am-Heh said that before I got distracted. "Oh, well. Is it something you can deal with?"

He shakes his head. "I believe your presence is required."

I stand up and brush off my rumpled t-shirt and wrinkled pants. It's not my best look, but I'm not an actual princess to worry about being decked out in a ball gown and tiara. "Fine." Mehen moves fast and I have to trot to keep up, but I follow without complaining. Mostly. He shows me to a large conference room off the main hallway on the first floor. "I assume you'll want your entire court here with you?" He lifts his eyebrows expectantly. "Excluding recent removals." He coughs into his hand.

Kahn left.

I still hardly believe it.

"Who are these people?" I ask. "I can't imagine you'd invite an Isis envoy inside these walls, so are these the leaders of Amun in the area? Or what am I about to walk into?"

John jogs down the hall, his chest rising and falling

quickly. Jesse's not far behind him, and Martin, Henry, Oliver, and Thomas are just behind them.

"The others are waiting inside already," Mehen says. And he opens the door.

I can't be bothered to pelt him with any more questions, not when the answers are right on the other side, so I walk through the door. And standing on the other side . . . is the King of England. Or at least, I think he's the King of England. I've only ever seen his face on the television. His dad died of a heart attack not long ago, and he's young. Not much older than I am, really. Ten or fifteen years, perhaps.

"Uh, hello," I say. "I'm Alora."

He holds out his hand, as if he wants me to shake it. "You're American, are you not?"

I nod, dumbly, but I do take his hand.

He pumps my arm enthusiastically. "I'm a huge fan. I've been watching the clips people were able to record over and over."

A huge fan? Of what?

"You go by Most Divine?" he asks. "Is that the correct title?"

I laugh. I can't help it. It's the most absurd interchange I've ever had in my life. Even in my dreams, I couldn't have imagined something as ridiculous as the King of England shaking my hand and asking whether he should address me as 'Most Divine.' I wipe at my eyes, embarrassed at my irreverence. "I'm not divine, not even close." I toss my head behind me. "These people can attest to that well enough."

Jesse snorts. I can always count on him to laugh at anything that mocks me, as long as I'm the one making the joke.

"Why are you here, Your Majesty?" I ask.

He opens his mouth and then closes it again, looking around the room as if someone else might help him. There are half a dozen people behind him, but I don't recognize them.

"I'm the Prime Minister," a woman with a red business suit and dark hair and eyes says. "We've come to make you a proposition."

"A what?"

"We know you're the daughter of Ra, reborn in modern times." The king swallows, his Adam's apple bobbing up and down. "And we know that, like him, you can assimilate —is that right?"

I shrug.

"You can take energy from others." He swallows again. "We saw that on all of the video footage."

I turn to look at John. "What video footage did they see, exactly?"

"Apparently quite a few of the residents in the surrounding buildings videotaped the standoff with Isis— the first and the second. That footage, from all sources, has gone viral, and has also been picked up by all communication networks under Amun control." John pulls a phone out of his pocket. "If you'd like to see it—"

"Absolutely not." I can't imagine anything worse than having to watch innocent people die and hundreds of soldiers wither on video. I had to live it—that was more than enough hideousness for me.

Are they here to reprimand me? It seems . . . arrogant at best, to confront the person responsible for so many deaths yourself. "What exactly is your proposition?"

"My family has ruled in Great Britain for more than twelve hundred years," the king says, "since King Alfred the Great."

"You think that's impressive? My dad had been alive for twenty-four hundred years . . . in three hundred and fifty B.C.E." I joke.

No one laughs.

Instead, the King, the Prime Minister, and the others who came with them bow.

They freaking bow.

"Please, please stand up," I say. "I'm not sure quite what's going on, but—"

"I beg your pardon, Most Divine," the king says, "but we're here to offer up Great Britain to you—for your leadership. It's clear that we're not able to protect our citizens, but you are."

This must be some kind of joke.

"We think the most obvious place for you to take up residence, with all your people, of course," the Prime Minister says, "is at Buckingham Palace. It's already fortified, and it's set up for press conferences, and dignitaries, and whatever else you might need."

"My wife is hoping we'll be allowed to retain Kensington Palace," the king says. "Our children have never lived anywhere else, and it would be—"

"I'm not going to live in a palace," I say, a little too sharply. But honestly, this whole thing is alarming.

"You should think this through," John whispers. "Tell them you'll consider it."

"Is he kidding?" I ask no one in particular.

"It does make sense," Jesse whispers. "They're right that you can protect the people in a way they can't."

The world has turned inside out.

"Let us discuss," I say. "Give me a moment." I turn for the door.

"Take all the time you need," the king says.

"No rush," the Prime Minister says. "But we do hope that wherever you decide you'd like to live, you'll take the governance of our people seriously. These are terrifying, turbulent times, and you seem to be the only person able to weather the storm."

If they had any idea . . .

But when I poll my supposed Council, every single one of them thinks I should accept. "You think I should be the *Queen* of *England?*"

"Emperor has a better ring to it," Am-Heh says with a smug smile. He's been spending every waking moment learning English, and I feel like he's starting to understand the basics, to my great dismay.

"Stop grinning," I say in Egyptian. "This is a mess. It's one more headache."

"But you'd be able to adjudicate disputes," Mehen says. "And you'd have access to the condemned, the evil, the villainous members of society at large, would you not?"

"Where are you going with this?"

"Instead of execution . . . " He glances at the stupid golden collar I'm still wearing. I really ought to hide this somewhere safe.

He has a point, though. If I had access to the bad people in the world, siphoning them would be justified. It could give me a justifiable and consistent well of power I could use to keep Jesse alive as long as I need . . . And thankfully, no one else has any idea what they're saying. "Fine," I say in English. "If you all think this is the way to go." I look around. "I guess we're moving. To Buckingham Palace. Go pack your things."

"Are you sure about all this?" Jesse asks softly.

"What choice do I have?"

"We always have a choice," Jesse says. "You could step away. You could run. Both of us could, right now in fact."

"But if we do that, Isis and Amun won't disappear. The struggle will go on, only those caught in the middle will have no one to defend them."

A great pulse distracts me—and I look down to see what I already know. The remaining power in the red stones set in the collar around my neck is gone. Ra has done it again, drained the power *I* replenished. It's starting to really piss me off. If I could figure out how to get to Rra from Earth, and then shift onward to Ā, I would do it right this second. I would give him a piece of my mind. Having to constantly support Jesse is hard enough without an incarcerated freeloader always draining my efforts.

But I can't deal with telling Jesse all of that, so I force a smile. "It'll be fine, J, I swear. Why don't you see if you can help Mehen and Am-Heh explain to all the Amun troops what we're doing and where we're going."

He doesn't argue further, but his eyes are kind. It's a balm to the raw edges of my heart.

I don't want to have to handle the details with the King and Prime Minister myself—it feels too awkward—so I grab John's elbow before he disappears. "Will you handle the transition or whatever? With them, I mean?"

"Don't you think maybe Mehen, or Am-Heh—"

I laugh. "In ancient Egyptian? Or Greek, perhaps?"

His smile is sideways—a little nervous, I think.

"What's wrong, John?"

"I'm not the right guy to be interacting with royalty." He looks at his feet.

"Why is that?"

"I'm not good enough to talk to them, and I'm certainly not good enough for the *Most Divine*."

"Oh please. I hate when people call me that. That's not me. Do you know who *is* me? The little girl who stood in your kitchen, lost and confused. The kid whose brother needed a job—needed a chance. The girl who eats way too many tacos. Those are me." I grab the collar of his shirt and tug him toward me. His eyes jump to meet mine, and there's the same electricity I've always felt around him. It's not the inferno I feel with Kahn, but it's still something special. And Kahn is gone. "That's someone for whom you've always been good enough. It's someone who feels blessed to have you in her corner."

"Even then," he says, "you were—"

I flatten my palm against his chest. "I'm the opposite of divine."

"You can assimilate," he says. "You're Fire Called. You're a Render, and you're the most powerful Lifter anyone has seen, Oh Great and Mighty Warden." His tone is mocking, but he's not really making a joke. His feelings of inadequacy are real. "You're fit for a rebirth of Apophis—your father's greatest enemy. I'm not fit for you, however."

"Kahn left." My voice sounds ragged. Barely sane.

"What? Why?" His eyes search my face intently.

"Remember I said I wasn't divine?" I drop to a whisper. "Jesse was fading and he forbade me to save him."

John's brows draw together angrily. "He what?"

"Duncan, through Kahn, convinced him that when I saved him it destabilized Terra. Jesse believed that his existence has caused all the problems we've been facing. That, combined with his guilt over all the energy I'm using to save him, was enough. He made me promise to let him go —Duncan's operating under the delusion that somehow if Jesse dies—" My voice cracks on the word. "—that will put Humpty Dumpty back together again."

"There's no way that you bringing Jesse—"

"I don't think so either, but Jesse isn't willing to risk it. He's never been willing to allow any harm to anyone else because of him."

"But he's alive now," John says. "Is he saying you can't in the future—"

I shake my head. "I already did it, I saved him again, even though I swore I wouldn't. It was maybe, or probably, the reason I raced out to confront the Isis army. I needed to recharge the batteries to save him." I can't quite believe I'm admitting this, but . . . "It's likely clouding my judgment about what and when to siphon, knowing that Jesse needs me. And I think Ra may be using that knowledge to force me to funnel more and more power his way."

"That's a lot of information to process," John says.

"It's worse than that," I finally confess. "When he realized what I'd done, Jesse was upset. Really upset."

John's baffled. "Okay."

"So, I erased it." I cringe, my face scrunching up. "I took his memory of what Kahn and Duncan thought, and I took his memory of me ignoring my promise and saving him. I stole the truth from my own brother."

"Which is exactly what you should have done," John says. "That's why they have medical powers of attorney, you know. Your brother Jesse's sick, and you have to make decisions for him until he's well again."

That, I did not expect. "You really think so?"

"Of course I do. How could anyone think anything else? My dad murdered your brother—it's probably his greatest regret, but it was a great wrong, and of course you're doing everything you can to reverse that great evil."

"But I can't know whether I'm influenced by my desire to save Jesse when I make decisions. I can't be sure, with the fate of the world hanging in the balance, that—"

John's arms wrap around me, drawing my cheek against his chest. "Alora, hush. Every decision anyone makes is influenced by the things they want, by the way they were raised, by their particular set of fears and wounds. It's impossible to make decisions in a vacuum. If your brother had died, do you think that wouldn't impact the decisions you'd make? You could destroy the entire world in your grief, and you'd be entitled to do it, too. Stop fretting. What you did was right based on what you knew, and what had happened to you. You're a good person."

"But Kahn—"

"Is a complete moron if he would walk away from you over something so stupid. He should be supporting you. He should be helping you in any way he can. Instead he's floating away on an island called the Moral High Ground. I hope he doesn't die on it."

"That's not true," I say.

"Fine." John smiles down at me. "I wouldn't be upset if he did. But you would, so I'll hope against it."

I swat his chest, and my heart still aches, but I do feel better. Kahn may not support me, but John's a good person and he *gets* it. He doesn't think I'm drowning in an ocean of grey.

I just hope, if Kahn is right, that I won't take the whole world down with me.

26

RRA

"Wake up!" Someone's shaking me, but their hands aren't very firm, and their voice is staccato, like it's not really an order. I roll over, unprepared to face another day, unwilling to fail again and again and again.

"Please." The voice is desperate this time, and I open my eyes.

Christopher's face is distorted, somehow, his unkempt, shaggy hair flying up in several directions, and his eyes wild, but that's not the most concerning part. No, what I struggle to focus on is how the edges of his body are . . . glitchy. They spark and twist in ways that are hard to understand, much less look at. I glance down at my own arm—a human arm. For the first time, I've woken in human form here.

That's odd.

"What?" I mumble. "What's wrong?"

"We aren't sure. Everyone's experiencing strange flashes of pain. Some of it's localized. Arms, legs, shoulders, whatever. Some of it affects the whole body. It's worldwide, from what the alphas can ascertain by broadcasts."

I shove myself up and run a hand through my hair. It's even more tangled than Christopher's. "I wonder if it has to do with the weird pulsing, sparking, blinking thing you guys are all doing."

"With the what?"

"I noticed it yesterday," I say. "When I would try to force a shift, your bodies would . . . unfurl or something. I can't describe it. No one else seemed to even see it, so I gave up trying to explain."

Christopher's expression is hard.

"Look, everything about this world has been strange," I say, "from the day I opened my eyes and killed a deer. I'm a human who can turn into a lion, for heaven's sake."

"What's strange about that?" He lifts one eyebrow, and it twists, sparking, pulsing, unraveling.

"There—it's happening. Does your right eyebrow hurt?"

He gulps, and then he nods.

"That's it, then." But what am I supposed to do about it?

I shove him out the door, dress in something more substantial than the plain, thin cotton pants and shirt I always seem to shift into for my first shift of the day, and emerge, prepared to endure more pleading and bombardment. I just hope that something I do today actually helps. It's beginning to feel like I'm stuck in some kind of bizarre punishment loop. Everyone expects me to save them, but there's no way to succeed. It's like I'm doomed to fail over and over and over as some kind of penance for being a bad person.

Am I a bad person?

I've killed several animals and many human-animal-shifters in my time here. I've tried over and over to do the right thing, but I manage only to mess things up.

But when I reach the dining hall, there are already dozens of people gathered, all of them staring at me from the second I walk inside, their eyes pleading, their posture sycophantic. What in the world am I supposed to do? How could I possibly stop their bodies from unraveling? They can't even see it happening.

"Yesterday, no matter what you tried, no one died," Christopher says, as he places a bowl of something lumpy in front of me.

"What is this?" I poke at it with the spoon protruding from the edge.

"All our resources have been diverted to trying to figure out why we're all stuck in human form," he says. "I'm sorry if our culinary stylings aren't up to your exacting standards."

I sigh and begin to shovel food into my mouth. But when a lump of I-don't-know-what wriggles and sparks as I'm putting it in my mouth, I drop the spoon into the partially empty bowl with a clatter. "Actually, I'm not that hungry. What's the plan for today? Should I make it my goal to kill a few people? Is that the only way you'll be satisfied I'm really trying?"

I'm about done being ordered to yell at and coerce people. The roaring, though? I feel like I could do some of that right now. "What we tried before clearly did nothing. Isn't that the definition of insanity? Trying the same thing over and over and just hoping the results will change?"

"Probably," he agrees. "Which is why we want you to try harder. You say that we're unraveling in front of your eyes? That we're sparking and flashing? We want you to lean in on that. Push harder, with a targeted force. Keep shoving on me until I've completely disintegrated."

"Have you lost your mind?" An image of the snake man exploding flashes through my mind, and I vomit up whatever bizarre thing I just ate into the same bowl from which it came. Before I've even finished wiping my mouth,

Christopher's standing in front of me, hands relaxed at his sides.

"Do it now, before you've had time to think it through."

Murder my one friend here, and don't think about it first. Seems like a good plan. "I—"

"Please," the dark-skinned goose-woman from yesterday says.

"Try." The short man who was standing in the back corner is behind her.

"Please," another man behind Christopher says.

"Gather us," a woman sitting across from me pleads.

They've all lost their sparky, unraveling minds. If I was experiencing localized, random pain, if I couldn't shift into human form and then I couldn't shift into animal form, if I had no idea what would happen to me today, let alone tomorrow, maybe I'd be this adamant. Maybe I'd try to bludgeon the one person who can see what's going on, who seems to have some semblance of control over the happenings of my life, into shifting me, too.

But I hate the whole idea. I want to crawl back to my room and hide under my covers.

I don't run, though, no matter how much I want to escape. I can't. How can I ignore these people when they beg and plead and look to me to save them?

It's hard, but I stand up instead, and I focus on Christopher, directing every speck of my power, every bit of my will, and every ounce of my resolve in his direction. *SHIFT,* I think. And then I think it again. *Shift. SHIFT. SHIFT! SHIFT!!!!*

And he does, only it's not into the lion shape I know so well. It's not even into the bowing, flexing, torturous writhe that I created so often yesterday. No, he begins there, but he keeps on moving, snapping backward in ways his body should never extend, and then there's a popping sound that it appears only I hear. I cover my ears and shy away from him, as a tiny golden light emerges from his slack body and rises upward, floating up, up, up.

It pulses and sparkles, and it's one of the most beautiful things I've ever seen. It's comprised of circles and spools of bright golden light, wrapped around one another over and over, and it beckons to me. I gather it against myself and it's *absorbed into me* in a way I can't understand, but I still feel it, along with a bizarre sort of tugging. My hands tremble, my shoulders ache, my head pounds, and then I look down, at Christopher's collapsed body.

His eyes are blank, his features slack.

I killed him—another person, gone.

At least I didn't explode him into goo.

The room has erupted into chaos around me, people shrieking and calling out, begging me to do something, to do anything. What they think I'm going to do, I don't know. I can still feel Christopher's light pulsing against my heart, like a tiny displaced star. I realize with a start that I need to take it somewhere.

But *where?*

Why isn't anything clear to me? Why is everything such a miserable jumble?

Then, right in front of my eyes, the goose woman's body begins to shudder, and her bright golden light emerges from her twisty, filament fraying body. It's just as brilliant and beautiful as Christopher's, but different too—more complex, and more nuanced. I reach for it and it flies to me as the woman collapses, bonelessly, silently.

The people in the room don't like that. The shrieking and wailing increase in frequency, until a large man with a dramatic beard lunges for me, and I dodge out of his way . . . and shift sideways into a doorway no one else can see. A path to another place. A path to . . .

Earth.

All of it crashes into me then.

Jesse. Kahn. John. Devlin and his men. Terra's collapse, followed by Erra's. That one nearly killed me, and it took days to gather all the souls. I don't have that kind of time, not to ferry *billions* of people over. I'm holding two souls right now, so I step all the way through the doorway and fall easily back to Earth. Once I've found it, the pathway's simple to reach, at least. But by the time I'm close, it drains me, as it always does. I make it, barely, but I know I have to head right back. If the bodies on Rra are ejecting the souls . . . this is going to be impossible. How can I possibly gather billions of souls before they've all died?

I'm doomed to fail, right from the start.

I race back, only to find that every single person who was near me is writhing, their bright golden souls shining and ready for gathering. I reach and grab them all, every last one, and then I reach further, as far as I can comfortably reach and then further yet. I gather a thousand souls. Two. And then I race back to Earth, freeing them as quickly and expeditiously as possible—but it drains me, right down to practically empty. When I return, I start to unspool the scenery, the large building where I'd been staying, even the dishes and the grass, and the sky above. Anything to fuel my efforts.

Even though I know already that they're ultimately doomed.

Isn't saving a few million people while billions die a total failure? Maybe not for the ones I save, but taken as a whole—I can't win.

I need help. I need it desperately. From someone who understands how a construct like this can exist. From someone who knows how to siphon energy, someone who will understand what I'm dealing with.

I need to see my father.

So instead of gathering more desperate souls with the energy I've siphoned, I shift the other direction, toward Ā.

Dad's got some explaining to do.

27

Ā

Ā looks nothing like I remember it. The last time I came, it was like a dark jar, filled with slugs, despair, and depression.

Now it's a cavernous room, well lit, with individual sections partitioned off like a caravan. Tents are sprinkled all over the space, and each one appears to be populated by a different person, all of them well-dressed and healthy. I'm standing in the center of the cavern on a polished stone floor, several dozen yards from the closest tent.

No one seems to have noticed my presence.

"Sekhmet!" Anat jogs from the largest of the tents, made from fabric of a vibrant sapphire blue. Her eyes are bright, her dark hair lustrous, and her curves as lush as I recall them being in ancient Egypt. "You're back. Praise be to Ra himself. I'm sure he's desperate to see you."

Heads pop out of every flap, all of them trained on me, most of them smiling.

At least they aren't dragging themselves toward me, claws outstretched, mouths drawn back into rictuses of horror. "This place has had a major upgrade."

"Thanks to you, I understand." Anat walks toward the

winding stairs I circumvented on my first visit. This time around, no one is prone on them, writhing in starvation-induced agony.

"What could *I* have done?" I ask.

"You pried the stone free and fed it to me," she says. "Ra says that's what caused—actually, perhaps your father should explain."

She takes the stairs with me, walking along the outside as if she's guarding me from any risk of a fall.

"I'm remembering things," I say softly.

Her gorgeous face, high cheekbones, flawless olive skin, and luminous dark eyes nearly overwhelm me when she turns to regard me more closely. "What do you mean?"

"I'm not actually Sekhmet." I hate how apologetic I sound. "I know I look like her—I mean, I suppose I *am* her, but I've been reborn. The life I remember, the one I've lived, it was on Earth in a very different time. I was born in a place called the United States of America."

"I know that, little one," she says, "but you'll always be Sekhmet to me."

We've reached the top. "I'm remembering things from that past life," I say, "and you're in some of the memories."

"Then you already know that I love you," she says.

"That's why I ripped that stone off and fed it to you," I say. "I couldn't bear the thought of you suffering in here, when you were always so kind to me."

Her hand cups my jaw, her fingers gentle, her eyes kind. "You would have done it for anyone. You've always been the most empathetic, the most generous, and the most kind and self-sacrificing person I've known."

I wish I deserved that praise. "Not in this lifetime," I say.

"The kind of girl who mourns for siphoned scorpions, who leaves treats and cookies for condemned prisoners, who has a kind word for everyone including self-centered courtesans—that kind of person doesn't change, not at her core. You're the same as ever underneath the armor you've constructed to keep yourself safe."

I wish she could be right.

"He'll be waiting for you. He's been so much more aware ever since you tore down the prison walls."

Tore down the what? Before I can ask, she's already trotting down the stairs. If I didn't have billions of people whose lives were resting on my getting answers here, I'd take a moment to prepare myself. I'd inhale and exhale slowly a few times. I'd compose myself.

But there's no time for that. I need Ra's help to figure out how I can possibly gather all those people before the prison collapses on their heads, so I grab the handle and shove, entering Ra's room without even gaining permission.

"Hello?"

Unlike the last time, he's not asleep. When he turns around, broad shoulders straight, golden eyes clear and alert, Ra's already smiling. "Sekhmet. I wondered whether I'd see you soon."

"I need help," I say. "And I'm in a hurry. A big hurry. People are probably dying at this very moment."

"People are always dying." Ra sits on the same bench where we sat last time and gestures for me to sit next to him.

I sit. "But this time, it's my fault they're dying."

"Why?" His expression is bizarrely serene, utterly unconcerned. "Did you put them in harm's way?"

"Actually, I might have. A lot of people think, since I'm the Warden, that I'm the one who made Terra in all its iterations. I don't recall doing it, so I can't be entirely sure."

His mouth curves into the half smile I remember. "But in this instance, you're not harming them, you're just not sure how to *save* them, right?"

"I don't have time to debate the semantics. Here's the

problem. When Terra started to unravel, I gathered all the souls of all the people there—Lifters, Healers, all of them—and I transported them back to Earth. It was stressful and exhausting, but I did it pretty quickly. There were only three hundred thousand or so locked into Terra in the first place. When Erra collapsed, I did the same thing, but it took me three days because there were so many more—around seven million, I think."

"That sounds terrible," he says.

"It was okay," I say. "But on Rra, there are many, many more. There are *billions*. Clearly I should have been taking them back to Earth for days and days, but I didn't know who I was or what I could do. They kept telling me I was She Who Gathers, but it meant nothing to me, and now, unless I figure out a better way, it's too late for most of them. No matter how fast I gather, no matter how hard I try, I can't save more than a fraction of the people who are dying."

"Perhaps the world needs no more than a fraction." He's so calm, so unconcerned at the prospect of killing billions.

"Of course that's not true. These people have families, lives, and loves. I can't let them die. There must be a better way."

"Then likely there is," he says. "I've been limited by my ability to process what you're saying by my location. It's hard to know how a house looks on the outside from the inside."

There it is—he's finally asking me to release him. "You want me to gather you right now and take you to Earth. Is that it? That's the price for your aid?"

His face falls. "Not at all. You think I'm trying to strong-arm you? That I mean to force you into freeing me?" He sighs. "I'm telling you my limitations, but within them, I'm happy to do all that I can to help."

"I find it hard to believe you," I say. "You know, since you lied to me so spectacularly before."

"Lied?" He blinks rapidly. "About what?"

"You tricked me." There's more hurt in my voice than I expected. Did I really think Ra would be a stand-up guy? He's locked in a prison, after all. That's not usually where good people wind up.

"How did I trick you, in particular?"

"I don't have time to go over the details of this daddy-daughter drama," I say. "People's lives are on the line."

"Sekhmet, think—"

"Please stop calling me that. It's not my name."

He stiffens. "I apologize. Alora, then." He inhales through his nose and exhales through his mouth. "It's a lot for an old man to process." He doesn't look very old. That's throwing me off.

"What I need to know is, how can I gather these souls faster? How can I save everyone before Rra collapses?"

"Have you ever been in a terrible rush before, Alora?" His eyes are calm. Clear, even.

"Of course I have."

"And when you were harried and stressed, did you make good decisions? Or bad ones?"

"What does that mean?"

"I find that, when people are stressed out and rushing, they drop things. They forget important pieces of information, and insight eludes them."

I force myself to sit back and listen to what he's saying. "You're right. If we're talking about billions of people, a few extra minutes trying to figure out a prudent approach isn't wasteful. It's the opposite. It's best to avoid hastiness and act with forethought." I nod. "Please accept my apology. What can I explain that might help you to help me?"

He beams. "Exactly, yes. You said you 'gather' them. Can you explain that to me?"

"Sure." I describe the process as clearly as I can. Maybe more than anyone else in the world, he might be able to comprehend, since he also sees souls. "Does that help?"

"You said they call you 'She Who Gathers.'"

"On Rra they do, yes."

He taps his lip. "I wonder whether you're doing it the wrong way."

"Doing what the wrong way?"

"Think about gathering. What does it mean?"

"To pick things up and put them in the same place, together."

"It can mean that, yes. You gather apples. You gather toys strewn across the floor."

"You know what toys are?"

His smirk surprises me. "They did have toys when you were a child, you know. In my time. I gave you quite a few."

Of course he did.

"But if you're wondering about my apple reference, they didn't have *those* in Egypt. So if you're wanting to know how I'm aware of them?" He tilts his head slightly.

"I am, actually. Yeah."

"I've been stuck here for a very long time. In your American prisons, they have people who bring things for the prisoners. They trade these contraband items for other things they want. Cigarettes form a currency of sorts, but smuggled goods are also bought and sold, including information."

"I really want to know how you know anything about that."

"I assumed you would. On Ā, I have been the one who could procure contraband. For many years, it was easy. I'd wait until there was a glitch in the system, a power surge, you might call it, and I'd push and pull quickly. I never knew quite what I'd obtain, and it was always a shadow of something real, something current, but once it arrived, I could always find a use for it. The surges became more frequent in past years, but I had less and less strength with which to push and pull. And the other inmates here grew less and less . . . healthy."

Thinking of the slugs from before disgusts me.

"Over the years, the things I've been most eager to obtain have been books, literature, or anything I could find to convey the popular culture of the time."

I look around the room slowly, taking note for the first time of the bookcases lining the walls. I thought them nothing more than decoration, or possibly an illusion, but now I see that was wrong. There are scrolls. There are old, heavy tomes. And there are even modern bound books, including magazines and newspapers. "You've been keeping up with things?"

"Studying new languages and cultures, yes, as best I'm able. I wanted to be ready when you needed me. And there's little else to do here, if I'm being honest."

Amazing. "You did all that so that you'd be ready to take over the world again as soon as you were free?" That kind of ambition is baffling to me.

He snorts. "Not at all. I did it so that I might be of use to *you* when you needed me."

"Then why double cross me?" I can't quite keep the hurt out of my voice, even though it's embarrassing.

"You said that before—in what way did I . . . " He trails off, and then exhales. "Oh. I told you to use my reservoirs, and then when you found them—"

"You stole every last speck of energy inside of them, forcing me to refuel." I frown. "And then you stole it all again. You played me, and like a sucker, I fell for it."

Ra stands up and walks to the window. "Look, child. Please."

He won't try to push me out the window or anything, right? That's crazy. He could kill me a million different ways. But now that he mentions it, I'm curious what *is* outside of Ra's windows. Each of the other prison worlds has been just the right size for the population. Which means . . . are there more Assimilators outside? More than the hundred and fifty or so who are currently inside? I cross the room and look for myself.

A barren wasteland stretches out in front of him, decorated only with lightning strikes and occasional spurts of inexplicable lava. "What is that?"

"That used to project an image of a beautiful field back to me," Ra says. "But after you left, it fell apart. The walls began closing in, literally."

"What?"

"Anat tells me you removed a piece of rock and *fed* it to her."

"They were starving," I say. "They looked *awful*."

"I'm aware of what it was like before your visit," he says. "I was doing the least I could do to keep them alive, rationing what reserves I had left. I could have fed them more once you appeared, knowing we didn't have to wait much longer, but you didn't mention freeing us, and you needed the small amounts of energy I had left, for Shu."

"Jesse," I say absently. "His name is Jesse, now."

"Jesse." The word rolls around in Ra's mouth. "I like it."

"So you're saying you didn't set me up?" I watch the lightning strikes—they're almost soothing. I wonder absently whether there's a pattern to them.

"Of course not," he says. "But I've needed to use the energy to keep the walls from coming down around us. When you removed that rock, it destabilized the entire infrastructure. It's been falling apart ever since. I could only keep it intact because of the energy I've siphoned from the reservoir. When you refilled it, I hoped that you were in a position to do so—because we'd all have died if I hadn't shored up the walls in here each time I did."

"Everyone is well fed and living in decorative tents," I say a little skeptically.

"They're Assimilators," Ra says. "They can sense the power surges, and they know how to siphon too. I can't keep them from skimming off the top, but trust me. Those little illusions cost very little compared to maintaining the walls."

He wasn't betraying me—he was cleaning up my mess. Maybe I can trust what he has to say. "I need ideas about how to increase my gathering speed. Did anything I shared help?"

He scratches his chin. "I've been thinking about the word 'gather.' You explained it to me as picking things up and aggregating them. But when I read it before, it seemed to me that the word could also mean . . . " He walks across the room to his bed and plucks the blanket off the top. He carries it over to me. "See this fabric?"

I nod.

He wiggles his hands together and a tiny needle with thread running through the eye appears. He takes the needle and weaves it through the blanket in a clumsy way, pulling and tugging through wide swaths of fabric, underneath and above, and then he presses the trailing end into my hand. "I didn't think to tie a knot, so hold this here."

I press my fingers together tightly, holding the far end of the fabric and thread.

"Now watch what happens when I *gather* the fabric." He pulls gently on the needle, tugging and yanking so that the fabric bunches together, the pieces he pierced all pulling flush against one another.

He gathered it—pulling the individual places together into one spot, bunching it together, really. Like the gathers of a skirt or pleated pants.

"You mean . . . " I think about what I know of Rra and Earth. "You think I shouldn't be trying to pick up each soul individually and ferrying them over to Earth in a bunch."

"You're limited by your capacity to capture and hold them all," he says.

"But if I were to tug Rra forward so that it was closer in proximity to Earth . . . "

"They could pour over themselves," Ra says. "Quickly. Efficiently. Without your individual ferrying of souls."

"And without the terrible losses of everyone I can't physically carry myself."

"Exactly," Ra says. "Now this is all theoretical. I'm not sure what it would take for you to bring Rra and Earth together, and before you leap to this conclusion, it might drag Ā along behind it, yanking us right next to Earth as well. Any attempt could result in freedom for every last one of us. That's not my goal—I'm trying to help you save the people you want to preserve, but it could be an unintended side effect of any kind of relocation of prison holding areas."

I throw my arms around his neck.

His eyes widen with surprise, but a beat later, his arms slide around me as well. He may only be a shadow—a collection of thoughts and feelings projected into a fake world where his powers are held hostage, but he feels real to me. His advice is sound, and I believe his love and affection for me are real.

"Thank you."

"Not a day goes by that you don't surprise me in some new way, little cub, and I love you for it." His eyes are sad. "I hope this works."

"Me too."

My arms tighten around his waist, and my tears wet his robes. And then it's time to go. To see whether there's any way for me to take the gift he's given me, the insight he's shared, and salvage the world that's crumbling all around me.

It's time for me to try to save the seven billion I've been unable to help for the past week or more.

"Thanks, Dad. I'll be back, I swear it."

I just hope I'm strong enough to honor that promise.

28

RRA

The second I step back into Rra, I realize that I have far less time than I thought. People flicker and roll, like an old broken video game. Sparking into existence and then winking out. I can't seem to focus on anything in particular, because anywhere I look, the objects that should be there are gone, and then back again.

Ra's idea is brilliant, and I hope he's right in his assumptions, but I'm not sure quite how to shift the entire prison world. He used a needle and thread for his demonstration, but I have nothing here other than myself.

Gathering my way, that I can do.

So, panicked by the deterioration around me, I fall back into what I'm capable of doing. I dart about, gathering and pulling as many souls to me as I possibly can. I tug and yank and suction, until I'm holding thousands. The strain is tremendous, so I siphon the flickering, degrading energy and use it to propel myself downward, to Earth.

Once there, I shove all the souls I've collected downward and prepare to launch back.

But I don't, not this time.

I have to take the time to find a better way, or billions will die. I can't rush and race and drop the ball.

If I do, it will be my fault.

So instead of racing back, I *look around*. Not with my eyes. They're useless here in this aether-based tunnel, but I cast about with my other senses. My ability to sense power, my ability to Lift, my ability to press my desires onto others, and somewhere in between all of those, I *feel it*. It's like a net, like a blanket, really, cast over everything. It connects Earth with Rra, and it secures them both, keeping them from spinning away. As I press on the fabric holding them together, it flexes and pulses and shifts, and a sensation very much like the pain of burning lances through me.

For being in a place where I don't have a body, it sure hurts like I have one. Without a needle and thread equivalent to focus my abilities, how am I supposed to drag these two places together? An image of rats fleeing over the edge of a sinking ship runs through my mind, and I shudder.

These aren't rats.

They're humans, and they really are drowning, even though their bodies aren't anywhere near water.

I have to drag this ship to shore.

I'm the only one who can.

I may not have a needle handy . . . but neither did Ra. He manifested it. Maybe I can do the same thing. I imagine a needle, and nothing happens. So I spread my invisible, mental hands apart and try again.

Still nothing.

I wish I had a brick wall I could bang my head against to try and dislodge some new ideas.

For days and days, I've been trying to figure this problem out with no success. Because I'm not strong enough. Not smart enough. Not *enough in any way*.

I should give up right now.

Jesse may have triggered these problems.

I may have collapsed the worlds saving my own brother —it really may all be my fault.

And now I can't save anyone.

I'm a failure.

That's all I'm capable of. Back in Egyptian times. Now. Forever. I failed Ra. I failed Kahn. I failed Jesse. And now I'm failing the entire world.

A memory floats to the surface of my exhausted, depressed, beleaguered brain. For one year of high school, the year before we ran away, Jesse and I were debate partners. I was lousy, and Jesse was good. Over and over, I'd lose us the round. I'd say the wrong thing. I'd take inconsistent notes. Jesse spent every moment of our preparation time trying to explain things to me, but the more overwhelmed I got, the less I could comprehend what he was saying. I knew I couldn't grasp his overall strategy—I wasn't smart enough.

So we lost and we lost and we lost some more.

Until one round, when I didn't get what he was saying, Jesse said, "It's fine. Don't worry about whether you *get* it. It's okay if you don't right in this moment. But while they're speaking, I want you to think about what I've said. Then when you get up there, don't be afraid to make them wait for it. People listen better when you make them uncomfortable. Go at your pace."

It worked. As the opponents spoke, I thought about how we could defend and counterattack, and finally, the response Jesse was explaining clicked, because I had the seed of the same idea myself. It was like drawing lines between the connect-the-dots pictures, but I couldn't find the start. Pausing, relaxing, it allowed me to find the first and second dots and connect them, and then I followed the idea through one by one until the end.

People really do listen better when they're forced to be uncomfortable, when they have to acknowledge their own failures, their own deficiencies. I know my weaknesses.

I'm unsure, I lack confidence, and I worry, sometimes too much, about doing what's right and what's wrong.

In that moment, it finally makes sense. Creating that needle took energy. I can't steal the energy I need from Rra, or it won't be different enough to pull through Rra and drag it to Earth. I need to take energy I've already taken, and use that to fashion my needle. Only energy not *of* Rra can move Rra through space.

So I do it—I tap into the power I've saved. I have no collar on here, but on Earth, I do. I make a needle, only it's not a needle. It's shaped more like a giant magnet, and I use it to *pull*, in a way I couldn't when I was on Rra. I was trying to use Rra to pull Rra, and that could never work, just as I could never pull myself up into the air from the ground.

And this time, when I reach, and I heave, it does something. Rra slides closer.

Only a hair.

So I dig deeper, and I craft a bigger magnet, and I do it again. I *gather.* This time, I manage a much bigger yank. A more impressive tug.

But it's not enough. So I drain the reserves all the way down to the bottom and I keep pulling, aware that now, I'm pulling on my own energy, my own life force. But this is bigger than me. It's bigger than the world. So I shape and I set my theoretical feet and I *PULL* as hard as I can, and with a great creaking sound, a monstrous shrieking, and a pain unlike any I've ever felt, I dislodge Rra from its foundation and shove it up against Earth.

It's almost close enough.

But not quite.

The golden lights can sense it—that they're within a hair's breadth of being safe. That home is just around the bend. They huddle in a bunch just at the edge of Rra, but if they leapt toward Earth, they'd plummet into nothingness.

I don't have the energy to move Rra any more. Not now. Not in this moment in time.

And Rra itself begins to unspool.

I'm out of time. I have no more energy with which to yank. So instead, I reach out and I stretch. I anchor the base of Rra to the edge of Earth and I beckon to the souls, to the shining life-forces gathered and waiting.

And the rats flee.

The tiny lights, some golden and pure, so bright they're practically unbearable, and some twisted and dark, they all flow like a river over the edge, scrabbling and racing and flitting across my back and dropping back onto Earth. Reconnecting with their bodies. Freed from the prison I made, or at the very least, that I've been running.

And just as Ra said, Ā is just behind Rra. But it's not touching. I could leave them—all those Assimilators. I could free the world from their yoke and their dominion. I could let them die, because with the reservoirs drained, there's nothing Ra can do to preserve them. He can't fix my mistakes anymore, not with nothing but empty batteries to bolster him.

They can't simply race across as the lights of Rra are finishing up with doing. Even with my life-force stretching from Rra to Earth, Ā is too far removed.

I could pull it closer to Earth as well, but I'm out of energy. The thought of trying to yank anything, to shift anything else—it overwhelms me.

Until I realize—I couldn't Gather the old way for billions of people—they raced across at light speed, and they're still escaping. But once they're done, once Rra is empty, I could easily gather a hundred and fifty souls from Ā and use the framework of Ā itself to power our return trip

Which leaves me with one question: do I want to save them, and more specifically, do I want to free Ra?

Kahn would say no.

He would tell me that I should use the energy I could siphon from Rra and the energy I can siphon from Ā to make a new prison, however rudimentary. I could probably make something stable that would keep the Assimilators imprisoned, for now at least. I could look into it, recover more of my memories, and stay in this holding pattern until I could recreate something even better than Ā.

I understand what he's saying, and it might make sense, but for one thing. The fly in the bowl of ice cream. The blighted spot on an otherwise perfect strawberry.

Only siphoning the energy of Terra and Erra until they disappeared truly freed the women. Their powers must have been powering Terra in all its iterations all this time. If I use the energy forming Rra and Ā to make something new, what happens to them?

Can I really justify keeping women in bondage to restrain Ra?

If he were here, Jesse would ask me whether that's really what all this is about. Am I making this decision based on what's *right*? Or what I *want*?

I may struggle to admit it back on Earth, but I want my dad back.

I'm desperate for someone else to rule instead of me. I want someone greater, someone more competent to be responsible for all these upcoming decisions, for all the impossible choices, for the mind-bending ethical questions.

And most important of all, only Ra has a chance of saving Jesse.

In the end, whether it makes me a bad person or not, I am who I am. I want to save my brother above all things.

I cross over to Ā, and I gather up all the glowing souls, and I siphon all of Ā's residual energy, gathering one bright soul last. A blindingly bright soul, with a few pure ebony threads running through the center.

I know it's Ra. I'm not sure how, but I know it.

The power from Ā fuels our trip home. I force myself back down the open path, and stop at Rra to form a bridge for the rest of the souls still waiting. I reconnect Rra to Earth, and I wait patiently as the last of the souls on Rra return to Earth. Then I siphon the last vestiges of the prison world that has held every human on Earth in check for millennia, brick by brick. Stone by stone. Tree by tree. And I funnel all of it into the stones I can't see or touch or feel. I funnel until it seems they can't handle a speck more, and then I keep funneling. I swell and grow and shift, and I keep pulling.

And finally, when I think I can't take a bit more, I pull one last time and Rra disappears, just as Terra and Erra and Ā have disappeared, and I sprint home, every part of me flush and brimming with power, with energy, with life-force I shouldn't have.

As I reach Earth, I have a decision to make—and I make it. Instead of trying to drag all that power back with me, I release it into the atmosphere, and the entire sky turns bright pink. The setting sun looks like it's exploding out of the horizon, the energy spreading out all around me like fireworks and dissipating into the atmosphere—and I slam back into my own body.

"Where's Ra?" I ask the second my eyes open.

"Ra?" John's eyes widen.

Jesse frowns. "You think he's here?"

"He's alive," I say. "I know he is."

"If he was like Mehen and Am-Heh," Jesse says, "he's waking up in a mummy case somewhere, waiting to be freed."

Ugh. "That's kind of nasty to consider."

"It really is," Jesse says. "But does that mean . . . what did you do?"

I turn toward the television. "You might want to turn that on."

"Why?" Jesse's brow furrows.

"Because I collapsed the whole dang thing. Rra, Ā, all gone. The world is back to normal, only it's no normal we've ever known. And our real father is finally free, for the first time in over two millennia. I'm guessing things are about to get really, really interesting."

<<<<>>>>

I hope you enjoyed Awoken! I'm working on the fourth book, Capsized, now. I hope you'll love what I think will be the epic conclusion to the Anchored saga. I'll update with a preorder link once I have one.

ACKNOWLEDGMENTS

Thanks, as always, to my husband. I would have quit writing a long time ago without him.

Thanks to my children for their unfailing support.

Thanks to my mom for her cheerleading and all the times she lends a hand.

Thanks to my editor, Carrie. Phenomenal work, as always.

Thanks to Christian and Lara both. I work with the best cover artists on Earth, and they both put up with me marvelously. They help my vision for these books come alive.

Thanks to my readers. YOU are the reason I do this. I love you. For reals. From the bottom of my heart. You're the reason I write.

Bridget's a lawyer, but does as little legal work as possible. She has five kids and soooo many animals that she loses count.

Horses, dogs, cats, rabbits, and so many chickens. Animals are her great love, after the hubby, the kids, and the books.

She makes cookies waaaaay too often and believes they should be their own food group. In a (possibly misguided) attempt at balancing the scales, she kickboxes daily. So if you don't like her books, maybe don't tell her in person.

Bridget is active on social media, and has a facebook group she comments in often. (Her husband even gets on

there sometimes.) Please feel free to join her there: https://
www.facebook.com/groups/750807222376182

The Finding Home Series:

Finding Faith (1)

Finding Cupid (2)

Finding Spring (3)

Finding Liberty (4)

Finding Holly (5)

Finding Home (6)

Finding Balance (7)

Finding Peace (8)

The Finding Home Series Boxset Books 1-3

The Finding Home Series Boxset Books 4-6

Children's Picture Book

Yuck! What's for Dinner?